the

blue caterpillar

Also by Sam Pickering

Books of Essays
A Continuing Education
The Right Distance
May Days
Still Life
Let It Ride
Trespassing
Walkabout Year

Literary Studies
The Moral Tradition in English Fiction, 1785–1850
John Locke and Children's Books in Eighteenth-Century England
Moral Instruction and Fiction for Children, 1749–1820

Sam Pickering

the

blue caterpillar

and other essays

university press of florida

GAINESVILLE TALLAHASSEE TAMPA BOCA RATON PENSACOLA ORLANDO MIAMI JACKSONVILLE

02 01 00 99 98 97   6 5 4 3 2 1

Library of Congress Cataloging-in-Publication Data
Pickering, Samuel F., 1941–
The Blue Caterpillar. / Sam Pickering.
p. cm.
ISBN 0-8130-1482-4 (cloth: alk. paper)
I. Title.
AC8.P66 1997
081—DC20   96-33049

The following essays by Sam Pickering are reprinted by
permission of the original publishers:
"Blue Caterpillar," *Homeworks: A Book of Tennessee Writers,* ed. Phyllis Tickle
and Alice Swanson (Knoxville: University of Tennessee Press, 1996).
"Down," *Dartmouth College Library Bulletin* 34, no. 2 (April 1994).
"Early Spring," *Virginia Quarterly Review* 70, no. 2 (Spring 1994).
"Gathering," *American Identities: Contemporary Multicultural Voices,* ed.
Robert Pack (Hanover, N.H.: University Press of New England, 1994).
"July," *Creative Nonfiction* 4 (Fall 1995).
A portion of "There Have Been Changes" originally appeared in "Wanton
Palfreys and Glittering Casinos," *Sewanee Review* 103, no. 1 (Winter 1995).

The University Press of Florida is the scholarly publishing agency for the
State University System of Florida, comprised of Florida A & M University,
Florida Atlantic University, Florida International University, Florida State
University, University of Central Florida, University of Florida, University of
North Florida, University of South Florida, and University of West Florida.

University Press of Florida
15 Northwest 15th Street
Gainesville, FL 32611

contents

preface

"Do they think, 'here comes the food lady'?" Vicki said, opening the barrel of birdseed. "Yes," I said, walking toward the woods and sniffing the air. "Soon, though, the snow will melt, *turdus migratorius* will reappear, and all creatures can fend for themselves." "By *turdus,* I take it you mean robin," Vicki said, kicking snow aside and casting a handful of cracked corn and sunflower seeds onto the ground. "Maybe," I said, disappearing into the scrub. During the night a heavy snow blew across Connecticut, rumpling yards and turning Valentine's Day white. The snow was winter's last hard blow. Above the woods the sky curved blue like an empty glazed bowl. Beyond the horizon March preened, pulling green shoots through the tweedy fabric of season and flicking clots of ice off rivers and creeks.

Essayists forage, and I roamed wood and field in hopes of harvesting a sense of season. Gusts of snow caught on the lip of Horsebarn Hill and, twisting, poured down the slope into drifts. When the wind shifted, the drifts stretched, and the top layer of snow peeled away before shredding white and fibrous into nothing. In the woods trees popped and snapped. A deer picked its way across a clearing, its hoofprints sharp as needlepoint. Beside a road clumps of snow clung like tissue paper to multiflora rose. Above ridges winds groaned and roared. In valleys stubble snagged the air and ripped winds into sharp, metallic breezes. On trees near the beaver pond lichens glowed yellow and green in the sunlight. Snow melted and froze in the furrows of bark, and tree trunks seemed to shake and tinkle like tall, frosted glasses, slices of lime and lemon sliding bright over crushed ice.

The sights were familiar, and although I wandered the woods for four hours, I stumbled across little I could blend into an essay. Walking home, however, took me past the School of Agriculture and the Ratcliffe Hicks Building, an arena built for livestock shows. Parked outside the building was a convoy of trucks and trailers. In the arena the Connecticut Pork Producers held their Annual Production Show and Sale. White metal pens turned the floor of the arena into a checkerboard, and the air was warm with the sweet and sour aroma of hog and sawdust. For a dollar I bought a cup of coffee and a chocolate doughnut, shreds of coconut rising sharp above the chocolate like bristles. I strolled through the pens. Behind rails hogs slept or rooted through sawdust: Poland Chinas; Berkshires; Hampshires, black with white hair falling off their shoulders in capes; Landraces; then Yorkshires, fleshy and lumpy, resembling bars of soap cobbled together from bathtub remnants. My favorite hog was the duroc, and for a long time I stood by a pen watching a gilt sleep, her belly spilling in front of her like a thick red moon.

Farmers, often accompanied by wives and children, roamed the pens, taking notes. The men wore brown overalls; sweatshirts; boots, deep cleats corrugating the soles; and then baseball caps. Stitched across the fronts of the caps were logos depicting hogs and the names of farms: from Connecticut, Break Hill and Long Ridge farms in Goshen and Northfield, respectively; Andrews Farms in West Greenwich, Rhode Island; and from Lebanon, Pennsylvania, Arnold Hog Farms. A duroc floated like a scarlet balloon across the front of a white cap while a Yorkshire rose in a cloud over the bill of a blue cap. Students from a chapter of Future Farmers of America wore colorful caps, the letters FFA silver and slumping like pitchforks tossed into a purple loft, the bill below resembling a dirt-red floor. A Feeder Pig was being raffled, and I bought a ticket for a dollar. The pig weighed twenty-five pounds. Usually the winner fed his prize through spring and summer, then butchered or sold it in the fall. My yard is modest, barely big enough to contain three children, a wife, and two small dogs. Still, we produce buckets of slops, and the pig would, I thought, furnish a larder rich with the toothsome stuff of essays.

Because the raffle took place at the end of the afternoon, I watched the sale. Although the auctioneer started the bidding for boars at three hundred dollars, no boar sold for more than a hundred dollars. In contrast, while bidding for bred gilts opened at one hundred fifty or two hundred dollars, the gilts sold for more than three hundred dollars. By the end of the auction my enthusiasm for raising a pig had melted into drippings. Happily I did not win the pig, or as my son Francis put it, "bring home the bacon and the crackling and the chops." Nevertheless, during the auction I scored the skin of story, and although I did not have time to boil and cure the narrative, I seasoned it for the page.

A host of characters from Carthage, Tennessee, wander my essays. Prominent among them is the Reverend Slubey Garts, owner of the Tabernacle of Love and other religious sundries. An entrepreneurial Christian, Slubey is forever searching for ways to glorify God on high while lining his pocket below. Last Sunday after church, he gave away "Paradise Candles," instructing parishioners to burn them at home. The candles, Slubey said, were gospel hounds, expert at treeing sin, making it stink with fear like a polecat. If people smelled anything bad while their candles were burning, then, Slubey warned, the old lewdster Satan was roosting in their rafters. "Clamp on the Helmet of Salvation and the Breastplate of Righteousness. Hurry to church," Slubey instructed, "and put a new song in your mouth." The next Sunday the Tabernacle bulged like a whiskey barrel. So much money was collected at the offering that the plate went through the congregation four times, the sound of the coins rattling like musketry. "And all because," Turlow Gutheridge said, "Slubey shoveled a little hog manure into the tallow when he made the candles."

The story is low. Despite attempts by publicists and occasionally by preachers to elevate the written word, most writers are ground-dwellers. When I write, I root about in the good muck of daily life, trying to turn up nourishing nouns and verbs. In spring I wander lowlands, the fragrance of *symplocarpus foetidus,* or skunk cabbage, as gourmets dub it, rising around me in a mist. In summer I tumble through gullies, the

song of *culex pipiens,* or mosquito, sawing the air about my ears. Throughout the year I rake through days, piling the doings of season, place and
family together into essays. My writing appeals, I suspect, to "grown-up
adults," as a child psychologist at the university puts it, people who have
watched decades stream behind them and who, instead of lingering in
the doldrums lamenting the passage of time, have sailed brightly through
days, joy billowing ahead of them like flying jibs. Some of my readers
probably resemble Miss Mabel Campbell, the Carthage town librarian.
"I'm not as young as I once was," Miss Mabel wrote me last week, "and I
don't believe I shall ever be that young again, even if I live to the age of
Methuselah." People who demand order from essays, and life, may find
their "nervous cisterns" overflowing with impatience after reading a signature of my pages. Perhaps folks who buy bathtubs with faucets at both
ends so that the water is always level should avoid my choppy prose. "A
writer," my friend Josh said, "must believe he is a quorum. If he worries
about the votes of potential readers, his books will be tabled and never
make it to the floor of a bookstore."

I suspect Josh is right. Be that as it may, however, after returning from
the hog sale and taking a bath, I sat down at my desk. I examined a Bible
I found in the basement of Vicki's parents' home in Princeton, New Jersey. Published in 1789, in Oxford, England, the Bible was bound in leather.
Stamped in gold across the front was the name of a stranger, Nancy Prior.
Much as I wandered hill and field, willfully following the vagaries of mind,
so I thumbed the Bible. Aside from the Apocrypha and the Old and
New Testaments, the contents of Bibles are miscellaneous. Things preserved in a Bible resemble the various activities of a day, bound together
not by the spine of a life, however, but by the spine of a book.

At the end of Ecclesiastes two leaves of low bush huckleberry turned
red, signaling the beginning of a fall long ended. Amid the Song of
Solomon lurked the business card of George Peirce, a "Piano and Organ
Tuner and Repairer" with an office at 162 Union Street in New Bedford,
Massachusetts. The card was four and three-quarters inches wide and
one and a half inches tall. Depicted on the card in what had once been
black ink but which had faded to gold was a square piano with ponder-
ous cabriole legs. Near the Sermon on the Mount I found a piece of
rough rag paper measuring five by ten and a half inches. Printed on the

sheet were eight stanzas of "An Original Hymn" composed "For the Ordination of Mr. Jonathan Cole, at Kingston." "Wrapt in the deepest shades of night / The wide creation lay," the first stanza read. "God spake—and lo! in glory bright / Shone forth the golden day."

The hymn was cheery, but the most striking verse I discovered was written by hand on a scrap of paper, foxed and yellowed by time. "I can cure the cholera, colic, or cramp," the lines declared. "I can cure the worst fevers: coast, typhus or camp. / I am death on the diarrhea, can physic off fits, / And drive off the smallpox, without leaving pitts." Would that essays could work such cures. At best, essays are nostrums for the mind. Still, as the hymn written for Jonathan Cole stated, words can transform night into golden day. If my essays make people smile and see that enjoyment blooms seasonless through ordinary life, then, by gosh, I haven't done badly.

the

blue caterpillar

gathering

I put two cloth bags into the basket on the bicycle, the first distributed as an advertisement for *Riverside Reader,* a textbook for college freshmen, the second given to students at Eliza's school in order to encourage reading. Printed in big blue letters near the top of the bag was NORTHWEST. Near the bottom appeared LIBRARY. In between a happy blue whale spouted a fountain of ink while swimming through a sea of letters reading A WHALE OF A SCHOOL. Later at the English Department I picked up two handfuls of rubber bands and sixty-eight "Reusable" envelopes, printed for the State of Connecticut in order to send "Interdepartmental Mail" from one agency to another. Nine and a half inches wide with pink lines dividing the fronts into thirds resembling pages torn from a small address book, the envelopes were just the right size for specimens.

The day was windy, and a cold rain fell. Weather rarely influences my little expeditions. Earlier in the week I decided to spend Thursday roaming the campus, looking at trees and gathering fruits. Although I could identify all the trees in the woods behind the sheep barns and along the Fenton River, I could not name some of the trees a quarter of a mile from my back door. After pushing the envelopes into the bottom of the library bag and buckling on my helmet, I pedaled to the Ratcliffe Hicks

Building and began my study. Six hours later I finished. I shivered in the cold, and by the end of the day my feet were almost numb, but the basket on the bicycle resembled a grocery of leaf and fruit.

I am not sure why I took the fruits home. Gathering, though, is part of my nature, and so long as I can remember, I have cluttered house and mind with things. Nowadays as memory stretches thin and becomes pocked with sieve-like holes, I gather more, perhaps trying to plug recollection with leaf and bark, or, if not that, then with a grout of stringy words. On the floor of the study between the television and red sofa, I displayed my harvest: the conelike fruit of the tulip tree resembling an ornament carved on an antique newel post; brown spiny balls from sweet gum; from the goldenrain tree small tawny lanterns, the seeds inside dark round bulbs; pods from the honey locust twisting like giant screws; next to them fragile silver pods from the redbud; and from the sweetbay magnolia, cones covered with loose red seeds ringing like maracas. Into a flat box I put a walnut; a twig heavy with the pitted red fruits of kousa dogwood; a hunk of bark from an amur cork-tree; green catalpa seeds seven inches long; and then from an osage orange, two hairy fruits, sticky and lumpy, resembling, Edward said, "gorilla brains." Into a smaller, deeper box, one which once contained a quart of peaches bought at Johnny Appleseed's Farm in Ellington, Connecticut, probably jayhaven or redkist peaches, I dumped twenty-six fruits from the yellow buckeye. Some of the nuts were loose, but most had not broken free from the spongy capsules which surrounded them like eiderdowns.

The floor of the study was bright as a Christmas tree. Near my desk were the green fruits of gallery pear. In front of the television, switches of English and Washington hawthorn, European mountain ash, and double-file viburnum glowed red with berries. Against a footstool leaned a fan of burning bush, the leaves scarlet and the fruits furiously orange. On the floor lay twigs from fringe trees, the fruits dark blue olives, and then swatches of basswood, the fruits clustered and resembling drops of green tea sloshed from a mug by a careless drinker. I opened the hairy pod of a beech and placed the seed alongside that of a silverbell. Although the seed from the beech was half an inch long and had three wings while that of the silverbell was one and three-quarter inches long and had four wings, the seeds resembled each other. Both had sharp needles at their tips, helping them, I thought, to slip through grass and dig into dirt when they fell from branches. Gingkoes had begun to ripen into fragrance. Eliza and I liked the aroma. Vicki and Edward did not, Vicki ordering me to throw the fruits outside, saying they smelled like "raccoon shit," something she has never sniffed and which I told her was marvelous, having little odor and often being radiant with the elytra of beetles.

From many trees I did not gather fruit. Instead I brought home impressions of bark: the sharp thorns on castor aralia; spongy redwood; three-flowered maple shredding into scrolls; then lacebark elm, raised dots peppering the surface like small pegs. I picked leaves off all the elms on campus: lacebark, American, slippery, Siberian, camperdown, and Japanese zelkovia. With its leaves sliced into sharp greens and yellows and its buds tight bundles along the twigs, a sprig of Siberian elm resembled a cutting of Victorian wallpaper. Twig and fruit often brought things homey to mind, the feathery leaves of dawn redwood and bald cypress reminding me of antimacassars, and the seeds of box elder resembling horse collars hooked and dangling around musty twine.

Gathering keeps me vital. If I did not pluck fruit and leaf, I would sag out of the present and settle into sentimental memory, into a past as comfortable as a bolster. Happily the bed on which I doze is often lumpy, even prickly. Last month when I snuggled up to Vicki, she pulled the covers tightly around her shoulders, making her, I thought at the time, resemble the fruit of a yellow buckeye. "Vicki," I started to protest. I got no further. "Sam," she said firmly, "just knowing that you are here in the bed with me is enough." "Oh," I answered, then added, "good night." "Good night," she said, "and sweet dreams."

The next morning I drove to Hartford to catch a plane to North Carolina. On the way I stopped at the Enchanted Bakery in Tolland and bought two amaretto truffle brownies. Unlike sugary dreams, desserts leave crumbs behind, something Vicki does not like to find either in a bed or on a car seat. To keep domestic life smooth, I sift carefully through hours, greasing minutes whenever possible. So that crumbs would not fall onto the seat, I leaned forward over the steering wheel to eat the brownies. In my left hand I held a napkin under my chin. In my right I grasped both brownie and wheel, pinching the brownie between thumb, index, and middle fingers while wrapping my fourth and little fingers around the wheel. By sliding my hand back and forth around the wheel and by dipping my head, I drove the brownie into my mouth while I steered the car along the interstate. And I did so without an accident. Not a single crumb drifted beyond the napkin and crashed against the seat.

Such care, alas, does not always insure a smooth bed or reception, and when I returned from North Carolina two days later, things at home were as bumpy as the bark on a hackberry tree. "Daddy," Eliza shouted when I walked through the garage door, "the brothers are taking my pretend people." "What?" I said, putting my suitcase down by the stove. "Edward and Francis won't leave Pillard-Pillard my seagull alone," Eliza said. "I told them that Pillard-Pillard had gone to Illinois to visit his grandmother. Then he went to the state fair and won a stuffed fish for her, but Edward does not believe me. He says Pillard-Pillard went to Florida for a vacation and Bob-Bob the alligator ate him." "What?" I repeated. "Daddy," Eliza continued, "tell Edward that you will spank him if he doesn't leave Pillard-Pillard alone. Also tell him to get rid of Bob-Bob. We can't have an alligator in this house. He frightens all the other pretend people."

After Edward promised to chain Bob-Bob to the desk in his room, Eliza calmed down, and soon her pretend people resumed wandering house and story. At dinner the next day, Pillard-Pillard sent a postcard from Honolulu. At the fair he entered a contest for best bird and won a two-week vacation in Honolulu. I envied Pillard-Pillard. Birds of a feather vacation together, and if I had not been collecting material for the Reverend Slubey Garts, one of the pretend people inhabiting my essays, I would have winged it out to Hawaii and strolled the white sands with old P-P, as I call him, now that I have gotten to know him better. To give my pretend people xylem and cortex, pith, phloem, and cambium, I spend much time gathering words. Minister of the Tabernacle of Love in Carthage, Tennessee, Slubey himself is fond of words. Not long ago he preached a fire and sorghum sermon, urging his flock to prepare themselves for the final shearing. "The fat isn't always going to be on the possum. Some cold morning," he declared, "tears as big as taters are going to roll down your cheeks. Doctor Sollows won't be able to help you then. Only the Lord can carry you from the sickroom to the living room."

Spring was in the air, and some of the lambs were frisky, so Slubey urged them to imagine the end, that morning when green pastures would sour and the wolf would break into the fold, carving congregations into chop and roast. "Some of you sisters," he said, "think you have got the wings of a locust and come Judgment Day can fly right up to the Pearly Gates. Well, I am here to tell you," he said, rolling his pupils under his lids so the whites of his eyes shone, "you aren't going to get as far as Red Boiling Springs. Just as soon as you heist yourselves out of the dirt, an old peckerwood will see you and flap down out of the sky and gobble you up. The soul isn't a magic hoe that works by itself. No, siree, you have to pull and chop. You have to fight sin all day. The cat doesn't wear gloves when she hunts mice. You have to seize the devil and shake him. The devil resembles the big snapping turtle Deacon Goforth found behind his outhouse last summer. The deacon chopped the turtle's head off and tossed it into the garden, thinking that would be the end of it. But it wasn't, not by a long shot. The next morning the deacon heard a terrible racket in the garden. He rushed out. And what did he see? He saw a sight that would make Bible birds groan," Slubey said, raising his hands above his head and wiggling his fingers so that they looked like fat baby snakes. "He saw that head trying to swallow a rooster."

Googoo Hooberry rarely left Carthage, and when Loppie Groat met Goo-goo outside Prunty's Store in Little Dover, he was surprised. "Googoo," Loppie exclaimed, "fancy meeting you here. Are you traveling around today, or are you just going somewheres?" Although I travel through books searching for story, I rarely let stories take me anywhere other than Carthage. Much as I spread leaf and fruit over the floor of the study, so I spread tales across my desk. Occasionally I keep a story, dumping it into an essay as potting soil in which to root pretend people. Loppie Groat was Clevanna Farquarson's first cousin twice removed, and when she applied for the job of cook at the Male and Female Select School, Clevanna listed Loppie as a character reference. After reading Clevanna's application, Judge Rutherford called Loppie to his chambers. "Loppie," he said, "can you vouch for Clevanna's veracity?" For a moment Loppie looked startled. "Judge," he said, "I didn't know such things mattered, leastwise for a cook, and to tell you the truth I just don't know her that way. Some folk say she do, and others say she don't. But why don't you ask her, Judge?" Loppie continued. "She'll give you a straight answer. She's as honest as the day is long."

Clevanna got the job, and a week later she cooked a celebratory lunch for Loppie. Although the drive from Little Dover to Carthage prevented Loppie from plowing, the day was not lost. Early that afternoon Barlow Warple fell into the hot wax vat at Walduck's candle manufactory on Spring Street. "Barlow turned hisself into a wick," Loppie told Clevanna later. "With all that wax on him he was as slick as owl grease and couldn't nobody get him out until Finster Mulrynne came up with the idea of using grappling hooks." That morning Mr. Walduck had seen Loppie in Carthage with his wagon, and after the accident he hired Loppie to deliver the corpse to Barlow's house in Buffalo Valley. Loppie had not been to Barlow's house before and had not met Mrs. Warple. On arriving at what he thought was the right address, he knocked on the door. When a woman opened the door, he took off his hat and said, "Excuse me. I'm not sure of my directions. But are you the widow Warple?" "My name is Warple," the woman replied, looking puzzled, "but I'm not a widow." "Ma'am, you just think you ain't," Loppie said, gesturing toward the road. "Don't say no more until you see the body I've got in that there wagon by the fence."

Almost every spring the Cumberland River flooded. Often people who lived along the riverbank below Carthage had to leave their homes for three or four days. Although a house was occasionally swept away, the floods were beneficial, depositing silt on bottomlands and providing farms with early crops of insurance, and fish. Before abandoning their houses to the water, farmers set out mousetraps baited with doughballs in order to catch catfish. Barrels of fish were caught and sent to restaurants in Nashville, so many fish that for a while Carthage advertised itself as "The Catfish Capital of Tennessee." Although I have never pulled a catfish from a mousetrap, I have netted a few piscatorial tales.

From the English Midlands I hooked the story of the fourth wise man, Kenelm. A legendary hero, Kenelm was hurrying to join Gaspar, Melchior, and Balthasar at the manger in Bethlehem when he turned aside in order to save Britain. During the Great Flood, a "hairless dog-headed worm" washed ashore near London. For centuries the worm remained small, causing only minor damage, laying putrid "windeggs" in wells and spoiling water. Suddenly, though, the worm grew monstrously large. Not only did its breath cause crops to mildew, but it suffered from an unquenchable thirst and threatened to drink the Thames dry. For six years Kenelm fought the worm unsuccessfully. Whenever he sliced the worm into bits, the pieces rejoined, forming an even larger monster. In the seventh year, though, Kenelm destroyed the creature. Britons constructed a huge bonfire. Once the fire was lit, Kenelm walked into the flames and remained in them until his armor was red hot. Afterward, when he fought the worm and chopped its body into pieces, the hot armor cauterized the wounds, making it impossible for the separate bits to join together as in the past. A charm protected Kenelm from the heat. A holy man removed a thorn from a white hawthorn and drove it deep into Kenelm's left eye. Although Kenelm lost sight in that eye, he remained cool and saved his country.

Kenelm carried two presents for the baby Jesus, a cage of doves and an ear of corn. While he fought the worm, Kenelm placed the gifts on the ground, and during the long struggle they vanished, at least people with ordinary vision could not find them after the battle ended. The loss of his left eye, however, was a blessing, giving Kenelm insight and making him farseeing. Not only did the Lord accept the gifts for his son, but He sent Kenelm a sign, showing his pleasure. On the spot where Kenelm set the cage of doves grew a new flower, the columbine, its blossoms resembling doves huddled together in prayer. The actual doves carried the corn to the Holy Land, where later it became known as Turkey wheat. Initially all kernels on the ear were white. At the crucifixion, however, many kernels changed color, some becoming red to represent the blood of Christ, others going into mourning and turning black, still others turning blue like the firmament, making the corn the most beautiful and desirable in the world.

Every fall, I travel around, to use Loppie's words, to several literary gatherings. I make talks, and I like to believe that I am going "somewheres." Not all my friends agree. Recently a novelist sent me a letter. "You should be using more of your time to write," he advised, "instead of running around and giving all these speeches." My friend writes books that have beginnings, middles, and ends. My essays meander, and as I wander, I harvest stories. Much as I pedaled across the university campus cramming bark and twig into envelopes, so I wheel into rooms and pluck phrases from conversations. At a recent conference in Massachusetts, adolescents read poetry. Although the authors were fresh and budding, the poems were a wintry glaze of unhappiness: accounts of suicide, murder, incest, and dismal love. "Does a person have to be middle-aged to laugh?" a man muttered. "*Lies* not *lays* on me," a woman said in response to a poem written by a cherubic eighth grader. "I don't care if your nipples are swollen citadels; he lies on you," the woman continued, talking to herself, before turning to the man and saying, "what is the world coming to? None of these children know proper English."

A month ago I spent a weekend in Florida. To raise funds, a library brought a handful of writers to town. During days writers attended a conference and read excerpts from their books. At night local people held dinner parties at their houses. The first evening an Armenian poet and I went to a large house on a riverbank. A string quartet played in the entrance hall. Before a window a silver lazy Susan reached to the ceiling, orchids dangling in streams from each shelf. Under a chandelier gleaming like a mall, our hosts greeted us, shaking hands with both of us, then pinning a white orchid on the poet's dress. "What did you think of them?" I said to my companion as we strolled into the study. "He is tall and thin. That's good, and she," the poet said, her voice suddenly rising, "she looks like she loves to fuck." "What?" I said. "You heard me," the poet said. "Now get me a drink, a tall Scotch with no soda water and only one ice cube."

When I handed her the drink, she was studying a painting of two pink-bottomed cherubs hanging over a sofa. "Thanks," she said, taking the glass and gesturing toward the wall, "now it is your turn. What do you think of this painting?" "It's a little dull," I said. "Right," she exclaimed, "it would be a lot better if they were fucking." This last word rushed outward like a wave of sound. Instead, though, of sweeping people away, it sucked them toward us in a great undertow, and when a crowd began washing around the poet, I drifted to the dining room. I filled a plate with smoked salmon, crabmeat, and lamb, and, sitting at a table, began signing posters advertising the conference. Participants in the conference signed posters. When friends of the library made donations, they received the posters as gifts. I had almost finished the stack of posters when the poet appeared on my right. "Let me have some of those things," she said, taking a heavy gold pen out of her purse. Over the i's in my name, I drew little hearts. "What's this?" the poet said, jabbing the pen at one of the hearts. "A heart," I said. "I put hearts above the i's to cheer people up." "Jesus," the poet exclaimed, "that's really corny." "Well," I said, the salmon having made me bold, "why don't you draw a phallus under your name? That wouldn't be corny." "What!" the poet shouted, glaring at me as if she were offended, "I will not draw dicks on these posters." When several people turned and stared at us, she pointed at me and said, "he wants me to draw dicks all over these posters, but I won't do it." I had two more posters left to sign. I hurried through them, omitting the hearts, and returned to the dining room.

I did not see the poet again until late the next morning. She was a member of a panel which discussed "Women and Literature." One of the participants disliked men, and afterward when I met the poet, I said, "that woman on the end didn't seem to care much for men." "Care for men!" the poet exclaimed. "That's putting it mildly. She hates to fuck." Again this last word had a whirlpool effect, pulling people toward us. As they circled and began to talk, I slipped away through an eddy in the conversation. Not until that night after the readings ended did I talk to the poet again. In the lounge of the hotel in which we stayed, several writers sat drinking wine and talking about the conference. I was tired, and I dozed on a couch, dreading the long trip back to Connecticut. Suddenly a voice said, "Get me a drink. You know how I like them." Then the poet sat down next to me with a thump.

I fetched the drink. When I returned, people were discussing a foot fetishist who came to the conference. After asking each of the women to sign one of her books, he said he was a shoe salesman. Explaining that he noticed her shoes when she read, the man asked if he could look inside the right shoe to read "the mark," a number, he explained, which revealed the date and place of manufacture. All the women let him examine their shoes. Once he held a shoe in his hands, he complimented the woman's bare foot. "Good Lord," Kaye said, "he told me my foot resembled a lily, and I just smiled and said thank you." "He told me my foot looked like a violet," Connie said. "How terrible." During the discussion the poet had been silent. Suddenly she sat upright. "He told me my foot was a daisy," she said, "and I told him to fuck off. Anyway," she continued, "looking at a foot doesn't amount to much. It's not fucking." "No, it isn't," I said aloud on the plane the next day, unaccountably starting to giggle, the dull flight exploding into brightness. "It certainly isn't."

"What are you laughing about?" the man sitting next to me asked. "Poetry," I said, "I'm laughing about poetry."

Although the trip home seemed short, traveling tires me. Often I am tempted to stop, not only running around and giving speeches, as my correspondent advised, but also gathering and writing. When Bob Dylan came to Storrs to give a concert, I bought tickets for Vicki and myself, telling friends that during the 1960s when Bob Dylan was really popular, I was too busy studying to notice. By attending a concert now, I explained, I would participate in the communal past of my generation. On hearing me mention the concert in the Cup of Sun, a student looked up from his coffee and said, "Dylan? Who would want to hear him? He is as old as you guys." I wrote the student's remark down in a notebook. Later, I read it and everything I jotted down about the concert to Vicki. "That's fine, Sam," she said, "but can't you do anything without thinking about it? Wouldn't it be more natural, and better, if you just lived days and didn't write about them?"

In part I long to take Vicki's advice. I would like to toss pencils and notebooks into the garbage can. Instead of roaming woods sliding from root to root over a sea of crumpled leaves, I dream of spending damp fall days inside, sitting in a comfortable chair, reading *Smithsonian* or watching the National Football League on television. If I stopped writing, life might be more natural. "When you come to children's soccer games," Mary told me last week, "one of the mothers always says, 'Here comes Sam. Be careful what you say. He'll write it down'." Because I write, I eavesdrop. Often I hear things I wish I had not heard. "When I was small," a man with a blue and green dragon tattooed on his right forearm said outside the Cup of Sun recently, "I used to pick chewing gum off the ground and eat it."

Even worse, so that I will have sentences to gather, I sow the seeds of narrative around myself. Last week when I walked into George's for a haircut, a man was giving Holly meticulous directions on trimming his hair. The man was a stranger, but that did not deter me from starting a story. "Don't listen to him, Holly," I said. "He's dotty and doesn't know what he wants. Just give him a Mohawk and be done with it." Later, a retired member of the English Department came into the barber shop. The man spent forty years writing about Edgar Allan Poe. "Eric," I said, "am I glad to see you, old buddy. I have been thinking a lot recently about 'The Fall of the House of Usher'. If Usher had hired a contractor and had a solid foundation laid down, everything would have been hunky-dory. Have you ever thought about that?" When Eric opined that the thought had not crossed his mind, I delivered a five-minute lecture on bricks, listing grades of building brick: severe weathering, moderate weathering, and nonweathering, or SW, MW, and NW, as they are known in the trade. I described pointing styles: flush, weathered, struck, concave, vee, and raked. I asked Eric if Usher knew anything about laying bricks on a sand base or with dry mortar and then suggested that before he wrote any more about Poe he go to Willard's and talk to Bob about home improvements. "Sam," Vicki said after I described my morning at the barber shop, "people will think you are moonlighting with Ringling Brothers."

Writing itself distorts life, much as makeup on a clown distorts the human face. Days are infinitely various, and moments do not tumble naturally into sentences. If I bade farewell to gathering, to wandering field and barber shop, to sculpting hours into subject and predicate, if I stopped traveling and talking, making speeches and saying silly things, perhaps my life would be more natural. "When the ox dies," Slubey Garts said last week at a funeral, "he is carved with a butcher knife. When a man dies, a mouth carves him." I am not waiting for a preacher to dice my days. I'm carving now, and I'm not using sterling silver either. My blade is the stainless steel of workaday adjective and adverb, of poetry's low, hard words. Dull in spots, the blade rarely slices cleanly. Instead it rips, tearing complexity and shredding people into hunks of conversation. Yet I am satisfied. Carving makes my days wondrous. If I put my knife away, doves would not huddle amid columbine in the spring, the fragrance of gingkoes would not fill my study in the fall, and cherubs as fat as grapefruit would not cavort through my imagination.

Three weeks ago I introduced the speaker at a dinner celebrating the hundredth anniversary of the *Sewanee Review*. During the introduction I read a poem. The word so frequently on the lips of my Armenian friend appeared once in the poem. Attending the dinner was an older woman, an acquaintance of my mother, who, I feared, might find the word offensive. Before dinner I spoke to her. "Miss Elizabeth," I said, "in my introduction there is a bad word. The word is not one I normally use, and if Mother heard me say it, she would roll over in her grave. The word, though, is in a poem, and I hope my reading it won't upset you." "Sammy, don't you worry," Miss Elizabeth said, patting my right hand, "I would not want you to say a bad word, but if it is in a poem, then that's all right."

How sad it would be if I did not record Miss Elizabeth's generous remark. If I did not scribble such things down, I would forget them. My life would be diminished, and so I will continue to gather, stuffing bits and pieces into envelopes and garish sermons. On Sunday Slubey preached on the evils of drink. The sermon was a rip-snorter. "Throw all your beer into the river," Slubey shouted. "Amen," responded Deacon Goforth. "Toss your wine in the river, too," Slubey continued. "Yes, Lord, amen," echoed the Deacon. "And chuck in your whiskey," Slubey concluded, seeming to follow his own advice by pitching himself against the front of the pulpit, then collapsing in a heap. For a moment the congregation was silent. Then Brother Goforth rose to the occasion. "Amen," he shouted, "praise the Lord. Now," he continued, turning to Mr. Billy Timmons at the organ, "let us all rise and sing 'Shall We Gather at the River'." When the congregation stood to sing, they were not alone. I was there, too, swimming open-mouthed through the crystal tide, praising King Jesus, keeping a weather eye cocked for Bob-Bob, and gathering, yes, Lord, gathering.

down

I shoveled snow because I was angry about Vicki's ears. "It's mutilation,"
I said. "Besides you'll look like you just arrived from the old country."
"I'm forty years old," Vicki said, putting the Frosted Mini-Wheats back
on the shelf and turning around, "and if I want to have my ears pierced,
I will. It has taken me fourteen years to realize that most of the time you
don't know what you are talking about. You are so forceful that people
assume you are right and don't question what you say. I am going to do
what I want for a change." "You could bore holes in your ears with an ice
pick for all I care," I said, finishing my granola. "I'm going outside and
shovel the drive." "Don't be an ass," Vicki said, "you'll hurt your back.
Then you'll be sorry." "Not so sorry as you will be when your earlobes
rot off," I said, standing and putting on my gloves. "Anyway if my back
goes out, you'll have to nurse me, and I guarantee I won't be an easy
patient, especially if you mutilate yourself."

For fifty minutes shoveling was easy. Then pain snapped down my back
and legs like cracks shattering ice, and I tumbled over beside the driveway. I had cleaned most of the drive, and, angry at Vicki, I was determined to finish the job. I turned myself into a ball, pulling my knees
into my chest. Then thrusting my feet out slowly, I inched across the

drive. When I got close to the remaining lumps of snow, I pushed the shovel across the asphalt and slid the blade between the road and snow, almost as if I were slipping a sheet of paper into the middle of a report. Once the blade was out of sight, I rotated the handle of the shovel from right to left in order to loosen the snow. Then after pulling the blade free from the mound of snow, I scraped the handle along the ground in a half-circle. When the blade reached my feet and the border of the drive, I turned it on edge and shook out the snow. Finishing the rest of the drive took thirty-five minutes. Three hours later I was inside the house, sprawled across the fifth step of the stairs, seven steps below the landing. My left arm was wedged under me on the fourth step, resembling a joist supporting a heavy rafter, my weight practically hammering my elbow into the carpeting. My right hand and forearm rested flat on the sixth step like a ridge board, one so weakened by time and carpenter ants that instead of furnishing a surface for rafters to bear against, it crumbled into shreds. Below me Vicki locked the balls of her feet against the stairs and pushed upward, her arms jammed against my bottom like studs holding up a top plate. From the landing the children's arms dangled down like hooks as they tried to hoist me upward.

I stayed in bed six days. Every time I moved, my back hurt. The thought of crawling to the bathroom brought tears to my eyes, so I stopped eating. Vicki had her ears pierced and steel studs stuck into the holes, but I hardly noticed. After the excitement of getting me upstairs passed, the children ignored me, preferring to play in the snow with George the dachshund. During my second day in bed not a child spoke to me until Vicki made them tell me good-night at eight-thirty in the evening. When I was sick in childhood, I listened to the Breakfast Club on the radio, and Mother fed me chocolate ice cream. Afterward she read the Hardy Boys to me. In Connecticut I felt sorry for myself, and I longed to be in Tennessee, with the hardy boys and girls with whom I grew up, those children who were my friends before I knew what a friend was.

As I lay in bed, my childhood seemed buried beneath a blanket of years and distance. Early in December I read John Sheldon Reed's collection of essays about Southern matters entitled *Whistling Dixie*. "Daddy," Francis said, seeing the book in my hands, "what's Dixie?" At dinner the next night Edward announced that he probably would not marry, explaining that he had not met anyone in Storrs he wanted to marry. "Don't worry, Edward," I said, "when the time comes for you to marry, I will ship you to Tennessee, and my friends will find a nice wife for you." "Oh, no!" Edward exclaimed, "I would feel funny around all those Southerners."

On the morning of the third day I received a telephone call. A writer for the *Hartford Courant* wondered if I still wanted junior after my name, "now," the man said, "that your father is dead." "Drop the junior," I declared, wiggling my toes and not feeling much pain. "It's time for a new me." Suddenly I smiled, remembering something Eliza said on Christmas Eve. "What would you do if you found us hiding downstairs tonight, waiting for Santa to see if he is real?" she asked, quickly adding, "we are not really going to do it, but what would you do?" Eliza's remarks often cheer me, and I remembered what she said the morning I shoveled the drive. After kissing me, she stared at my face, narrowing her eyes and wrinkling the flesh around her cheekbones. "Daddy," she asked, "when I get old are my nostrils going to be as hairy as yours?" "No, Eliza," I thought as I lay in bed, "you won't have an oriental rug in your nose. What you will get will be a letter like the one Francis received yesterday."

Atop a stack of mail on the bedside table lay a letter from the United States Achievement Academy, congratulating Francis on winning "a National Science Merit" award and inviting him to have his "personal biography printed in the appropriate volume of the United States Achievement Academy National Awards Yearbook." For $32.95 plus $7 for processing, handling, and shipping, Francis would receive an eight-by-ten-inch "commemorative certificate suitable for framing" and the yearbook, which included not only his "biography" but his photograph, one of his family's choosing. For the retiring student who did not want his picture printed, the certificate and book, complete with biography, were available for $28.95, plus the $7 handling fee. If a child did not wish to purchase the yearbook but still wanted his picture to appear in the volume, the cost was $9.95. No charge was made to the student who merely filled out the biographical sheet. Such students, the Academy assumed, were rarities, writing, "Your parents, grandparents, other family members and friends may want their own copy of the book in which you appear." For two copies, complete with biography, pictures, and one certificate, the handling fee was waived, and the charge was $74.95. "Because this award is of significance to your entire community, the Academy," the flyer stated, "will prepare a news release for your local newspapers, school newspapers, and broadcast stations announcing your USAA award. This release will be sent directly to you so that you can control its distribution to news outlets you yourself select." "Recognition by the Academy of our Nation's outstanding young people is an important contribution to America," declared a former president of Morehead State University.

Four or five times a year commerce stumbles across my doings and creates a distribution of honorific words in order to pick my pocket for a yearbook. I have never purchased a book, not even one of the red leather volumes with gold lettering. Still the flyer interested me, and before balling it up and pitching it over the edge of the dresser in hopes of swishing a domestic three-pointer into the waste can, I skimmed the biographical chart. What achievements, I wondered, did the Academy deem worthy of recognition? The chart listed 193 possible achievements. Students could choose up to eight for their biographies, including among others, Pom Pom Squad, Freshman Class Historian, Powder Puff Football, Model U. N., Weight-Lifting, Civic Air Patrol, Karate, Leo Club, Twirler, Betty Crocker Award, and Future Business Leaders of America. "What should I do, Daddy?" Francis said, seeing me reading the list. "I just make good grades." "Do this," I said, crumpling the flyer and taking a set shot from the prone position. I missed the waste can, but I took two more shots, missing the first with a postcard assuring me I had won an "all-expenses-paid two-week holiday in Hawaii" but making the second with a letter informing me that either a motion-picture camera, a set of luggage, or a new Chrysler was mine, just for calling a 1-800 number.

Francis was not the only family member to have his achievement recognized. Although I did not win an award, I received a prestigious nomination, or so a mass-produced letter on the bedside table informed me. "Dear Princetonian," the letter began, "You were recently nominated for consideration as a candidate to stand for election for Alumni trustee this coming spring. The Committee has met twice and has concluded its deliberations. I am sorry to say that your name was not selected for further consideration this time around. Your name will be kept in our active file for two more years, so you will again be considered without having to be nominated. Each year," the letter continued, "the Committee receives several hundred nominations for just six slots on the two slates. It's a formidable task to choose from among such an outstanding group of talented and successful Princetonians. The University is indeed fortunate, and I wish that we could have had better news for you this year. In the meantime, on behalf of the Committee let me thank you for participating in the process. Your continued interest and support are much appreciated." Because I did not know about the nomination until I received the letter, participation in the process was simple, about as simple as balling up the paper and trying to kiss a high one off the mirror above my dresser and into the waste can.

The first two nights I was down, pain woke me in the middle of the night. Falling asleep again was difficult, and the first night I spent the early morning hours in a sour mood, chewing over remarks that provoked mental indigestion. Statements made by an acquaintance at Thanksgiving gnawed my palate. "You just can't get anything with two bedrooms," she said, "for less than a million dollars." "Park Avenue," she gushed, a sip of wine later, "has become such a family neighborhood." Full of silly, alkaline compliments for me and mine, the mail, however, drove the acid out of my system and so sweetened the second night that when I awoke I quickly fell back asleep. At dawn I woke again, not because of pain, though, but laughter. "Are you all right?" Vicki asked, hearing me chuckling and seeing me sitting upright in the bed. "You are not choking, are you?" "I'm fine," I said. "I dreamed about your earlobes and that gave me indigestion and made me choke. But I've recovered, for the moment at least."

Although just a pillow away, Vicki's ears were far from mind. What I really dreamed about was Cousin Kathryn and her forty-five-year-old daughter Ann. In the dream Ann lay in a knot on the floor of her mother's living room, her arms extended above her head and wrapped around a table leg, a bowed leg with an old-fashioned claw and ball foot. When Ann grasped the leg, Kathryn pushed her around it. Soon Ann spun rapidly around the leg, making thumping noises, the sound resembling a worn belt whirling around a flywheel in the motor of a car. Atop the table sat four china figurines: a green lion wearing red boots, two frogs sprouting yellow wings, and a blue turtle with gold eyes. Although Ann's activity tickled me, it did not interest the menagerie, and they remained silent and aloof, too dignified to glance at the human clattering around the floor two and a half feet below them.

The next morning I decided to read until the mail arrived, and I began M. F. K. Fisher's *The Gastronomical Me*. Alas, her spicy accounts of dining across Europe were too rich for the bedridden me determined not to eat. Saving Fisher for a time when my back was well and I would not have to pick my way through hours à la carte, I asked Vicki to bring me the catalogue from Forestry Suppliers in Jackson, Mississippi. Four hundred thirty-two pages long, the catalogue contained much I coveted: heavy-duty brush cutters, thirty-four inches long and weighing seven and a quarter pounds, and then "Gator Chaps" and "Wire Mesh Snake-Proof Leggings." After reading the catalogue, I almost bought a Victor Tin-Cat Repeating Mouse Trap. Hordes of mice colonize the attic in winter and burrow into my imagination, so short-circuiting reason that sometimes my fire alarm goes off and I wake up in the night thinking I smell smoke. Certain that mice have chewed through electric wires behind the walls, I roam the house sniffing the air. I am preternaturally alert, ready to race into the children's rooms, pull them from their beds, and, throwing them across my shoulders, bound downstairs and out into the dark before the house dissolves in a whoosh of blue flame.

On shelves in Eliza's room the lamb dozes beside the lion, and cat and mouse frolic together. After studying the catalogue, I knew the Tin-Cat would not be welcome. "Multiple catch trap will hold up to 30 mice. No poisons, bait or resetting required," the description stated. "Trap is constructed of heavy-gauge galvanized steel with hinged lid and can be immersed in water for disposal of mice." Although the description put a damper on my desire for mouse traps, my back was better, and I was in an up, buying mood. During fall deerjackers roam the university woods, disregarding "No Hunting" signs. One hunter even raised a shooting platform in a tree on which the game warden posted a sign. The woods are popular, and families wander them throughout the year. By ignoring signs, hunters endanger lives. As a result I decided to buy a Buck knife, the "Bowie-style" with a seven-and-a-half-inch blade and weighing one and a quarter pounds. Raised by a series of heavy ropes and pulleys, shooting platforms are temporary. Although I tried to fell platforms in the past, I wasn't successful. With a Buck knife I could slice through ropes and drop platforms.

I ordered a Buck knife. By the time it arrived, however, deer season was over. Still, once my back was healthy, I strapped the knife to my belt and went platform hunting. Although I did not gut any platforms, I wasn't disappointed, for accompanying the knife was a gamy leaflet. "The fantastic growth of Buck Knives, Inc. was no accident," the leaflet explained. "From the beginning, management determined to make God the Senior Partner. In a crisis, the problem was turned over to Him, and He hasn't failed to help us with the answer." "What do you think?" I said after reading the statement to Vicki. "The Senior Partner sure took care of you, Samson," Vicki said. "Nobody but a fool would think about chopping people with guns out of trees."

When I first went down in the back, I tried to pass time by making up stories. Conclusions eluded me, though, and I didn't get far. I spent hours thinking about a man who drank too much eggnog on Christmas Eve and fell out drunk in his driveway where the UPS truck, making a last-minute delivery, ran over him and killed him. I brewed the eggnog, buying the rum, bourbon, and brandy, beating the egg whites and whipping the heavy cream. I planted hemlocks along the drive and churned up a squall that sprinkled the man with snow, just like confectioner's sugar, he thought, opening his mouth to catch a flake just before the truck flattened him. What I could not do was decide what the truck was delivering. Nothing seemed right, not the "Sunshine Assortment" from Harry and David or a four-layer, chocolate peanut-butter cake from Swiss Colony.

"Never Sharpen" a Buck knife "on a power-driven grinding wheel," the junior partners warned. Use a honing stone, they urged, and move the blade in an "even circular stroke." Harry and David were the stuff of fashionable, power-driven stories. In trying to give my tale a sharp, contemporary edge, I dulled the narrative, and so after I ordered the Buck knife, I pulled a handful of familiar characters out of the past and turned them slowly through the familiar grit of Carthage, Tennessee. From a butcher in Lebanon, Hink Ruunt bought a coatrack of aged hams and sold them out of his barn. When Loppie Groat returned his ham, saying it had gone bad, Hink protested. "You must of cooked it wrong, Loppie. There ain't nothing wrong with this ham. Why it was only cured last week." "Maybe," Loppie said, looking Hink hard in the eye before spitting into a milk carton, "maybe so, but it's done had a relapse."

Hink was a notorious miser. Four or five spindly trees of Arkansas black apples grew at the edge of his pasture. "I got a hankering for apples,"

Derma Tureen, his second wife, said to him one day, "and I think I'll go down to the grove and pick a handful." "That's all right," Hink said, "but don't you pull any except wormy ones." "Supposing there aren't any wormy ones, Hink," Derma said, putting on her bonnet. "Well, then you'll just have to wait until some of them go wormy," Hink answered. "We can't afford to eat apples that's worth eight, maybe nine cents a pound."

Like many tight-fisted people Hink forever came up with schemes to make money. Each spring when the residents from the school for the afflicted in Buffalo Valley visited Carthage, he staged an exhibition in his barn and charged the poor souls five cents to enter. One year he penned up a deer and, after painting the unfortunate creature white, hung a sign on the side of the barn reading, "See The Unicorn With Two Horns." In a stall next to the deer were a goose and her goslings. Nailed to the rafter above the stall was a piece of cardboard on which Hink wrote, "See The Amazing Goose What Can Suckle Eleven Goslings." Near the cesspool one May he buried a chipped hatchet. The next spring he dug it up, and after wiring it to the wall, so, as he explained, "it can't be stole," claimed it was the hatchet with which George Washington chopped down his father's cherry tree.

Although residents at the school weren't up to much history, most had heard of Washington, so Hink made Washington a specialty. In Nashville once Hink obtained the skull of a monkey. No one knew where Hink got the skull, although LaBelle Watrous, who went to Nashville on the same day as Hink to see about her adenoids, said that while she was waiting to see the doctor she looked out the hospital window. "And, Lord help me," she recounted, "down there behind the Vanderbilt Medical School a man about Hink's size and figure was rooting through the bins. Every once in a while he stuffed something into a brown paper sack. But whether he was putting in big toes or monkeys' heads, I couldn't for the life of me tell you." Be this as it may, however, Hink had a shiny white skull, and that spring he exhibited it, declaring it was Washington's skull. "Hink," Turlow Gutheridge said when he saw the skull, "you've gone too far this time. This skull is small, and I've read that Washington had an extraordinarily large head." "Oh, Mr. Gutheridge, you are right. Washington did have a big head," Hink said, not batting an eye, "but this here is the skull he had when he was a little boy."

Hink had the misfortune to pay funeral expenses for seven wives. Under such a succession of financial blows most misers would have buckled and dropped their coin purses at least once. Hink was made of more penurious stuff. When she was dying, Derma Tureen asked Hink to send her body to Morgan County so she could be buried in the family plot at Sunbright. "I know it's a lot to ask, Hink," she gasped, "but I couldn't stand to be buried here in Carthage among all these strangers." "Honey," Hink replied, "it is a lot to ask, but you've been a good wife to me, and I want to be fair, so I'll tell you what we're going to do. We'll just try you here in the graveyard in Carthage and see how you like it. If you don't lie quiet, then I'll move you to Sunbright."

Vicki does not like my stories. After I tell her one or two in bed, she buries her head under the pillow and won't remove it until I stop talking. Although pillows are soft, they seem hard when one's earlobes are tender, and during the last nights of my convalescence, I had my narrative way with Vicki, introducing her to the linguistic delights of Loppie Groat. One afternoon when Loppie and Googoo Hooberry were fishing at Dunphy's Pond, Loppie saw a man sitting on the back of a Hereford. "Googoo," he said, "look at that fellow riding a cow." "That ain't a cow," Googoo said, squinting into the sun, "that's a bull." "The hell, you say," Loppie responded, "that's a cow. I know it's a cow by his teats." Loppie was no fool, and he realized that his remarks occasionally strained the patience of people like Vicki. "It's not for want of ignorance that I speak nonsense," he once told Turlow Gutheridge. That same day he explained why he did not own a dog. "Turlow," he said, "I never saw a man what had a dog that didn't get to bragging about him sometime, and that's the reason I don't have a dog. I haven't got no gift of bragging." On hearing that Royce Farquarson got decapitated in an accident at the sawmill, Loppie was silent for a moment before he spoke. "Royce's head weren't no great shakes of a head, but still," he said, "I guess it was a sad loss to him."

When I finished this last story, Vicki did not say a word. She just stared at me. "I can see," I said, "that the tale has left you speechless in admiration. Well, you haven't heard anything yet." When Vicki shut then opened her eyes, the pupils resembling pools of quicksand, I swam into my next narrative. In Ankerrow's Café one lunchtime, I began, Loppie grabbed Ennion Proctor's toothpick and started digging at his teeth. Turlow saw

Loppie pick up the toothpick and, nudging him, whispered, "Loppie, I beg your pardon, but you are using Ennion's toothpick." "Great God, Turlow!" Loppie exclaimed, turning toward him, "don't you know me? This is your friend Loppie. I ain't going to steal the toothpick. As soon as I get through using it, I'm going to return it." At the end of the story Vicki was stone-faced, and I started laughing. I kicked the covers off my legs and, leaping out of bed, began hopping around the room. Not until Vicki reminded me did I remember my back. The pain was almost gone, and the next morning I ate a big breakfast, in honor, I told Vicki, of my buddy Loppie.

For another week my back stayed tender, and I remained hobbled, close to home. Still both life and I were looking up. Instead of being power-driven by the grinder of commerce and false compliment, the mail turned joyous and personal. From Alabama a grandfather who read one of my books sent Eliza a recipe for lemon squares. "I think she will enjoy trying it," he wrote. "I keep copies in my wallet to give to children about her age." "I'd like to meet you the next time you are in my neighborhood," a lawyer wrote from Richmond. "We could eat at the Smoky Pig in Ashland. The Pig isn't listed in any guide to fine restaurants. All you can find there are cole slaw, barbecue, hush puppies, and people who talk, these last occasionally stretching the truth but somehow still managing to circle around and embrace it in the end." "So that you will know what is on the minds of your readers, I am enclosing a slip of paper I found in one of your books in the Gainesville Library," a man wrote from Florida. Three inches wide and five inches tall, the paper was pink. Written neatly in pencil across the top of one side was "take chicken out of freezer."

The simple and the informal bring me more joy than the ornate and the carefully planned. I roam the university library, rummaging shelves, searching for stories about my buddies in Carthage. Folded between pages fifty-four and fifty-five of the first volume of "The Centennial Edition" of Rowland E. Robinson's *Works*, published in 1933 by the Tuttle Company of Rutland, Vermont, was a piece of green note paper, measuring four by six inches. Printed in thick letters across the top of the paper were the words "a hasty little note." At the bottom hung a checkerboard border, five-eighths of an inch wide and resembling oil cloth sliced off a kitchen table. In the middle of the paper was a note, written on December 31, 1933, by Mary Titcomb from her home at "1 Maple Street, Sanford,

Maine." "Dear Mr. Henderson," the note began, "I thank you very much for the book you gave me this Christmas. I got many nice presents. I got a ski suit, skates, a geography globe, hankies and a pocket book. I wish you a very happy New Year." My heart leaped when I read the note. What I found did not matter to the great world. To me, though, Mary's Christmas seemed important, and the dusty shelves of the library bloomed with poinsettias, and carols rang like crystal through the silent corridors.

Until my back was completely healed, I did not stretch my tether farther than the library. Instead of my going to their offices, people who wanted to see me visited the house. One morning a reporter from a foreign newspaper came. She arrived at 10:04 and left that afternoon at 1:26, making her visit three hours and twenty-two minutes long. She drank a cup of black coffee and ate a blueberry muffin and two Pepperidge Farm cookies. During the interview the woman went to the lavatory three times, a fact that broke down into one visit every sixty-seven minutes and twenty seconds. When I feel good, I play with numbers, and as I kept track of my interviewer's doings, I knew my back was practically mended. That afternoon in the mail I received a video tape. An acquaintance sent it, stating in an accompanying letter that he was sure I would find the video "provocative." In the tape a "futurist" preached about commerce. The message was clear: to remain competitive "in the global marketplace" a business had to foster originality and flexibility. Instead, however, of simply stating that creativity should be encouraged, the futurist declared that businesses should expand their paradigms. *Paradigm* is not a word that trips lightly from my tongue or the tongues of my friends. In the tape the futurist mutilated the definition of paradigm then painfully drilled the word through my ears, using it ninety-two times in a thirty-eight-minute lecture, for an average of 2.42 paradigms every minute, or one paradigm every 24.8 seconds.

I don't have deep thoughts about education. I simply cope with what the classroom thrusts at me. In the interview the woman raised "meaningful issues." A school board in New York City recently fired a superintendent because he insisted that elementary schools teach positive lessons about homosexual as well as heterosexual families. Did I, she asked, think schools ought to teach such lessons? "The homosexual family," I said, taking a deep breath and praying that oxygen would flood my brain, "is but one configuration of that larger social entity, the alternative family. Here in Mansfield," I said, "there are many alternative families. I know several, all of whom have children. In that white house at the corner," I said, gesturing vaguely toward a side window, "is a family consisting of two men, five women, and a clutch of children. I am not sure of the exact number of children," I added, as the woman's eyes widened and her pencil moved rapidly. "One of the women, as you might guess, is often heavy with child, so the number varies. Down the street is a very pleasant Episcopal family of three men, two women, and four children. Episcopalians don't breed so irresponsibly as other groups, and from what I understand the number of children in this family will not increase. On the other hand," I continued, "a Catholic family, consisting of six or seven women and a varying number of men, lives just across the South Eagleville Road. Because all members of the family are orthodox and refuse to practice birth control, the number of whelps is extraordinary. In spring they scamper across the highway like squirrels. Occasionally one is mushed and sent back to his maker, but, no matter, he is soon replaced. Thus," I said in summary, "you can see that the number of configurations that alternative families can assume is immense. To teach children about all the existing variations in just this small community would fill the entire academic year and probably rupture the educational system. Until the school year is expanded and July and August are strapped like trusses onto the calendar, perhaps teachers should, for the time being at least, concentrate their pedagogical energies on lesser matters, say, such things as reading and arithmetic."

More often than not topics thought profound are simply reflections of low current events, reconstituted and linguistically elevated but low events nonetheless. Recently, blather over sexual matters in the military has soiled front pages. Shortly after the interviewer left, Josh visited me. Josh believes that the military is beneath libidinous concern and thinks debate over soldiers' hormones moronic. Josh does not hover over his opinions like a mother hen. Resembling a starling on a bird feeder, he rakes his mind through controversy, pushing ideas about like millet and cracked wheat. "How would you like to take a shower with a homosexual?" an economist recently asked him in the locker room. "Heterosexual, homosexual, that does not matter so long as the man belongs to my social class," Josh retorted. "I couldn't bear to shower with someone from a lower class. You never know what will happen with inferior people. Rarely can they be relied upon to behave decently."

Josh's visits stir dyspeptic thoughts, and the best palliative for them is a walk in the woods. My back no longer hurt, and the next morning after breakfast I went for a purging stroll. Flocks of house finches and juncos gathered at backyard feeders, ebbing and flowing with alarm and hunger. Nuthatches ran up and down trees, digging into blisters for insects. Titmice and chickadees skittered through scrub while woodpeckers scratched along limbs. A blue jay gargled and squawked, and a pair of cardinals perched on bittersweet. White-throated sparrows huddled in forsythia, and English sparrows squatted on drainpipes, turning their eyes along sidewalks, searching for tasty bits of litter. A mockingbird crouched on a bramble, looking as knowing as a gypsy. Amid blackberry canes west of Unnamed Pond a goose lay dead. A bone in the upper part of the bird's left wing was splintered, and the goose was probably a cripple. Wounded by a hunter hiding in the brush atop Bean Hill, the goose rode the air across highway and pond before breaking and tumbling to the ground. One foot of the goose was pointed and tightly pinched. The black leathery skin rolled in folds like ridges of fingers, and the foot resembled the shadowy head of a duck plastered to a bedroom wall, a figure shaped by a child's raising a hand into a beam of light. During the walk I found several broken things: a pink toilet, a bloated raccoon, and then a pigeon downed by a hawk, kernels of corn ripped from the bird's craw and scattered like yellow bits of tile amid an insulation of gray feathers.

As I looked at the goose, the pond grunted and snapped. Unlike the bird the pond was alive. Gasps of air rose through buckles of ice accompanied by throaty abdominal rumblings. Because the day was quiet, I noticed sounds: George's dog tags tinkling in the cold, his feet small drumsticks pattering across the rime; then down the ridge behind the sheep barns small creeks running like tinfoil. Late in the afternoon a breeze hurried across the ridge. Branches clacked together. Afterward knuckles of ice fell and, shivering across the frozen snow, rang like harpsichords. Gray rocks on a ledge were green with ferns: Christmas and marginal wood fern, common polypody, Alpine woodsia, and rock cap fern. A pink plastic ribbon dangled from a bird's nest twelve feet off the ground. Sunlight shined through the bark of yellow birches, turning the shreds pale gold. The trees themselves resembled rolls of linen, long forgotten in attics but now pulled out into the day and tattered in the process. The nests of fall web worms unraveled like socks at the tips of branches. Winter creeper changed bare branches into lively bushes, making me forget the season and imagine spring.

The Fenton River was high. On hemlocks growing along banks, snow hardened and became heavy, pushing the lower branches into the water. Ice formed on the limbs, decorating them with pearly knobs and trains of sharp-cut lace. A gray and white hunting cat picked a silent path through brambles. A kingfisher swooped over a pool in the river. A short-tailed vole bustled into sight and, darting across a patch of ice, vanished down a hole in the snow. When George and I walked across the beaver pond to the lodge, a yearling beaver clambered up the air vent and growled. I stayed in the woods until early evening. At dusk three mallards flew fast overhead, their wings rising and falling in a rhythmic beat and whistle. The moon rose low and full and burned a cold yellow hole through the blue night. I turned home, and as the moon climbed high, a green halo melted around it, softening the sky and candying the hills.

I was now well out of bed, and little aside from a snow shovel could topple me, not even a rushed, overnight trip to Chicago. I left Connecticut late one Thursday afternoon in order to deliver a speech Friday morning. Once my back healed, appetite returned, and I finished *The Gastronomical Me.* Traveling makes me imagine myself sophisticated, and at dinner in Chicago I decided to become a culinary voluptuary, similar to M. F. K. Fisher, or, if not quite that, at least to keep track of what I munched. I began my meal with "Bruschatta Caponata—a Garlic Rusk with a Medley of Warm Eggplant, Tomato, Fresh Basil, and Pinenuts." For the main course I ate "Grilled Medallions of Swordfish"; for dessert, "Tiramisu—Lady Fingers soaked in Espresso with Mascarpone Cheese Filling and Chocolate with Vanilla Sauce." For good measure I tossed down two glasses of wine, the first white and the second red. Alas, at the end of the meal, the juices of digestion did not waft me aloft to bed and the poetic sleep of the satisfied. Instead my innards groaned like Unnamed Pond, and I staggered from the restaurant, feeling as if I were stuffed with bird shot. Much as wild goose should be soaked in milk to remove the fishy taste from its flesh, so I needed to wander soft hours to purge biliousness from body and mind.

The second stop on the Women's Professional Billiards Tour, the Chicago Classic, was being played in my hotel. Never had I seen men play billiards, much less women, so I bought a ticket. For two hours I watched the tournament, basting myself with Coca-Cola in hopes of reducing dinner to a simmer. In two rows of six each, twelve Kasson game tables filled the Chicago Ballroom. Nine feet long with grayish Formica sides, the pool tables resembled chunky tubs, stored so long outside a warehouse that rainwater filled them, allowing algae to grow across their surfaces in furry green mats. Over the tables hung racks of white imitation Tiffany lamps. Suspended above the lamps were two cords resembling clothes lines. Nine Styrofoam balls were strung along each line. All the balls were white except the fifth one in each line, which was orange. Whenever a competitor won a game, she reached up with her cue and pushed a ball from left to right along the line. In order to win a match, one had to win nine games. By looking for the orange balls, spectators could tell the progress of a match. Larded with ropes of glass and bulb, six chandeliers hung heavily from the ceiling and threw so much light over the room that brightness seemed to gather in corners like silt. Tacked to walls, flags advertised Marshall Field's; Chris's Billiards; Muddler's Pool Room; Huebler, "The World's Finest Cues"; and McDermott Cue Manufacturing of Menomonee Falls, Wisconsin.

People watching the matches spoke in whispers, and aside from the bang and metallic slap of pool balls, the room was silent. Once or twice I shut my eyes and imagined myself on the shore in Nova Scotia, the sound of racks jostling balls against each other reminding me of stones pulled down a beach by undertow. The players dressed similarly, many wearing loose dark trousers, white blouses, and black vests. Most players were slender, and when they leaned across tables to shoot, they resembled grasshoppers, their legs bent and flexed at the edge of flight. To hold their cues, they twisted their fingers into arthritic knots. After shooting they relinquished the table to opponents and, sitting in stiff chairs, poured glasses of ice water. Usually they did not watch their competitors' shots; instead they gazed into space. Although opponents occasionally smiled at each other, they rarely talked, at least not while their match was going on. Most spectators were family members or officials, editors of *Pool and Billiard* magazine, or representatives of sponsoring organizations, most prominently Kasson Game Tables. A few lone men wandered the room.

Most were pudgy and middle-aged and, wearing leather jackets, seemed to think they were younger than their years. As I watched them, I remembered something Turlow Gutheridge said to Hink Ruunt when he heard about one of Hink's schemes for making money. "How dreadful!" Turlow exclaimed, "a man at your time of life behaving in this manner." "Mr. Gutheridge," Hink responded, "I ain't a man of my time of life."

After two hours, I, on the other hand, felt old and went to bed. At breakfast the next morning M. F. K. Fisher did not come to mind, and I chopped a banana over a bowl of granola. The company to which I spoke managed more than a hundred business associations, among others, the World Airline Entertainment Association, the Popcorn Institute, the American Association of Women Dentists, and the Cremation Association of North America. On my mentioning this last group to a company employee, she responded, "Oh, yes, death care is a lively field." Like a cue ball slamming through the foot-spot, the woman's remark started a carom of words. Slubey Garts would never let a paradigm grow weedy under his feet, I suddenly thought. He would be aware of the commercial possibilities of death care.

That afternoon I did not need the World Airline Association to make the flight home entertaining. Instead I amused myself, polishing an account of Slubey's sharp dealings. Haskins was the biggest funeral home in Smith County, and the day after Luburl Haskins was buried, Pearline, his widow, sold the home to Slubey and started packing for Florida, where, as Turlow Gutheridge put it, "she could grieve in a little more comfort." Luburl was a gloomy man, and Pearline hankered for gaiety. "You have no idea how I regret to see you wearing these habiliments of woe," Judge Rutherford said to her at the graveside. "You can't be as sad as I am," Pearline answered, reaching up to flick an inchworm off her veil, the diamonds on her fingers sparkling in the sunlight. "I look worse in black than any other color."

Before he planted any of the gospel brethren, Slubey refurbished the funeral home. He bought a big rock in Crab Orchard and drilled a hole into it, turning the rock into a fountain by running a length of hose through the hole and attaching one end to a sink in the basement. He set the fountain in the entrance hall; on the wall above he fixed a plaque reading, "The Rock in Horeb." Next he hired Isom Legg to paint the ceiling of the chapel. A coal dealer in Orphan's Friend, Isom was a competent craftsman, good enough to paint signs on the sides of barns urging tourists to chew Bull of the Woods Tobacco and to see Ruby Falls and Rock City. However, he was not an artist. Although he tried to follow Slubey's instructions and paint the Lord showing Moses the Land of Gilead from the top of Pisgah, he wasn't entirely successful. Pisgah looked like Battery Hill, just outside Carthage, and Moses was cross-eyed and had a swollen red nose, bearing a striking resemblance to Isom's sometime drinking companion Hiram Povey. As for the Lord, Isom painted Him as a dove, replacing His wings with hands, the fingers of which were extraordinarily long, the middle finger of the left hand running from the center of the chapel roof over the choir stalls to end in a sharp nail pointing at the altar. On the Lord's right hand the middle finger was shorter and stubbier; still it stretched from the middle of the roof almost to the lintel above the entrance. Hiram was recognizable, but the Lord puzzled some viewers. When Proverbs Goforth first saw Him, he exclaimed, "Great God Almighty, what a big rooster!"

In the vacant lot next door to the funeral home Slubey dug a pond. After dumping in a tub of goldfish and planting "Bible flowers," day lilies and jonquils, along the shore, Slubey set benches around the pond and erected a sign reading "The Fishpool in Heshbon." From a mail-order house in Arkansas he bought an ornamental gondola. When Slubey told Proverbs he planned to buy a gondola, the deacon reacted enthusiastically, urging him to purchase two, saying, "They might breed." Proverbs was cistern deep with advice. After the ploughing season ended, he urged Slubey to rent Jeddry, Loppie Groat's mule, and tie him to a stake near the pond and hang a sign on his back saying, "Balaam's Ass."

Slubey's most successful improvement was the marquee he erected over the front door. Whenever someone was "in the nuptial bed waiting to marry the Lord," as Proverbs expressed it, Slubey put his name on the marquee in capital letters, full names, too, no matter how long, "not just no middle initial," Proverbs bragged. When business was slack and the "honeymoon suite" vacant, Slubey publicized local events, reminding neighbors of the dance at the Elks Club or the Eastern Star's bake and book sale. When the high school basketball team played in the state tournament in Knoxville, he printed "Go Owls" on the marquee. Unfortunately one of the Mrs. Ruunts died suddenly, and Slubey was forced to change the marquee before the tournament ended, and Carthage lost in the semi-finals to Lenoir City, a team they beat earlier in the season. Slubey's civic concern brought rewards. In a ceremony at the Male and Female Select School, just two years after he bought the funeral home, he was made "Knight of the Upper Cumberland" and was awarded a shield embossed with two crossed swords.

Not all members of Slubey's Tabernacle of Love approved of his success, and when he buried the fifth Mrs. Ruunt on a Sunday, a small part of the congregation accused him of "profaning the Sabbath Day for the merchandise of silver." When Slubey refused, as the dissenters put it, "to set his standard again toward Zion," they broke away and formed the Church of the Chastening Rod. Slubey, their spokesman said, "had forsaken the stream of living waters. Gadding about with Methodists, he trimmed his ways to seek fame." Proverbs Goforth told people that he expected the breakaways would soon drape themselves with sheets and "take up serpents." For his part Slubey said that although he expected the breakaways to harvest a heap of sorrow, he did not think they would be misguided enough to handle reptiles. "Or if they did," he reckoned, "it wouldn't be nothing more serious than fence lizards, Jimmy Bullard's box of toads, and then on special occasions like baptizings, a big shiny rat snake."

The secession disturbed Slubey more than he admitted. A good religious name was better than precious ointment, and so he wrote his old friend Pharaoh Parkus in Memphis, inviting him to hold a revival at the funeral home. "Tinker the hearts and churn the sensoriums," Slubey instructed, concluding his letter, "may Jesus turn your intellect into a volcano and redden its lava and widen its mouth." Pharaoh accepted the invitation and delivered a sermon that made Carthaginians forget Slubey's problems. "You are all cavalry," Pharaoh declared, "galloping down the rapids of mortality. The dewdrops of disease are bright on your foreheads, and your hearts are blacker than tassels on the buggy of death. Only the artillery of Jesus loaded with holy shot can ticket you for glory and write your names in italics in the newspapers of Heaven." "Did you hear," he said, "about the woman in the hospital who was getting better when she died suddenly and the doctor said she died of improvements? Don't improve. Stay as you are. You don't want to be strong enough to climb the parapet of Hell. Pray for wounds as resplendent as vermillion and odiferous as musk. Forsake the orgies of the kennel. Be a hero gnawed with rust and digested by insects but polished for glory."

"You've poured the water of gall over the Chastening Rod," Proverbs said to Pharaoh at the end of the sermon, "and it will wither on the vine." For my part I am not quite ready to assign the church to the Cremation Association. Still, Slubey had leaned on his Senior Partner, and the Senior Partner proved a stout champion. Pharaoh dulled the two-edged sword of Slubey's critics on a grinding wheel rough with grainy words. As a result death care remained on the cutting edge of Slubey's enterprises, and at a gathering of the Knights held shortly after the revival, Slubey was awarded a pennon, two garlands, and a skull to accompany his shield.

"Daddy," Eliza said when I returned from Chicago, "Koala has a surprise for you in your bedroom." Eliza's stuffed koala sat on my pillow. Propped open in front of him was *Babar's Anniversary Album*. "Koala will read to you if you hurt your back again," Eliza explained. Dixie and childhood seemed near. Unknowingly Eliza opened the *Album* to an illustration that made me laugh when I was young. While Babar and Queen Celeste were on their wedding trip in *The Travels of Babar*, Arthur, Babar's small cousin, started a war by tying a firecracker to the tail of Rataxes, king of the rhinoceroses. Until Babar returned from his trip, the war went poorly for the elephants. Babar realized the way to defeat Rataxes and his chief of staff, General Pamir, was not through force but craft. Accordingly Babar painted the tails of his largest soldiers red. Afterward he drew two huge black and white bull's eyes on the bottom of each soldier. While Babar painted, Arthur made green and red wigs. On the day of the battle, the faces of six monsters rose from behind a hill, terrifying the rhinoceroses. In the illustration the monsters stared over a yellow slope, their tails resembling carrots and their "hair" tufts of crabgrass. In the foreground the rhinoceroses tumbled over each other, rolling down the hill in gray clods, trying to escape. "This is wonderful, Eliza," I said, squeezing her tightly and kissing her. "Babar is an old friend." The next morning was sunny. Spring seemed in the air, and I drove to the mall and bought Vicki a pair of earrings. Little honey bees dangle from minute silver chains. Vicki says the earrings are "sweet" and promises that she will wear them as soon as her earlobes stop stinging.

early spring

Catalogues shape the seasons of my mind. In January when Spring Hill's *Planting Guide* and White Flower Farm's *Garden Book* poked budding through the mail, I pulled the rumpled snow off the yard and, folding it, stored winter away on a back shelf of thought. In imagination my rocky half-acre turned loamy and, breaking out of its tight, dull skin, stretched fresh through meadow and across hillside. I lined the long driveway of dream with twenty-four kousa dogwoods, all fully grown and in bloom, white clouds thirty feet tall. Trumpet vines dangled from the well house in red clusters. Over them hummingbirds paused then swung like batons, softening the notes that seemed to blow brassy down the long blossoms. Amid sweet William by the back door, Eliza held a tea party. Kitty, Fuzzy, and Penny Panda sat in chairs around a small table while Cowboy galloped on his rocking horse through a patch of baby's breath, worried that he would miss the Oreo cookies his friends were munching. Along the stone wall at the edge of the pasture, shrub roses bloomed like Easter bonnets. The roses were old-fashioned: damask Celsiana, pink Félicité Parmentier, Louise Odier, Marquise Bocella, and Rose de Rescht, its double blossoms puffs of powdery fragrance. The scents drew the family like bees, and on cool evenings we strolled along the wall, our conversations hives of contented murmurings.

The meadow behind the house dipped down then swept out to a creek. In the soft dirt above the creek thickets of winterberry and sweet pepperbush thrived. Through the shrubs curved a path bordered on both sides by lilies: Golden Sunburst, Scarlet Emperor, pink Montreux, and Top Hit, the blossoms of this last white as ironed sheets. Between stones at the edge of the creek yellow flag bloomed. The hillside across the creek was damp. In spring rivulets of water blew down it, resembling silver ribbons tied to a fan and streaming out in the breeze. Early on June mornings a haze hung over the hillside like a web. By noon the haze had burned off, and lupine gathered the sunlight, turning it pink and purple. Throughout the meadow I scattered golden yarrow, coreopsis, and ox-eyed daisies. In my mind blossoms bloomed and faded by the hour. The planting and hoeing tired me, though, and one morning after transplanting boxwood, I decided to buy horses. The children liked to ride, and I owned so much land that I bought Bashkir Curlies. I told friends that I bought Curlies because they could endure long rides and were gentle. Although I did not tell people, I also purchased the breed because every horse owner I know owns Morgans or quarter horses, and as spring rose prancing through my veins, I imagined myself doing a bit of showy high-stepping, or at least prancing at a gait beyond that of the plodding herd.

I did not keep horses long, however. Soon after I raised the barn, the Grant Mitsch catalogue arrived from Hubbard, Oregon. An hour later oceans of daffodils rippled and broke across the meadow. In spring I prune concern for expense from my imagination. Scattered across the field were three hundred white Chaste daffodils costing forty dollars a bulb. Princeton and American Heritage bloomed in clumps, the former costing seventy dollars a bulb and the latter ninety. Daffodils with white appealed to me this year, and I planted Cedar Hills and Refrains throughout the field, the cups of the former yellow at the edges but darkening to green eyes and the cups of the latter ruffling with pink and orange. With their split coronas pasted pink against white perianths and resembling splotches of lipstick, Shrikes stood garish beside First Formals, dignified and demurely white. As the flowers tossed and curved through the field in rainbows, their names rang like poetry: Ice Chimes, Carib, Desert Bells,

Moonflight, and Hillstar, Verdant Meadow, Pink Valley, and Night Music. From Smith and Hawken I bought a teak lawn chair. I placed it at the edge of the meadow under a stone arch waxy with wisteria. On sunny days I sat in the chair and read my mail, the wisteria waving blue and the field beckoning like a table set with sweet fruits, the perianths platters and coronas cups beading with color.

In January the letters I received bloomed like snowdrops and warmed days. From a nursing home in Pennsylvania Miss Frances thanked me for my letters. "It is not genius, or even love, that makes a person great," she declared, "but kindness." Even in New Hampshire sap was rising. "It's an embarrassment," an acquaintance wrote from Concord, "that our generation of literary intellectuals is the first in nearly two centuries to have contributed little or nothing to the elucidation of *Hamlet*. I have remedied the situation." Snow melted in Illinois, and wags generated spontaneously from the mud. "Mr. Pickering," Glenn Tree McGhee wrote from the prison in Marion, "me and a fellow human being Mr. Duke Crawford is on a hunger strike and been on for 3 week. No one has showed no human concern for our human life. We are asking that you come out to here and call myself and Mr. Duke Crawford out to talk with us. This is all we ask and well come of this hunger strike. If you do not come we will die soon. Do not have our blood on your hands. You will go knowing you did not save us but we died." For a moment the letter startled me, but then I recognized the imagination of a friend, one whose thoughts turned to pranks in the spring, much as mine turned to flowers. If I could not visit the prison, Mr. McGhee instructed, then I was to pledge money to "Carts for Weenie Dogs Foundation," a nonprofit organization established to aid crippled dachshunds. "Make the donation in the name of the Stanky family," Mr. McGhee explained, "Roy Leroy, Wanda Towanda, Fern Laverne, Gene Eugene, Earlene Lurlene, Cecil. Pray for this troubled family sick at heart and afflicted with the sugar diabetes, sinus, and diarear. You could get a jar of salve if the money was big enough."

Winter mail also brought catalogues to the children. Imaginary possessions did not satisfy them. Francis wanted "Turbo Pascal for Windows," version 1.5, a programming language for computers. For his part Edward coveted a green tee-shirt with the logo of the Florida Marlins baseball team printed on the chest, a marlin leaping through a gray buoy, the

center of which resembled a baseball with orange stitching. From the
Aston-Drake Galleries catalogue, Eliza selected a doll: Mary, the oldest
of the Ingalls children in the Little House on the Prairie books. Wearing
a brown sun-bonnet and a calico dress, Mary held a blue apron sagging
with apples. "I know Helga and Octavia would invite her to their tea
parties," Eliza said. "She would give them slices of apple, and they would
give her Fig Newtons."

So that the items they wanted would not remain as hazy as the flowers
that bloomed through my mind, Edward and Eliza drew up an "Allowance Scheldue" and handed it to me one day with the mail. Thirteen
payments were listed. "Scrubbing the bathtub" earned twenty cents, and
"Watering Mom's plants," fifty cents. For "Taking the garbage out," the
children asked five cents. "Feeding George" was ten cents. While "Making parents' bed" was a hefty seventy-five cents, the most costly item on
the list was "Cleaning up the twigs in the yard" at five dollars. The children felt guilty asking money for chores, so they also compiled a list of a
dozen "Allowance Deductions." Some penalties were stiff, and fifty cents
seemed the standard deduction, being assessed for "Teasing," "Forgetting to do our homework," "Getting into deep trouble at school," and
"Watching over 1 hour a day of TV." The penalty for "Playing the computer for over an hour" was sixty cents while "Getting phone messages
mixed up" cost forty cents and "Bad manners at the table," a nickel less.
The most expensive deduction was five dollars for losing a library book
while the least costly were "Not putting tooth paste top on" at ten cents
and "Not putting a new roll of toilet paper in" at fifteen cents.

The mail also brought a royalty check from the University Press of
New England. During the previous six months I earned $14.89 for two
books, eleven cents less than the children would make for picking up
sticks, twice in the fall and once in the spring. "Everybody," I said, looking at the check and feeling spring-like, "let's make a night of it and go
to the girls' basketball game at the university." Vicki and Francis did not
want to go, and so that evening Edward, Eliza, and I attended the game.
The check did not cover expenses. I spent a dollar and fifty cents more
than the cost of a Starthroat daffodil bulb: eleven dollars for tickets, five
for an adult and three for each child; ten dollars and fifty cents for treats,
two hot dogs at a dollar and seventy-five cents apiece, two soft drinks at

a dollar and fifty cents each, and three Eskimo Pies at a dollar a pie, one of these last for Edward, the other two for Eliza. For myself I bought a cup of "Colombian Supreme" coffee costing a dollar.

Spending the royalty check at one swoop emboldened me. At summer's end my sabbatical began, and I planned to take the family to Australia. Airplane tickets cost eight thousand dollars. Unlike many acquaintances I have never earned money from writing, much less been able to convince a foundation to award me a fellowship. Spring, though, was in the blood. As I blew the check at the game, so others, I thought, might also feel expansive and open their purses for me. During the week after the basketball game I put together a packet of material, including reviews, articles about my little doings, and a copy of my last collection of essays. In the packet I also stuffed a letter from a press agreeing to publish any book I wrote about Australia. I mailed the packet to United and Qantas airlines; to the United States Information Agency, the cultural branch of the diplomatic service; and then to automobile companies: Ford, Mazda, Chrysler, and General Motors. For tickets or the use of a car I offered to barter speeches and paragraphs, even whole chapters of the book. United Airlines, General Motors, and Chrysler answered by return mail, saying they rarely sponsored junkets like mine, Chrysler explaining to my embarrassment that they did not "distribute vehicles in Australia."

"Sam," a literary man said to me in January, "you hide your learning better than anyone I've ever met." Would that the other corporations I wrote concealed their opinions of my plans as well as I hid my learning. Unfortunately they all resembled the literary man and had strong reactions to my offer, so strong they did not acknowledge receiving the packets. At another time of the year the lack of response might have irked me. Little upsets me, however, during catalogue season, and I raked cars and planes from my imagination and resowed days, planting butterfly bushes on the hillside above the lupine, and then to the surprise of neighbors, buying horses again, this time Lippizans because I had a few tricks with which I planned to startle readers accustomed to ordinary literary dressage.

At the end of February I flew to California and spent a week at Stanford University. Real spring blossomed, and I roamed the campus, much as I wandered catalogues, turning the grounds into my garden. Brown towhees and scrub jays scratched through bushes. Brewer's blackbirds hunched on limbs outside a snack bar, whistling and rolling their eyes over picnic tables in hopes of finding crumbs. Behind a ridge the sun glowed yellow, melting the hills and making the horizon flow soft and cloudy like candle wax. While acacia bloomed in long cool fingers, saucer magnolias spread red and fragrant. The early morning light pulled pools of color from deep within Chinese elms, turning the bark orange. At dawn blue welled out of fissures in the bark of live oaks. By noon the color had drained back into heartwood, and the bark was gray. I spent much time looking at eucalyptus. On one tree leaves resembled silver awls while the bark twisted upward and turned red like skin stretched taut by an Indian burn. From the bark of another tree sap oozed then hardened black, appearing singed. Clumps of scarlet blossoms hung behind bunches of leaves, licking at the edge of sight like small flames. Resembling shags teased from country rugs, strips of bark curled about the trunk of another tree. The tree was huge, and walking around the trunk took eleven long paces. The limbs themselves were massive, and patches from which bark had peeled were white, resembling great bleached bones through which blues and grays flowed, shadows of clouds laden with weather.

One morning I roamed Jasper Ridge, a biology preserve in the foothills above Stanford. Although I knew the wildlife could not survive in New England, I wanted to graft a scion of California onto the stump of my Connecticut. Flowering before plants in Mansfield, the graft might force me to words earlier than usual. I studied Jasper Ridge, seeing leather and blue oaks for the first time, marveling at valley oaks, the bare limbs curving heavy then suddenly shattering into nests of twigs, fibrous against the pale sky. Clots of mistletoe grew in valley oaks, and acorn woodpeckers fluttered between trees, their faces clowns' masks painted red, yellow, white, and black. Moss wrapped green around the trunks of live oaks, and from limbs ramalina lichens hung in long creamy nets. Bark cracked open across madrone and, pulling loose, rolled into scrolls, turning branches umber. Along a slope above a creek, poison oak grew in grabbing snares. In a grove of redwoods, shreds of bark absorbed water and sound, cooling and quieting the day.

A California newt clung to greenstone above a stream. Yellow banana slugs as long as my hand ate glistening paths across rotting leaves. Runoff from the hills wore smooth, throat-like channels into limestone. Beards of moss covered rocks above the channels. Through the beards California polypody pushed then sprouted in green falls, a double row of orange seed dots beneath each leaflet. Wild cucumber spun tendrils and, hooking twigs, wound itself up through stronger plants. I chewed bay laurel then pitcher and California sage. I sliced open a fist-sized oak apple gall, pitted by the gray larvae of parasitic wasps. While the flowers of buck brush had not opened and resembled clusters of small rattles, sprays of white urn-shaped blossoms speckled manzanita. Beneath oaks clustered red brushes of Indian warrior, the leaves at the tops of the plants cut sharply, the flowers below smooth paddles. While a black phoebe turned after insects above the lake, two coots glided slowly along the shore, their bills white in the sun.

My Jasper Ridge was a gallery of impressionistic paintings, the soothing colors spreading across hours, making me feel kindly. As milkmaids and trillium blossomed modestly, so I was drawn to people who drew nourishment from their years and bloomed with story, spring people who delighted in life and who concealed only their learning, not themselves. My host in California was Ted Harris, an old friend and head of the Department of Medicine at the Stanford Medical School. Late one November night some years ago, Ted recounted, his mother telephoned him. "I've just heard the news," she said, "and I wanted to tell you how sorry I am." "Sorry?" Ted answered, rubbing sleep from his eyes. "Sorry for what?" "I'm sorry," she said, "that you didn't win the Nobel Prize." For the next five years Mrs. Harris telephoned each November to offer Ted condolences for not winning the prize. In the sixth year, however, Mrs. Harris needed an operation. She was old, and odds were good that she would not survive surgery. While she was in the hospital, the Nobel Prize for medicine was announced. "Ted," she said when he visited her just before the operation, "I'm sorry about the prize." "That's all right, Mother," he said, telling a green lie, "this year I finished second." "Oh," she said, smiling as the orderly wheeled her toward the surgery, "how very nice."

For students hibiscus blooming on the university grounds appeared spring enough. During my week at Stanford I did not see a single couple holding hands. Moreover I saw so few children on campus that I suspected that both faculty and students had been inoculated against spring fever. At least no signs of the infection came to notice until the day I left. Each morning I ate in a university dining hall. Students always ate with me, and at breakfast that last morning when I said that I had to eat hurriedly because I was scheduled to talk to residents at the medical school, Jill, a slender blooming freshman, smiled modestly then spoke. "Would you mind doing some shopping for me?" she said, turning her fork upside down and pulling it slowly through syrup atop a blueberry waffle, the tines cutting soft, sticky gullies into the batter. "Do what?" I said. "Shopping," she answered. "Find me a doctor. I don't care what his specialty is just so long as he is good-looking."

Suddenly hormonal spring seemed not only in the air but in the blood, even at home in Connecticut where it was, to my mind at least, not weeks but decades early. "Daddy," Eliza said when I returned from California, "Jason kissed me today at school." "When did he kiss you?" I said, sitting down at the kitchen table. "In math," Eliza said. "I was subtracting four-digit numbers. Jason isn't good at math, and he can only subtract one-digit numbers." "Oh," I said, wondering if subtraction led to kissing in the second grade what multiplication would lead to in the sixth grade. "Anyway," Eliza said, interrupting my reverie, "he is not Tarzan."

Since the seventeenth century educators have preached that childhood reading shapes adults. Despite thinking it suspect, I have paid lip service to the notion. For nine years I read to the children. Along with entertainments I occasionally selected books which attempted to teach lessons. This world seems a harder and colder place than the one in which I grew up, and I wanted Eliza to be self-sufficient. To this end I read scores of books to the children in which heroines were tough and independent. The examples did not take. Children are more complex than theory, and Eliza fell in love with Tarzan. Instead of thrusting strong-willed through life, she imagines herself swooning before Tarzan, a man with prehensile toes who is happiest swishing naked through the tops of trees.

Because the telephone began ringing and continued to ring through dinner that evening, I did not think long about Eliza's infatuation. The calls were for Edward. Lucy, a girl in Edward's fourth-grade class, wanted to know if he "liked" her. "For heaven's sake, Edward," I said, "tell her you like her. That will make her feel good, and these damn calls will stop." "I don't know, Daddy," Edward began. "Just do it," I interrupted when the phone suddenly rang again. "If you don't, you cannot have dessert." "Well?" I said when Edward returned to the table. "What did she say?" Edward's face was red. "What she said was inappropriate for a nine-year-old," he replied. "It might be all right for a fifteen-year-old. But for a nine-year-old, it was inappropriate, and I can't tell you."

In public right-thinking parents subscribe to privacy. In private they rummage through children's lives and desks. "Edward," I said, "I respect your right to be silent, and if you don't wish to share Lucy's remarks, that is fine with me." Then I put my fork down, and standing said to Eliza and Francis, "Let's play *Memory.* Edward can join us when he finishes dessert." If people were divers and secrets pearls, Vicki would be a millionaire. Before Edward even nibbled dessert, she pried him open and pocketed the conversation. "What gives?" I said to her thirty minutes later while the children were upstairs waiting for me to read to them. Edward's response, Vicki recounted, pleased Lucy. "I am so glad you like me, Edward," Lucy said, "but I don't think we should do it, yet." "Great God from Gulfport!" I exclaimed, "I'm sending Edward to California!" Not all the children were roused by hormones baying at winter's traces. With eyes only for keyboard and screen, Francis was oblivious to charms other than those possessed by Turbo Pascal. When Evan constructed a "Flirt Chart" at school, rating his friends from active, or ten, to inactive, or zero, Francis fell off the chart, scoring minus five.

Reared by an ape, Tarzan was a primitive suitor, and not long after I returned from Stanford, I changed my opinion and decided pagans interested Eliza more than primates. On the coffee table in the living room she erected a garish altar, built, she explained, to welcome Persephone back from the underworld. Over the table she spread a red silk scarf decorated with fat tongues of color and with wildflowers resembling butterflies. In the middle of the table stood Josephine, a doll eight inches tall. Josephine wore a ruffled dress. Perched on the back of her head was a straw hat, a ribbon dangling from it in yellow and green curves. From her waist hung a blue apron, speckled with minute purple and red birds. Josephine was a priestess. Around her Eliza arranged an altar rich with offerings: three cloth poppies, the stem of each eighteen inches long, at the tips red velvet blossoms; a granite rock, a green owl painted on it; a ceramic cat made in Mexico and five and a half inches tall; three bright 1993 pennies, Lincoln's head face up; four seashells, one, a measled cowry, the others, orange and white olives; and then a porcelain mask, the face of a woman, her hair black and white resembling keys on a piano.

Josephine had as much to do with Poseidon as Persephone. At Josephine's feet Eliza placed a tribute made from clear plastic. The tribute was an inch thick, two and five-eighths inches wide, and three and three-quarters inches long. Inside was a reef of sea creatures: two pearly snails, a seahorse, lacy threads of seaweed, a starfish, a limpet, and two small pink cockle shells. Balanced on top of the plastic and resembling an umbrella was a sand dollar. Sometimes I think modern life more pagan than that in ancient Greece. In March Edward's class saw a film which celebrated the changes that occur as girls mature and become capable of having children. That night at dinner Edward described the movie, seasoning his description with terms such as ovary, womb, and fallopian tube. Not only did he use the word *period,* something I cannot do, but he explained the workings of the unmentionables in clinical detail. During Edward's account Eliza's mind drifted from lower bodily regions to Lower Egypt. Only when he described the period did she pay attention. "Well," she said when he finished, "I wonder who invented that thingy-do, that pyramid."

Not only was sap rising through my family, but some of the vascular creatures inhabiting my essays had awakened from winter naps and begun to percolate about town. Horace Newell married Mozelle Burn. County treasurer for two decades and one of the best friends, as Turlow Gutheridge put it, that money could buy, Horace discounted scores of tax assessments. For her part Mozelle was a person of a generous and democratic nature, a woman never reluctant to accept remuneration for certain therapeutic services at which she was remarkably adept. "Great God!" Turlow exclaimed on hearing about the marriage. "That scoundrel Horace will never stop robbing the public."

For the first time in months Cora Tilly did not ask Vester McBee to shop for her at Barrow's Grocery. Instead Cora put on shoes with rubber soles and walked uptown and shopped by herself. Cora was a careful shopper, and before buying a vegetable, she pinched all the produce in the bin. Nothing irritated Lowry Barrow more than people's squeezing vegetables. Often when business was slow, he left the cash register and crept along the aisle past canned goods until he reached fresh vegetables. Slowly he peeked around the corner, and if he saw someone fingering the vegetables, he spoke sharply to them. On this particular occasion Cora held a big tomato in her left hand, and when Lowry looked around the aisle, she thumped it with the index finger of her right hand. Lowry paid handsomely for his tomatoes, buying them in Lebanon from Maury Stonebridge who grew them in his greenhouse. "Cora," Lowry barked, "put that tomato back!" Cora was so startled that she gasped and jumped upward, breaking wind with a loud bang. "And," Lowry continued, jumping himself, "you can put that back, too."

With the coming of spring people felt healthy enough to visit doctors. Isom Legg traveled to Carthage from Orphan's Friend to see Dr. Sollows. "You've got to help me, doctor," Isom pleaded. "I'm near-sighted and ruptured and suffer something awful from varicose veins and boils. I've got a liver complaint, an aching back, Bright's disease of the kidneys, dyspepsia, neuralgia, and the green bronchitis, not to mention a pain in the shoulder bone of my flank." "Have you talked to Doctor Chism in Lebanon about your troubles?" Dr. Sollows asked. "Yes, indeed," Isom replied, "I've consulted all the doctors in Lebanon. I have also been to see a homeopath, four chiropractors, and when I was up to Nashville, a podiatrist. I've tried store-bought medicines, too: Sloan's Liniment, Doan's Pills, and Heiskell's Ointment. This winter I wore red flannel underwear, and last summer Pharaoh Parkus baptized me once at Pleasant Shade then again at Horseshoe Bend. But that didn't do no good. All that water done was to put me in a flux and give me the rumbling catarrh." "Mr. Legg," Dr. Sollows said after Isom finished describing his ailments, "you best go home and rest in peace. If you have tried all these things and are still alive, I don't know of anything that can kill you."

Dr. Sollows's prescription did not go down well with Isom. Later, when Turlow Gutheridge saw Isom outside Read's drugstore and asked him how he was doing, Isom replied in a surly manner, "I am as well as you or anybody else can be that is in no better health than I am." Season, not Dr. Sollows, was responsible for Isom's irascibility. Along with flowers weeds sprout in the spring, both in gardens and characters. In March teachers in local schools assigned "units" on the American Indian to students. "I am tired of Indians," Eliza complained, "they are too good. Weren't there any bad ones?" "I have studied Indians for six years," Francis said, "and I have never met a real Indian." "That's because you have never been to a casino," Eliza answered. "Many people in Mansfield come from

Poland and Italy," Edward said. "Why don't we ever read about them?" "Yes," Francis added, "and why not the Irish or the Germans, or Jewish people?" "I wish we could study Greeks," Eliza said, "especially their myths." At breakfast the next morning I found a piece of paper in the middle of the table. Drawn on it were three "warriors": Pee-Pee Hawk, Do-Do Bear, and Chief Sitting on the Pot. Like a socially responsible gardener, I fetched my intellectual hoe and chopped at the weeds, but I am afraid I did not cut the taproots. My back wasn't in the task, for I, too, had grown irritable. "Real education," I told Vicki, "would nurture thought from seed. Schools purchase ideas from social garden centers. All the plants come from the same rootstock. No wonder lessons bore children."

Although diced weeds can spice a day, they do not blend well with ambition. The next morning I received a telephone call from California. A producer was putting together a series for public television. Already "on board," he informed me, were two "stars," and he wondered if I would become part of "the team." The people he mentioned were famous, and just to sail once across the screen in their company, I would have signed up for a voyage with Captain Bligh. Or at least I would have, had not spring and weeds arrived. "Next Wednesday we are having a luncheon in New York," the man continued, "and we'd like you to join us. Will you be able to attend?" "No," I heard myself say. Like runners rolling out from hawkweed through a lawn, my words were uncontrollable. "No," I repeated, "I never go to New York." "Besides," I continued, "I have to clean the yard. My daffodils are coming up, and I did not rake the leaves off them last fall." "You could have hired the children," Vicki said later. "They only wanted five dollars for tidying the whole yard."

Spring is wet in Connecticut. No matter how withering the foolishness of a day, rain falls and buds unfold. In the woods behind the house hazelnut bloomed, the male catkins turning yellow and the small female flowers wrinkling into scarlet threads. I raked leaves off the daffodils and amid the distracting bustle of the season forgot about the television program. An opportunity to promote my books had vanished, but something else, I knew, would soon blossom, for spring is wonderfully various. Just yesterday Tanya brought her pet ferret, Sabine, to class. After class she put Sabine on my shoulders and suggested I write about pets.

"A ferret," she said, "would be a change from flowers." "I don't know anything about ferrets," I answered. "What would I say?" During the conversation Sabine twisted over my back and around my neck. Abruptly, though, she stopped and, perching on my collarbone, leaned forward, dug her claws into my shoulder, and urinated down my back. "Oh, Lord!" Tanya exclaimed then grabbed her pet. "Professor," she said, her face redder than a Chrysler Imperial rose, "Sabine has never done this before. She has never peed on anyone, and I don't know why she did it now." "Tanya," I said, stepping out of the puddle at my feet and starting to unbutton my shirt, "wonderful things happen in the spring. Now I have something to write about."

the
blue caterpillar

I took *The New Yorker* to the first rehearsal. I had started reading an article describing the murder of a partner in a distinguished New York law firm. The man led two lives, one public and heterosexual with a family, the other private and homosexual. A piece of rough trade killed the man in a sleazy motel in the Bronx, stabbing him thirty-two times. I didn't finish the article. The spire of the church in Lebanon rose clean above the common, resembling a sharp white cattail pushing through a green pool. Dressed in leotards and tutus, little girls bustled out of cars and fluttered into the church, mothers and fathers swirling about them. In the good afternoon sun the article seemed dank and soiling, and before going into the church, I dropped the magazine into a garbage barrel at the edge of the green, a blue barrel with a swinging, hinged top, the kind that makes second thoughts and retrieving trash impossible for all except the simian.

June and the annual concert of the Lebanon School of Dance had arrived. Nancy Baldwin, the director, divided the concert into halves, selections from the *Sleeping Beauty* ballet for the older girls and for younger girls ages three through nine, *Alice's Adventures in Wonderland*. On Friday the 18th of June and again on Saturday the 19th, students performed. Sixty-seven girls and one adult danced in *Alice*. Eliza was the Queen of

Hearts, and I was the Blue Caterpillar. I was excited. Never had I been in a ballet. Fifty-two years is a long time to be a chrysalis, and I was eager to split the pupal shell, pump up my wings, and flutter through an auditorium. I am not light of toe or hind leg. Upstroke and downstroke, glissade and pas de chat were beyond my furcae, and the best I did was bask at the corner of the stage like a satyr or hairstreak, wings folded and body sideways to the audience.

In truth my costume was so heavy that I could hardly manage a hop much less the slow bob of a swallowtail. Instead of ballet shoes I wore bedroom slippers, the brown kind sold by L. L. Bean, fuzzy with wool and costing forty-five dollars. I also wore a green athletic shirt, presented to people who ran a road race in Norwich, Connecticut, in 1985. Since Eastern Savings and Loan was printed in big white letters across the chest, I wore the shirt inside out. On my head sat a green bathing suit. Stuffed with cotton, the suit rose to a point. Through the leg holes on the sides poked antennae, two curved ten-inch springs, atop each a ping-pong ball dipped in silver glitter. For the performances I bought my first pair of tights. I wanted a yellow pair, but the only color that TeeKay's in Willimantic sold that fit me was gray. Still, I enjoyed wearing them, and when I first put them on, I leaped through the house. Domestic reviewers did not rave. When I stopped, rising to what I thought was a dreamy, otherworldly soutenu, Eliza turned to Vicki. "Ugh," she said, "I hate that lump that men have in the front when they wear tights."

At the performance I wore blue bathing trunks over the tights. Even without the trunks the lump would not have been visible, for wrapped around me and trailing after me was an ancient brocaded curtain. In a previous dramatic incarnation at the Rectory School in Pomfret the curtain had stalked the stage as a dragon. Stapled on as trim was a thirty-seven inch tail thicker than an eiderdown. While a heavy yellow beanbag was attached to the end of the tail, a ruffle of diamond-shaped orange scales ran up a seam to the back of my neck. Despite these reptilian attributes, my costume remained a curtain, lined and so heavy that I sometimes thought it still contained rods, and not plastic rods but heavy walnut or brass rods, removed from a great-aunt's country estate. Stitched across the body of the curtain were gold designs, some resembling thin, leafless Chinese trees, others onions sliced in half. At the bottom of the curtain hung a deep border. Green cord twisted through the border in a series of doodles, all of which turned into eights the longer I looked at them. While a double row of green tassels switched above the floor, a strip of lead half an inch wide insured that the curtain would not wobble lightly.

At the Bench Shop in Willimantic, I bought makeup, for two dollars a tube of luminous blue Harlequin Colors cream makeup, a white grease crayon for a dollar, then for $1.95 a black "Eyebrow Eye-Liner Pencil." Before each performance I painted my face, neck, and ears blue. With the eye-liner I blackened wrinkles and crevices. Afterward I colored my eyelids white and highlighted my cheekbones and forehead. Next I drew a white line along the center of my nose down to my upper lip. Lastly, I clipped two plastic earrings to my ears. The earrings belonged to Eliza. Gold-colored and two inches in diameter, the earrings formed bright circles, making my caterpillar swashbuckling, transforming him from the larva of a dull swarthy or dun sedge skipper into that of a fritillary, maybe even that of a spicebush or tiger swallowtail.

I began my *Adventures* by walking down the aisle of the auditorium. I carried several vertebrae of tail in my left hand; in my right I held one of Francis's school notebooks. Vicki covered the notebook with red and green paper, the kind of paper used for wrapping presents at Christmas. Inside were prompts for my steps. Once I reached the stage, I opened the notebook and read an excerpt from Lewis Carroll's poem "Which Dreamed It?" Afterward I sat on an orange mushroom-shaped stool at the left front corner of the stage. The stool was so low that my knees were almost as high as my chest. Surrounding me were four cloth mushrooms borrowed from the School of Puppetry at the University of Connecticut and ranging in height from one and a half to two and a half feet. After I arranged my curtain, the dancers tripped through the theater like dreams: the youngest children bumblebees in yellow leotards and black tutus speckled with gold sequins. Attached to their shoulders were gauze wings. Fluttering behind the bees were butterflies, five dressed in lilac and three in apricot. Close behind them hopped rabbits, pink and white ears flopping over their heads. Next came dodos spinning in bright colors, green, yellow, purple, red, and blue. Once the dodos bounced through the curtain, a garden of flowers bloomed, daisy chains of creamy petals wrapped around their waists. Diamonds followed wearing sashes decorated with red sequins. When the hearts danced into the theater wearing long white dresses, my heart pounded. To love a child as much as I loved the bright Queen of Hearts was almost painful. Alice was the last dancer to slip down the aisle. When she approached me, I wriggled, startling her, and asked, "Who are you?"

My role was small. I introduced nine dances by reading short excerpts from *Alice's Adventures*. I spoke a total of 736 words. Although I did not leave the stage during the ballet, I tried not to move. I was merely gena and mandible, the horny functional stuff of a caterpillar. The dreams, to use Lewis Carroll's words, were "golden" on the stage and in their parents' imaginations, and I did not want to drain "the wells of fancy dry" by calling attention to myself. Only once did I leave my mushroom, and that was to retrieve three little bees who strayed far from hive and choreography to bumble about dangerously near the front lip of the stage. When the curtain closed at the end of the ballet, I gathered my costume and walked to the middle of the stage. I started to go behind the curtain, but then I turned around and, facing the auditorium, asked the audience, "Who are you?" Three minutes later I led Eliza out for her bow. The caterpillar had vanished. I was now Daddy, proud, adoring Daddy.

Although I knew who I was at that moment on stage, Lewis Carroll's Alice could not answer the caterpillar's question about identity, explaining that she was confused because she had changed size several times "since getting up in the morning." Ours is an age besotted with the desire for answers. Today Alice could consult a government survey and amid statistic and percentage could find an identity. "Not a very satisfactory identity," Josh said on my mentioning Alice's problem to him. Josh has little regard for surveys except for those which he conducts. "Seven out of eight women," he told me recently, "will rock in their seats on a Ferris wheel no matter what you tell them." Josh's conclusions are always deduced from personal observation. Because he reaches conclusions only after years of observation, the small number of participants in his surveys is, he assures me, beside the point. "Despite my requesting that they not rock the seat once we were aloft, seven females did so at the apex of our orbit, and did so, laughing fiendishly. The only woman who did not misbehave had a husky voice, a hearty, pleasing personality, and threw the javelin when she attended college. Only once in all my experience," he continued, "has a man rocked the seat. And he was a vegetarian, raised poodle dogs, and wore bow ties with horrible little dots on them." Josh enjoys the large conclusion. "Unlike man," he told me yesterday, "woman does not stop pumping gas when the nozzle first cuts off. At the absolute minimum woman will pump until the nozzle shuts off six times. Even then she will squeeze out drops until the last digit of the bill reaches either zero or five. Any other number at the end of a gas bill offends the female of the species. I would not be surprised to learn," Josh concluded, "that estrogen plays a significant role in this matter."

For a price commerce will provide an identity. Indeed molting children arouse commercial hormones, and businesses swarm out of mailboxes in hives to parasitize young larvae. While some parasites inject larvae with pride, others slosh pheromones over glitter, both types hoping to attract youth to the fertile mating of dollar and product. The best protection for naive childhood is a hard exoskeleton: parents who say *no*. This past fall Francis received a letter from the United States Achievement Academy, congratulating him on winning a "National Science Merit" award and offering to print his "personal biography" in one of the Academy's yearbooks. The yearbook and a certificate "suitable for framing" cost $28.95 plus $7 for a handling fee. When Francis did not reply to the Academy's offer, I assumed the matter would end. Alas, shedding merit is not easy for a sixth grader praised by the Academy as "one of our nation's most outstanding science students," especially when that merit is attached thorax and abdomen to commerce. In June the Academy sent Francis a flyer listing "Custom gifts for national award winners." For $99.99 plus $5 for shipping and handling Francis could purchase the "Men's Celestrium USAA Ring." While Francis's initials would be engraved inside the band of the ring, the setting featured "a fire blue stone." Celestrium, the Academy informed young scientists, was a "silver-white jeweler's alloy—a tarnish-free, durable metal of the 90's." If the ring did not appeal to him, Francis could buy an "Official USAA Key Pendant" for $16.95, a belt buckle with a pewter finish for $15.95, a jacket for $34.95, or a Wall Plaque, this last, the flyer stated, "Silkscreened 8" by 10" brushed silver finish plaque mounted on walnut finished board. Personalized with National Award Winner's name."

Eliza plays with the Barbie dolls Vicki owned as a child. Three years ago I gave Eliza two dollars, and she joined the Barbie Club. The mail that brought Francis the flyer from the Academy brought Eliza a letter from the Danbury Mint. "Dear Collector," the letter began, "Step back in time for a moment. What were *you* doing in 1960?" Since Eliza is eight years old, she remembered little about her activities in 1960. On the other hand, the director himself was learning to ride a bicycle, and his sister, he informed Eliza, "was playing with a brand new doll that was creating a sensation throughout the country. Her name," he continued, waxing nostalgic, "was Barbie and to little girls everywhere, she was pure magic!" "No Barbie outfit," he stated, "was more cherished and desired by collectors than her '1960 Solo in the Spotlight' glittering black evening gown."

For $26.95 Eliza could buy "an enchanting new figurine portraying Barbie in this stunning gown!" The figurine was "the premier issue in a landmark new series entitled The Classic *Barbie* Figurine Collection." If Eliza bought the doll, she would acquire not simply an "enchanting figurine" but the option "to acquire all subsequent figurines in this collection." As Francis at twelve was too young to sport a talisman proclaiming him to be one of the nation's best science students, so Eliza was too young, and too poor, to become a collector. Better for her to flutter through childhood as a checkerspot one night and the Queen of Hearts the next than to become a collector.

"Explain yourself," the caterpillar ordered Alice in Carroll's book. "I can't explain myself," Alice answered worriedly. Today's Alice need not worry if she cannot explain herself. Plenty of other people are certain they can explain her and provide a solution not only for her difficulties but for all the problems of life itself. Instead of acknowledging the complexity of existence, people often embrace platitude and slogan, statements which either describe experience or solve problems in so artless a fashion that they at first seem revelatory, if not profound. Not long ago I was in Chattanooga, Tennessee. Parked outside the Elkins Building on West Eighth Street was a Lincoln Towncar. Stamped across the vanity plate on the front bumper of the car was "Tell the Child about Jesus." Printed beneath the command in smaller letters was "Loving Friendship Missionary Church, Bro. S. Peagram, Minister, 349 Spencer Avenue." On the left side of the plate stood a cross, flecks of red rising about it like sparklers. I thought about the command on the plate. What, I wondered, should I tell my children about Jesus? I had read them stories from the Bible, but I told them little about Jesus himself. For a moment I thought about visiting Brother Peagram's church, but I knew I would not find his view of life satisfactory. Truths are simple, but moral systems are never complex enough. Instead of acknowledging that life forever molts out of rigidity, system forces experience into narrow, recognizable patterns, offering emotional and intellectual walkers to people bothered because they cannot explain themselves or their doings.

The plate told me more about the owner of the Lincoln than it did about childhood and Christianity. Words both define and reveal identity. "Let's soak up some rays at the electric beach," I heard a student say recently, urging a friend to accompany her to a tanning salon. "He is generous with his time and conversation," Josh said, describing a mutual acquaintance. "He is always willing to enlighten me about things I already understand." As the caterpillar's solemn questions and grand statements revealed him to be pompous and self-centered, so people examine words for clues to character. Among the papers Eliza brought home from school in June was a story she wrote as an exercise in class. "One day," Eliza began, "I made a snowman. It came to life. It was out to kill me! It made more snowmen. I made a snow cannon. They broke it. How would I make it to the bus stop in the morning? I just had to get them tonight. I grabbed a hose and froze them in their evil tracks! I was safe until next time. Somehow some killer snowmen avoided being frozen. They wanted revenge! Out of the corner of my eye I saw them. I asked if I could borrow Mom's hair dryer."

Parents force identities upon children. "Not bad," I thought after reading Eliza's little tale. "Writing is in her blood. She's my daughter." "Each year I mean to reform and make better grades," a girl said to me this past semester, explaining why an essay was late, "but then along comes some boy." In this house along comes Daddy. Vicki gave Eliza a diary to take to camp this summer. "My name is Pickering," Eliza wrote on the first page, "Eliza Pickering, 8 going onto 9. It was the summer of 93. . . ." Filling in the space above the dots may not be easy with me around. I am dogmatic and like Carroll's caterpillar always have "something important to say." Edward is a graceful baseball player, a pitcher who throws strikes and a shortstop whose glove attracts balls like mud puddles butterflies. At least he is a good player when I am not around. Whenever I watch a game, he strikes out, and slow grounders roll between his legs. To give Edward relief during games I wander into the woods at the edge of right field. Spectators assume that I go to the woods to relieve myself, not Edward, and my friend Michael said the woods ought to be renamed "Sam's Whizz Park." Maybe someday Edward will not notice me at a game, but I doubt it. The more loving the parent, the more difficulty a child may have ignoring his presence. "I really missed you," Eliza said when I returned from Chattanooga, "but now that you are home what will I do with you?"

Alice was too young to know who she was. Only seven, she had not lived long enough to have a past. If she had been aware of her past, she might have answered the caterpillar's questions better. I spent the last weekend in April at the Blooming Grove Hunting and Fishing Club in northeast Pennsylvania. Founded in the early 1870s, Blooming Grove consists of 23,000 acres of wood, lake, and stream. Bill Weaver, my oldest friend, owns a cottage at the Club, and he invited ten middle-aged Southern men to spend the weekend with him fishing, both for trout and, as it turned out, for our old selves. We had known each other ever since we became aware of friendship: at Parmer School and Montgomery Bell Academy in Nashville or in college at Sewanee. We knew one another's parents and had been in each other's weddings. In 1955 Wylie was my Big Brother in Alpha Chi, a high school fraternity. We had nicknames: Bony, Redneck, and Field Pea. Twenty years had passed since last I saw some of the group. When we met, though, I realized that little that mattered had changed. Bill was in a wheelchair, but he was still the grand guy I loved. Selfless as ever, Garth did not fish the third morning, even though he traveled to Blooming Grove from St. Louis. Instead he roamed the banks of the Shohola, taking pictures for us to show wives, children, and grandchildren.

While at Blooming Grove, I walked around Lake Giles twice a day. Spring azures puddled along the path then flickered up in whisks of blue. Turtles fell off logs. Catbirds whined, and a green heron looped along the shore ahead of me, probably thinking I was following him. Towhees scratched under laurel, and, resembling waiters in cutaway jackets and bibs, black-throated blue warblers let me approach close to them. Deer turned sideways to watch me while turkeys hurried into brush, pushing their necks forward like sprinters approaching the finish line of a race. Nights were silver, and after dinner the first evening, Hill, Garth, and I went canoeing. Now a banker in Kentucky but once a camp counselor with me in Maine, Hill decided to demonstrate intricate canoe strokes.

Once Garth and I stepped onto the dock, Hill spun the canoe around and promptly rolled over. His glasses disappeared into the lake. Before breakfast the next morning he and I searched for them, Hill turning the canoe slowly while I leaned over the side peering into the shallows. After thirty minutes I found the glasses.

We fished from mid-morning to late afternoon on the Blooming Grove Stream at places named Burnt Mill, Twin Rocks, Boundary Line, and Beauty Pool, then on the Shohola at Bradley Spring and Shook House Run. For lunch we ate fried potatoes, slaw, and trout. I ate in my underwear. Because the hip boots I wore resembled tubs and caught water by the buckets, my trousers and socks were soaked by lunch. One noon I varied my diet slightly. After planting a bag of worms in my pocket, Bill announced that he had learned that one of his guests had strayed from the ways of right-acting fly fishermen. When no one was looking, this person, Bill recounted, removed the fly from his line and fished with earthworms. "No honorable man," Bill said, "would do such a thing." Although he regretted the vulgarity of searching our jackets, Bill said that he felt obliged to do so, if only to restore the besmirched honor of his guests. On the discovery of the worms in my jacket, I rose open-mouthed to the bait. I seized a can of Coca-Cola and washed the dirt off the biggest worm, a fat fellow five inches long. Holding the worm between the thumb and index fingers of my right hand, I raised it above my head. Then I rolled my head back, opened my jaws, and slowly lowered the worm into my mouth. When my fingers reached my lips, I released the worm. He wiggled, and I swallowed, spitting out the hook Bill set for me and in the process adding a moist tidbit to my lunch.

While I had never fly-fished, others in the group were experts, having wandered streams in Alaska and Montana, even New Zealand. Bill assigned a guide to Taylor and me, the two novices, and I caught my share of fish, a dozen or so brook trout during the two and a half days. Blooming Grove ran its own hatchery. Although the streams were not baited, as some cornfields are for dove, trout meandered through pools in universities, not schools. The group was too old and comfortable to compete by keeping track of the fish caught, and throughout the days friends laid rods aside and, taking me to good pools, taught me technique. Although tying lures and leaders remained difficult, by the end of the weekend I could differentiate between a Woolly Bugger and a Mrs. Simpson or a

Yellow Muddler. The hours were green and gold. Water rolled in knots over rocks then unraveled into currents, twisting and looping like loose twine. Black and white warblers scurried through trees along the shore, and often as I stood in mid-stream, I watched pine warblers hunting bugs along overhanging branches. In the sunlight the warblers glowed and crinkled like colored foil. The fret of other days and places softened and drifted downstream. Fishing even eroded worries about health. If one of us became ill, however, the group could supply all the doctors middle-aged men usually needed: a urologist and a cardiologist.

I played minnow-like pranks on Hill, my roommate. On his pillow I spread pancake-shaped lichens. The lichens were green and so meaty with yellow lumps they made the pillow look as if it had served as the sickbed of some small creature suffering from stomach problems, a squirrel who gnawed a wormy nut or perhaps a rat who had feasted upon aged fish entrails. I stuffed Kleenex into the tips of Hill's shoes, not enough paper to be immediately noticeable but enough to cramp toes and make a sedentary banker think the unaccustomed activity with rod and reel had made his feet swell.

The first night we ate dinner at Bill's house. From Nashville he brought a trashcan filled with turnip greens, and we ate biscuits and greens, fried chicken, then fudge cake. We were a community sharing a past longer than our fifty years, a past that reached back through parents to grandparents, a community that spread broadly through the South. Every night we reminisced, telling stories about friends, the boys and girls with whom we grew up. "He'd shoot anything with wings," Hugh Hunter recounted of an acquaintance. "If an angel flew low enough, he'd shoot it." We told jokes, the kind that Southern men seem to appreciate more than other groups, earthy, absurd stories that in their absurdity deflate pretension and obliquely level, rendering all people ridiculous, no matter the social rank, thus creating a world in which genuine community is possible. Raleigh Lane, Bob began, was standing on the first tee at the Belle Meade Club when suddenly he saw his friend Clay Ferris stumbling up out of the rough. Divots had been whacked out of Clay's cheeks; his nose was a red water hazard, and his forehead looked like a putting green on a public golf course. "Clay, what happened?" Raleigh said, propping Clay against a tree. "I played golf this morning with Mary Crabtree," Clay said, wobbling like a bad backswing. "I got a double bogey on the second hole.

But then I birdied three and four, and things went well until eight. Then, woe is me, Mary and I both sliced our drives badly. I thought we hit them out of bounds into the cow pasture that borders the hole, so I searched along the fence. For a while I didn't find anything. But then suddenly I heard a moo and looking up saw a ball stuck in a cow's ass. I crawled under the fence and once I was on the other side lifted up the cow's tail and shouted, 'Mary, does this look like yours?' And Lord help me, she leaped the fence and began hitting me with her mashie."

A caterpillar's munching a worm smacks of cannibalism, but then I did not become the Blue Caterpillar until June. Still metamorphosis does not occur overnight, and I may have long harbored vermicular hankerings. In April I gave blood to the Red Cross. The blood drive was held in the ROTC hangar at the university. When I was a child, shots made me faint. Even worse, nurses frequently had trouble locating veins from which they could draw blood. The floor of the hangar is concrete, and, nervous that I might collapse if a wildcatter drilled a series of dry holes in my arms, I wore my bicycle helmet while giving blood. Made from Styrofoam with holes cut in it and covered with a black and white net, the helmet resembled the head of a caterpillar. While the blood drained from my arm, I pinched my legs together, locked my free arm against my side, and did not move. From a distance I resembled a pupa, my shoes a cremaster attaching me to the wall at the end of the cot, the black netting on the side of the helmet my eyes, and the white centerpiece my frontoclypeus.

Humans are sorters, taxonomists addicted to cataloguing and classifying. Impatient creatures, we are baffled and irritated by complexity. In the quest for simple classifications or definitions, we lump matter together in great piles. As a result different or unclassifiable behavior is almost always criticized. Although I thought wearing the helmet reasonable, people looked at me oddly, staring then turning away when I glanced at them. To such people I was the sort of person who should not be allowed to donate blood. Turning my platelets loose in the bloodstream of some tepid, unsuspecting Methodist might transforms his veins into rivers, polluted with laughter and butterflies, angels with buckshot in their wings, Ferris wheels rocking, the Queen of Hearts dancing, and cattle floating ass up, golf balls white as snow in their fundaments.

Of course action does, in part, shape identity, no matter that the iden tity is foisted upon a person by the glib or the hurried. If Eliza resembles me, she will become a collector, not of Barbie dolls, though, but of place and story. Life is richer if a person reads license plates and the landscape, or at least tries to puzzle out some of the natural letters which color the earth like print marks pages. Late in May I traveled to Sheridan, Wyoming, to address the Friends of Fulmer Library. The day after my talk I hiked into the mountains above Big Horn, following a path running alongside Little Goose Creek. I started at six in the morning. Cock pheasants scratched in a field beside a dirt road while turkeys picked around the edges of a pasture. A magpie rowed the air over a damp green field, the white patches on his wings rolling like water churned by oars. A Lazuli bunting perched on a small plum tree, his breast orange amid a mist of blue and gray feathers. From a grove of aspen house wrens bubbled like seltzer. A meadowlark sat on a fence post, his song starting clearly but breaking into a scratch at the conclusion, almost as if something exasperated him, a dark cloud perhaps, blowing in from the west and threatening the bright day. A pair of black-shouldered kites hunted over alfalfa, dipping and gliding like gulls buffeted by a choppy wind. A Bullock's oriole flew into a cottonwood tree while a varied thrush swept across a damp gully and a green-tailed towhee fluttered through shrubby river birch. Prairie dogs bustled around low red mounds. A pair of weasels scampered up a creek bank. Before running to their burrows, marmots studied me, the white on their muzzles giving them an analytical, intellectual expression.

Spring was blooming: chokecherries and hawthorn along a lonely road and then, turning a long, rocky slope blue and yellow, lupine and arrowleaf balsamroot. I imagined the air bouquets of colors, fresh from the refrigeration of high valleys and wrapped with ferns spilling out moist and green. First, yellow, sometimes tangy and cindered but also sugary: fawn lilies and violets, Oregon grape, sulphurflower, caragana escaped from a garden, and sweet yellow pea. Next purple and blue, silky, smooth as a slow night rain, sometimes dark like thick glass: shooting star, mountain bluebells, larkspur, penstemon, and virgin's bower, this last seemingly nodding in humility but thinking about, even planning, the fibrous, entangling snarls of late summer. Finally, white, rinsing bars of sun pouring over gray rocks, conjuring up enchanted lands: loco, star lily, false Solomon's seal, wild lily of the valley, fairy bells, and baneberry. On baneberry flowers bloomed together in thimble-like brushes. I counted the number of blossoms on three brushes, finding seventeen on the first, twenty-one on the second, and thirty-eight on the last.

Although a few spring beauties lurked shy and pink in the bouquet, I am partially colorblind, and so I plucked no reds from the air. In truth missing the pushy, peppery reds did not bother me. I have hovered about for half a century, and my wings are tattered. Let youth flutter about red, sipping hot nectar and singeing feelings. For my part I prefer cooler colors, the blue letters printed on two wooden signs standing beside a driveway in Big Horn: "Please Watch for Old Dog," and "Please Watch for Old Cat." When Alice started to walk away from the Caterpillar, he called her back, saying, "I've something important to say." When she turned around, he said simply, "Keep your temper." The advice didn't seem weighty to Alice, at least not when she was changing sizes and stumbling into fabulous and frightening landscapes. "Is that all?" Alice answered curtly. Unlike Alice, who probably would not have noticed them and certainly would not have thought them important, the signs struck me as emblems of a decent life, a slow life in which little things mattered: pets, wildflowers beneath mountain ridges, friends in wheelchairs, family and community, those soft, dancing dodos and bumblebees over whom everybody should watch, and watch carefully.

From high in the Big Horn Mountains streams rushed toward Little Goose Creek, falling over ledges and breaking on rocks in twists of white. From a distance the streams resembled ribbons of snow, but as I climbed and the day darkened and became chilly, the streams turned into thin vibrating bands of steel. Indeed except for elbows of aspen bending green and blue through ravines, mountainsides seemed metallic, lodgepole pines cutting sharp against the sky like the barbs on arrow plate wire. The higher I climbed the more barbed the landscape became. Jagged rocks along stream beds appeared bound to the currents, their thorny edges wrapping the water, slicing up and out like the edges of greenbriar wire. Hiking became more difficult the higher I climbed. Around each bend was another obstacle, here a broken boulder jagged as a spur rowel, there a fallen pine, the trunk a roll of lazy plate, splintered limbs sticking up from it in stakes.

The next morning the Maguires, my hosts, took me to a branding on the Crow Reservation in Montana, just across the Wyoming border. Hills rumpled into soft knobs, rocks slipping and crumbling down dry slopes. Resembling tacks being pried out of the ground by time, a few trees grew along the Turtle River. The landscape looked so old and worn that everything appeared fragile. Near the river trees pinned down a blanket of green. Corners of the blanket had frayed, creating the impression that a strong wind could tear the grass loose and, rolling it back, strip the hills to stone.

I was guest of the Padlock Ranch. One of the biggest cattle ranches in the country, Padlock leases grazing land from the Crow. Early that morning cowboys rounded up cattle, and by the time I arrived, three hundred red cows and their calves were milling about and bawling inside a heavy metal portable corral, erected in the middle of a green pan of land bordered by a creek and dry hills. The branding crew consisted of fifteen men, three on horseback, two roping and one driving branded calves and their mothers away from the corral. The other twelve men branded. The crew had been branding for eight days and would do so for another seven. On a hill above the corral grazed the cowboys' horses. The ranch owned some 220 horses, including twenty teams of draft horses, Percherons used for delivering hay to cattle in winter. Draft horses, the manager of the ranch said, "start on cold mornings." The crew were full-time employees, and the branding went efficiently. Once all the calves were branded, the men would break down the corral and load it on a flatbed truck to be driven to the site of the next day's roundup.

The person who erects signs urging passersby to watch out for pets would not enjoy a branding. On the bed of the truck were three tanks of propane gas, burned to heat the branding irons. The cooker for the irons stood on heavy metal legs. Four and a half feet long and a foot in diameter, the cooker resembled a hunk of iron pipe, one side of which had been cut open and pealed back and up into a flap so that irons could be inserted and heated in the burning gas. The top of the cooker served as a grill for testicles, or Rocky Mountain oysters, as they are called. The day was damp, and to keep warm I ate fifteen or so oysters. Wrapped in a stringy membrane, an oyster resembled a big man's thumb or better yet a jumbo shrimp without head or legs. Heat dried the membrane surrounding the testicle while causing the testicle itself to swell. Eventually the membrane split, and the testicle puffed out through the rupture, resembling soggy, partially cooked popcorn but tasting liverish.

Although I dined on the fruits of the cowboys' harvest, I did not participate in the branding. Eating is easy. Branding is hard, dangerous work. Six men handled a calf. One man rode into the corral and lassoed the calf low on the hind leg and as near to the hoof as possible. Once the rope was tight, the man turned his horse and pulled the calf out of the corral to the entrance, where the calf was flipped over. Immediately a cowboy kneeled on the animal's body and pressed the calf's head to the ground. At the rear of the animal another cowboy controlled the calf's legs, preventing it from clambering back to its feet. Leaning backward the man jammed his left boot into the socket of the calf's right hind leg locking it forward. He then controlled the calf's upper leg by yanking it back toward him, using his own right leg for balance, sometimes laying it across the calf's left leg. As soon as the animal was pinned down, a man burned a bar into its muzzle, the calf crying all the while, its tongue curving upward in a semi-circle, the flesh blue under the strain as the animal tried futilely to reach the searing pain. Next a bar and a sketch of a padlock were burned into the hide on the left side of the calf's body, the smoke rising in a hot fog. Simultaneously another man vaccinated the calf, one injection being stuck under the animal's left front leg and the other in the left hip. The injections covered a ward of viral and bacterial plagues, diseases of which I had never heard but which evoked images of charnel houses and knots of bloated cattle bumping slowly together, caught on a snag after a flood, the only sound around them the buzzing of flies: bovine rhinotracheitis, virus diarrhea, parainfluenza3, respiratory syncytial virus, leptospira canicola, grippotyphosa, hardjo, icterohaemorrhagiae, and pomona.

A plastic identity tag was stapled to the calf's left ear. If the animal had horns, the man pushing its head to the ground cried "horn," and another man chopped the horns off, dusting the calf's head afterward with disinfectant. The other cry heard outside the corral was "bull." Castration was simple and quick. A cowboy sliced off the animal's scrotum with a sharp knife, tossing the, to use words kindergarten teachers apply to children's dolls, warm fuzzies on the ground behind him. Next he reached into the animal and, seizing the membrane which held the testicles, stretched the membrane so that the testicles were six or so inches outside the bull's body. Then taking an instrument resembling a monkey wrench, he cut the testicles off, the device crimping the blood vessels together so tightly that the calf did not bleed much. Two lavender buckets stood outside the corral, one containing water, the other disinfectant. After castrating a bull, the cowboy dipped the blade of his knife into the disinfectant and dropped the testicles into the bucket of water. When we arrived at the branding, the bucket was half full of testicles, and the blood had turned the water red, not a thick red but a clear, light red resembling cherry Kool-Aid.

Before leaving the branding, I picked six fuzzies off the ground and stuffed them into the side pocket of my jacket. Because they were the right size and were covered with reddish hair, they would make, I told Vicki, nice covers for door knobs. Much as my grandmother replaced the oriental rugs in her house each summer with thick straw mats, so we could put the covers, I suggested, on doors in the winter. Vicki did not think much of the idea. In any case rain washed away my plans. I wanted to cure the fuzzies in the sun. But after two damp days they gathered flies and odor, and so after showing them to the children, I buried them in the backyard.

Scrotums were not the only things I brought home from Wyoming. I bathe quickly rather than carefully. While taking a shower the day after returning home, I discovered a tick in my navel. Travel had not disturbed the tick's appetite, and despite the long flight, he dined well and enthusiastically. When the children did not comment on the scrotums, I was disappointed. The tick, though, was different verbal matter. Jumping out of the shower, I dried quickly and, wrapping a towel around my lumps, front and back, hurried into the kitchen where the children were setting the table for dinner. "Look at the little fellow in the manhole," I said, first sucking my stomach in then inhaling so the flesh around my middle rose like bread overdosed with yeast. The children's reactions did not disappoint me. They bubbled like male wrens in the mating season. After I pulled the tick out, Edward wanted to put it and the side of beef the tick extracted from my navel into a jar and keep it as a pet. "My daddy is strange," Eliza said. "No one in second grade would believe me if I told them that he danced around the kitchen in a towel with a tick on his belly button."

I am not strange. I am ordinary. Sometimes, though, I feel estranged, like Alice disgruntled with the odd doings of Wonderland. When I am out of sorts, I walk. I crimp myself so firmly into place that bile cannot seep out. Early in May I roamed the campus, looking at trees and shrubs. By the end of the walk I had forgotten what irritated me, the plants tacking me, not grass, down, preventing gloomy mood from flapping loose and obscuring the sunlight. Shucks of seeds dangled from camperdown elms. Carillons of white blossoms swayed on silverbells, their waxy orange stamens clappers ringing not to the ear but to the eye. In the middle of each lilac blossom were two yellow mounds, baking in the sun and rising like loaves of lemon cake. Resembling small red wings, stipules twisted above the leaf-stalks of Japanese zelkovia, straining, it seemed, to catch the air. In the center of sassafras flowers stood translucent goblets, veined and frothy with yellow. A red dew of buds covered cornealian cherries. On Korean Stewartia bark flaked and formed pools of still, soft color, gray and blue, brown and orange, arctic in their serenity. On tulip trees knuckles of buds unraveled and stretched upward in long, thin fingers. From the new growth on Osage orange, color streamed toward the trunk in bright pinstripes.

The Blue Caterpillar was wrong. Knowing place is more important than knowing self. When a person knows a place, not only does he become part of that place, but others get to know him so well that questions about identity are meaningless, having almost nothing to do with daily life. During winter my lawnmower froze to death. By the time I bought a new mower, the yard was a hay field. In order to cut the grass, I pushed the handle of the mower down to my knees, thus lifting the front wheels and the front half of the blade a foot off the ground. Then hunching over I leaned forward and, inching the mower along on its back wheels, attempted to cut off the top third of the grass. Every ten or so feet a bale of hay clogged the blade, and the mower shut off, exploding in an aneurysm of clanging and acrid white smoke. I was trying to restart the mower for the twentieth time when suddenly a tractor appeared in the yard. On it sat a man who took care of lawns for his living. "Mr. Pickering, you don't know me," he said, "but while I was driving by, I saw you trying to cut the grass. You are never going to finish the lawn, and so I am going to mow it for you for free. Will it be all right," he added, as he turned his tractor, "if I dump the cuttings in the woods behind your house?" "Yes," I said.

Two days later Dave knocked at the screen door. "Sam," he said, "I've got something to show you and the children." I don't know Dave well.

Like me he swims, and I see him a couple of mornings a week at the university pool, where we chat about college doings. Dave had never come to my house before. I didn't think he knew where I lived, and I could not imagine what he had in his car. An old leather briefcase sat on the front seat of the car. Piled next to it were its former contents: two books, a stack of loose papers, a notebook, and yellow pencils in a rubber band. As I looked in the car window, the briefcase shrugged. Dave reached over, picked the case up, unzipped it, and took out a box turtle. "I found him on the road," he said, "and I thought you and your family would like to see him before I turn him loose." Years ago I wrote an article for *Yankee Magazine,* describing a person who rescued turtles from roadsides and who placed signs along highways reading, "Turtle Crossing. Please Slow Down." Once or twice a year since the appearance of the article, acquaintances telephone and ask questions about turtles. In truth I am a bit of a turtle person. Since childhood I have rescued turtles from roads. Only last week I stopped traffic and removed a painted turtle from the middle of a state highway. Box turtles have finer feelings, or at least they are capable of more aristocratic restraint than painted turtles. Dave's box turtle did not soil his briefcase. Not having a satchel in which to place him, I put the painted turtle on the floor of my car. Before I turned him loose in Tift Pond, he created a lake and several creeks, urinating almost non-stop.

The Memorial Day Parade is, as a friend put it, "the event of events" in Mansfield. The route of the parade is short. Starting at Bassett's Bridge Road, participants march a quarter of a mile along Route 195 past the old graveyard. On Cemetery Road the parade turns right and proceeds a tenth of a mile to the new graveyard. Along the route mothers and fathers sit in folding chairs, and children play atop old stone walls. The parade itself isn't lengthy, this year consisting of a handful of marchers representing the Eastern Star, Lodge No.14 in Windham, Connecticut, one of whose members wore a top hat and looked like Abraham Lincoln; the mayor riding in a jeep driven by a retired Army sergeant; a smattering of veterans; a five-man color guard; and two bands, one from the middle school, the other from the high school, both playing old favorites: "Anchors Aweigh," "Yankee Doodle," and "The Marine Hymn." Following the bands were five antique cars; volunteers with the Eagleville Fire Department, triangular patches sewed on their left sleeves depicting a white eagle spreading its wings under which was printed "We Protect"; and nine trucks manned by firemen—pumpers, a hook-and-ladder, but also a small green truck with "Forestry 117" printed on the side in yellow, then a pickup truck towing an aluminum boat equipped with an outboard motor, used to rescue people in difficulty on ponds. Most marchers were children, Girl and Boy Scouts, Cub Scouts and Brownies. One Cub Scout pulled his sister in a Radio Flyer decorated with small American flags. A Brownie pushed a baby carriage crammed with a zoo of stuffed animals. Marching behind the Scouts in happy disorder were children who played baseball in the town recreational league. Among them were Eliza and Edward, Eliza wearing a blue shirt and a blue cap, on the front of the cap a white M standing for Mansfield, and Edward wearing a green shirt, yellow letters on the chest spelling TCBY, the name of the yogurt store that sponsored his team.

In front of the stone walls along the parade route daisies bloomed. Red-winged blackbirds nagged marchers from perches atop cattails in the shallows of Echo Lake. Standing beneath a sugar maple in the graveyard, the mayor introduced the speaker, a colonel in the Army Reserve. The mayor promised that the colonel's speech would be brief. "When he loses the attention of the Brownie Scouts," the mayor said, "he cuts it off." In his talk the colonel implied that the United States had lost a sense of purpose and maybe identity. He asked God to "give us a vision." No, I thought. Visions are too distant and abstract. People need to see and appreciate the immediate. Identity and purpose do not lie beyond the horizon. They inhabit backyards. Instead of being handed meaning, people should seek it themselves. Wonderland does not lie inaccessible in dream or down a rabbit hole. When a child flutters awkwardly across a stage and smiles at her daddy, that's Wonderland. When a man hides behind an oak at the edge of a baseball field and watches his son bat, that's Wonderland, too. Wonderland is a boy, a good science student standing in a graveyard talking to his best friend about computers, in the background a nice man praying for a vision, a red-eyed vireo singing, sunlight yellow on hemlocks, the new growth molting, flickering like candelabra.

july

In June Eliza's dancing school staged a ballet version of *Alice's Adventures in Wonderland*. Eliza asked me to be the Blue Caterpillar. I sat on an orange mushroom at the edge of the stage and before each dance read a selection from Lewis Carroll's book. My role was functional. The evening belonged to the dancers and their families. All I wanted was to be good enough not to draw attention to myself. I succeeded. People smiled at me after the performance. Some even waved, but few spoke. "Quite a caterpillar," a man said in the men's bathroom as I washed blue makeup off my forehead. "Good going," a woman called as Eliza and I walked toward our car.

Before the ballet I read the chapter of *Alice's Adventures* in which the Blue Caterpillar appeared. Resembling the sticky pads brush-footed butterflies spin before metamorphosing, bits of the chapter clung to mind weeks after the dancers themselves molted, fluttering off the stage and into scrapbooks. When the Caterpillar asked, "Who are you?" Alice had trouble answering, explaining that she had changed sizes several times since morning, then adding, almost desperately, "I can't remember things as I used." Alice was too young to realize that forgetfulness is a blessing. A good memory makes the good life impossible. Without forgetfulness I would be so plagued by guilt that I would be unable to pull myself out of bed in the morning. All the stinging words that the tongue tossed carelessly at others would rise like jellyfish through the subconscious and lash me into paralysis. Forgetfulness frees a person from the past, allowing him to live in a fictional world peopled by many selves, flexible and ever-changing. "Sam, you skunk," a man said recently, approaching me at Southeast School while I watched Edward trying out for a baseball team, "you were quite the lad at Princeton. I'll never forget some of your antics." Not only had I forgotten the doings mentioned, but the man himself was a stranger, so much so that not even forty minutes of talk quickened recollection.

One summer thirty years ago I escorted twenty-four college girls through Europe. Three weeks ago one of the girls came to Storrs for a conference on education. She looked me up, and after describing her children and the years that had passed since we were young, she reminisced about the European trip. After mentioning several girls on the tour, half of whom I did not remember, she said, "I'll never forget the time I got you out of jail in Paris, and I guess you won't forget it either. What a night!" The remark startled me. Aside from the occasional simulated lockup in a museum, I could not recall ever seeing the inside of a jail. If gendarmes had slapped me behind bars in Paris, wouldn't I, I thought, remember the event? "Yes," I answered, smiling as if I were both slightly ashamed and slightly proud of the past, "yes, indeed, that was a real night."

Forgetfulness enables people to delight in the present. Forgetfulness transforms the old into the new. Because of forgetfulness life is forever fresh, and the ordinary becomes Wonderland, inhabited not by Mad Hatters or Cheshire Cats but by plain husbands and wives. Because of forgetfulness seasons startle. Flowers that have bloomed in dells or along driveways for a decade waylay and awaken joy. Life, of course, falls into patterns, rhythms which can lull observation but which like a fugue can also build contrapuntally into appreciation. For me July is a quiet month. With the bustle of teaching over and the children at camp in Maine, I roam Mansfield, delighting in sights I have seen many times.

Early in July I spent a day in the Storrs Community Cemetery. I did not wander the graves. Instead I walked beside the stone walls, looking at shrubs and vines. Virginia creeper bloomed, the four petals of the blossoms resembling ballet slippers. In the leaf axils of winterberry, blossoms clustered in small bouquets. While fruits ripened on older twigs, flowers bloomed on the new growth of alder buckthorn. Petals wrapped the flowers in dusty green, and over the pistils stamens rose, hooded and white. Fruits curved in sickles on staghorn sumac, green and orange blinking through the cherry color like distant moons flickering through clouds on a red night. On pignut hickory leaves were fresh as rain, and ribs splashed through them like spring creeks. While the new growth on sourwood cut limber through the air, the edges of zelkovia leaves rolled forward scalloped, resembling waves threatening to swamp leaf tips.

I read only one tombstone, a small rectangular marker engraved with the name of a man and the dates of his life, 1917–1990. Attached to the stone and rising half an inch above the granite was the outline of a train engine. Made from iron and turning orange with rust, the engine was old-fashioned. Two wheels on each side powered the engine, and a cowcatcher stretched in front. The headlight bulged like an eye, the smokestack spreading above in a soft funnel. Balanced on top of the boiler were a bell and two lumps resembling samovars. The engine pulled, I thought, that gospel train which rolled through the mountains whistling, as the old hymn puts it, urging people to buy tickets. Although I wasn't quite ready to set off for the station, I looked around the graveyard and thought about where I wanted to be buried. I wanted a plot with a view of trees and flowers. The graveyard was on a hill. Beneath it stretched the university, a landscape dominated by brick and chimneys, and then, strikingly, by the silver dome capping the basketball arena. I could live for a few years with the chimneys. Eventually the university heating plant would stop burning oil, and the chimneys would be removed. The dome was a different matter. The emphasis the university placed upon athletics trivialized learning, and seeing the dome for decades would gnaw my vitals worse than a bucket of night crawlers. Bury me, I decided, over the lip of the hill, close to Unnamed Pond, amid poison ivy, in the shade under the raccoon tree, near where orioles nested each spring.

I didn't fume much about athletics in July. For me graveyards are happy places, and a turn among tombs always brings stories to mind, sometimes sad stories but more often than not humorous ones. Not long after purchasing Haskins Funeral Home, Slubey Garts bought the eastern slope of Battery Hill in order to establish a cemetery. Calling his graveyard

The Pillow of Glory, Slubey hired Loppie Groat and Hoben Donkin to clear the land. Loppie preferred the old graveyard near the high school with its boxwood and big cedar trees. "I'd rather die than be buried in a place like this," he said to Hoben while they were wedging up a boulder. Hoben belonged to Slubey's congregation at the Tabernacle of Love. "Well, it's just the opposite with me," he said, dropping his crowbar and wiping his forehead with a dish towel. "If I'm spared, I'll be buried nowhere else."

When Squirrel Tomkins died, Coker Knox was in the hospital, recovering from a gall bladder operation. Coker and Squirrel served together in the Tennessee legislature for thirty-two years, and soon as Coker was able to get about, he visited Squirrel's grave. Above Squirrel the grateful citizens of Hardeman County erected a statue of Solon, the Athenian statesman. A local artist carved the statue. Since the ancient Greeks were not large people, he made the statue three feet high, no matter that Squirrel himself was six feet two inches tall. Moreover since the artist had never left Hardeman County, much less visited Athens, he dressed the statesman in the only robe he had ever seen, a white sheet rising to a pointed hood over the head, not just transforming Solon into a pigmy but initiating him into the Ku Klux Klan as well. The graveyard was empty when Coker visited it. The quiet made him melancholy, and Coker did not notice the finer details of Squirrel's memorial. Coker had, however, recently completed the advanced course in poetry at the YMCA night school in Nashville, and his thoughts were elevated. "How sad," he said when he saw the grave, "not a worm, not even a blood-red cherub parades around this desolated sepulcher." Coker's thoughts lay, as he put it, "too deep to geologize." "My feelings," he later wrote Squirrel's relic Minnie, "marched like telegraphs to the drumsticks of a better world, feathered songsters wobbling in its tepid glens, its creeks festive with seraphic ripples and crowded with the rowboats of paradise, in a sacred grove of hackberry trees a celestial choir on its knees, doxologizing and whistling salvation, in the brothers' hands, Bibles, sweet cordials of the grave."

In July when the children were at camp, hours occasionally gaped like graves. Whenever a day seemed empty, I planted it with story, shoveling in character and place. During her first year at Ward-Belmont in Nashville, Orene Hamper published two poems in the college yearbook. When she returned to Carthage for summer vacation, Orene showed the poems to Vester McBee, who cleaned and cooked for Mrs. Hamper. The poems impressed Vester. No one in Gladis wrote poetry, and when Vester visited her grandmother MaudyMay, she mentioned the poems, saying, "Miss Orene has shocked us and turned out a poet." "Good Lord! Who would have thought it?" MaudyMay exclaimed, before asking, "did you find out who with? And she has the nicest parents in Carthage, ever so polite and well-educated. Well, I never." Clearing boulders from Battery Hill made Loppie's and Hoben's muscles sore, and the day after they finished the job, they decided to walk to Samson's Wells and soak in a mineral bath. The day was hot, and after walking three miles Hoben started complaining. After two more miles he sat on a rock beside the road. "Loppie," he said, holding up his right leg, "would you pull off this boot? My foot aches something terrible." Loppie pulled off Hoben's boot and after shaking it out examined Hoben's foot. "Hoben," he said, "there ain't nothing in this boot or on your foot that could hurt you." "Well, then," Hoben said, "pull off the other boot. I'm sure one of my feet is sore."

Early in July I hunted snakes, catching garter; black racers; northern water snakes, their undersides mottled with orange, brown, and purple; then my favorite, ring-necked snakes, their bellies and necks bright yellow, their backs blue in the shade but green in the sun. One day I found a black racer with two bulges in its stomach, probably baby birds. Under a piece of plywood I found the skin of a racer four feet seven and a half inches long. Searching for snakes, I turned over rocks and boards. In the damp under a rock curled a black and white marbled salamander. A wolf spider scurried into dry leaves, young clinging to its abdomen and resembling an infestation of warts.

Paper wasps built nests under rocks, and once when lifting a rock, I slapped my hand over a nest and was stung. Stings rarely burn longer than a quarter of an hour, and I ignore them. Being stung is part of life in July. While picking raspberries I bumped a hornets' nest and was stung again. I moved six yards away and continued picking. Friends warn that bee stings have a cumulative effect, saying that someday I will have an allergic reaction. I don't think I will. As a child on my grandfather's farm in Virginia, I roamed summers barefoot and half-naked. Hives of wasps and hornets stung me. Now when I am stung, the pain does not so much startle as trigger association, awakening memories of hazy days spent building huts, climbing silktrees, or picking spiders out of mud daubers' nests.

Insect season begins in Connecticut in July. During the first part of the month eye gnats swarmed about my face. Deerflies spun around me when I was in the shade. Since deerflies tried to bite me on the neck or head, rather than on hands and arms, I wore a hat and ignored the buzzing. In contrast George suffered. Flies dug into his ears and hind quarters. At the beginning of July I examined small insects: adelgids clinging cottony to hemlocks; on alder, woolly aphids clustered white and thick as heavy cream; carpenter ants carving logs into delicate lattices; and a crab spider glistening like a pink and white pearl. Early in the morning blossoms on swamp rose trembled, bumblebees shaking them, bathing, almost as if the pink petals were tubs floating with yellow pollen. Bristly larvae of ladybugs clung to spikes of timothy. Nearby the heads of flies shined like dew. I marveled at the hair on red milkweed beetles. I watched spotted ladybugs hunt along leaves, their black backs dotted with pink like a gay necktie worn at a summer party, a July party held under a striped tent, the sound of ice tinkling and glasses beaded and bright with half-moons of lemon and lime.

Eyespot galls stained the leaves of red maple and white oak brown. The midges that caused the galls had left the trees, and many galls had dried and sunk. Still, on oaks the centers of some galls remained red while a levee of leaf tissue rose yellow around them. Resembling granola, brown galls peppered alders looking as if they had been shaken over leaves to season the trees. On cherries spindle galls twisted upward, resembling not simply spindles but also small worms wiggling upright. When a breeze stirred the leaves, the galls danced, vibrating like thin, improbable belly dancers. By July the galls were empty, their inhabitants having escaped through holes bored near the tops of the galls.

Early in July black-winged damselflies perched on spicebushes along the Fenton River. By the middle of the month dragonflies bustled hurriedly over ponds and preened on twigs. One morning six white tails clung to a dead tree. Bark had peeled off the tree, and the wood had dried bony and blue. Each white tail was two inches from its neighbor, all so still they seemed painted, turning the tree into the border of a delicate Chinese screen. Some afternoons I squatted on the banks of ponds and watched dragonflies. Often they seemed to play with light, catching it on their wings then flicking it quickly away in bursts of sparkles.

While I sat watching insects, I listened to birds. From damp woods fluttered the calls of wood thrush, veery, and ovenbird. Through meadows bounced the whistles of field and song sparrows. Crows ripped the calm of late afternoon, and the screams of the red-tailed hawks slid through the air. At dusk a lonely screech owl whinnied. Every evening from behind our house a wood peewee called, and Vicki and I stopped what we were doing to listen. The call was sad, and we wondered how to cheer him up. "Maybe," Vicki said, "we could introduce him to house wrens or red-eyed vireos."

One morning at Tift Pond a cardinal cried loudly, the repetitions slapping across the water. A green and a great blue heron fished the beaver pond in the Ogushwitz meadow. Nearby a northern water thrush nested in shadows under a bank of the Fenton River. A pair of kingfishers sputtered over wet lowlands, the female often sitting on a branch reaching up from the riverbed. The end of the branch was splintered, and from a distance resembled an open hand. Indigo buntings rummaged the scrub wrapping the cornfield on Bean Hill. A willow flycatcher sat alert on a cattail at the edge of Unnamed Pond. A pair of kestrels carried mice to their young in an oak tree. Late one afternoon a glossy ibis circled low over Unnamed Pond, its body black against the sky and its bill long and hammered into a curve like a dagger.

Places did not remain constant throughout July. Along the shore of Tift Pond the white trumpets of swamp azalea wilted sticky by the middle of the month while sweet pepperbush burst into fragrant vanilla spikes. July was hot, and during the month the beaver pond shrank, drying into puddles, trapping tadpoles in mud. Unnamed Pond pulled into itself like a bull's eye. Just behind the willows, though, blackberry canes glistened moist with berries. One afternoon I picked eight quarts. Vicki refused to eat the berries because seeds wedged between her teeth, and so I ate them, blackberries for breakfast, lunch, and dinner. With the exception of raspberries I eat all the foods I bring home from walks. The first week in July I dug ramp or wild leek in the wet woods above the beaver pond. Ramp has a strong onion flavor, and although Vicki chopped some into a salad she prepared for me and then the next night fried a handful with Polish sausage, she would not taste ramp.

In the Ogushwitz meadow flowers broke July into three seasons: milkweed season followed by seasons of Canada thistle and Joe-Pye weed. Of course other flowers bloomed at the same time: fleabane and water hemlock; sprays of forget-me-not, raised yellow bowls in the centers, silver running in veins through the petals; black-eyed Susans; stinging nettles; both yellow and white sweet clover; steeplebush and meadow sweet; bristly St. Johnswort; and vervain, from a distance its tall spikes seeming to float above the meadow in a soft blue fog. One morning I stood in a circle of swamp candles eighteen feet wide, yellow sweeping out from me like a skirt. When I stepped beyond the bright folds, a dappled fawn bounded out of the grass, the smell of wild mint lingering behind him.

Although other flowers streaked days, Canada thistle, Joe-Pye weed, and milkweed marked July with the richest colors and spread fragrance in melodies, drawing hives of bees and butterflies clapping like hands. Sometimes I stood in patches of thistle and listened to bees. Often I watched butterflies: monarchs, swallowtails, sedge and silver spotted skippers, cloudy wings, cabbage whites, sulfurs, pearly crescents, fritillaries, and painted ladies. At the same time Joe-Pye weed bloomed in the meadow, its purple flowers throaty and hot with summer, chicory and Queen Anne's lace blossomed leggy along the road behind the dairy barn. At the top of Bean Hill green buttons of pokeweed aged purple, and Japanese beetles chewed multiflora rose into lace.

My walks were collages, papering hours with small pictures, making days pleasurable but never reaching high truth or accurately chronicling the flow of time. Profound truths are beyond me. When a choice exists between simple and complex explanations, I always choose the simple. I resemble Horace Armitage in Carthage. One spring Horace decided to grow a beard. Although Horace did not shave for ten months, his beard remained thin and as yellow as runoff from a paper mill. "Horace, why don't you see Doctor Sollows," Googoo Hooberry said in January. "He'll tell you why the beard won't grow, and he'll prescribe fertilizer for it." "Hellfire, Googoo," Horace replied, "peat moss isn't going to do this beard any good. Besides I already know why it's scraggly. This fat nose of mine casts a big shadow, and the beard don't get enough sunlight to do any real growing."

On walks little things captured my attention: a dead bat an inch and three-quarters long; a painted turtle sunning on a tire in the pond behind the piggery, duckweed covering the surface of the pond, making it resemble a meadow; the bark of American chestnut, seams blistering proud from the ground; leaves of Amur maple resembling backs of cassocks;

then in the middle of the woods, a tan, fibrous bag split, white chicken feathers spilling out in a rush. The feathers had lost fluff and clung to quills in damp, suffocating mats. July is quiet, and as I noticed small things on my ambles, so little matters interested me at home. From Maine a student wrote, saying he spent twelve days near Mt. Baxter. The number of days, he said, was not long enough "to learn to think like a mountain," though, he added, "a medium sized hill is not beyond access, if my experience is the norm." A girl wrote from Oregon and asked if I were a dragon. "Have you always been like this," a woman wrote from Michigan after reading one of my books. I wanted to answer that I was smaller when I was a child and did not have as much hair on my back, but I didn't.

Hair was on mind as well as back. Several people who live in nursing homes write me regularly. Although small matters make walks enjoyable, they are not the stuff of entertaining letters. The dead bat that soars quick through imagination in the woods bores on the page. For the person who lives a quiet life finding interesting things to write strangers about is difficult. One day last winter Eliza commented on the hair in my nostrils, hoping, she said, that when she was an adult she would not be so hairy. In July I wrote Miss Frances in the Grand View Health Home in Danville, Pennsylvania. In the letter I quoted Eliza's remark. Miss Frances answered by return mail. Enclosed in the envelope was an advertisement for a "Rotary Nose Hair Clipper" costing $7.95. The clipper, the advertisement declared, was "for careful grooming in the privacy of your own bathroom." A "professionally designed, precision-made personal grooming instrument," it trimmed "nostril hair without so much as an ouch."

Although I resembled Alice and followed most rabbits that crossed my path in the woods, grass and wildflowers were the stenciling linking one walk to another. In July I noticed several flowers that I had not seen before: black cohosh; orange grass; gooseneck loosestrife and lance-leaved coreopsis, both escaped from gardens; mild water pepper; enchanter's nightshade, the blossoms dangling loosely from small green clubs, delicate hairs curling over the ends like silver flame; colicroot; sweet William catchfly, the blossoms a flat cluster of long, pink horns, corrugated and sticky; and then broad-leaved helleborine, the blooms growing up a tall spike and opening wide like the hands of a boy playing softball without a glove. In the middle of each blossom was a purple well, above it a yellow cap with a bill, below, a pouting pink lip. I looked closely at flowers I neglected in the past: spreading dogbane and Canada lily, ribbons of pink striping the bells of the former, fifteen ribbons in all, five bands of two ribbons alternating with bands of one; the anthers of the latter flower resembling flat loaves of reddish brown bread, the edges crusty and overcooked.

During July I read Edward Hoagland's collection of essays *Balancing Acts.* Hoagland visited Belize and Yemen. He paddled the Okefenokee Swamp in Georgia, rode horseback through the Absaroka Mountains in Wyoming, and traveled the Black and Porcupine rivers in Alaska in a flat-bottomed boat. On his trips Hoagland met soldiers of fortune and lion tamers turned environmentalists. I don't know such people. My friends are teachers, students, lawyers, real estate agents, and coaches. During July I talked to few people other than Vicki. For a while after finishing *Balancing Acts,* I envied Hoagland. But then as I stood at the corner of a cornfield and looked at yellownut grass, its bristles wet with dew and sparkling in the sun, I forgot envy. My words and roots are local. They don't stretch far, but they twist through tussock and great fringed sedges, reed meadow and blue joint grass, agrimony, horse nettle, and poke milkweed.

Vicki and I are different. I like knickknacks and clutter. If Vicki had her way, she'd live in a house as bare as a sauna. I go to bed at nine-thirty and read, always falling asleep before ten-thirty. Vicki putters and watches television, coming to bed after midnight. I get up at six in the morning. Vicki sleeps until nine. For the first years of our marriage children were blossoms, their fragrance pulling us close. Over time, however, our roots have become entangled, and differences have hybridized into friendship. When not roaming hill and field this summer, I hung out with Vicki. After dinner we took short walks on the campus. Some nights we ate in restaurants: driving to Tony's Too for pizza and Everyday Books for dessert, or walking through the woods and across the parking lot to the Cup of Sun for pasta. Once before going to the Buckland Mall to buy suitcases we ate Vietnamese food at the Lotus in Vernon. When Vicki's father visited, we drove to Brooklyn, Connecticut, and ate dinner at the Golden Lamb. Two or three nights when Vicki came to bed, I was awake, and when she undressed in the dark, I barked, making her jump and scream. I wore short pants around the house. The pants were baggy, and my legs dangled like worn-out bell clappers. "Are those the pants Vicki wore when she was pregnant?" my friend Tom asked.

One Saturday Vicki had a tag sale, selling boys' clothes. Vicki plans ahead and buys clothes on sale. She stores the clothes in the attic, and sometimes she does not find them until the children have outgrown them. Occasionally clothes bought for a distant summer will only fit a boy in winter. Sometimes the boys don't like the clothes she buys, and they refuse to wear them. As a result many clothes in the sale had not been worn. Nevertheless, in order to clean out the house Vicki set low prices: twenty-five cents for shorts; trousers, a dollar; and shirts, fifty cents. Vicki made $162, and three women gave her their telephone numbers, imploring her to call them before the next tag sale. The day after the sale Vicki boxed the clothes that were left and donated them to Windham Area Interfaith Ministries. While she carted clothes to Willimantic, I bicycled to the Catholic Church and gave blood. I stayed for a longish time, eating doughnuts and chatting, not with former mercenaries and carpenters become lepidopterists but with our family doctor, the secretary to the dean of the College of Arts and Sciences, a member of the English Department, an art librarian, and the mothers of two of Edward's friends, one friend a member of his fourth grade class, the other a forward on Mansfield's ten-and-under soccer team. That evening I piddled about the yard.

During July I spent much time in the yard, levering up rocks in order to plant flowers in the dell, turning compost in the woods, and pulling weeds. I pulled weeds almost every day. One night after dinner I timed myself, and in an hour I removed 421 weeds from the front yard, most plantain but a few dandelions and a handful of hawkweed. Often I yanked up bittersweet, or Connecticut kudzu, as I call it. The trouble with removing bittersweet was that it led to more strenuous doings. One afternoon after pulling bittersweet near the Morrones' property line, I crossed the yard and began digging forsythia near Mrs. Carter's driveway. From forsythia I progressed to small trees, sawing off branches that blocked sunlight from the dell. One long, thick branch caused problems. After much bending and muttering, I pinned the end of the branch to the ground with my foot. Then I leaned forward and started sawing well up the branch near the trunk of the tree. "If this limb breaks," I thought, "it will do serious damage to my face." "I'll have to be extra careful," I concluded. The next thing I knew my shirt and shorts were splattered with blood, and my mouth was numb. Before I sawed through the limb, it broke, and, snapping like a rubber band, whacked me on the chin. Flesh wounds bleed heavily, and by the time I reached the back door I was gory, not a sight in which Vicki delighted.

In ninety minutes five friends were coming to dinner. Vicki prepared a feast: curried apple soup, rice with pinenuts, sautéed zucchini with carrots, lemon and ginger pork loin, and key lime cheesecake. As various as the seasonings were, they were not eclectic enough to include white and red corpuscles. "Jesus!" Vicki exclaimed, "what have you done now? Don't even think about coming in the house until you stop bleeding," she added, handing me a towel from under the sink. By pork, two hours and a can of bandages later, I stopped bleeding. The next morning my chin resembled a redbelt fungus, jutting out from my face and dusty with dried blood. To show Vicki how stalwart I was, I dismantled the children's swing in the backyard. The swing had stood for ten years. The bolts were rusty, and I used a maul to dismantle it. In the process a strut fell and, hitting me on the jaw, started my chin bleeding again. Although blood ruins most pies and soups, I did not let it spoil my work. By the time I reduced the swing to pasta, my shirt was red, and Vicki refused to let me eat in the house, from the basement fetching the towel she gave me the day before and making me dine al fresco on the back steps.

At the end of July I went to a funeral at the Congregational Church. A neighbor died. I did not know him well. But on Halloween he and his wife gave the children apples and candy, and whenever he drove past our house, he smiled and waved. Flowers turned the church into a garden, blossoms spraying up through ferns toward the altar: gladiola, bushy spikes of liatris, lilies, chrysanthemums, and daisies, some white and yellow, others yellow and orange. The neighbor was popular. For fifty years he worked to make Mansfield and the University of Connecticut better places, and the church was crowded, mostly with older people who had visited each other for many Julys. When a woman sat in the pew behind me, a friend greeted her and asked about her health. I heard a little of the woman's response. "A touch of arthritis," she said, "but that's part of it." The first hymn sung was Isaac Watts's fine, old standby "O God, Our Help in Ages Past." "Time, like an ever-rolling stream, / Bears all its sons away," the fifth stanza began. "Yes," I thought when I sang the words, "being borne away is part of it. But that's not all of it." Being rooted like my neighbor was another part.

People also slip from memory, or, as Watts wrote, "They fly forgotten as a dream / Flies at the opening day." At the end of her adventures Alice woke up. She described her dream to her sister then ran home for tea, high-spirited and forgetful. Her sister sat longer by the river bank, "watching," Carroll wrote, "the setting sun, and thinking of little Alice and all her wonderful Adventures, till she too began dreaming." August has arrived. In a week the children return from camp. "Nature," as Coker Knox put it poetically, if not logically, "vies with Creation to render the scene of unmitigated splendor." Goldenrod has turned the Ogushwitz meadow yellow. Stars of virgin's bower twist through swamp dogwood, and the dell is lemony with horse balm. I will take the children for walks even though they won't remember what I show them. Perhaps they will dream a little. Perhaps when they are grown, they will roam August by themselves, wads of mint in their mouths, hands swollen from stings, maybe even a ring-necked snake turning green through their fingers. Perhaps a rabbit will scurry before them into a patch of blackberries, and they will remember me, not with highfalutin words but simply, maybe oddly, as Horace Armitage remembered his old buddy Hiram Povey, saying, "Hiram won't a man to keep his talents hidden in a napkin."

change
of reading

In college I read with purpose. The future stretched before me like an alluvial plain. In the distance hills lifted in stairs toward a blue flecked with gold. To pluck achievement from the air I had only to buckle knowledge about myself and stride through decades. Thirty years have passed, and my reading has changed. Instead of plunging lidless through the night following a schedule of improving reading, I sleep. No longer do I dig through Cicero and Livy, Herodotus, Plutarch, and Thucydides searching for nuggets of truth. Instead I set the clock radio to the classical music station in Hartford and switch off the light. What sort of person was the I, I sometimes wonder, who studied Hobbes, Mill, Rousseau, Adam Smith, and John Locke. Nowadays I don't even read editorials in newspapers. Politics seems a low muddle, and those theorists from whose books answers once stood out like exclamation points now themselves seem question marks. Certainty is for the young. To the middle-aged, certainty seems naive, at best the harvest of inexperience.

More often than not nowadays my reading is random. In August Vicki and I drove to Maine to fetch the children from camp. On the way we stopped for a night in Portsmouth, New Hampshire. We arrived in Portsmouth in late morning and spent the afternoon roaming the town. Pasted to the window of John's Barber Shop on Daniel Street was a cardboard sign advertising "Clinton Haircuts" for two hundred dollars, the price the president supposedly paid for a haircut in California. Taped below the sign was a white paper, red letters stretching neatly across it in thin lines. To benefit Mercy House and Mercy Shrine, the Knights of Columbus sponsored a raffle. Three tickets cost a dollar. First prize consisted of fifteen lobsters, and second, ten lobsters. On August 7, 8, 14, and 15, the Hackmatack Repertory Theatre in Dover, another poster announced, was staging *Winnie, the Pooh.* Tickets cost five dollars for both adults and children. After reading the posters, Vicki and I walked to the Ceres Street Bakery, and, while drinking coffee and eating a slice of cardamom cake, I studied the table at which we sat. Twenty-five inches square, the top of the table consisted of sixteen ceramic tiles. In the center of the table beat a blue heart from which orange pulsed outward to the edge of the tiles, only to clot on a picket fence of blue slats.

Not only has my reading become random, but the pages I scan occur less often in books than in the past, the nouns and verbs I notice occurring not in sentences but in fragments joined by mood rather than grammar. In July I flew to Columbus, Ohio. I changed planes in Philadelphia. Terminal C was being refurbished. Ventilation worked poorly, and smokers squatted along the hallway in ridges, smoke rising above them diffuse and gray, resembling stratus clouds. From the walls masking tape dangled in loose, silver vines. Tubes of pipes draped from the ceiling in ladders, and fluorescent lights blinked then glared like dead suns. With a large marking pen a workman had written numbers on air conditioning ducts, 8541-4, for example, followed by AH 92 and 2, these last two figures being circled. Yellow tape slipped down columns like loose belts, the print sagging lumpy in bundles of black letters. I stretched a tape out flat in the hallway. It read, "CAUTION—BURIED ELECTRIC WIRE." Stains turned the rug in the waiting area outside the gate paisley. Near the entrance, cups lay on their sides, an orange one, then a blue one with "Maxwell House" printed on it in white letters. A bottle of powder had been overturned, and passengers walked through the dust, tracking white throughout the room. Trash washed around chairs like overflow from a landfill: popcorn; peanuts; newspapers crinkled and torn, the sports sections missing; and Ritz crackers, half-chewed and smeared with peanut butter.

To cheer travelers USAir pasted posters on the wall, advertising Dayton, Seattle, London, and Universal Studios. London was red and furry with Beefeaters while a stack of five crabs turned Seattle pink. Five biplanes dawdled above Dayton. "We'll fly you to the stars," the poster for Universal Studios declared. The waiting area was a cinder-block place, so heavy and dark that imagination could not escape the immediate much less imagine the faraway. "Do what you got to do," an old woman told her son, her voice gritty with exasperation. A man with his shirttail hanging over his backside kissed a heavy woman in a purple dress, their mouths slapping together, the sound broken only by the cranking laughter of a man standing in the hallway. Eight feet in front of the counter a young couple dumped their daughter onto the carpet and amid the grime of foot and trash changed her diaper.

Despite parsing place more than I did years ago, I still read. The subjects of my reading have changed, however. As a boy I never read about medicinal matters. "There is a disc herniation at the C 6–7 level posteriorially and to the right of the middle," I read recently. "In addition there is moderate narrowing of the foramen at that level (the canal through which the C 7 root traverses), as well as some bony overgrowth at the C 6–7 level." Whenever I notice an article about the prostate, I start to read it, though halfway through I usually wince and put the article aside. I subscribe to several magazines, all gifts. These I peruse from back to front. As a boy I read magazines from front to back. Nowadays order seems less important than in the past, an illusion contrived by editors, having little to do with life. Years ago I finished every book I started reading. I particularly enjoyed novels. Today I rarely read novels, and when I start a novel, I usually read only four or five chapters, or at most half the book. The unfinished no longer seems incomplete. By half the book I know the quality of the writer's mind, and plot is not now the hook, baited with mystery and anticipation that once pulled me through narratives. I spit out even the most highly crafted illusion of life. At the slightest distraction, George's barking at the back door or the scent of honeysuckle on the air, I slip books and close covers.

I subscribe to two newspapers: the *Hartford Courant* and the *Willimantic Chronicle*. At breakfast I read the *Courant,* starting with the sports page. I begin with athletics because they don't matter. Who is up or down in the National Football League is insignificant. I don't care who hits the most home runs or wins the batting title in the American League. Consequently I spend hours during the week reading statistics, forgetting them almost as soon as I read them. On the front pages appear stories which are sometimes important, stories which are difficult to forget, at least for someone who imagines his family in the plights of others. There but for luck on that pallet in Boston lies Eliza. But for fortune Edward would be huddled in the sand in the Sudan and Francis would be under a sheet on a rainy corner in New Haven. When the *Chronicle* arrives in the afternoon, I read the obituaries. Often I read only the ages of the deceased. When a person my age dies, I feel uneasy. But when I find three or four people who died at eighty or above, I am reassured and almost hopeful. Because I was born and have spent half my life outside New England, most people mentioned in the obituaries are strangers. Old friends, however, mail me obituaries from the South. These I read carefully. Last month great-aunt Lucille died at ninety-three. Until I read the obituary, I did not know that she and my grandmother were from Abingdon, Virginia. Aunt Lucille attended Stonewall Jackson High School, and I wondered if Grandmother went there also.

During the Second World War Aunt Lucille was a Red Cross volunteer, accumulating, the article stated, 542 hours of service with the Richmond Office of Civil Defense. Little facts appeal to me now. In small doings, those often neglected by novelists cramming poignant events into narrow chapters, lie character and life itself. I read letters carefully, not selected letters of the famous but those sent to me by ordinary people. Recently a man wrote from Diamondhead, Mississippi. He was, he said, "a reader, gardener, widower, housekeeper, classical music lover, and an expert, experienced, and generous taxpayer." "The other day while driving somewhere along this Gulf Coast," he passed, he recounted, "a large truck with this sign on it: PICKERING REFUSE COLLECTION." He wanted "to capture the address and the phone of the company" but traffic prevented him from doing so. Still, he declared, the truck brought my books to mind, "rich with similar collections." Along with letters I read notes, most domestic, not artistic, written by Vicki and pasted to flat surfaces throughout the house. Two nights ago "Did you floss?" was taped to the mirror in the bathroom. Inside a tub of chocolate ice cream in the freezer of the icebox was a slip of paper in a plastic wrapper, reading, "STAY OUT.

THIS ICE CREAM IS FOR THE CHILDREN." On the counter taped to a box of prunes was the warning, "These prunes must last a week."

Instead of studies of social and political theory I read handbooks describing the natural world. Not only do I read such books, but I buy them. Place interests me more than idea. While understanding ideas, indeed fabricating them, is easy, understanding, even seeing, place is difficult. For twelve years I have struggled to know Mansfield, Connecticut. Although I couldn't identify an ash and had never seen a scarlet tanager a decade ago, I pontificated in class. Now after having walked ridges and riverbeds, I teach with more humility. I believe less and marvel more. I want to name things rather than answer questions. Description attracts me more than explanation, no matter how intricate the latter. Little seems more suspect than certitude, and whenever a writer becomes absolutist and preaches truth, I shut the book and open the door for a walk. Last week I wandered the Ogushwitz meadow. Early fall was on the breeze. Canada thistle shredded into down and, blowing like thin cirrus, caught on goldenrod and Jerusalem artichoke. A swallowtail hovered black over Joe-Pye weed, spots at the edges of its wings faded and tired. Summer had worn the wings of fritillaries threadbare, and when I pushed my finger between a fritillary and a purple blossom, the insect crawled atop my knuckle. Berries on swamp dogwood had begun turning blue. Virgin's bower dangled through elderberry in milky crinkles while hops bunched in clutches, resembling green shingles. Bees bored into turtlehead, and dodder garroted nettles, the thin orange bands choking the green stems. On highbush cranberry, berries which faced the sun reddened around the stems while backs and bottoms, those parts of the fruits shaded by bushes, remained yellow. The caterpillars of monarch butterflies grew fat on milkweed. Carolina grasshoppers sputtered along the shoulders of dirt roads, and a pair of barred owls called at dusk. Summer had been dry, and the beaver pond pulled inward, leaving behind chains of puddles which shrank then dried into flakes. A fist of mud remained damp in the bottom of one puddle. Tadpoles turned slowly in the mud, a haze of flies about them, the buzzing so loud that it resembled singing. I scooped up a handful of tadpoles and dumped them into the pond. I hoped water might revive them. Alas, the tadpoles were too weak to survive. Instead of thrashing into life, they sank heavily into the pond.

Although I rarely read novels, I gather stories, fictional tadpoles. Few become frogs but in wiggling for a moment amid the mud of adjective and verb, they entertain me. One morning Waycross Tayler and his brother Jodrell cut beams for a new tobacco barn. Although Waycross was a fine sawyer, he was addicted to drink. "Waycross never was worth a damn after twelve o'clock," Jodrell said later. Early in the afternoon Waycross lost his balance while perched on a limb. He fell and, bouncing down through the tree, slapped hard against the ground, breaking his neck. Jodrell hurried to Haskins Funeral Home and after giving Proverbs Goforth directions for fetching the body informed Waycross's wife, Antiguny, about the accident. "If I told him once, I told him twenty times not to drink and stand on limbs," Jodrell said, "but Waycross was stubborn. I did all I could. Why just this spring I bought Waycross a ticket to the cake raffle and fried chicken supper sponsored by the Daughters of Temperance. I would have made Waycross go, too, if I hadn't been troubled by a pleurisy in the side. It gives me fits, and Doctor Sollows can't do nothing for me. Waycross never did pay me no mind about it, but I guess that's neither here nor over yonder what with Waycross's neck being snapped like a wishbone. But I reckon things could be worse. Waycross didn't let go of the ax when he fell, and it is only the grace of God that prevented him from cutting himself when he hit the ground."

On Saturday morning Slubey Garts preached a funeral sermon for Waycross at the Tabernacle of Love. There not being much good that could be said about Waycross, Slubey talked around the deceased, urging the congregation to prepare for the coming of the King. "The Lord doesn't stand on ceremony," Slubey said. "He'll jerk you out of a tree like Brother Waycross or out of a field when you are ploughing like Sister Skidzun last month. The Lord sticks closer than a cocklebur. When Jesus broke a strap on one of his sandals in Bethlehem," Slubey continued, "he took the sandal to a cobbler to be mended. Like Waycross the cobbler liked drink, and when he was working on the sandal, he sliced the middle finger off his left hand. The finger fell into a pile of sawdust and leather shavings on the floor, shaking like a tail cast by a lizard. 'Oh, God,' the cobbler moaned and grabbed his hand as the blood spurted. Right then the Lord came to his aid. As soon as he said 'God,' the finger poked its nail out of the trash and sniffed about like the nose of a hound tasting the air. Before the cobbler could say 'Jumping Jehosophat,' the finger hopped up and attached itself back to the cobbler's hand. The King of Glory washed the cobbler's blood away, and after the accident all the cobbler was left with was a scar shaped like a cross at the joint where his finger joined his palm. After that whenever Satan tempted him to drink, the finger stiffened and rose up before the cobbler like one of the cedars of Lebanon, pointing toward the heavens and glowing red with the Blood of the Lamb."

"Here comes the Lord Jehovah," Slubey shouted at the end of the sermon, "make way for Jehovah." Hink Ruunt and Googoo Hooberry spent the previous evening at Enos Mayfield's Inn in South Carthage grieving for Waycross. Consequently they dozed through Slubey's sermon. "Who's that?" Hink said to Googoo, jerking awake when he heard Slubey say Lord Jehovah. "Oh, he's that foreigner who came up from Nashville, the Englishman who bought the Timeout Café in Red Boiling Springs and turned it into a restaurant. He probably donated a bundle to the church. He must have come in the rear door, and Slubey is paying him back."

I enjoy short tales because I can repeat them to others. Each morning I go to the Cup of Sun, drink coffee, and talk to my friends, Ellen, Roger and George. Not long ago Ellen went to the races at Saratoga. Outside town, she recounted, stood a sign advertising a "Christian Magician." For a while we speculated about the magician's tricks. Next we talked about insults, and I quoted the worst insult I had heard in some time. "He is so low," a man said, describing his brother, "that he looked up and saw a snake's asshole and thought it was the North Star." The quotation was a bit rough for the group, so before leaving I told a story about Carthage. Two weeks after Dr. Sollows vaccinated Hiram Povey for smallpox, Hiram drank too much, stumbled into the Cumberland River, and drowned. "I can't see what use this vaccination is," Albert Hennard said at the funeral. "It didn't do Hiram no good."

I left the Cup of Sun in order to write. Unlike the front page of the newspaper, writing distracts and cheers me. To write one must have free time, and I was able to write because Vicki banished me to the study. While the children were at camp, Vicki wanted to clean the house, something she insisted upon doing by herself. "Write a silly story," she said. "That will keep you out of my way." "Should I write about Jodrell Tayler?" I asked. "He worried so about his cows during the calving season that he slept in boots and overalls in order, as he put it, 'to keep myself awake'." "Or I could write about Hiram," I continued, seeing Vicki's eyes glaze.

"One evening a fox broke into the chicken coop at the Poveys and ate a fine Golden Sebright hen. To protect the chicks Beevie Povey took them inside the house and put them in a big bowl on the kitchen floor. Hiram spent all day at Enos Mayfield's Inn. When he got home that night, he'd had so much to drink that he staggered into the kitchen and threw up into the bowl containing the chicks. After the first wave of sickness passed, Hiram looked into the bowl. 'Oh Lord,' he moaned, 'I remember the sweet potatoes and the kale. But when did I eat all these chickens?'" "Into the study," Vicki said. "I have work to do."

The older I get the more stories life contains. In the cleaning or my absence from the cleaning was the stuff of tale. Although Vicki refused help, she resented working by herself. Because she worked hard, she was tired at night. Not having been assigned any chores, I came to bed full of energy. A tired wife and a bouncy husband do not a harmonious couple make. "I spent the entire day working for you and the children. Can't you see how tired I am? Now when I want to sleep you have to tell me a story. My God, you are insensitive," Vicki said one night after a day of cleaning. "To quote Googoo Hooberry," I said, "'I ain't going to bed it no longer'. Unless I tell a story I will stir around the house and keep you up all night. This past summer," I began, "Quintus Tyler considered retiring from teaching at the Male and Female Select School in Carthage. The board of education interviewed candidates for Quintus's post, and Proverbs Goforth applied." Proverbs, I told Vicki, did not do well in the interview. When Judge Rutherford asked him if he had read *Romeo and Juliet,* Proverbs replied, "I've read *Romeo.*" After telling the story, I rolled over onto my side and slept well. Despite being tired Vicki tossed about and was muttering when I fell asleep.

Maybe I read less because I am busy living. When Vicki and I retrieved Eliza from camp in August, the director spoke to us. "Eliza," she said, "enjoyed a fine summer. At first she carried a book with her everywhere. She read during meals and took books with her to activities, even swimming. But," the director continued, "by the end of the summer she laid books aside and participated wholeheartedly in everything." "At the beginning of camp," Eliza's counselor added, "Eliza was standoffish. She wouldn't participate in skinny dips. She said they were 'totally inappropriate'. By August she was the first girl in the lake in the morning." Eliza's participation went further than skinny dips. Not only did she put books down, but she also dropped her shorts, becoming, as she told me at dinner one night, "the best mooner in the cabin." An eight-year-old's forsaking reading and become adept at showing her behind may not be improvement. What I do know is that on a shelf somewhere stands a book that takes such matters seriously. I won't read the book. I will be too busy telling stories and raising the bubbly glass of life to my lips, turning it bottoms up in the sunlight. "Proverbs," Judge Rutherford asked, "how do you explain the origin of the prairies out west?" For a moment Proverbs looked puzzled and his chin sagged, but then he smiled knowingly and spoke. "Herds of mammoths ate the trees," he said, "and made the prairies."

Much as I don't read so much for instruction, so I now turn less to books for entertainment. On airplanes books are therapeutic, and like lithium, calm jittery nerves, enabling me to get through the highs and lows of turbulence on an even keel. At night books are soporific. The book I take off the bedside table at nine-thirty tumbles to the floor by ten. Still, I continue to read, not, though, in order to educate or shape myself. Instead I read so that I will not, as the English poet Matthew Arnold wrote, be left "in the sea of life enisled." As I age and the society in which I grew and thrived changes, I often feel dissociated from time and place, even Mansfield despite my wanderings. And so I read to escape the sense, as Arnold put it, that "we mortal millions live alone." I dig through signatures of books searching for runners that bind me to other people.

Recently I read an autobiographical account of a woman's travels to, among other places, China, Kashmir, and Ethiopia. I was envious when the woman described the culinary delicacies of Mongolia: hot candied camel's hump, camel's feet braised in brown sauce, and bull's penis liquor. Last year I snacked on sea urchins in Papua New Guinea and green ants in northwest Australia, and I longed for a tray of Mongolian canapés. Instead, I settled for a Granny Smith apple. The ravenous fit passed, and the book was slipping from my hands to the floor when I read a description of the woman's traveling companion, a man, she described as the producer and director of the movie *Pumping Iron,* a film about bodybuilders. "George," I said aloud. I had not seen George for seventeen years, and once the woman mentioned him, I read the book carefully. Instead of paying attention to the author's ideas, though, I read through pages to memory. Because his father did not attend the premiere of *Pumping Iron* in New York, George decided to have a premiere in New Hampshire. Body-builders flew to Hanover for the evening. Two posed before the showing, and strawberries and champagne were served afterward. I taught at Dartmouth at the time and invited members of the English Department to the festivities. Three attended. Arnold Schwarzenegger came to the premiere, and I ate dinner with him. "You ate dinner with the Terminator," Edward said when I mentioned the meal, a fact which boosted my masculinity considerably in Edward's opinion. "Old buddy," I said to Edward, "in my younger days I was something else, practically a T-1000."

Last month I read Sydney Lea's *Hunting the Whole Way Home,* a collection of essays about writing, hunting, and family. I read the book because I know Sydney though I have not seen him in eighteen years. Like me Sydney is middle-aged, and now when he hunts, he points his shotgun but does not shoot. Years have taught him control. The last time I went hunting was with Sydney. In 1973 we hunted woodcock. He shot one bird, and I didn't shoot anything, something that was typical since I have always been a terrible shot. After reading Sydney's book, I told Vicki that I wanted to the roam the woods again with a gun. "Why do you want to kill things?" she asked. She did not understand when I explained that I would not shoot, that I had spent most of my life not pulling triggers, not acting and not writing about matters because they would cause pain. I wanted to smell moldy leaves and to wear my old hunting jacket, shotgun shells bulging in a row across my chest. I wanted to turn Mother's twenty-gauge through my hands, the barrels smooth as night. Most of all I wanted to wander paths long sunken in memory.

Not only did *Hunting the Whole Way Home* make the past vital, but the book made me nostalgic for what never occurred. Sydney and I taught English at Dartmouth in the 1970s. Teaching with us were Jay Parini and Robert Siegel. During the seventies the University Press of New England began publishing, and Sydney and Jay founded and edited *The New England Review.* Dartmouth fired the four of us. Since leaving Dartmouth, we have written some forty books among us, many celebrating family and place. Had we remained in Hanover we might have helped each other grow. We might even have been the source of literary stirrings, much as the Fugitive poets were at Vanderbilt in the 1920s. On the other hand, if we had stayed at Dartmouth, we might have drowned in slippery critical words, and parochial interests might have clogged our thought. Instead of writing about place and family, we might have devoted ourselves to professional guild and literary abstraction.

Not long ago George Core, editor of the *Sewanee Review,* asked me to review Lincoln Kirstein's memoirs, *Mosaic.* Kirstein founded the magazine *Hound & Horn* and has been celebrated as "the father of American ballet." Years ago I stopped subscribing to *Gourmet.* Descriptions of places I could not afford to visit and accounts of fabulous meals I would never taste made me dissatisfied with wholesome domestic fare. Vicki dreaded the arrival of *Gourmet,* noting that for two days afterward I was melancholy. *Mosaic* crackled with famous names and resembled an intellectual and social *Gourmet.* Kirstein sat at tables so high that I could not imagine them. In 1916, however, Kirstein attended Camp Timanous in Maine. For five summers in the 1960s I was a counselor at Timanous, and now Francis and Edward go there each summer. After showing pictures of Kirstein at Timanous to the children, I read *Mosaic* with delight. Instead of being excluded by wealth, I felt part of Kirstein's world. In a summery room in the past he and I were boys together.

Shortly after Hiram's funeral Albert Hennard and Loppie Groat went to Nashville for the weekend. On Sunday they rode the streetcar out West End Avenue to Centennial Park to see the replica of the Parthenon. Cannas bloomed in red rows, and a pair of swans glided through the duckpond, resembling white question marks. "This is a great sight," Loppie exclaimed. "Yes," Albert answered, "it's fine in its way, but I once saw a turkey buzzard with a wooden leg." As I totter along the shore of contemporary doings, I have eyes for wooden legs, those odd bits of paragraphs that support me and make me feel part of the bookish main. Yes, my reading has changed. Rarely do I finish a book that does not flash upon recollection and warm the night.

home again, home again

Universities are impersonal. Faculty who retire are quickly replaced and forgotten. "I haven't seen Charles Huddlestone recently," Richard said to me, mentioning a prominent member of the history department. "If you see him," I answered, "run like hell. He has been dead three and a half years." I spent the past twelve months in Australia. Almost no one noticed my absence. "Sam," Chuck said in the locker room, "you've not been in the pool recently. Have you had a cold?" "You had a sabbatical, didn't you?" a member of the English Department said the other day. "Did you go anywhere or did you stay in Storrs?" I liked Australia and on arriving home felt depressed. Self-centered people inflict their moods upon others. I did not want my feelings to affect the children. I wanted them to look forward to school, so I went for a long walk the morning after we returned.

Alone in the woods or at the end of a field, I think myself part of the natural world. Among people I sometimes feel estranged, and so I roamed the woods behind the sheep barns. I wandered for several hours, walking beyond mood and into place. Spotted cort pushed damp and purple through brown leaves, and destroying angel gleamed white. Two black racers curled in knots under a piece of plywood. When I lifted the wood, the snakes remained motionless for a moment. Then raising their heads off the ground, they glided up to my legs before slipping around my boots into the brush. In November after snakes hibernated, mice took up residence under the board, and one afternoon I counted seven. In the Ogushwitz meadow goldenrod was high as my chin, and bees were so thick the air throbbed like a bass speaker on a record player. Paths I wore through the meadow in previous years were overgrown. As I beat through the goldenrod, three bumblebees crawled under my shirt and stung me. Never before had bumblebees stung me. Each year insects sting me in the woods: paper wasps, yellow jackets, and white-faced hornets. The stings raised welts on my back. When I returned home, I showed the welts to the children. "Just like two years ago," Edward said, "when we returned from Nova Scotia and five yellow jackets bit you the next day. Things are the same."

The university had bulldozed the beaver dam in the meadow, but Edward was right. Little had changed. The ROTC still played military games in the woods. Nailed upside down to a small oak at the foot of Bean Hill was a tin can. The can had been painted red. Inside the can a baggage label dangled down. Printed on the label was "C3 Mechanized Infantry." Attached to an ash in the middle of a corn field was another can. "Ji Aviation" was written on the label inside. Letters were visible beneath the red paint, and after tilting my head sideways to compensate for the can's being upside down, I puzzled out the lettering. The word SYSCO circled the tops of the cans, and CLASSIC the bottoms. Each can once contained 3.06 kilograms of pineapple chunks.

On my walk I noticed small changes from the past. Loggers had cut down red pine and white oak. Tacked to every other fence post around Horse-barn Hill were signs warning people about rabies. "Because of the current rabies epizootic in Connecticut," the sign stated, "we advise you not to feed the animals." Barn animals over three years old had been vaccinated. Younger animals could not be vaccinated, so, the sign urged, "Please help us protect you and your children by taking proper precautions when you visit our barns. Look but DO NOT TOUCH!" By the middle of August, twenty-two rabid raccoons had been killed in Mansfield, and people were nervous. My neighbor Mrs. Carter set out a Havahart trap during June, "not because of rabies," she said, "but to protect the garden." During the month she caught six ground hogs, four raccoons, a possum, a skunk, and a feral cat.

No matter the clouds, days brighten when I roam woods. One damp Saturday in September I took Edward to soccer practice at Lions Field. The day was cold, and I wondered how I could endure the practice. For a while I watched Edward play sweeper, neatening the field like an erasure. "Not a bad comparison," I said to myself, suddenly looking up. Trees shed leaves like raindrops, color falling to the ground in red and orange splats. Blossoms hung from New England asters in soggy blue baskets, and purple drained out of Joe-Pye weed, turning the plant brown as burlap. Spiders, *Epeira insularis,* hide themselves under leafy tents, looking like orange and brown nuts, single strands of silk stretching to their webs. Smooth puffballs clustered at the edge of the field. Blister beetles crawled through the grass. When I picked beetles up, they pretended to be dead. Red-humped oak worm caterpillars shredded leaves of scrub oaks into lace, their orange and blue stripes turning them into small candy canes.

A daddy-long-legs trod daintily across a leaf, his second pair of legs reaching forward and tapping lightly ahead of him, his pedilaps moving, holding and adjusting bits of food that I could not see. Witchhazel bloomed in small yellow snarls, and catkins hung down from ironwood and hornbean, resembling Christmas ornaments made from bits of cardboard threaded on a string by a child at school. A flock of bluebirds bathed in a puddle, tossing blue about them like petals. "How was the practice?" Vicki asked when Edward and I returned home. "I bet you were cold." "No," I said, "I didn't notice the temperature."

The morning after the bumblebees stung me the stings itched. I was too busy, though, to scratch. Batteries in both cars were dead. Marty started the Mazda, but he had to tow the Plymouth. Eight hundred and seventy-nine dollars later, the cars ran, the Mazda smoothly with a new battery, the Plymouth jerkily, a death trap stopping in the middle of intersections. Eleven years old, the Plymouth had been driven 61,154 miles. In 1984 I bought it for $10,098.38, including taxes and fees. I decided to buy a new car. "Buy another car if you want; I'm not having anything to do with it," Vicki said, before stipulating that a new car had to have a roof rack and space inside for the children and George the dog. I bought a Toyota Camry at Middletown Toyota, an hour and fifteen minutes' drive from Storrs. The car was a station wagon with dual airbags, antilock brakes, a six-cylinder engine, and a roof rack. I visited several dealerships. The manager of a Volvo dealership in East Hartford was rude, and when I asked to see the factory invoice at several places, salesmen balked, and I left. In Middletown "George" showed me the invoice immediately. Thirty minutes later I wrote a check for $23,810.02. "Gray will go nicely with the black Mazda," Vicki said when the car was delivered. "You could moonlight at Potter Funeral Home in Willimantic."

Sometimes I think I spend more time tending cars than I do family. As soon as Marty fit the Mazda and Plymouth with new batteries, I drove them to Danielson for emissions tests. Both passed, but the drives filled two mornings. Not long after trading in the Plymouth, I took the Mazda to Morande for its fifteen-thousand-mile checkup. While the car was being serviced, I walked up Main Street to The Whole Donut. I nibbled a chocolate doughnut, sipped coffee, and read Maxine Kumin's collection of essays describing life on a farm in New Hampshire, *Women, Animals, and Vegetables*. I left the shop when an afflicted man changed seats and, sitting behind me, read over my shoulder and said, "what is ringbone?" The man had a cast eye that resembled a mulberry, and his hair hung off his shoulders in braids as fragrant as garlic. When I replied that ringbone resembled arthritis and lamed horses, the man said, "I have never had arthritis, but I have had a tough time, let me tell you." I bolted my coffee, and before the man could gallop into a narrative, I was out of the gate on my way back to the customer paddock at Morande.

The paddock was dreary, and the other two customers seemed broken to saddle and quirt. A middle-aged man wearing a blue windbreaker sat immobile, staring at *Sports Illustrated* but never turning a page. A younger man in gray slacks, a long-sleeved blue shirt, and brown tasseled loafers dug through a stack of papers eighteen inches high. Occasionally he stopped and used a pocket calculator after which he wrote a figure down with a ball point pen. A beige telephone sat on a low table to the man's right, and several times he called numbers, reaching answering machines and confirming appointments, all of these last seeming to be scheduled for ten o'clock.

The air in the room was so dry that the pages of Kumin's book felt brittle, and I stopped reading. On a table in front of me lay a copy of *US News & World Report,* the issue for 21 November, focusing on the results of the fall elections. I picked up the magazine, but then put it down unopened. Instead I decided to read the room. Three gum machines stood along one wall, all operated by the Lions Club. A handful of salted peanuts cost twenty-five cents, and round gumballs, ten cents. Fruit Skittles were also twenty-five cents. The candy came in different colors: green, red, orange, and blue. Pasted across the top of the machine was a decal declaring "The Rainbow of Flavors."

Unlike Skittles the room was colorless. I sat on a plastic sofa bleached out of color. Suspended above the window behind me was a white bowl, English ivy hanging dusty over its sides. Beside the telephone stood a brown plastic pot containing a small philodendron. On the ceiling were two racks of fluorescent lights, each rack holding two long bulbs. Between the racks water spigots jutted down in triangles. Nailed to the walls were two aging plaques listing employees of the month for the years 1990 and 1991. David Raczkowski was employee of the month in September 1990 and again in March and July 1991. A door on one side of the room led upstairs. On the door was a blue sign, white letters stamped on it declaring, "Office Personnel Only." Across the room another door led to the "Service Write-Up Area." Signs decorated the room. Enterprise Rent-A-Car offered "Special Rates on Rental Cars," and Morande was a member of the "Greater Manchester Chamber of Commerce."

Behind the man using the telephone hung three enlarged photographs, all depicting Hartford during the 1920s. I counted fifteen streetcars in one picture. In another picture a truck with a tarpaulin raised over a flatbed backed into an alley. Painted on the side of the truck was "Byrolly Transportation." On the building above the truck stood a billboard, urging passersby to "DRINK MILK." I could not see the pictures clearly from the sofa, so I walked across the room and leaned over the man talking on the telephone. The man put the telephone down and started to arrange his papers. When I realized that he thought me one of the afflicted, I kicked up my heels. "Uhhh!" I said loudly, the sounds coming from my throat in a bubbling gargle. When I shuffled my feet rapidly across the linoleum, the man grabbed his papers and calculator and hurried through the door to the write-up area.

For the first six weeks home I lived mechanically, grinding through days on an axle bending under errands. I took the lawn mower to Morneau's for repairs. I calculated income taxes and wrote the Superior Court in Rockville, asking to have jury duty delayed until December 13, the day after I stopped teaching. Although I have been called for jury duty several times and have not applied for a release, never have I served on a jury. I looked forward to the experience. "In a democracy," I told Vicki, "one must not shirk his civic duty." "All you want," Vicki said, "is to gather material for an essay. To use people's misfortunes for your benefit is lousy. You are worse than a lawyer." Vicki refused to listen when I recounted how Father once made justice prevail when he served as foreman of a jury. A cook at the Maxwell House Hotel in Nashville made a batch of apple pies. To cool the pies the cook set them on a window ledge. Unfortunately when she was bringing the pies back inside, the cook knocked a pie off the ledge. The pie fell on the head of a woman walking along Church Street. The woman sued the Maxwell House claiming the pie damaged her brain, making it impossible for her to stop blinking. At the trial she blinked nonstop.

"She had the worst case of blinking imaginable," Father said. The trial began late in the morning, and the judge recessed the court for lunch. Father did not want to eat downtown, so he drove to a restaurant on the Nolensville road. "I had just started eating," Father said, "when I glanced across the dining room and saw the woman eating lunch with her lawyer. She wasn't blinking." Not once during the meal did the woman blink. Father ate quickly and left the restaurant. He knew what he saw was privileged information and not admissible in court. He realized that if he told the judge he would be excused from the jury. An alternate would replace him, and the woman would win a big sum of money. "So I did what any decent person would do," he said. "I kept quiet, and when the jury reconvened after lunch, I spoke first." "This is a clear case of neglect," Father said. "The pie caused this woman to blink terribly, and I think we should award the poor soul a lot of money to prevent this kind of accident from happening again. I suggest we give her two hundred and fifty dollars." The rest of the jury agreed with Father. "The verdict and the award," Father said, "cured the woman but did serious damage to her lawyer. She stopped blinking for a moment, and he started blinking."

Home is where doctors are, and I spent almost as much time driving humans for checkups as I did cars to garages. After a year of being free from asthma, Eliza and Edward started wheezing twenty-four hours after reaching Connecticut. Edward ran a fever and had nightmares. One evening wild women chased him from room to room, skating across ceilings on roller blades, their arms swinging below them like vines. After Edward and Eliza visited the allergist, the whole family had physicals. Donna cleaned our teeth, and Dr. Weeks replaced Edward's braces. Francis had a hemangioma removed from his chest. A bundle of veins, the hemangioma resembled a red pearl. The doctor cauterized it in nine seconds and charged $110. "Home again, home again, jiggety-jog," Vicki said as we passed in the driveway, she returning from taking Edward to one doctor, I on the way to another with Eliza.

So that home would seem familiar, we repeated patterns of behavior. Vicki bought chrysanthemums for the front steps: yellow Jessica, white Tracy, and Radiant Lynn, this last orange and red. I ordered daffodils for the side yard, fifty each of Arctic Gold, Lunar Sea, Bravoure, Accent, Ceylon, then twenty Gigantic Stars. Daffodil companies always ship more bulbs than one orders, and instead of 270 bulbs I planted 356. The soil in the yard is poor, consisting mostly of till with a splattering of dirt between stones. Before planting the bulbs, I dug and wedged rocks out of the yard, filling in long beds with compost, wheelbarrows of which I shoveled out of the woods behind the house.

Till of all sorts clings to home. Before leaving Connecticut for Australia, I cleaned my desk. Yet when I opened the top right-hand drawer, I found Father's Social Security card wedged under a wooden divider. The card was issued on "12-10-36," and Father's number was 578-07-6883. Father's signature was firm and youthful, the letters slicing upward in straight lines then curving backwards, resembling scapulars on birds rowing through the air. I unpacked carefully, but like stones tossed out of a gully by a cloudburst, bits of things from Australia turned up in corners. Behind my desk I found a sheet of yellow paper. On it were written the titles of five gift books, each measuring four and a half by six inches. One afternoon at the bookstore of the University of Western Australia I saw them lined up beside the cash register: *The ABC of Loving Yourself, How To Play Mah Jong, The History of Farting, Chess Made Easy,* and *Finding Balance.* Despite occasionally pretending to bumble about, I am balanced. When I took the College Board Examinations, only one point separated my score in English from that in mathematics. "Too balanced," Don said recently, "your writing could do with tipping."

Don was wrong. The doings of a day are tipsy enough without my being out of balance. Four nights ago, while we ate dinner, the doorbell rang. A woman stood amid the chrysanthemums on the front steps. Her hair eddied over her shoulders in brown strings. She wore tweed trousers and a heavy jacket from which tassels hung in rough shucks. She was raising money for Greenpeace. I told her that we already were members. "Oh," she said and looked pained. She pivoted to leave but then turned back toward me. "Could I use your bathroom?" she said. "I am in trouble." After the woman left, Vicki fetched the Lysol from under the kitchen sink and, going into the bathroom, scrubbed the toilet bowl. "Everybody ought to live naturally," Vicki said as she served dessert, "but that woman looked too natural to me."

I received little mail in Australia. In Storrs mail gushed out of the box. A man in Pennsylvania graded *Trespassing,* my latest collection of essays, and gave it a B+. Late in 1991, the University of Missouri Press published *Let It Ride,* another collection of essays. Waiting for me when I arrived home was the royalty check for the first half of 1994. Returns outnumbered sales, and my royalty was a minus $60.39. "What are you going to spend it on?" Vicki said when she saw the statement. I telephoned the publisher of *Trespassing.* "I am back," I said to the director of the press. The director is a man of few words. "Good," he said, ending our chat. I asked to speak to the publicity director. "I hear you had a good time in Australia," he said when he answered the telephone. "Yes," I said. When he didn't respond, I said that I was eager to help publicize the book. "That's good," he said, and the conversation ended.

The mail was swollen with advertisements. From Pennsylvania, came an advertisement for Christian Chimes, "The Chimes for a Lifetime." While eight-inch chimes cost $29.50 plus $1.75 for shipping and handling, eighteen-inch chimes sold for $59.50, the shipping and handling adding $4.50 to the bill. *American Girl* sent Eliza a card. "Please send my American girl her FREE issue of *American Girl* magazine and enter her one-year subscription (5 more issues for a total of 6) for just $19.95," the card stated, adding "if she is not completely delighted with her FREE issue of *American Girl,* I'll simply write 'cancel' on my invoice and return it. I will owe nothing, and the FREE issue will be hers to keep." FREE was printed in red. "When companies promise free gifts," I explained to Eliza, "hold your wallet tightly. This *free* costs $19.95."

The children received much mail. Before leaving Australia Francis entered the "Australian Schools Science Competition" sponsored by Esso

Australia and administered by the University of New South Wales. Francis finished with "High Distinction," putting him in the "top 1%" of ninth-grade science students in Western Australia. The headmaster of John XXIII, Francis's old school, announced the results in a weekly assembly. Andrew wrote Francis and described the assembly. "High Distinction," the headmaster declared, "to Lee Bowers and Francis Pickering, who has since left us and returned to the States." Before the headmaster continued, Andrew wrote, "Mrs. Waverley said, 'Thank God' and the hall roared." Francis seems to impress people. "Once a month while you were in Australia," Aaron told him, "we celebrated high-socks day. We pulled our socks up and wore them as high as we could in your memory."

A herpetologist sent me an article he wrote analyzing "blood-squirting in a horned lizard." When threatened by a predator, the horned toad, as the lizard is commonly known, ejects blood from a sinus cavity by the eye. Accompanying the article was an eight-by-ten-inch color photograph of a toad squirting blood. A solid fountain of blood two and a quarter inches high erupted from the toad's eye. Beyond the solid mass of red, the blood broke into twenty-one scarlet droplets. To provoke squirting, the herpetologist used a yellow Labrador retriever, a female between two and three years old, and himself, a white male of German ancestry, approximately forty-five years old. The lizards, he explained, were placed in the center of "an arena." Then the dog, or the herpetologist "on all fours" mimicking the dog, barked at, approached, chased, and physically manipulated the lizard. The herpetologist will not make his fortune on the stage, at least not in productions of *Bob, Son of Battle* or *The Hound of the Baskervilles.* On all ten occasions when the Labrador "manipulated" them, lizards squirted blood. Only twice did lizards respond to the herpetologist, no matter the fervor of his tail-wagging, bottom-sniffing, or whatever "canid" behavior the herpetologist imitated.

The herpetologist's letter raised my spirits considerably. But what really made me glad to be home was a chair. I have a bad back, and for years my friend George Core has urged me to buy a better chair for my desk. My house is a graveyard of chairs, most with sagging bottoms or sprung backs, but chairs nonetheless. One more chair would, I thought, force another chair into the furniture mausoleum in the basement. While I was in Australia, George wrote literary friends of mine, asking them to help him buy me a new chair. Friends sent money from Ohio, Virginia, Iowa, Vermont, New York, and Tennessee. Late in September the chair arrived. "A welcome home present," George said. A present, I should add, that brought a mist of appreciation to my eyes. "That is the nicest thing I have ever heard of," Vicki said. "I contributed to it," Jay said, "because it is the only university chair you will ever have."

I spent many hours in the chair. In Perth I wrote a book of essays describing our year. The manuscript consisted of 615 handwritten pages. I wrote on yellow paper, each page measuring twelve by eight and a quarter inches, thirty-four lines to a page with no margins. On September 29, I began typing the manuscript into the computer. Thirty-two days later I finished typing. I recorded percentages of the manuscript that I typed. I kept Vicki apprised of my progress, telling her several times each day how much I had typed. Vicki does not enjoy numbers as much as I do, and the progress reports were the source of domestic discord. Nevertheless I continued the reports, in fact doubled them when I realized they irked Vicki.

I am a chip off my Father's DNA. Once a month Father ambled into the kitchen late in the evening and, opening a cabinet, banged pans against each other. Never did Mother fail to respond, rushing into the kitchen and asking, "What are you doing?" "Just looking around," Father always said, "seeing if I can find more efficient ways for you to store pans and manage the kitchen." Father never intended to move the pans. Much as I informed Vicki about the progress of my typing, so he rattled pans only to irritate Mother. Such are the ways of husbands with wives in good marriages. Thus on that first day, September 29, I typed 20 pages, or 3.25 percent of the manuscript. By the seventh day I had typed 121 pages, 19.67 percent of the book. On the fourteenth day I reached 228 pages, 37.07 percent. Ten days later I had typed 448 pages, 72.85 percent. By the 26th day I was at 525 pages, or 85.37 percent.

After typing the manuscript into the computer, I printed the pages, the total being 288 pages, thirty-six lines to a page. I then revised the manuscript, twice by hand on the printed pages then once in the computer. I reduced the manuscript to 249 pages, cutting 13.54 percent of the original manuscript, as I informed Vicki. To revise the manuscript I almost wore a hole in the seat of my new chair, usually taking thirteen hours to revise an essay, or, for the fifteen essays in the book, approximately 195 hours, or, as I again informed Vicki, eight and one-quarter full, twenty-four-hour days.

I enjoy counting, an activity that reflects, I suppose, the balance on my College Board examinations. Papering the wall at Little Caesar's restaurant is a huge picture of a pepperoni pizza. Last week while waiting for two family-sized pizzas, I counted the slices of pepperoni seasoning the pizza on the wall. A seam jutted out from the wall, dividing the pizza and making counting difficult. The number of slices of pepperoni on the pizza was sixteen. I counted four times to be sure. A tall man and a woman with a basket of clean laundry were also waiting for pizzas. Neither noticed the wallpaper, leading me to conclude that they probably did poorly in mathematics in high school.

Edward and Eliza cried when we left Australia. Now they would be upset if we left Storrs. Once school began, our lives slipped into familiar routines. Francis spent hours in the Interest Center at the Middle School fiddling with the computers, among other things changing the files for a game called Commander Keen 4C. While the Commander himself became Kentucky Fried Chicken, the files Order and Readme became Home Delivery and Chicken and Potatoes, respectively. "The game is silly," Francis said, "and the saucerhead kids play it all day and are very annoying." Eliza started the obligatory Indian project. Vicki bought a slab of balsa wood at Phil's, and while Eliza stretched out on the floor in her bedroom and reread the *Odyssey*, Vicki sat on the back stoop and carved a kachina doll, a figurine used in rituals by the Hopi Indians. Vicki painted the doll and then glued on a headdress made from grouse and blue jay feathers. Eliza helped paint, mostly, I am afraid, smearing lines. "Indians don't interest me," she said. "I'd rather read Greek myth."

Reading is Eliza's love. Teachers in fourth grade assign students a number of pages to be read each month. If the student completes the reading, she wins a certificate to Pizza Hut, awarding her a small pan-style pizza. While some students won pizzas for reading two hundred pages, Eliza has to read five thousand. Reading five thousand pages is easy for Eliza. She always accomplishes it during the first two weeks of the month. Since first grade Eliza has carried books with her everywhere, and Vicki and I have to confiscate books at dinner each night. We worry about her reading but know there is nothing we can do. "Your father was just the same," Uncle Coleman told me. "Samuel always had a book with him."

Thought and place are linked. When I returned home, I began saying things which had long been the matter of household patter but which had dropped from conversation for a year. While driving the family to the Seventh and Eighth Grade Science Fair at the Middle School, I mounted a familiar platform, telling the children that I came from a couple of rungs higher on the social ladder than their mother. "When you know who you are and where you are from, you are confident," I said, "and don't worry about what other people think about you." "Is that why you fart so much?" Eliza asked. "Absolutely," I answered, "breaking wind without concern is one of the privileges of belonging to the aristocracy." Few privileges, I should add, remain. Indeed the word *aristocrat* mystifies most folks. Recently Coker Knox traveled through East Tennessee raising money for the Democratic party. Preachers are the best fund-raisers in small towns. When Coker Knox went to a town in which he did not know anyone, he introduced himself to the minister in charge of the biggest Christian temple. "Are there any aristocrats hereabouts?" Coker asked the minister in Hard Acres. "Nary a one," the preacher answered. "We are broad-minded people here in Hard Acres and haven't got nothing against aristocrats. But this is a family town. An aristocrat would be more comfortable in New York or someplace north where there's all kind of folks. Still, I'd welcome an aristocrat if he could play the organ. Tell you what, if you run across an aristocrat in your travels, ask him if he plays the organ. If he does, send him here. He'd have a real future in Hard Acres. He couldn't teach school or nothing like that, but the congregation would pitch in and help him open an antique store." "No," Coker said, "I am afraid that you misunderstand me. By an aristocrat I mean someone born with a silver spoon in his mouth." "Born with a silver spoon?" the preacher repeated. "That might be all right, but most people around here would prefer a good pull at the titty."

School stamped routine upon our days, Francis walking to the high school for mathematics every morning at 7:15, and Edward and Eliza catching buses at 7:35 and 8:15, respectively. The lives of parents mirror those of children. Every day I got up at 6:00. I swam in the university pool at 7:00 and taught at 8:00. At 9:30 I rode my bicycle to the Cup of

Sun. Ellen was there writing, and Roger, Caroline, Lee, and George were usually there, too. I ate a muffin, drank two cups of coffee, and talked. Ellen read excerpts from her novel. Roger put on makeup on his birthday, so he looked like the Ancient of Days. Before flying to Colorado for Christmas, George read a poem he wrote when he was fifteen, "Grandma's Potato Salad." Conversation was always gentle and pleasant. We had aged beyond zeal and ambition, beyond caring what ladder, not to mention rungs, we stood upon. One morning we decided rugs were floor hangings. Another day Ellen said one of her former students spelled *voluptuous* as *volumptuous*. "That's me," Lee said. "Age has made me volumptuous." We speculated about the discoveries we would make if we could examine the spell checkers on people's computers and see what words they added. "Who would have thought it?" and "I always suspected" were the sorts of remarks we imagined making. Last week I coined the word *pre-empty*. Modeled on the word *pre-owned* used by car dealers to sell second-hand cars, pre-empty means full and should be used when buying, say, candy, in a phrase such as "I would like a pre-empty box of chocolate nougats, please."

The activities of the children forced structure upon afternoons and evenings, and Vicki and I became drivers, not parents. On Wednesday afternoon Edward and Eliza took piano lessons. Eliza also started playing the clarinet. Her teacher told her that she probably would not make a sound for three months. The teacher was wrong. That night screeches slashed through the house, sounding like the death cries of a large furry animal. "I didn't think I could reach high notes so soon," Eliza said to me, "how did they sound?" "Wonderful," I said. In October the children began ice-skating lessons, Eliza's lesson occurring at a different time from that of the boys. In November Eliza returned to ballet, going to Lebanon twice a week. She began dance late because she played on the Mansfield eleven-and-under girls' soccer team. The team practiced on Wednesday afternoons and played games Saturday mornings.

Edward also played soccer, on two teams, the recreational team with two games a week and the town eleven-and-under boys' team, practicing once a week and always playing one but often two games a week. For two and a half months Vicki and I did not have a day free from driving. The lives of other parents resembled ours. Our childhoods, as least as much of them as we remembered, had been different. We stood on sidelines and discussed changes in society. We wondered whether doing so many things was good for children. "When I was a boy," Henry said, "my parents did not take me anywhere. I played with the kids in the neighborhood." "Children don't have chores now," Betty said, "and playing sports is more educational than another Indian project."

In much of Mansfield neighborhoods don't exist. Houses line streets, but people who live next to one another are not friends but acquaintances. By making it easy to visit someone living six or eight miles away, the automobile has removed community from neighborhood. Only at schools and at children's recreational activities do strangers meet. By November Edward was tired of soccer, telling me he wanted the season to end. I didn't. I liked talking to other parents. We told stories and enjoyed watching our children scamper through days. Vicki and I spent Columbus Day at a soccer tournament, Edward's team finishing second, losing on a penalty shot called against Edward for a handball. "What a wonderful way to spend a holiday," Susan said as we left the field after the championship game. Eliza's team lost all three games in a tournament in Coventry. Each girl received a trophy though. "Look what I won," Eliza said running to me, her hair bouncing around her head.

In a tournament the boys defeated a team from Willington. A week later Willington trounced the boys. Yet parents had fun. The day was crisp, and maples were red. "What gratitude," we said during the game, "after all the driving we have done and the boys play like this. Never again." Of course we dreaded the *never again,* that time when we would truly be on the sidelines, the children playing in fields far from our lives. "Once children leave school," John said, "Mansfield ceases to be a community. That's why Abigail and I spend so much time in New York."

On the fifth and sixth of November, Edward's town team ended the season playing in a tournament in Barrington, Rhode Island. All other teams in the tournament were "elite" teams composed of the best players from several towns. Mansfield played well, winning two out of three games. The first day I picked up Michael and his son Ari. Michael navigated while I drove. I parked beside a field. Six-year-olds were playing. "Get in his face, Kevin," I heard a father shout to a little boy in a green shirt. Between games we ate calamaris then wandered the grounds of a farm owned by the Rhode Island School of Design. We walked to the shore. The water rippled and rolled silver and green in the sunlight. During our last game Charlie yelped when an official made a poor call. "For heaven's sakes," a parent of a boy on the other team said, "it's only a child's game." Charlie paused then said, "You are absolutely right. I apologize." "What a good guy," I thought standing next to Charlie. "It is nice to be home."

Involvement with sports bounced beyond soccer fields. Edward said he wanted a season ticket to football games at the university. I agreed to buy a ticket. Immediately Eliza said she also wanted a season ticket. "Those babies," Vicki said, "can't go alone." I bought three season tickets. Vicki and Francis did not get completely off football. I bought tickets for them for the opening game and for homecoming. To all the games I took apples and candy bars, usually Mounds. At the stadium I bought sodas, popcorn, hot dogs, and ice cream. The afternoon games were sunny, and often I dozed, much as I do at concerts. Occasionally something exciting happened. The day I bought the Toyota I sat on row 30, seat 21. I slept peacefully until suddenly hands stretched around me, and I woke with a start. Spiraling toward me was a white plastic football, six inches long and ten inches in circumference. Without thinking I stuck my hands out and caught the ball. I had not moved from my seat, but others had. A man behind me stumbled in the aisle and whacked me above the right kidney. A boy three rows in front fell backwards into the lap of a woman wearing a sweatshirt with "Huskies" printed on it.

Written on the side of the football was the number 41. I had won a prize Edward told me. The prize was a gray tee-shirt donated by "Xtra Mart Convenience Stores." Printed high on the left front of the shirt was "Xtra Mart," the X red, all the other letters blue. The catch was the highlight of my season. Connecticut played two games at night. At half-time of both games there were fireworks displays. The fireworks were set off some distance from the north end of the stadium. Paperbark birch grew at the end of the stadium, and leaves blocked the fireworks from the sight of most people at the games.

Homecoming is small and familial, and Vicki and I and the children never miss it. We stood at the corner of Hillside and Gilbert roads. From garages all over town convertibles are brought out and shined for the parade. Two young actors in a daytime television serial called *One Life to Live* rode in a black Corvette. One actor seemed nothing but white teeth and brown hair. "That guy needs a haircut," Edward said. "Yes," I said, "he looks like a bum, but a handsome bum." "Thank goodness," Sherry said sitting on a wall behind me, "I said he was a ten, but my family disagreed with me." Miss Sweetheart Connecticut rode in a white convertible. "She looks sweet," Eliza said. White, Francis informed me, was the favorite color for convertibles, noting that six white convertibles appeared in the parade. Announcers from the Willimantic radio station rode in a pink Volkswagen beetle. Atop the roof of the car was a square of green carpet. Three pink plastic flamingoes and two small American flags stood on the carpet. "A patch of real America," Vicki said.

Dressed in buckskin a group of Mohican Indians marched in front of a trailer pulling a wigwam. "Drumming up support for a casino," Francis said. Uncle Sam staggered by on stilts. Students whirled around him on roller blades. Engine 322 and Tower Truck 122 from the University Fire Department crept slowly along, their lights flashing. A milk truck owned by the Mountain Dairy followed them. The truck had wooden panels on the sides and was almost fifty years old. The Cycle Unit from the Sphinx Temple of Shriners in Hartford drove red Kawasakis back and forth across the road. Strapped to the seat of one motorcycle was a pink dinosaur. A stuffed gorilla wearing green and white checked boxer shorts clung to the back of another motorcycle.

The university band marched past looking like tin soldiers painted blue and white. They wore new uniforms, these smacking of the 1890s rather than the Crimea. The old balaclava helmets had been replaced by hats resembling buckets turned upside down and wrapped with blue paper, topped off with white chicken feathers. Beside the band strutted a battalion of girls twirling poles, at the ends of which were triangular flags. The flags were red and gold. In the center of each flag, a white *C* curved like a waning moon. The girls themselves wore blue sequined outfits, resembling one-piece bathing suits. Instead, though, of appearing long-legged and somehow soiled, the twirlers came in sundry shapes, tall and thin, short and dumpy, and resembled baby-sitters, wholesome girls from around the corner.

This year I was more involved in Homecoming than ever before. In September I was invited to the Royal Tea to judge "Royalty" for homecoming. Despite being an aristocrat, I had never met royalty, so I accepted the invitation. The tea took place in the Jorgensen Art Gallery. Seven judges rated fourteen candidates. While judges munched brownies, the candidates wandered the room talking to us, trying to make good impressions. Officials of the Student Union Board of Governors supplied judges with a list of a dozen "Possible Issues," questions such as "Who would you rather be for a day, Mother Teresa or Donald Trump?" and "Does the government have the jurisdiction to make a ruling about abortion?" I stuffed the list into the side pocket of my sport coat and chatted with the students, one of the best conversations focusing on how to cook turnip greens. The tea lasted from 3:30 to 7:00. When conversation flagged, I explored the gallery. On the walls were grim photographs, among others, pictures of street urchins in Bogota, urban guerrillas attending school in Buenos Aires, and a dank graveyard in San Salvador.

My choices for royalty differed from those of some of the other judges. The candied, physical or mental, does not appeal to me, and I looked for sunlight beaming from eyes, not simply the light of intelligence but light that brightens days for others. "Sunbeams," Slubey Garts declared in a sermon, "support the rafters of heaven." A week after the tea my friend Josh dropped by the office. In his right hand he shook a piece of paper listing the results of an "ASSESSMENT SYMPOSIUM" held at the university on October 21. Teachers attending the symposium wrote down phrases describing "The Ideal Student." Printed on the paper were the results, a list of twenty-two phrases, among them: Active Listener, Focused, and Invested in their Learning. "A stack of sheets was on a desk in the writing office," Josh said, "at least three hundred sheets, ready for mailing, envelopes beside them. I removed two sheets from the stack and between 'Fun' and 'Reachable' printed 'Naked'. Then I slipped the sheets back into the pile. The bare truth is," Josh continued, "that we don't have any idea what constitutes good teaching, much less a good student. And so we clothe ignorance with threadbare phrase and platitude."

This fall I taught a class that met three times a week at eight in the morning. One hundred ten students took the course. I enjoyed them so much I arrived fifteen minutes early to chat. I don't know how much, if anything, students learned. In fact what students think they learn does not interest me. I resemble Proverbs Goforth. When asked what he thought about Communism, Proverbs replied, "I don't care which nor whether about it." What I do know is that when the semester ended I was sad. Sunbeams vanished, and for a moment the heavens sagged. I thought a lot about teaching during the semester, concluding that in arts perhaps the best teaching is the absence of teaching. In Australia Edward and Eliza rarely had homework. Because school was easy, they piddled about at night, Edward often worrying that he was falling behind friends in Storrs, and Eliza writing sheaves of stories and poems. "When Edward gets home," I told Vicki, "he will have homework, and he'll stop worrying." I was wrong. Edward worried more. One night he worried so much about homework he threw up.

For her part Eliza quit writing stories to do homework, ordinary assignments about square roots and bones in the body. Eliza started but did not finish stories. On her desk I found a notebook containing first lines. "Once there was a foundling named Silva. She lived in a hut with her cat Nightstar," a story began, and ended. Maybe Eliza, Edward, and the children in my eight o'clock class would be happier and more creative, I thought, if they did not have homework. I underestimated Eliza. The stories had not stopped. They had only changed.

One night I drove Eliza and two of her friends to ballet. When we started home, Rachel and Sarah asked Eliza to tell a story. Eliza's first story was about Wolfgang Amadeus Mozart. "Wolfgang," Eliza explained was the most important part of the composer's name. "Wolf music was his real music," she said. At night when people listened to *The Magic Flute* or *The Marriage of Figaro,* he crept into graveyards and sang, calling wolves to his side. Wolfgang's career rivaled that of Don Giovanni, ending with his being pulled into a cold grave instead of a fiery pit. Silva reappeared in Eliza's other story. To escape poverty she married a brutal woodcutter who beat and starved her. One morning he ordered her to cook liver for his dinner. The meat smelled so good after being cooked that Silva could not resist tasting it. Once she tasted it, Silva could not stop, and she ate all the liver. After finishing, she was terrified, knowing that her husband would flog her when he returned home that night. The meat, however, became food for thought. Silva remembered that she lived next door to a funeral home. Carrying her kitchen knife, she climbed through a window in the back of the home. On a slab lay the corpse of Mrs. Pendleton. Silva chopped out Mrs. Pendleton's liver, took it home, cooked it, and served it to her husband.

"This is the best liver I have ever eaten," he said, smacking his lips. "I won't beat you tonight. But tomorrow I want heart." The story then repeated itself, the Pendleton family furnishing Eliza with a counter of delectables: brains, kidneys, and pancreas in addition to heart and liver. By the end of the story Silva had recovered from starvation and become so strong that she left her brutish husband. When he tried to stop her, she knocked him down. Evil ways bring evil ends. As Silva vanished over a hill, the Pendleton family, all corpses newly risen from the grave, entered her husband's house. They seized him and tore him to pieces, taking back the parts of their bodies that "had become his bones and blood."

Knickknacks furnish days. One evening I spoke to students at the Honors House at the university. There being no lectern on which I could set my notes, students taped shut flaps on a plastic garbage can. At six-thirty one morning I appeared on a local radio station. In talking to the announcer, I mentioned that I visited Papua New Guinea twice during the past year. Immediately the telephone at the station rang. On the line was a man who had fought in Papua New Guinea during the Second World War, and he wanted to give me his recipe for lemon-and-banana cheesecake. I spent an afternoon with my friend Pat Ferrigno walking across a hilltop he planned to turn into a dozen lots for houses. Pat and Donna could not decide on a name for the development, and so Pat asked me for suggestions. The next morning I sent him a list of sixty-six names, including Biscuit Hill, Sunny Top, Broken Plow, Pumpkin Field, Morning Glory, Spoon Hill, and Sweet Clover Ridge.

The highlight of fall, however, was the horticultural show staged in the Ratcliffe Hicks Arena by the College of Agriculture. Each fall the horticultural club covers the floor of the arena with dirt and wood shavings and creates a series of gardens. The title of this year's show was "Gardens of the World." Students divided the arena into seven gardens: Japanese, South of the Border, Tropical, American Rock, Italian Water, English Herb, and Native Connecticut. I spent two and a half hours at the show. The tropical garden brought Perth and travels to Fiji and Papua New Guinea to mind. Instead of twisting high into palms, its leaves broader than the shells of sea turtles, philodendron leaned over green plastic pots. I recognized banana; croton, veins thick and taut with yellow on the top leaves, pink on the lower leaves, the color seeming to seep through the walls of the veins, forming shallow pools; fiddle-leaf fig; golden trumpet; ixia, blossoms rising in spikes of pink stars; and gold dust plant, its green leaves speckled with clumps of yellow.

From a balcony water fell into a pool, and mussaenda hung down in pink bunches. At the edge of the pool stood a clump of spathiphyllum, the blossoms rising and bending like small white sails in a choppy breeze. South of the Border was bright with blue indigo; torch lilies flaring pink; yucca; and Rose of Sharon hibiscus, the petals of this last snowy, the centers dark red. Boxwood trimmed to resemble pompoms surrounded the Italian garden. In the center of the garden stood a statue of a young girl with a pageboy haircut. The girl leaned over a fountain, a flagon in her left hand. Water streamed from both flagon and fountain and collected at the girl's feet in a scallop shell. Finger-length goldfish swam through the pool, gathering in shadows at the base of the statue then suddenly flaring out in quick slivers of yellow before drawing together again. I counted the goldfish twice. The first time I counted twenty-five; the next, twenty-six.

White stones curved in lines through the Japanese garden like slow, shallow streams, drifting past a red Buddha then an incense burner resembling a shrunken temple. A student raked the Japanese garden. He wore a green tee-shirt. Printed in white letters across the chest of the shirt was UCONN HORTICULTURE. A thick, silver cross hung from a chain around the boy's neck, and two gold earrings clung to the side of his left ear, resembling the edges of snail shells. On his head sat a white baseball cap, a yellow hornet on the front, and on the right side in gold, the letters GT, standing for Georgia Tech.

Saplings stood throughout the arena, their leaves bright with color: white oaks, black birches, and red and sugar maples. Plywood lay across bales of hay, forming tables. Bags of apples sat atop the tables, each bag holding half a peck of Spartans, Macintosh, Red Delicious, Macoun, Empire, and Jona Mac. An orange mound of pumpkins rolled out lumpy from a corner of the arena. Rows of chrysanthemums filled the bleachers above the arena: Bravo, a deep, blackened red; Ginger, sandy and yellow; blue Adorn; and Naomi, pink and white, to name but a few. In the "Cut Flower Garden" stood metal florist cans of flowers: orange gladiolas; bird of paradise; yellow Gerber daisies big as wheels on tricycles; ornamental ginger; delphinium; green bells of Ireland; and protea resembling suns hammered out of gold. I bought the children candy canes, Eliza, grape; Edward, spearmint; and Francis, clove. Vicki then took the children to

Willimantic to buy ice skates. I stayed at the show and ate lunch. For $1.50 I bought a chili dog smothered in onions. I sat outside on the grass, leaned against the trunk of an oriental cherry, munched the dog, and waved at friends.

In September Bill Dearborn, Father's and my close friend, wrote from Nashville. In an old file he found a snapshot of himself and Father taken during a snowstorm in Carthage in 1944. Bill and Father wore gray slacks and short dark windbreakers. They were bare-headed. They thrust their left hands behind their backs, making them resemble officers in the British army. Each held his hat in his right hand pressing it to his chest. On their faces were whimsical smiles. With the picture Bill sent a postcard Father mailed to him from Carthage on September 14, 1944. On the front of the card was a photograph of Horseshoe Bend on the Cumberland River, "4 miles North of Carthage." On the back of the card Father wrote, "We're OK except for me. Have spent 1 day in bed—let my content get too low. K. & S. fine." *Content* referred to alcohol, antifreeze that could protect the body against cold. "We'll be back by the 23rd," Father continued, "so kill the catted falf. Let bacchanalian revelry reign—every man a king. Nothing doing except a church revival. Have the opportunity of going twice a day and hitting the sawdust trail. Regards to you and the distaff side."

Postage for the card cost a penny, George Washington staring rocky and noble from the right side of the card, behind him a green fertile carpet. Fifty years have passed since Father wrote Bill from Carthage. Aside from the cost of postage, little has changed. In September, I, another Sam Pickering, visited Carthage. I traveled in imagination, not fact, however. Despite buying the Toyota, I don't drive much, and most of my visits are imaginary. At the Tabernacle of Love Slubey Garts led a revival. "One blessed day when Slubey was in swaddling clothes," Proverbs Goforth told visitors, "he fell asleep with his mouth open. Bees made a honeycomb in his mouth, and ever since his words have been sweet."

Slubey believed Tennessee a Christian state to be defended against predations of unbelievers, primarily Catholics and pagans, and in Carthage itself against apostates. In the spring six families seceded from the Tabernacle. They accused Slubey of trafficking with the world and Methodists and founded the Church of the Chastening Rod. During the revival Slubey doused, as Proverbs put it, "that mutton what left the fold with bitter herbs and an asafetida of words." "They have fed on thistles and nettles and swallowed so many grapes of gall that they have become as crazy as Abraham, telling folks the Lord speaks to them," Slubey said. In the Land of Moriah Abraham said the Lord spoke from the heavens and told him to cut the throat of his child Isaac. "What that old coot really heard was indigestion and pride," Slubey declared. "You would be better off squatting in the pea patch, listening to okra and turnip greens, as to pay attention to stiff-necked apostates."

According to rumor a priest had been seen near Chestnut Mound. Turlow Gutheridge said the man was probably a Mason out on a spree, not a priest. Nevertheless Slubey singled out "Romanists" for chastisement. "A red fox can buy a white coat at Cain-Sloan in Nashville," Proverbs said, adding that "the good shepherd can never be too careful." "Most of what you hear about Romanists isn't true," Slubey said. "They are not the get of Eve's fornicating with Adam's corpse. No," Slubey continued, "Catholics are almost like us except we don't believe that mushrooms come from lightning bolts striking the earth. We wash in well water, not holy water, and we don't kiss the big toe of the Basha of Rome, traipsing about in a red nightgown, three tails switching behind him."

The week before the revival Gunth's Traveling Show came to Carthage. For two nights the show camped on the high school football field, and townsfolk wandered through the exhibitions, including among other things, a monstrous pumpkin, a kangaroo, two tame canebrake rattlesnakes, a bear with a peg leg, a rooster in a ten-gallon jar, and finally a wax museum. The museum was the most popular exhibition, containing statues of Robert E. Lee and Abraham Lincoln; the head of Mary Queen of Scots; Pocohontas, the face of Captain John Smith tattooed on the inside of her right thigh; and a gigantic alligator, two feet sticking out of its mouth, red streaming down to the toes from above the ankles. By the exit to the museum stood a statue of Judas Iscariot, his hands cupped before him and reaching out for silver. Although no Carthaginian put silver into Judas's hands, people dropped in so many pennies that the take compared favorably to the collection at the Tabernacle on a cold Sunday, something that so rankled Slubey that he preached against superstition.

"Some people in Smith County," Slubey said, "care more for wax idols than the host of cherubim and seraphim." Slubey said he knew parents who stuck children's baby teeth in corn cobs and threw the cobs over the roofs of their houses in order to bring the children good luck and did so, he declared, "even before the babies were baptized." To keep old Nick from getting them, other people put matches in their hair before going to sleep. People who practiced such superstition were going to simmer in hell, Slubey said, if they did not burn their houses down first. "A paper sack of nail parings and hair clippings can't be bartered for a pass through the pearly gates," Slubey said, assuring the congregation that he was only against superstition, not medicine. Nothing could settle a swamp fever faster, he declared, than mixing a spoonful of dried tortoise "in a cup of Temperance Liquor, God's own clear water."

Slubey warned people against drink and greed. "A crate of money in Nashville in the First American or the Commerce Union won't do you any good on Judgment Day; only bills drawn on the banks of the Jordan establish credit in glory." "No corn juice," he said, "is pure. No matter how you filter it, no matter the charcoal, there is always adultery in it." "Sheep and men," he said, "are born to tremble. You have to repent to get to heaven. You have to fall on your knees and shake. You might as well hunt for goobers on a goose or try to bore through Battery Hill with a boiled carrot as attempt to sneak past St. Peter without calluses on your knees." "You have got to hunt Satan with the gun of the gospel," Slubey said one night. "You have got to tree him with the hound of righteousness."

Funerals boomed in Carthage this fall. No one was able to account for the high number of deaths. Loppie Groat said "that it is just a fact that a great many people died this year who didn't die last year." Anak Tooker wept when pallbearers lowered his wife, Keturah, into the grave. "I've lost a chicken house of Buff Orpingtons, half a herd of Guernseys, and a prime Hereford bull," he sobbed, "but I have never had anything cut me up like this."

Lowry Barrow comported himself with more dignity when his wife, Ofelia, died, putting a notice into the *Carthage Courier.* "Ofelia Barrow," the notice stated, "died after a mercifully brief illness, leaving behind four children and a grieving husband. I beg to inform customers that the grocery will be furnished as well as formerly, having entrusted the business to Ofelia's beloved brother Ofellow, who is intelligent and as well versed in meat and produce as the deceased herself. P. S. Canned apricots have just arrived, and Blue Peter sardines are expected on the next train from Nashville." Isom Legg was the gravedigger at most of the funerals. Isom suffered from a racking cough, one, Loppie Groat said, that sounded like gravel being thrown into a washtub. "Isom," Slubey said as Isom smoothed the clay atop Keturah Tooker, "you have got a terrible cough." "Yes, it's bad," Isom said, leaning on his shovel, "but as bad as it is, there's a passel of folks hereabouts who would like to have it."

In Australia Vicki sat on our back steps and fed Fred the kookaburra. The bird became so tame he ate out of Vicki's hand. In November Vicki filled bird feeders. A whirlygust of birds, as Loppie might put it, descended upon the backyard: chickadees, goldfinches, white-throated sparrows, juncos, starlings, house finches, titmice, and nuthatches. One morning I counted fourteen mourning doves eating corn. That afternoon eight blue jays landed in the bittersweet, their cries as raucous as the orange berries. Usually seven cardinals appeared at dusk. High overhead geese honked. Crows swooped out of the woods when Vicki put out stale bread. Downy woodpeckers drilled into the suet hanging beneath an eve while a red-bellied woodpecker hitched up a black birch. A sharp-shinned hawk lurked in the woods. One morning I saw him on the ground beside a chipmunk's hole. Occasionally he swooped through the yard like a tight line, and in the dell I found feathers torn from a dove.

Often I stared out the kitchen window and watched birds. The flutter of home is endlessly entertaining. Last Sunday a student missed the final examination, this despite my having informed the class of the time and place of the exam every morning for three weeks. When the student telephoned me at home to request a makeup examination, she giggled. I agreed to give her an exam the next day but told her that missing tests was not a matter for hilarity. She taped a note to her examination. "I write to thank you for giving me the opportunity to take the examination. I apologize if you thought my giggle over the phone was out of amusement in this situation. It was a nervous reaction. My only other reaction would have been to sit down and cry about everything again because my nightmare of a semester had not ended yet." The student did well on the test, and that cheered me. Last night Eliza danced in *The Nutcracker.* She wore a purple dress with a white fringe, and two of her friends told her she looked like Miss America.

january

"After the preparations for winter are all made, and before those for spring," a correspondent wrote in the *Country Gentleman* in January, 1895, "there comes a delightful 'between-time' that is full of pleasant possibilities—long evenings beside the fire, with the sound of storm and wind outside." Because I worry about setting the chimney ablaze and burning the house down, I do not use the fireplace in the living room. In the backyard the woodpile molders. During fall puffballs and turkey tail bloom at the ends of logs, and gray squirrels scurry across the top of the pile, searching for the stale bread Vicki puts out for crows. After Twelfth Night the family abandons the living room, returning in May to look through the windows at the daffodils blooming in the dell. For me January often seems a "between-time," not, however, a period flickering with possibility so much as a functional link, a hard, confining pipe of gray days, Christmas red and green at one end, spring yellow and blue at the other.

Much as January itself is a transitional month, so this Christmas marked change. In the past all the family went to the annual Christmas sale at the Horse Barn. We drank hot cider, ate sugary doughnuts, and bought wooden trinkets for the tree. This year Edward and Francis stayed home,

Edward preferring to watch professional football on television, and Francis upstairs, creating a newspaper on the computer. Eliza went with Vicki and me. But when the Christmas elves rode out of the barn to fetch Santa Claus, the Morgan horses prancing, white fog blowing from their nostrils, Eliza was somewhere else, playing with her friend Rachel. When Santa Claus rolled along Horsebarn Hill in a four-wheeled cart, Vicki and I looked for Eliza but could not find her. At the barn Santa Claus handed out red and white candy canes. A crowd of parents and children milled about him, the hands of the latter waving and tossing. Eliza was not in the crowd, and for the first time Vicki and I stood apart, leaning against a fence by the riding rink, the ages and changing interests of our children separating us from the excitement. "Daddy," Edward said when I walked through the back door, "the Patriots are winning." "That's super," I said.

Christmas Day was also different this year. Gone were the mounds of small, inexpensive presents, the surprises Vicki unearthed throughout the fall. This year Francis received Corel Draw 5, a "graphics package" for the computer. Not only did Francis order it himself, but he checked through the package when it arrived. For his part Edward received a Sony radio and stereo system. Edward did not select the Sony, but he accompanied Vicki to Caldor when she purchased it, just to be sure she bought a system capable of playing six compact disks. Edward also received Doom II, a computer game. Stamped in red and yellow letters across the box containing the game were the words "Let the obsession begin. Again." "The wait is over," advertising on the box declared. "In your hot little hands, you hold the biggest, baddest Doom ever—*DOOM II; HELL on EARTH!* This time, the entire forces of the netherworld have overrun Earth. To save her, you must descend into the stygian depths of Hell itself! Battle mightier, nastier, deadlier demons and monsters. Use more powerful weapons. Survive more mind-blinding explosions and more of the bloodiest, fiercest, most awesome blastfest ever!"

On the front of the box a super hero with a jagged haircut, the ends of which resembled teeth on a saw, fired a thick, double-barreled gun at an inhabitant of the netherworld, a Cyberdemon with sharp canine teeth, goat legs, and blue horns shaped like those on a water buffalo. The hero's shot thudded into the demon's belly, searing flesh and exposing muscles resembling uncooked sausages. The Cyberdemon belonged to an army of "bad guys," including, among others, Hell Knights, Lost Souls, Specters, Arachnotrons, Mancubuses, and Former Humans. "The only good thing about" the Mancubus, the instruction manual stated, was "that he is a nice wide target. Good thing, because it takes a lot of hits to puncture him. He pumps out fireballs like there was no tomorrow." When Edward plays Doom, explosions reverberate, and shrieks ring like bells. Even worse, Doom resembles a paramecium and endlessly recreates itself. Edward now owns D!Zone, "an adventure beyond belief," adding "over 900 new levels," challenging even "the most battle-hardened among the DOOMED."

After I read the description on the box, I did not want to buy the game. "Doom is one of the few things Edward wants," Vicki said. "He asked to buy it for himself several times." Time has loosened duty's apron strings. Buying the game was easier than cinching myself, and Edward, to principle. Two years ago I would not have purchased the game. "The babies are not small anymore," Vicki said, "they have become people with lives apart from ours." "People," I said, "whom I am not sure I like."

At nine Eliza is still a little girl. Yet even her Christmas was more commercial this year. From "The American Girl's Collection" of dolls she wanted Felicity Merriman, "a spunky, sprightly colonial girl." The price for Felicity and a set of six paperback books describing life in colonial America was $104. Much as the heroes of Doom carried an arsenal of weapons, including chain guns, rocket launchers, plasma rifles, and mysterious devices called BFG 9000s, so Felicity appeared with a wardrobe of accessories, among other things, a blue Christmas gown and stomacher for $22, a riding habit and hat for $24, and, costing $98, "a tall-post bed with tester." Instead of a gunrack of accessories for Felicity, however, Eliza received her other request, a Syrian hamster.

Eliza named the hamster Dusty. So far the name has not stuck. The boys call it Dustbin, and Vicki, Hamsterabi, after the codifier of laws in Babylon. For my part I call it Hammy, the name of a hamster Mother and Father gave me one Christmas when we lived in the Sulgrave Apartments in Nashville. My hamster was supposedly a boy, but in January, he gave birth. The little hamsters did not enjoy long lives. Two days after they appeared, Hammy ate them. Shortly thereafter Hammy herself vanished. I did not want Vicki to buy the hamster, warning her that the creature would not only set off Eliza's asthma but would also put George's muzzle out of joint, at least, I said, "until he snapped up the little rodent."

I underestimated George, and myself. George does not bother the hamster even when it scurries across the floor. And I have played with Dusty more than Eliza has. Aside from throwing droppings with his teeth, Dusty does not do much that is interesting. Occasionally he runs up the sleeves of my sweaters, something his predecessor did forty-eight years ago. While he crawls through my armpit and around my back, I remember the past and Mother and Father. This Christmas I talked to them a lot, saying, "I miss you" and "I wish you were here to see how the children have grown." I talked to my parents this winter because the boys, in particular, have grown apart from me and I felt lonely.

I made no New Year's resolutions. My character has formed, and I am not going to change, a realization that sometimes cheers me, and other times depresses me. In the wild, Eliza's guide book states, hamsters run up to five miles at night searching for food. An exercise wheel sits in Dusty's cage. Six inches in diameter and painted yellow, the wheel is metal. About eight o'clock every evening Dusty climbs in the wheel and, dashing forward, spins it rapidly. The sight of Dusty racing nowhere made me long for the end of January and the start of spring when change blossoms every day. Early in January as I sat in the house, Connecticut spinning metallic and damp about me, I dreamed of elsewheres, open places where I could roam. I read the "Wranglin' Notes" from Eatons' Ranch in Wolf, Wyoming. Three years ago Vicki, the children, and I stayed two weeks at Eatons'. We spent days riding through the Big Horn Mountains, valleys sliding blue off the sides of hills, the ridges above us lumpy shadows. A travel agent in Boston sent a brochure describing trips to Greece. Snapshots covered the front of the brochure like window panes. In one picture the sun set soft and purple behind a black coastline. In another delphiniums flowed out from the wall of an old church like a blue cassock. In a lower pane three men sat in a taverna drinking pale retsina. Through the distance stretched a row of Doric columns, their sides pitted, the capitals pushing up against the sky like open palms. Aside from brochures I received little mail in January, so little that in hopes of perking me up, the secretary of the English Department sent me an anonymous note, reading, "You are the One."

A pall smothered the first two weeks in January, making me gloomy.

On the campus a new archives building rose atop the stumps of white oaks. Two sides of the building were solid brick, and the construction hung over Whitney Road like a cloud. Some mornings I sat in the study. Although I tried to read, I dozed, my back seeming to harden and freeze to the chair like a mat of leaves to the ground in the woods. Waking resembled melting. Instead of gradually flowing into individuality, I seemed to seep out of awareness and be absorbed into the chair, much as damp from the leaves vanished into the warming earth. Perhaps I did not so much seep out of awareness as consciously bury myself. From the kitchen came the jangle of public radio, the conversation always about politics and the voices of the announcers strident, sounding like the clatter made by a boy dragging a stick along a picket fence.

My friend Josh visits in January. On my telling him that the noisy silence of political talk had clogged my brain, he said, "not brain but bowel. Politics is too low to affect thought." Josh suggested a home remedy for my problem, one, he assured me, that was "extremely popular on estates in Fairfield County." "Take a hunk of cheese in the right hand, holding it between thumb and index finger. Then bend over and insert the cheese into the fundament," he instructed, adding that "the older and ranker the cheese, the more salubrious the treatment." "Next swallow a hungry rat. The rat will smell the cheese. In his eagerness to obtain a meal, the rat will rush through the intestines, pushing all impacting talk about Democrat and Republican out ahead of himself." If the blockage was so severe that the rat had difficulty gnawing his way to daylight, Josh suggested swallowing a second dose, this time not of rodent, but of feline. "And not," he instructed, "a cultivated dose of pet Siamese or Manx, but of stray American Tom, preferably an experienced ratter with shredded ears."

Medical matters infected Josh's thoughts this January. Tennessee elected a heart surgeon to the Senate. The man was a Republican and a conservative. During the campaign he promised to stitch up liberals suffering from "bleeding hearts." "If Bill Clinton had a hair within scratching distance of his colon," Josh declared, "he would say, 'now that the Republicans have sent a cardiovascular surgeon to Washington to operate on bleeding-heart liberals, we Democrats should seize the rubber glove of community service and do our benevolent part by electing a proctologist to loosen up some of these conservative assholes'."

Josh does not belong to a political sect. January, however, seemed operating season on conservatives. Early in the month he wrote me from Greenwich. He had spent a fortnight in Fairfield County collecting folk remedies for dietary ailments. He discovered the most primitive remedies at country clubs, most of the habitués of which, he said, "were once removed from dancing with rattlesnakes on Sunday morning." That theological observation aside, however, Josh began his letter, writing, "Sam, you are a popular writer, one whose readers, a friend on *The New York Times* assures me, number in the tens, perhaps hundreds of thousands. Write an essay entitled *Where Have All the Episcopalians Gone?* The government of this country needs a good purging. Pepper the piece with words like *decorum, grace,* and *integrity,* all of which you will have to define if readers in other parts of the country are as nouveau as these in Darien and New Canaan."

Josh does not discriminate against people impoverished by wealth or success. He spares no one. An article describing cafeterias at the university recently appeared on the front page of the student newspaper. Accompanying the article was a picture of a boy seated at a table eating. From a mound on his plate the student scooped up a fork of what appeared to be sandy sludge. The boy's jaws spread wide and toothy, his maw resembling the entrance to a muskrat's nest. The boy's tongue hung over his lower lip in order to catch any nubs that sloughed off the fork. The tongue resembled a banana slug. Even worse the boy wore a baseball cap. "Can you imagine," Josh wrote, "eating inside with a hat on his head! Such Goths are incapable of learning." Josh overstated the truth. Occasionally a student who wears a hat inside makes a D. In my classes many boys wear caps backwards, the bills jutting over the backs of their necks. "They wear their caps backwards," Edward said last Thursday at dinner, "because they don't know the difference between front and back."

Medicinal concerns occupied my thoughts almost as much as they did those of Josh. January is sinus infection month. For fourteen days I took antibiotics. For weeks matter ran down the back of my throat like water sliding over a gutter, pulling clots of leaves and twigs to the ground. For days I struggled without medicine, coughing and snorting, "harvesting greens," as Vicki put it. Eventually, I went to Dr. Dardick. A sinus infection chills the blood. In the waiting room stood an empty baby carriage, a parent having taken the baby into an examination room. As I slumped down wearily, a mother bundled her two offspring into thick, winter coats. The children were a boy, aged four, and a girl, two. While getting into their coats, the children looked at the carriage. "Where do you think that baby has gone?" the children's mother said, her voice naggingly soft as arsenic. Before the children answered, I spoke. "That baby has gone to my stomach. I ate the baby," I said. The children drew back from the carriage toward their mother. "He's joking," she said, reaching out to touch them reassuringly. "No, I am not joking," I said, feeling better. "I like to eat plump babies for dinner, especially when they are cooked with onions and carrots." The woman did not speak. Instead she zipped the children into their jackets quickly, so quickly that she almost caught hunks of arm and chin, making her liable, I thought, for child abuse. Then she pushed the children toward the door. Just before leaving the room, the boy turned back toward me and said, "You are a bad man." I did not reply. Instead I smacked my jaws together, swallowed, and rubbed my stomach as if I had just devoured a little blond-headed, blue-eyed morsel. Suddenly the day warmed, and my sinus stopped throbbing. Also resuscitating me was a conversation Josh had with a professional gardener and amateur banker in New Canaan. The banker was a catalogue of vegetable lore. Josh is fond of potatoes, and one night at dinner at the Fairfield Country Club, he asked the man, "do you put manure on potatoes here in New Canaan?" "Some people probably do," the man replied, "particularly if they are accountants or heart surgeons whose taste has been vitiated by drink. For my part, though, I prefer salt and butter."

Even in Carthage people were concerned about medical matters. One Friday shortly after New Year's Day, Dr. Buzzard and Daddy Snakelegs appeared in town, driving a black wagon. Painted on both sides of the wagon in gold letters was the phrase ANSWERS TO YOUR PROBLEMS. Over the phrase on the right side of the wagon a red sun set above a green pond, while tears shaped like eyes complete with pupils and eyelashes oozed from the lower rim of the sun. On the left side of the wagon a hand amputated at the wrist flattened a centipede. A fat pink tube burst from the side of the centipede, and a sliver of white bone stuck up from the wrist. The back doors of the wagon were white. On them was painted a black hen. Attached to the top of the wagon near the front were two wooden statues, on the right side a two-foot-tall bird, its wings spread, the bird itself appearing half owl, half vulture. On the left stood a man nine inches tall. The man's belly was round. Set in the middle was a clock, the hour hand at twelve, the minute hand pointing just to the left of twelve. The little man, Turlow Gutheridge later explained to regulars at Ankerrow's Café, was Unkus, Mary's second child. The son of John the Revelator born after Joseph divorced Mary, Unkus was the spirit of the atmosphere, the patron imp of quacks and conjure men.

Dr. Buzzard and Daddy Snakelegs were nondescript. While the doctor was short, Daddy was tall. The doctor's face was fat, and his eyes sank into his cheeks like butter into hot biscuits. Daddy's face was long as a shovel, and clustered about his chin was a handful of warts resembling gravel. Inside the wagon was a pharmacy of nostrums and potions: Five Finger Grass, White Horse Hoof, Zodiac Incense, Adam and Eve Paradise Root, Cerome Dust, Drops of St. Rita, Go Away Powder, Solomon Water, and Heart's Cologne, among others. On trees along Main Street, Dr. Buzzard nailed posters advertising a meeting at Butler's Lowlands on Saturday night at eight o'clock.

The doings in Carthage being almost as exciting as those in Mansfield in January, a crowd attended the meeting. Sticking out of the ground around the wagon were torches made from pine knots. Daddy Snakelegs preached, his sermon concentrating on body rather than soul. "When the frost is on the horseturds and you feel weaker than a span of pismires and colder than a tree frog, when the croup promiscuous seizes the goozle pipes, visit Doctor Buzzard and he'll set you back on your feet. In no time he'll have you roasting turnips and feasting on ashcake and corn dumplings." Preaching is hard work, and throughout the sermon Daddy paused to sip from a bottle he kept in his back pocket. The bottle was pint-sized and amber. Inside, Daddy said, was a little two-headed man who spent days brewing "The Springs of Inspiration." Although Daddy did not share drops from the Springs, every time he dipped into the Inspiration he attempted to peddle a cure-all. Van Van Oil, he said, was the world's best scalp invigorator. "One dose," he declared, holding up a bottle filled with orange liquid, "will heal a mangy dog's bottom and hair it over in twenty-four hours."

Licensed physicians are the enemies of Faith Doctors, and throughout his sermon, Daddy lambasted "book medicine." "You might as well hunker down before a mirror with your eyes shut to see how you look when you are asleep as think a school doctor can cure the aches of winter. Squeeze blood out of a shadow; tie smoke to a tree; trust a City Doctor when the fever grabs your bones and days are so cold that candlelight freezes."

To persuade his audience to buy potions, Daddy described the foolishness of licensed doctors, his favorite physician being "Oldbutton Groggins," supposedly a graduate of Vanderbilt Medical School who practiced in Murfreesboro, Tennessee, a man, Daddy said, "who ate so much fried chicken he broke out in feathers." When Oldbutton died, Daddy said, he wanted his savings to go to folks who had been his patients, so he left everything to Central State, the lunatic asylum. In hawking Lucky Bones and Spirit Traps, Daddy described spells and ghosts. He told a story about a wife who massaged "Terrapin Grease" into the skin of her faithless husband. Nine days after the husband visited his lady friend, the friend died. When doctors sliced her open to discover what killed her, they found a white tortoise eating her liver.

Another man, Daddy recounted, ridiculed Faith Doctors. When Sister Grace warned him that a Haunt was after him, he scoffed and threw out the Go Away Powder she gave him. That night when he fried eggs on the fire in his shack, he heard a noise on the roof. When he looked up the chimney, he saw a black shadow. Suddenly a deep voice bellowed, "I'm going to drop." Almost immediately the front legs of a huge black cat fell down the chimney. The legs crawled out of the ashes then sat on a chair by the hearth. Once the legs were comfortable, the voice spoke again, saying, "I'm going to drop." The hind legs then tumbled down the chimney. "It's getting kind of tight in here," the man said as the legs crawled to the chair. "I'm going to drop," the voice replied, and the body of the cat fell. "It's tight in here sure enough," the man said. "Yes, but you just wait until my head gets there," the voice said. "The back legs is here; the front legs is here; the body is here, but when that head comes down," the man said, running toward the door, "I'm going to be gone." "The man was fast," Daddy said, a tremor in his voice, "but the head was faster."

The effects of words cannot be predicted. Instead of convincing listeners to shun conventional medicine, Daddy so scared folks that he drove them to Dr. Sollows. When Dr. Sollows opened his office at nine o'clock Monday morning, a line of people hurried into the waiting room, all convinced by signs and omens that they were about "to hop the twig."

LaBelle Watrous discovered snail tracks on her front stoop. When Loppie Groat fetched wood for the stove on Sunday night, he saw two white rabbits sitting side by side in the moonlight. Other people had frightening dreams, Piety Goforth dreaming of a butterbean pie, and Jodrell Tayler of a black cucumber. People think more about medicine in January than during any other month. Because January is the first month of a new year, individuals dissect aches, treating pains as signs revealing what they can expect as the year unravels.

Instead of contemplating the future, I spent the first part of the month dismantling December. For Christmas relatives sent us six boxes of grapefruit from Pittman and Davis in Harlingen, Texas. From early December until January 13, we ate grapefruit every night for dessert. Along with the fruit we ate Vicki's cookies, tins of homemade chocolate swirls; crescents, snowy with confectioner's sugar; and sugar cookies in a variety of shapes, stars, reindeer, spruce trees, snowmen, and candy canes, some covered with pink frosting, red and green blanketing others. Dismantling the cookies was sweet work. Stripping Christmas from the house was gloomy. Vicki had turned the inside of the house into a garden. Every window ledge bloomed. Wearing red caps, elves and small woodland creatures scurried across corner tables. Atop the table in the dining room, a menagerie of wooden animals gathered outside a barn in a white New England village. Animals ambled out of woods: a black bear; three deer, one of these last a buck, the others a doe and a dappled fawn; a porcupine; and a marbled tomcat. A sheep resembled a cotton ball, and a cow, a mottled lump of sugar. To reach the barn some animals traveled great distances. A hedgehog came from England, an elephant and a giraffe journeyed from Africa.

Decorations in the house resembled dahlias, gladiolas, and corn lilies. Once the festive season wilted, I lifted them, and wrapping them in tissue, placed them in boxes and stored them in the attic. One morning I dragged the tree out of the house and tossed it on the brush pile in the backyard. I walked around the pile. Amid sticks and branches lay the remnants of four other Christmas trees. Yellow and dry, they snapped easily and seemed as fragile as memories of Christmases past. Not only had the Christmases of my childhood become mulch, but recollections of recent Christmases resembled twigs, brittle fragments: a smile red as an apple on Eliza's face, Edward sitting on the floor handing George a yellow rubber ball, and Francis, not even a person, but just large pale hands delicately removing gold wrapping paper from a flat box.

The first week of January was stormy. Instead of returning to the house after putting the tree on the brush pile, I pulled the garden cart out of the garage and loaded it with sticks. I stayed outside most of the day, filling the cart eleven times. Leaves clogged the ditch that ran through the dell. Years ago I dug the ditch so winter rains would not cut channels through my daffodils. After picking up the sticks, I cleaned the channel. While I worked in the dell, Vicki put paperwhites and poinsettias on the front stoop. White scale pocked the poinsettias, and I put them on the pile, one on each side of the tree. I took the paperwhites to the compost mound in the woods. I battered through the frozen surface of the ground with a heavy crowbar. Then I dug a hole and buried the paperwhites upright. Throwing flowers away is difficult for me. If the paperwhites sprout this spring, I will transplant them. Vicki also put two amaryllis on the stoop. Although I didn't tell Vicki, I did not throw the amaryllis away. After cutting stalks and leaves off, I hid them behind a box of letters in the basement. Next December I will put them upstairs in the bedroom window. Vicki does not hesitate to throw bulbs away. Scattered across the yard are clumps of hyacinths that I have rescued from the trash. I am older than Vicki. My blooming season has ended, and I worry that when I wilt, Vicki will get rid of me just like she does Christmas flowers.

Plants were not the only flowering thing Vicki tossed out in January. For Christmas I bought her a bread maker and a flannel nightgown. Over the nightgown bloomed a garden of yellow flowers, crosses, she said, between tulips and roses. The first week in January Vicki returned the nightgown to Lord and Taylor and the bread maker to Lechmere. "Our kitchen is the size of a window box," she said. "Nothing else can be planted in it." Rarely has Vicki kept a present from me, and the return of the gifts reassured me. Time changes oaks into coffins, but this Christmas, sap still pulsed consistently through my character. In fact January's sameness was reassuring.

The beginning of school imposed comfortable routine upon life, transforming Vicki and me from individuals with sinuses into roles. Once more we became drivers, taking children to basketball, soccer, ice skating, piano, and "Math Counts." I spent Sunday afternoons sitting in bleachers in the gymnasium at Parish Hill High School while the

Mansfield eleven-and-under boys' basketball team played teams from neighboring towns: Lebanon, Colchester, Andover, and Willington. Not only were the boys on the Mansfield team familiar, but I recognized players on other teams, having seen Edward play soccer against them in the fall and baseball against them in the spring. Banners hanging from the walls of the gymnasium were also familiar. Green with white letters, the writing on the banners said the same things it did on banners in gymnasiums throughout eastern Connecticut: OVC NORTH CHAMPIONS SOFTBALL 1979 and SOSNOWSKI SPORTSMANSHIP AWARD. At school fourth-grade boys still buzzed about Eliza, trying to draw affection with words, calling her "3-D Woman," "the Mutant from Dimension X," and once when she had a pimple on her nose, "Rudolph."

When a new girl entered Eliza's class, I told Eliza to befriend her. When Eliza spoke to her, the girl did not reply. Still, I urged Eliza to try to befriend the girl. "That would be the right thing," I said. "Daddy," Eliza answered, "I can't always do the right thing." January suddenly seemed more interesting, a month to enjoy for itself, not to look beyond. A student wrote me, trying to get into one of my classes, rather than out of something. "I am in my tenth semester (tenth and FINAL! barring unforeseen obstacles and Acts of God) with an individualized major in Art and Human Expression," she wrote, "and to graduate I need to take one writing class that has something to do with my major. So far you are it! If I don't get to take this course then they won't let me graduate, and I'll be doomed to a life of manual labor and no doubt die, starving and alone, in a homeless person's shelter at a very young age."

Late one afternoon I drove to the Pomfret School in the northeast corner of Connecticut. Gray clouds billowed like fenders and hung low over the hills, hugging the land, silver sweeping through them in polished chrome bands. Beyond a brown knob a band splintered into golden shards. Slowly the clouds turned pink and bled into purple before being pulled through the seam stitching hill and sky together at dusk. I went to Pomfret to listen to a poet. In his lecture the man said "a mystical sense of landscape" inspired his poetry. The particular, not the mystical or abstract, pervades the world I see. The audience at Pomfret was middle-aged. Men wore wire-rimmed glasses, brown penny loafers, corduroy trousers, and sport coats. Women wore skirts and cable-knit sweaters. Most did not wear earrings, and those who did wore small pearls or modest gold pendants. Women's hair was short. Years having leached the glow out, their hair resembled snow that sat so long on the shoulder of a road that it slumped out of season and texture into part of a broad, anonymous landscape. The two women sitting in front of me wore long coats, one coat pink, the other green. The collars and shoulders of the coats hung back over the chairs in which the women sat. Although the labels were upside down, I leaned forward and tried to read them. The pink coat was manufactured in Korea for Anderson-Little while the green coat was a Misty Harbor "original," made, I think, for a fold of the collar obscured part of the label, in Thailand.

In the mail that day I received *The Garden Book,* White Flower Farm's spring catalogue. After returning to Storrs from the lecture, I read the catalogue. As I turned pages, I dreamed of a bigger yard in which I planted an imaginary, not mystical, garden. Much as Vicki returns her Christmas presents, so I plant such a garden each January. Along the edge of the woods I planted fairy candles and trumpet lilies, these last Golden Sunburst. Tiger swallowtails bobbed yellow and black around butterfly bushes. By the side door silver sparkler daisies opened in smiles. Maroon hollyhocks towered over the front stoop. Bleeding heart tumbled over the ditch running through the dell. I considered planting cosmos along the ditch, but the blossoms seemed bland, not so quick as the daffodils that bloomed like puddles in the spring. I imagined a stone wall tumbling across the backyard. Beside the wall grew tree peonies, baskets of yellow, white, pink, and red. At fifty-nine dollars apiece, the peonies were expensive. The more flowers a man plants, so the old saw states, the more he forgives. As a result I did not begrudge money for the peonies. Still, I did not buy the yellow clivea Sir John Thouron, each plant costing $950. My imaginary wallet isn't that deep, so I bought an assortment of clematis and hung them in full bloom over the corners of the new screened porch.

Almost as soon as the imaginary plants rooted, the "between-time" itself opened and blossomed into identity. For Christmas Vicki gave me boots with thick soles resembling the treads on tractors. The next morning I put the boots on and began wandering January. Pools of glare ice lay black under a dusting of snow. Animals wrote themselves across field and slope. Squirrels scratched exclamation points as they scampered along fallen trees. A feral cat circled the edge of a wood in a big question mark.

Like a run-on sentence tracks of beaver wound across a frozen pond until they ended abruptly at the lodge, itself a bushy period. At dusk the runs of voles twisted under a glaze of snow and ice, resembling veins pulsing blue across the forehead of an old man. Some nights snow fell through street lights like a filigree of yellow silk. Other nights fog blew in billows, white but opaque, winter's darkness visible. The Fenton River was high. Ice clotted in quiet swirls, sticking to snags for a moment, then unpeeling slowly and floating downstream, almost as if the swirls were hands being pulled loose from the snags one finger at a time.

Creeks rushed off ridges, rocks along their beds garish with bowls of ice. On the flat lands below ridges creek beds widened, and ice spread out from the bank in trays, transforming streams into translucent tables. One morning I cut the index finger on my right hand. Cold numbed the finger, and I did not notice the cut until I got home. My glove was awash with blood. Vicki held the glove under the faucet so the fingers filled with water and the glove resembled a cow's bag, blood rather than milk, streaming from the teats. George accompanied me on walks. One morning we wandered the woods for three hours during a snowstorm. Eight inches of snow fell. George measures nine inches from the bottom of his front paw to the top of his shoulder, and he had to walk in my foot steps. Once during the worst part of the storm he crawled under a log, circled, and lay down. I stuffed him under my jacket and warmed his head in my armpit. He recovered, but the morning was hard on him. For a day blood oozed from the cuticles surrounding his claws.

Often I walked in rain. On such days I did not meet anyone in the woods or see any dog other than George. I liked being alone. I drifted across the landscape, rain crinkling in fields then ticking in woods as it tumbled onto slabs of frozen leaves. In the rain I talked to Mother and Father. Often we talked about Edward. I worried about him. He is moody. Little things—a broken drawer, paper on a clean floor—depress him. Only occasionally will he tell me what bothers him. I don't know what to do to make him feel better. Some nights when he goes to bed, I sit beside him and hug him, though he does not respond, then I rub his back until he falls asleep. Despite writing personal essays I could not dump worries into the lap of an outsider, and so I talked to Mother and Father.

In rain red fruits on barberry and winterberry glistened as if they had been varnished. Ovals of water sagged into silver drops on the canes of brambles. On stones and trunks of trees lichens bloomed like ancient flowers, yellow wall lichen and wrinkled *sticta amplissima,* plucking moisture from the air and glittering like bushes of diamonds in the early morning. Mosses that moldered out of sight in summer spilled over ledges in warm mats and tumbled across stumps and boulders, wrapping them with green and filling the woods with light. From creases in stony ridges polypody poured out in scoops, the underside of each frond dotted with spongy reddish spores, resembling clumps of gingerbread. In the woods Christmas fern lay pasted to leaves by ice. The cycle of thawing and freezing pulled ferns in different directions so that many fronds seemed disjointed, resembling green spines bent by spondylosis. While puffballs collapsed out of identity into the bark of brown logs, ruffles of *stereum complicatum* transformed dead twigs into dandies, tripping through winter, orange and gold bands at the edges of the brackets waving light-hearted in the breeze. On clear days the seedheads and long stems of goldenrod turned the Ogushwitz meadow brown, as if the field were a loaf of bread and goldenrod the crust. Near the beaver lodge the stems of ditch stonecrop shined red in the sun. Above the stems seed pods poured out in strings of small red and white lanterns.

In the fall I had placed small sheets of plywood at the edges of the meadow. Voles nested under the wood. On walks I lifted the wood, never failing to see several voles. Their runs spun through the grass, and when disturbed the voles raced along the runs like furry mechanical toys. Aside from voles, gray squirrels, chipmunks, and the occasional deer, I saw few animals. Among briars and along bushy runs I found a score of wooden traps, the doors latched open. During fall a biologist caught rabbits in hopes of determining the population of New England cottontails. Most rabbits in Mansfield are Eastern cottontails. Unlike the New England cottontail who has a black spot on his head, the Eastern cottontail has a white spot. Human droppings cluttered wood and field: in a depression atop a stump, a "Cherry Flavored ChapStick"; stuck into a bank, four white golf tees forming a cross; and tossed under brambles, a hospital bedpan. Wired to spicebushes in a rocky marsh were two dozen soft metal tags, each tag three-quarters of an inch wide and three and a half inches long. Pressed into the tags by pencil point were numbers, on one tag, for example, "83—64"; on another, "155—82." Dogs and sundry four-legged animals mark their territory with urine. Male college students mark territories with beer cans. Shiny scats had been dropped throughout the woods. Often several two-legged animals shared a territory as scats clumped together in barrows, the remains of Budweiser collapsing against those of Miller and Coors.

I didn't notice many birds aside from the usual visitors to backyard feeders, juncos, cardinals, mourning doves, and white-throated sparrows, among others. One morning I watched a hawk circle a field. The hawk had dark carpal patches on its underwings, and I thought it a rough-legged hawk, the first I had seen. Rough-legged hawks rarely appear in Mansfield, and now I suspect the bird was a red-tailed hawk. Often I heard blue jays imitating the cries of red-tailed hawks. Blue jays scrambled through woods almost in packs, swooping from tree to tree then dropping off ledges down slopes into cool glades. According to a Canadian folk tale, blue jays were once part of the sky. At the crucifixion a black storm wept across the heavens. To avoid the storm, bits of the sky broke away, becoming blue jays. Hot tears rained from the clouds and, falling on the jays, burned away color, leaving white splotches on some of the birds' feathers. Because jays fled before the storm, refusing to mourn the death of Christ, they were forced to do penance in Hell. Satan slung yokes around their necks and made them pull wagons loaded with cinders to help him build a bridge spanning the gulf between Hell and earth. The yokes were hot and seared the feathers around the birds' necks, creating a ring of black. The heat of the underworld also burned the jays' throats, and when they returned above ground, their voices had become harsh. Ashamed of the sound they made, they learned to imitate the calls of other birds. Penance is not atonement, however, and blue jays are never free from guilt. Storms remind them of the crucifixion and their failings. Before a storm breaks, they cry loudly and stir through trees, twigs slapping their backs painfully.

This fall I taught children's literature. A girl in the class was an all-American basketball player and a Phi Beta Kappa student. A journalist at the *Hartford Courant* wrote a profile describing the girl. The girl suggested to the journalist that he interview me. When he did, I said sunlight shined from her eyes. "She was," I said conventionally, "a credit to her family and to herself." Words transform. The page plucks teachers out of small clapboard houses and pushes them into tale. In the *Courant* the writer said I once ate a bouquet of flowers in a class. "A pitcher plant of milkweed, butter-and-eggs, and a side order of skunk cabbage, seasoned with peppergrass and spicebush might pass for breakfast," Vicki said after reading the article. "But," she continued, "if you have been sniffing around Dutch-man's breeches, nibbling on sweet William, or dallying with Jack-in-the-pulpit, don't make doll's eyes at me anymore." From little rhizomes grow beds of exaggeration. At dinner twenty-five years ago, when hormones fertilized me root and romance, I ate a forget-me-not. Sweet Cicely sat across the table. Instead of trying "to startle the stuffy and the boring," as the article in the *Courant* said, I hoped my munchy would warm the corn cockles of her heart, provoking her to let down her lady's tresses and, tossing touch-me-not on the compost pile, to behave like her country cousin bouncing Bet.

For years I have criticized big-time athletic programs at universities, thinking they trivialized learning. In truth sports are popular because they are trivial. Because so much on the front pages of newspapers is sad or disturbing, readers turn to sports pages and like blind Samson pull the columns down, burying themselves in anecdote and statistic in hopes of deadening thought and conscience. For their part universities have become bureaucratic corporations concerned more about continuing their existences than serving individuals or society. The old platitudes upon which temples were raised celebrating the benefits of education have crumbled. The problems countries face are so complex that they seem not only to defy solution but also to lie beyond man's abilities to cope. On the sports page life is clearer. The quick win races, and the hard-working occasionally triumph. Rather than struggling to elevate learning so that it serves, helping individuals to control their lives, perhaps even to better the neighborhoods in which they live, managers of universities have devolved into promoters, Philistines satisfied to entertain and divert.

January, however, as the writer in the *Country Gentleman* put it, is a "between-time full of pleasant possibilities," not a month for ardor. Along with describing my student, the article in the newspaper called attention to a basketball game to be played between the women's teams from the University of Connecticut and the University of Tennessee, the Huskies and the Volunteers as they are dubbed, respectively. Both teams were undefeated. With a record of 16–0, Tennessee was ranked first in the nation. At 12–0 Connecticut was second. Tennessee beat nine teams ranked thirteen or higher. Connecticut's schedule was easier. But the Huskies led the nation in scoring offense and not only beat opponents by an average of 42.4 points but also out rebounded them by 22.1 rebounds a game.

"Even if I have to eat a philosophic bouquet of cat's ear, goat's beard, pussytoes, turtlehead, and lizard's tail," I told Vicki, "I'm going to this game. In summer I will have plenty of time to purge with colic root and rinse my mouth with soapwort." All seats in Gampel Pavilion, the basketball arena on campus, had been sold, 8,241 seats to be exact. "You won't be able to wedge in sideways," Josh said. "All the black cats in New Canaan have been killed by brokers trying to conjure up seats. The Hunt Club in Westport has sold out of Lucky Bags. Even the Hartford Country Club has run short of Alligator Root and Holy Mammy Oil." "I have not spent two score years in universities for nothing," I said. "Education may not make the man, but it will grease hinges on doors to a basketball arena." Two days later, January 16, I was correspondent for the *Nashville Banner*, holding Media Pass 117 and sitting behind a table courtside, the correspondent for the *Knoxville News-Sentinel* on my left, on my right, the correspondent for the *New York Daily Post*.

Although the game did not begin until one o'clock in the afternoon, I arrived at the Pavilion at 10:30. Cheerleaders were practicing. In the middle of the basketball court compact girls posed atop triangles of boys. The cheerleaders who bounced through my school days have now become acrobats and dancers. Choreographers have replaced captains of cheerleading squads. "Keep it short," the choreographer said as the dancers swayed back and forth, their personalities seeming to sink into their pelvises, reducing them to shank and bone. The hearty "Rip them up; tear them up" cheer that rolled through gymnasiums when I was a boy has vanished, shattered by a "blastfest" of rock music.

I picked up a blue pompom and shook it. Shreds on the pompom were plastic, not crêpe paper. The Husky dog, a student in a goofy white dog costume, practiced for his performance, running around the court then throwing himself across the floor so that he slid on his stomach from one end of the court to the other. I found my seat. On the table in front of my chair lay a blue card, five inches tall and nine inches wide. Printed on the card was "Welcome to Connecticut Basketball." Beneath the phrase someone wrote "Sam Pickering, *Nashville Banner*." Blankets with the names of schools belonging to the Big East Basketball Conference sewed on them hung off the fronts of courtside tables. I sat behind the blanket with Villanova stitched on it. The blankets hid the feet of sports writers from view, and during the game several kicked off their shoes and sat in their socks.

I suspect they removed their shoes because they ate heavy lunches. In a corridor behind the stands at the south end of the Pavilion, the Athletic Department set food out for the press: deep stainless-steel platters roiling with bacon, scrambled eggs, link sausages, fried potatoes, chili, and beef stroganoff. Soft drinks and ice filled three red barrels. Resembling the belly of a middle-aged man, a long table sagged under a burden of sweets: blueberry muffins; doughnuts, plain and frosted, these last ranging from chocolate to bright cherry; cheese puffs; sweet rolls dripping jelly; and chocolate chip cookies as broad as hams. Trays of fruits and tossed salads sat on another table, beside them bowls of dressings and cardboard boxes containing packets of snack food: Wise White Cheddar Cheese Popcorn, an owl staring from the top of each bag; Multi Grain Huskies Lightly Salted Tortilla Chips; and something called Doodle Twisters with a "New Nacho Cheese Flavor." For the children I took three packets of Tortilla Chips, and for Vicki, who is more of a culinary adventurer, a bag of Doodle Twisters. I was not hungry. Still, I filled a plate with red grapes and slices of pineapple. Along the corridor reporters sat at cafeteria tables eating and talking. Wondering what real correspondents thought about the game, I pushed my way into a seat. Instead of discussing athletics, however, the reporters planned dinner, the restaurant of choice being a steak house on the Manchester side of Hartford.

Because I got to the game early, I explored the Pavilion. Throughout the building stood groups of temporary employees wearing yellow raincoats. Printed on the backs of the coats in large black letters were the words EVENT STAFF. I recognized two of the staff, a secretary from the Publications Department and then Bernie Marlin with whom I served six years on the Mansfield School Board. For being part of the staff, Bernie received a ticket to the game and six dollars an hour. "I recommend this for all retirees," Bernie said. For helping set up tables for correspondents and sweeping up after the game, students received $5.35 an hour. "I made sure you had a good seat," Daniel, a student in my children's literature class, said when he saw me.

I tried to be a competent reporter. Two university policemen stood by the north entrance to the gymnasium, eating ice cream cones, one cone chocolate, the other strawberry. "No quotes today," one said when I asked him about the game. When I asked an older woman checking tickets what she thought about the game, she said, "I'm not as quick-witted as I used to be." "Neither am I," I said, wondering whom I should next approach. I walked down to the court and looked at the backboards. A man working for public relations said the school kept eight backboards in the gymnasium. Each cost seven thousand dollars. When clocks and electronic paraphernalia were attached, the cost shot up. Folded down, the backboards resembled frames of pickup trucks, snow plows jutting out in front. Springs operated six backboards. Two were hydraulic, hydros, they were called. Springs were better, the man told me, because they did not leak oil.

The basketball court itself was sunken, seats rising above it like terraces in an amphitheater. Clustered about corners of the terraces were small stands. At Omar's Gourmet Coffee, a cup of Colombian Supreme cost one dollar while cannolis cost two dollars and a cappuccino two dollars and fifty cents. One of Edward's soccer coaches managed an ice cream stand in order to raise money for the elementary school. Sundaes with strawberries and whipped cream cost two dollars and fifty cents while fudge bars were two dollars. Pizza Hut sold pepperoni or plain cheese pizza for two dollars a slice. Almost as soon as people entered the Pavilion, they began eating. Hot dogs were the most popular food. People stuffed them in, the doughy bread curdling into balls and people's cheeks billowing like sails on a gusty afternoon.

The souvenir stand was named "Huskymania!" Two high school boys ran it. One had a Mohawk, and I asked him what his parents thought about the haircut. He said they were used to his doing odd things with his hair. "That's right," his friend said, "some days he comes to school with purple hair, other days with green. It's fun, and we laugh." I did not know the boy with the haircut, but he recognized me and asked when my next book was being published. The stand resembled a closet hung with clothes and knickknacks, selling among other items, tee-shirts, sweatshirts, stuffed Husky dogs costing $19, and eleven different "UCONN" baseball caps, the one-size-fits-all cap suitable for wearing backwards, the prices ranging from $15 to $18. For $6 a fan could buy a large Husky paw made from Styrofoam, the index claw on the paw pointing up, resembling the number one. For $3 one could purchase a blue and white tattoo of a dog's face. Students pasted them on their cheeks; some students went further and painted their entire faces blue and white, usually the left side of their faces, blue and the right, white. I did not price earrings shaped like dogs or pacifiers, these last with small, "nonallergic" puppies stamped on them.

I wandered corridors behind and beneath the seats. Along one corridor was a Press Corner. Above two tables twenty-three electric sockets stuck out of a wall, most with portable computers plugged into them. At the end of one corridor, a camera crew arranged lights for interviews. One cameraman wore a black tee-shirt. Printed across the shoulders in white letters was "Real Stories of the Highway Patrol." I talked to the man. The cameramen were free-lancers, working, he said, on assignment for ESPN, the television channel that concentrates on athletics. "I get to travel everywhere, but I spend a lot of time on the telephone telling people I am available," the man said, adding, "but when you are young, the life isn't bad."

The gymnasium filled rapidly after noon. Posters appeared on walls, warning Tennessee supporters to "Beware of Dog" and declaring "This is no *Conn* game. This is UCONN." Southern New England Telephone gave students tee-shirts with orange basketballs printed on the fronts. Stamped on the backs was "Battle of the Best." The telephone company also handed out small blue and white megaphones with the face of the Husky dog printed on the side. I took three megaphones home to the children. By the time the teams appeared, the stands buzzed like goldenrod in late summer. Children bounced about, and the crowd was good-natured. Many people were middle-aged and older. On the row behind me sat the grandparents of my student. "She is a good girl," they said, "and we are proud of her." Players from both schools knew each other, having been on the same national teams. During warm-ups they shook hands and chatted. A Tennessee player stretched out on the table in front of me, and a trainer bent her legs. I ached watching her. The teams wore heavy shoes. Under the heels were yellow, translucent bubbles. Connecticut wore black shoes with white streaks breaking across them like lightning. Edward wanted a pair of shoes that resembled them. The shoes cost $95 a pair, and he did not get them.

A color guard marched to the center of the court, and a fine arts major sang *The Star Spangled Banner*. The only times I hear the national anthem are at athletic events. The American flag hung down from the ceiling of the gymnasium. Also hanging down were thirty-seven blue and white banners, recording past basketball successes in, for example, the Big East Conference or the National Collegiate Athletic Association tournament. University graduations are held in the Pavilion. Place shapes tone, reducing educational achievement to the equivalent of three-pointers and slam dunks. At graduation parents and relatives become raucous fans, students become players, and the faculty, coaches. What, I wondered, was the effect of associating not only education but affection for country with athletics? The singer's voice rang, and I did not wonder long. The crowd roared, and my ears ached. Students sat at one end of the court. When the players from Tennessee were introduced, students opened newspapers and feigned indifference. When the Connecticut players were introduced, cheering erupted. Once the game started, sound never eddied, pushed along, in part, by the UCONN Pep Band, six trombones, three tubas, and a glittering assortment of other brass instruments.

During the game correspondents behaved differently. Some wrote in notebooks; others used laptop computers. A few did not take notes. The man from Knoxville divided his pages in half, drawing a line down the middle. On one side he kept track of the doings of Connecticut; on the other side, those of Tennessee. I wanted to appear knowledgeable, so I started writing on an eight by eleven-and-a-half-inch yellow pad with thirty-two lines to a page, the kind of pad on which I write my essays. I wanted Connecticut to win, and the game was so fast and exciting that I wrote little.

Actually taking notes was unnecessary. During the game wads of paper appeared in front of me. By the end of the game I had received a stack of paper seven-sixteenths of an inch high, containing, among other things, sixteen pages of *Media Notes* from Connecticut and twelve pages from Tennessee, these last printed on both sides of the paper. Facts surrounded me like mist. Clear throughout the game, however, were the players. Hands and legs never stopped churning, turning my inexperienced vision buttery. Tennessee started the game with four quick points, but after two minutes and forty seconds of play Connecticut crept ahead and never lost the lead. In the second half Tennessee drew within five points four times. Once or twice Connecticut lost poise, the words "here comes Tennessee" unspoken but hovering loud in people's minds. Tennessee ran and ran, and Connecticut swarmed. Not until the last forty seconds did the game seem won. Then the crowd started cheering louder than ever. Seven minutes after the game, people still cheered. I stood among them and wondered why winning a basketball game was so pleasant. "Basketball," Josh said, "gives academics sexual satisfaction."

The truth was that the game was just a game, something that did not matter, an event people could enjoy without thinking. After the game sixty reporters clustered in a narrow room for a press conference. A reporter asked my student what the victory meant. He wanted an inflated answer, one that would so elevate the importance of the game that it would diminish the day, at least for me. The girl disappointed him. "It's January 16," she said simply, "and this is another win." "Some people are too bright to let school ruin them," Josh said later, "and she is one of them." By the time I left the press conference, the crowd had drifted away. Outside the Pavilion gray clouds oozed rain. I walked home. Two crows flew over the graduate school in black lines. A brown creeper bustled around an oak, and juncos dropped out of forsythia like periods falling out of a paragraph. "Daddy," Eliza said when I opened the kitchen door, "you should see me make the cat's cradle." "Did you have a good time," Edward asked, "and are you going to become a sports writer and go to the Super Bowl someday?" "No," I said, "the afternoon was fun, but this is my last game. Tomorrow I am going to the Ogushwitz meadow and study voles. Now do your homework. Don't forget that you and Francis have ice-skating tonight, and I have to drive you." At twelve-thirty that night I faxed two thousand words to the *Nashville Banner.* "Here is the piece about the basketball game," I wrote the editor of the sports page. "Actually I did not describe the game so much as what went on around the game. Use it if you want. If not, just pitch it in the waste can."

Later that morning I wandered field and wood with George. Under plywood in the meadow I found six fat voles. That afternoon I went to the university library. I spent much time in the library in January. Once spring comes, I wander wood and field and forsake the library, taking, as a correspondent of the *Country Gentleman* put it in 1895, "an inventory of Mother Nature's cupboard." In January I plucked old books off shelves. Jas. S. Howe of Greenwich gave R. M. Ballantyne's *The Wild Man of the West* to G. Andrew Cheney, "his true friend," on January 29, 1864. I read the book. The novel blossomed with euphemisms. A trapper named Big Waller said whangskiver rather than kill, particularly when he referred to "children of the wilderness." Trappers forever fell into the clutches of Indians. One night when Redhand and Bounce crept out of an Indian camp, Redhand saw a familiar rifle leaning against a hut. The moment smacked of the graveyard scene in *Hamlet.* "An expression of deep sorrow overspread Redhand's countenance. 'Ay,' said he mournfully, 'I know it well. It belonged to young Blake.' Glancing quickly up at a place where several scalps were hanging on a pole, he took one down, and after gazing at it sadly for a few seconds, he added in a tone of deep melancholy— 'Poor, poor Blake! Ye had a hearty spirit an' a kindly heart. Your huntin' days are soon over!'"

My hunting days lasted the month. I like the musty smell of attics and storerooms, and I spent afternoons and mornings in the basement of the library roaming pages of old periodicals. In hopes of seeing days afresh, I read issues of journals published in January, 1895, and 1845. I first noticed advertisements. "FAT FOLKS" who took "ANTI-CORPULENE PILLS," an advertisement in the *Country Gentleman* declared in 1895, would lose fifteen pounds a month. The pills didn't cause sickness, contained no poison, and had never failed, Wilcox Specific, the manufacturers, assured customers. "Worms kill more sheep than dogs do," Moore Brothers informed readers, urging them to purchase their Worm and Tonic Powder. For five dollars a reader could buy a Hand Mill from Wilson Brothers in Easton, Pennsylvania, and grind his "Own Bone Meal, Oyster Shells, Graham Flour and Corn." For two dollars and fifty cents, including postage, G. P. Pilling and Son in Philadelphia would send readers a "Set of Instruments, with full instructions" describing how to "CAPONIZE." Heiskell's Ointment "positively cured Pimples, Freckles, Blotches, Ringworm, Eczema, Scald Head, Tetter, and all other skin disorders." Dr. Pierce's Golden Medical Discovery, an advertisement in the *American Agriculturist* (1895) stated, "cures ninety-eight percent of all cases of Consumption, in all its Earlier Stages."

Many advertisements focused on animals. On January 10, 1895, the

Country Gentleman contained advertisements for Red-Polled, Jersey, Brown Swiss, Guernsey, and Holstein cattle, then Berkshire, Jersey White, Chester Red, Poland China, and Yorkshire hogs. Packs of dogs gamboled through advertisements in *Forest and Stream:* Gordon, Irish, English, and Gildersleeve setters; beagles; mastiffs; Italian greyhounds; pointers; fox and rabbit hounds; cocker and Cumber spaniels; English pugs; St. Bernards; collies; French poodles; Skye, fox, Irish, and wire-haired Scotch terriers; and lastly Chesapeake Bay Duckling Dogs.

In 1845, the *George and Henry* docked in New York loaded with Peruvian guano from Chincha Islands. "Warranted pure," the guano was available at Thompson's Stores in Brooklyn or in large parcels at Edwin Bartlett at 42 South Street. For the past two years I have not fertilized my daffodils. A few are puny, and a touch of guano, I thought, might buck them up root and blossom. Some advertisements made me covetous. In 1895, *Forest and Stream* advertised sheets from Audubon's *Birds of America,* elephant folios, "the originals of the edition of 1856." "For a sportsman's dining room a selection of these plates appropriately framed makes," the magazine stated, "a *Superb Ornament.*" *Forest and Stream* advertised sheets depicting 120 birds. Wood wrens, white-throated sparrows, and black and white warblers cost four dollars a sheet; puffins and purple finches, five. The belted kingfisher and glossy ibis were seven dollars while the green heron, mockingbird, pileated woodpecker, and rose-breasted grosbeak cost a dollar more. For ten dollars one could buy a red-tailed hawk, for two dollars more a black vulture beside the head of a deer. Priced at fifteen dollars, the most expensive bird was the wood duck.

Although the prices of prints have risen, news has remained the same. St. Louis, the *Country Gentleman* related in 1895, had a "bloody Christmas record. In addition to 2 murders, there were 30 cases of cutting, shooting, robbery, and ordinary assaults innumerable. At midnight every police station in the city was full, while common drunkards were turned away for want of accommodation." Justice seems to have been swifter in 1895 than now. Vigilantes kidnapped Barrett Scott, "the defaulting treasurer of Holt County, Nebraska." Scott, the *Country Gentleman* said, had stolen eighty thousand dollars from the county. Sentenced to five years in prison, he was free on bail. "He was driving with his wife, daughter, and a niece," the magazine recounted, "when the party was fired upon from ambush." Scott's horses were shot, and while one bullet hit Scott himself in the ear another went through the "clothing of his niece." After attaching new horses to the wagon, the vigilantes drove over the prairie, eventually freeing the women near a farmhouse. "Scott," the article continued, "has not been seen since" and "is supposed to have been lynched and his body thrown into the Niobrara River." Also "taken by force" was Edward A. Woolston, this event occurring not on the Great Plains but in the Racquet Club in New York. "The well-known New Yorker," the account explained, was "committed for examination as to his sanity," adding he was "alleged to have been acting strangely." In contrast, college presidents in Indiana acted rationally. At a meeting in Indianapolis they "decided to prohibit intercollegiate football games in the future."

Much news focused on farming matters. In its issue for January 19, 1895, the *American Agriculturalist* reported that three turkeys and several chickens were stolen from F. P. Andrews in Coventry, Connecticut, just across the railway tracks from Storrs. The turkeys were recovered in Manchester, and Arthur House was charged with theft and "sent to jail to await the next term of court." The news reported to the *Country Gentleman* from S. B. Keach in Hartford County was not cheery. "A neighboring farmer, a fine specimen of a man physically, and much esteemed by all who know him," Keach wrote, "has just been stricken down with typhoid fever, and three physicians doubt if they can save his life. His sickness and death, if he must die, ought to be a significant and startling warning to every other farmer whose well is across the danger line and fatally near the barnyard." Keach was a regular correspondent of the *Country Gentleman*. "The substitution of electric cars for horse cars," Keach declared in a note, "will throw many street-car horses upon the market in Hartford as well as in other cities. This tends to lower the prices, especially of work horses, and will enable farmers to buy horses for spring use at cheap rates."

In a column entitled "Dog Chat" *Forest and Stream* (1895) reported that "during the Lexow police investigation, Capt. Schmittberger testified that he did not owe his promotion either to money payments or to political pulls, but to the fact that he found Commissioner Wheeler's lost dog. Another proof," the reporter noted, "that the dog is man's best friend." *The Rural New Yorker* (1895) urged readers to "hurry the limed eggs to market." While good celery was scarce, the magazine stated, "feathers of all kinds" were dull and prices low. Moreover, the journal added, "the big turkey has had his day in this market." In *The Cultivator* for January, 1845, W. R. Gilkey of Windsor, Vermont, challenged readers to match the hog raised by his neighbor Mr. T. B. Otis. On April 24, 1844, Otis bought a five-week-old pig weighing nine and a quarter pounds. He fed the pig corn meal and slops from the house. When the pig was slaughtered on November 18, the pig weighed "dressed, 350 lbs., making an increase of *pork,* deducting the weight of the pig when bought of 340¾ lbs." In the 208 days that Mr. Otis owned the animal, it gained an average of one pound ten ounces a day. "Best this who can," Gilkey said.

In January people remain in houses more than in other months, and if they resemble me, they graze through days. Articles about food seasoned magazines. In the *Country Gentleman* readers described cooking mush. In New York, one correspondent said, yellow meal finely ground gave the "best results" for mush desserts and mush waffles. "Plain fried mush," another correspondent declared, "is a very nice accompaniment of veal cutlets or hot boiled steak." "The white southern meal," another reader opined, was "too delicate to stiffen nicely." Many recipes appeared. My favorite was for jubilee pudding. "Make a pint of claret jelly," a writer instructed, then "cool it in a border mold if you possess one; if not, four patty-pans or small dishes will serve up prettily." Next, the writer explained, mix an ounce of candied cherries with a few strips of angelica, preserved ginger cut small, and "any dainty materials of this kind at hand. Stir these into a pint of whipped cream." After letting everything cool and "just before serving," put, the writer concluded, the "jelly in a handsome glass dish—at the four corners if it is molded" or, if not, "in any tasteful manner and heap the cream high in the center."

Much advice given to cooks was commonsensical and could be applied to things baked far from the kitchen. "The important thing in making cake is *to get ready,*" a correspondent explained in the *Country Gentleman.* "Be sure, first of all, of your fire. A good heat in the oven is the first essential. Then, when any particular cake is decided on, be quite sure that the materials are all at hand. It is very awkward to find that when a rich cake is partly put together that some essential ingredient is lacking." *Forest and Stream* devoted much space to dietary matters. At "certain Adirondack hotels," people refused to eat "deer meat" if it was listed on the bill of fare as venison. When described as "mountain mutton," however, customers never dreamed "of making any bones about it." C. H., a correspondent of *Forest and Stream*, described a feast held on Christmas day at Hotel Chattowka in New Bern, North Carolina. Served to gourmands were twelve kinds of fish and twenty-one kinds of game "with oysters in variety, winter radishes and asparagus." "Bear meat, wild turkey, venison and opossum figured prominently, all of them home products," C. H. reported, "while the quail, woodcock, goose, mallard, pintail, redhead, butterball, canvasback, brant, and Carolina dove all come from our fields and waters." The account resembled notes, as C. H., probably suffering from acute dyspepsia, needed a regimen of ANTI-CORPULENE PILLS. "Thermometer at noon 63 degrees," he recounted. "Negroes hilarious with horns, firecrackers and persimmon beer. Sunday School children happy and every one enjoying the charming weather and bright sky." At the end of his account, C. H. provided a full menu of dishes. The twelve fish included trout, shad, redfin, white fish, redsnapper, sturgeon, eel, pickerel, drum, mullet, halibut, and flounder. Among the meats were ham of black bear, leg of mountain sheep, buffalo tongue, this not being, C. H. assured readers, *bos Americanus* but the Carolina buffalo "found all along the Carolina coast," saddle of antelope, both loin and tongue of venison, then finally possum and wild turkey. In addition to the birds mentioned earlier on C. H.'s menu, celebrants could sample grouse, Wilson snipe, and Virginia partridge.

"There is more education in a walk over God's land with eyes wide open, than in many, many primers and slates," an essayist wrote in the *Country Gentleman*. Heat in the library made me dozy. Some days I had trouble keeping my eyes open, particularly after reading accounts of feasts and recipes for sweets like ginger cream and cold cabinet pudding. Still, I enjoyed roaming the periodicals almost as much walking around Mansfield. During the cold day animals hid in burrows. In the warm library I flushed coveys of intriguing columns. I have aged beyond hormones into wisdom. Not only do I relish giving advice, but I also enjoy reading it. In the *American Agriculturalist* appeared a column entitled "Mothers and Daughters." On January 12, 1895, a correspondent advised couples to end their spooning by ten o'clock in the evening. "Not only are the occupants of the house where the young folks are doing their billing and cooing likely to have their slumbers broken," the writer argued, "but I've got lots of thought and sympathy for the folks at the other end of the line. When the wooing party returns to his home, he has a horse to put up most likely. Then ten to one if no refreshments were offered where he had been he finds himself hungry at midnight and goes burglarizing in the pantry. Then he creeps upstairs, and no matter how softly he treads a board will creak somewhere or his shoes will squeak, and if he is not shot as an intruder somebody's got to be waked up."

In the periodicals doings in the parlor were second to doings in field and barn. "Do you realize what is going on in your barnyard this winter?" a correspondent asked in *The Rural New Yorker*. "Your manure bank is out there. The stock are the depositors and the firm of Water and Drain are drawing checks on the bank, payable to the brook." Crawling generations interested readers more than the rising generation. In *The Cultivator* (1845), a correspondent described his method of ridding fields of ant mounds. Just before frost he cut the top off the mounds with a bog hoe after which he dumped a shovel full of unleached ashes on the spot. Lye in the ashes caused the ants' "utter destruction." The mound itself should then, he said, "be removed from the meadow to the compost heap, or placed in some ditch or hole for the purpose of making the meadow smooth and level." Rats were a greater nuisance than ants, and in the *American Agriculturalist* (1845), R. H. Henderson of Middletown, Ohio, suggested keeping coons. "A good lot of pet coons," he wrote, were "much preferable to cats to kill, eat, and drive away rats," adding that "we were nearly devoured by rats until we got coons."

The smaller the animal, the more it troubled people. Moles were a great nuisance. "A neighborhood full of prowling cats is the most effectual way to get rid of moles," an editor of the *American Agriculturalist* wrote in 1895. For readers living in neighborhoods in which coons outnumbered cats, the magazine suggested a second way to get rid of moles. Soak grains of sweet corn until they were soft. Then, a writer instructed, split the germ ends with a pen knife and insert "a small quantity of strychnine. Then close the split and drop five or six grains in the freshly made runs of the moles." Spring, the writer assured readers, was the best season "for this work." Animals suffered from wards of ailments. "My young pigs have worms. I found sixty-six worms in the intestines of one small pig. What will kill them?" A. P., a native of Vineland, New Jersey, asked *The Rural New Yorker* in 1895. One teaspoon of turpentine for each twenty-five to thirty pounds of pig, the magazine replied, "give on an empty stomach and thoroughly shake up in milk or oil." Hogs were the subject of many letters in *The Rural New Yorker.* One concerned courtship. "How shall I feed young sows of about eight months so they will take the boar?" P. D. wrote from Ronkonkoma, Long Island. "I have two sows of this age, but they do not come in heat. I feed them with bran, corn meal, white bag meal, equal parts, and apples, and they look very fat." "Your hogs," a writer for the magazine answered, "are evidently too fat, and they probably also lack exercise."

Dr. Buzzard probably was familiar with some of the cures prescribed by periodicals. In 1845, Mr. Harmon, a farmer in Genesee, New York, sent his cure for fistulas in horses to the *American Agriculturalist.* "Procure a large warty toad, and having a thick glove or mitten on the hand, take up the toad and hold his back on the fistula for one or two minutes," Mr. Harmon suggested. "Take it off for a short time, then put it on again, and rub its back slightly over the affected part and continue to rub it thus for about an hour by which time the toad will be dead and should be buried." The horse would be "uneasy" at the beginning of treatment, Mr. Harmon noted, adding that after a few minutes "he will stand quietly." Care, he warned, "should be taken not to hold your head too near or over the place of application, as the fumes are somewhat sickening. A milky fluid, said to be poisonous, exudes from the warts on the back of the toad." For three or four weeks after the "operation," the fistula would drip pus, but then "the place will heal speedily." Toads hopped through periodicals. Most were long-suffering and short-lived. Toads, C. S. Brimley declared in *The American Naturalist* (1895), were the favorite food of the hog-nosed snake, who sometimes ate, he noted, three at a meal. If interfered with in the wild, hog-nosed snakes frequently disgorged "one or more toads." "Personally," he concluded, "I have never known them to eat anything else."

Articles in the periodicals were restrained, resembling January itself. Occasionally, though, a storm blew across a page. In the *Country Gentleman* (1895), several readers attacked "butter imitation." In Worcester, Massachusetts, a correspondent reported, dealers in "the fraudulent article are placing it on the market uncolored." "The better class of trade will probably let it alone, but among the poor the cheapness of the butterine may offset the lack of color. A curious result of the oleomargarine traffic came to light recently. A woman who keeps a large boarding-house in Worcester came to her dealer almost with tears in her eyes and asked if it was true no more of this product could be sold. She said her saving on that article alone enabled her to send her son to college, which would be an impossibility were she obliged to pay 28 cents a pound!"

Once or twice I wanted to add my breath to a storm. In *The Auk* (1895), a journal published for "The American Ornithologists' Union," a correspondent criticized the use of Latin names for animals. "Many of them are so long and overwhelming," he wrote, "that if a man does not want to be laughed at, or accused of wanting to 'show off,' he must choose his hearers with care before using them." "Tell a newspaper managing editor that you have got a *Taxidea americana neglecta* [a badger], and the chances are ten to one that he will think it is some kind of tapeworm and advise you to go and see a doctor right away." "Recent Additions to North America Land Mammal Fauna," a list of 155 species discovered in the years 1884–92, were the worms gnawing the correspondent's bowels. Eighty-five, he noted, were "launched upon the English-speaking world with no English names whatever, and with no names understandable to any but really good Latin scholars. In other words, the eighty-five new species have to about 999 persons out of every thousand, practically no names whatever!"

In January indignation is as enjoyable as a warm fire. In 1895, in *The American Naturalist* Charles Bessey reviewed *Wild Flowers of America* and *A Practical Flora for Schools and Colleges.* The books set him ablaze, their puffery furnishing matter for hot criticism. Of the first he wrote, "in spite of the extravagant claims upon the title page, as to the *special artists and botanists* who are said to have prepared it, and the *leading artists of America and Europe,* who are said to have approved it, as well as the *university botanists of both continents* whose *endorsement* is alleged, we venture to affirm that no one with any artistic ability whatever, or even the slightest knowledge of the science of botany could *approve* or *endorse* the hideously inartistic monstrosities here gathered together." "Of the illustrations" in *Practical Flora,* Bessey wrote, "little need be said, more than that many of them are *trade cuts* from the catalogues of seeds-men, many of them possessing the characteristic exaggeration of such cuts. The figure of Indian Corn on page 287, with *fourteen ears,* will not tend to give one confidence in the truthfulness of the illustrations."

Occasionally stories appeared in the periodicals. In the *Country Gentleman* (1895), a woman recounted drifting apart from her husband. "I used to have ecstatic feelings when his foot was on the stair, and I sat sewing little baby clothes." Now, she moaned, "when our lips meet, it is like two pieces of dried pith coming together." *Forest and Stream* published the biography of Uncle Bill Hamilton. Uncle Bill lived "by the side of the great Yellowstone." "No human being had a grander physical constitution." Having been offended by one of Bill's pranks, an Englishman "who had rather stilted ideas about affairs of honor" challenged Bill to fight a duel. "In a country where duels usually began synchronously with the challenge, this struck Bill as being rather funny and he accepted promptly, naming the conditions himself. The contestants were to fight that night by moonlight in the street. Both were to be stark naked and were to fight with swords or knives if swords could not be found. Before fighting each man was to jump four times naked through the ice into the Missouri River (it was in the winter), four holes having been cut for each man." The town turned out for the fight. The duel was short-lived. The first dip took "all the fight" out of the challenger. When the challenger crawled shivering out of the hole, Bill who was standing comfortably with his chin just above the water yelled, "Git into your next hole. Git in or I'll claim the fight." Shaking with cold, the challenger stuttered that he would not fight "this way to please no man." He then broke and ran "up the street in the moonlight with Bill chasing him, swinging his sword around his head and uttering yells of triumph."

A writer who signed himself "Seventy" contributed my favorite story to *Forest and Stream.* One evening a group of men sat around a fire talking about strange things that happened on fishing trips. A man named Trimble had a large, hooked nose. "I was fishing one hot day," Trimble recounted, "and becoming thirsty kneeled over the water to drink. Just as my lips touched the water a trout seized me by the nose and gave it a strong yank." "Yes sir!" Trimble declared, embroidering the account, "he held on and shook my head from side to side. I could have landed him but I was so astonished and scared that he got away." When Trimble finished the tale, the group was silent for a moment. Then his friend

Roper spoke. "Trimble," he said, "you have abused our intelligence. That story can't be true. No trout that swallowed your nose could ever escape. There is too much hook in it."

Reading itself is barbed. One book hooks another. A reader asked the *American Agriculturalist,* "Could you tell me where the poem 'She Died of Mortgage' by Will Carleton can be obtained?" The magazine did not provide an answer, at least not in January. I looked Carleton up in the *Dictionary of American Biography.* He was born in 1845 on a farm "two miles east of Hudson, Michigan." He grew up, Charles Dinsmore wrote, "a delicate dreamy boy, more inclined to deliver orations to the cows than to follow the plow." After graduating from Hillsdale College, he became editor of the *Hillsdale Standard* and the *Detroit Weekly Tribune.* In his spare time he wrote poetry. In 1873 Harper's published his first collection, *Farm Ballads.* The book sold forty thousand copies in eighteen months, and Carleton's career as a popular poet began. Although I did not find "She Died of Mortgage," I discovered several of Carleton's books in the university library. I liked Carleton. He dedicated *Farm Legends* to his father, writing, "To the Memory of A Nobleman My Farmer Father."

The most popular poem in *Farm Ballads* and probably Carleton's most successful poem was "Over the Hill to the Poor-House." After "The Lord of Hosts took poor John," her husband, a seventy-year-old farm wife was destitute. The wife remained on the farm with her son Charley until Charley married, and she "couldn't make it go" with her daughter-in-law. The old woman lived for a while with her daughter Susan, but having to take care of three children of her own and her husband's sisters, Susan neglected her mother. Her grandchildren's "sauce" drove the old woman from the home of her son Thomas. Next the farm wife begged shelter from her children Rebecca and Isaac, both of whom lived in the West. Although the children's homes were only twenty miles apart, they refused her request, one explaining that the climate was too cold, the other that it was too hot. "Over the hill to the poor-house—my child'rn dear, good-by!" the poem ended. "Many a night I've watched you when only God was nigh: / And God'll judge between us; but I will al'ays pray / That you shall never suffer the half I do to-day."

In Carleton's *City Ballads* Farmer Harrington traveled from the country to the city. The farmer kept a Calendar in which he wrote notes describing his journey. Harrington had "very little book learning," but he had "a clear brain, a warm heart and independent judgment, and a habit of philosophizing." The city shocked him into poetry. He began a section called *Want,* writing, "Want-want-want-want! O God! forgive the crime, / If I, asleep, awake, at any time, / Upon my bended knees, my back, my feet, / In church, on bed, on the treasure-lighted street, / Have ever *hinted,* or much less, have pleaded / That I hadn't ten times over all I needed!" In a section entitled *That Swamp of Death,* the farmer met a laborer, a man who worked "for food and rags and sleep," a man who hardly knew "the meaning of the life I slave to keep." The man's only daughter had just died. "Why, she lay here," the man told the farmer, "faint and gasping, moaning for a bit of air, / Choked and strangled by the foul breath of the chimneys over there; / It climbed through every window, and crept under every door, / And I tried to bar against it, and she only choked the more." On returning home, the farmer told his wife, Mary, to set the table "an' let the cloth be white; / The hungry city children are comin' here to-night; / The children from the city, with features pinched an' spare, / Are comin' here to get a breath of God's untainted air."

In the introduction to *City Ballads* Carleton addressed the reader, saying he hoped the book would "rouse your pity of pain, your enjoyment of honest mirth, your hatred of sham and wrong, and your love and adoration of the Resolute and the Good." Carleton was not a good poet, but his poetry moved people. "Superintendents of poor houses reported to him that their inmates were decreasing in numbers because children were withdrawing their parents from these institutions, shamed into filial duty by this ballad," Charles Dinsmore wrote, commenting on the popularity of "Over the Hill to the Poor-House." Aesthetics and sophistication may have little to do with good poetry. Maybe really good poetry turns people into Farmer Harringtons. On my desk lay a letter soliciting contributions for a summer camp which sent city children to the country "to get a breath of God's untainted air." For six weeks the letter had lain on my desk. The day I read *City Ballads* I mailed a check to the camp.

In 1895, Angus Gaines wrote *The American Naturalist* and described habits of the hog-nosed snake. "I have seen," he said, "the Heterodon platyrhinus turn up soil with its trihedral rostral with as much facility as a rooting pig." Josh's snout is flatter than that of the hog-nosed snake.

Nevertheless he digs into people's affairs and, rooting through the low soil of society, turns up customs richer than truffles. In January, I received several letters from Josh. Life at the country club appealed to him, and his research went better than expected. Golfers, he reported, were particularly good sources of information. "Although they have burdened their children with hyphenated names, even Wednesday afternoon golfers," he said, "hanker for the past, those simpler times when people had names like Ducklegs, Horn-buckle, and Teakle."

Unlike most anthropologists Josh did not need a warehouse of equipment for field work: camp stoves, air-tight Pelican cases, Eureka tents, bush cutters, and tetracycline. All Josh took to Fairfield County was ten cases of Wild Turkey and eight bushels of Brown Mule chewing tobacco. "You can't educate the twist out of the grapevine," Josh wrote. "Give these old boys a glass of Wild Turkey and a chew of Brown Mule, and they will tell you anything you want to know, no matter what they shot on the back nine." Josh discovered much about brokers and investment bankers, all of whom seemed to have sojourned at Harvard at one time or another, most at the Business School.

"Daddy Snakelegs and Doctor Buzzard can't compare to the nicknames students give tenured Faith Doctors in the Business School," Josh wrote. "So far golfers have told me about Dog Face, Humpadee, Ready Money, and Turkey Gobbler." The bald man does not need a comb, and Josh is so distinguished he does not have to lie or interview people more ignorant than yams in order to establish a reputation. Several Episcopalians told Josh that during the recent recession research at the Business School concentrated on hoodoo economics. Humpadee and a barn full of laboratory assistants discredited the theory that washing one's hands in milk from a black cow would make a person wealthy. In contrast Turkey Gobbler's study of the effects of reading Revelation backwards was inconclusive. Many of his subjects broke down at the walls of the New Jerusalem, not knowing how to pronounce chrysoprasus, sardonyx, and chalcedony, or susarposyrhc, xynodras, and ynodeclahc, as they were spelled when read backwards. Other subjects gave up the ghost at the seventh seal.

Fathers-in-law, of course, make more brokers than does education. Still, Harvard's influence upon Wall Street is great. Every banker in New York, Josh wrote, has studied the Sixth and Seventh Books of Moses. Hanging on walls next to diplomas and under oars are mojos, or charms, the pro-tractors and slide rules of a business school education. More common in brokers' offices than *Barron's* are money needles, most cut from hickory but occasionally an antique needle made from mahogany. Hanging from the chandelier in the waiting room of an old-fashioned Keynesian is the yellow skin of a chicken snake, red devils painted on it. Many bankers, Josh reported, wore lucky dimes, females, the golfers reported, wearing them above the knee, males, below.

According to duffers at Birchwood Country Club in Westport, 78.63 percent of all traders on Wall Street keep a jar of buzzard lard on their desks. More important to success than macro or micro models is the manner in which the lard is applied to the traders' hands. After killing his buzzard, the economist, Josh explained, must bury it in the ground for three days. At the end of the three days, the economist unearths the buzzard and boils it in water ladled out of a creek which runs due north. "If such a creek cannot be found, Perrier Water makes an acceptable sub-stitute." In applying the charm the broker must put three mounds of lard on the back of each wrist. Then starting with the left hand, he rubs the lard forward over the top of his hand until the lard reaches the fingertips, all the while repeating, "In the name of the Father, Son, and Holy Ghost." Once the lard is applied, the broker is ready to wrestle the Dow Jones.

Josh spent much of this year's "between-time" in smoking rooms at country clubs. He spent, as the correspondent of the *Country Gentleman* suggested, "long evenings beside the fire," not, however, listening to "the sound of storm and wind outside," but eavesdropping on the wind in-side. In a letter written on the last day of January, Josh described a con-versation he heard at Green Knoll in Litchfield. The name of one of the speakers was Ruckelshaus; the name of the other, Van Dusen. "Despite their names," Josh wrote, "neither could hit a chip shot worth a damn." Not able to crow about their skills on fairway and green, the men bragged about family. "The Van Dusens have been here since the beginning of time," Van Dusen said. "Were they around before the flood?" Ruckelshaus asked. "What flood?" Van Dusen responded. "Noah's flood," Ruckelshaus said, adding, "the Bible doesn't mention any Van Dusens boarding the ark." "Pshaw," Van Dusen sniffed, "who ever heard of a Van Dusen who did not have a boat of his own?"

crank

"Making Dessert Pizza is," the advertisement stated, "Mott's of Fun." The advertisement arrived in a packet of coupons delivered with the *Willimantic Chronicle* on Saturday. "I thought this might appeal to your literary taste," Vicki said, handing me the advertisement at dinner. In the middle of the advertisement was an illustration of the pizza. A pool of apple sauce scarlet with food coloring sloshed against the sides of a "ready-made pie crust" shaped like a bird bath. Through the bath swam a small school of six "gummie fish." The gummie fish resembled neon tetras. Two were orange; two, red; and two, green. The fish splashed over the surface of the pool, feeding on coconut, the shreds resembling white, crinkled worms. "I think the fish are after the raisins, not the coconut," Vicki said. "There are eight raisins, and they look like tadpoles." Vicki may have been right. In any case the pizza was awash with tidbits, enough, advertisers hoped, to send a school of children into a slurping frenzy. Floating atop the pizza alongside the raisins and the coconut were eight large red hearts and thirty small sugar stars, ten of these last blue, the rest yellow.

Attached to the bottom of the picture was a coupon. For one dollar and ninety-nine cents and "One (1) Mott's proof-of-purchase," I could purchase *Mott's Low Fat Baking.* The coupon instructed readers to send checks to "Favorite Brand Name Recipes," listing a post office box in Wisconsin. The next evening I wrote a letter to the "Creator of Dessert Pizza," mailing it to the box. In the letter I said I tested the recipe on the ears of my eight-o'clock class of 250 students. The recipe enjoyed a loud, if not enthusiastic, reception. "Moans and sounds of primitive beasts suffering from dyspepsia punctuated the reading." Although demons could not force the pizza down my esophagus, no recipe had given me or my friends, I declared, more pleasure. A distinguished lady, an habitué of the Cup of Sun, a café in Storrs frequented by culinary and literary adventurers, copied the recipe, declaring that she planned to serve it with cognac at a formal dinner party, telling guests that it was an "old family favorite." I ended the letter by asking the chef if he had other recipes of similar quality, explaining they would make palatable material for an essay.

Twenty-three days later I received a reply from Stamford, Connecticut, the corporate headquarters of Cadbury Schweppes, the owners of Mott's Apple Sauce. Enclosed in the envelope were two yellow coupons good for jars of apple sauce. The man who wrote was pleasant, an amateur grammarian who wondered about punctuation and suggested that when I began a sentence with *in short* I should place a comma after the word *short.* Forever in flux, punctuation rules are always matters of interest. Unfortunately by the time the man responded to my letter, my concerns had blundered beyond commas to deeds. At the Cup of Sun Mott's Apple Sauce had served as matter for conversation, moving up from intellectual dessert to the main course.

Once a gummie fish is hooked, the angler must keep his line taut. I answered the letter from Stamford by return mail. Friends at the café and I planned, I wrote, to hold a Mott's Apple Sauce piñata party in May. We spent two mornings, I recounted, pondering whether to have a free-range or a feed-lot piñata, finally "settling upon the latter as the former was too gamy for our conservative tastes." Nevertheless problems remained, and "since you pay meticulous attention to particulars, including, among other things, commas," I wrote the man, "we are asking you to guide us through a thicket prickly with difficulties, the primary thorn being design. A retired artist," I continued, "suggested stuffing apple sauce into balloons and afterward forcing the balloons into the piñata. Not only has the artist not suggested how to squeeze Mott's into the balloons, but even worse, he has spent years photographing male nudes, and I am afraid the shape of the balloons he has in mind might disturb Messrs. Cadbury and Schweppes." After asking my correspondent to design the piñata, I provided a guest list for the party, including among others, a native of Colorado. Early in January in the Cup of Sun, this man, I recounted, read "Grandma's Potato Salad," a poem he composed when he was fifteen. "Even though decades have elapsed since the stanzas were first pared, the potatoes have not lost their savor." With the letter I included a snapshot taken during the reading. Lastly I said that I would furnish champagne for the party, "only American champagne but bubbly nevertheless."

The man to whom I addressed the letter did not reply. He passed it on quickly to a "Consumer Services Manager" who sent me another coupon for apple sauce and a booklet of Mott's "Best Recipes," *A Better Way to Bake: Delicious Low Fat Recipes,* selling for $2.95 in the United States and $3.00 in Canada. On page seventy-four, he wrote, you will find a recipe "more suitable to your taste." The recipe was for "Lots O'Apple Pizza." Gone were the stars, hearts, food coloring, coconut worms, and gummie fish. The tadpole-like raisins remained, this time not eight but two-thirds of a cup, all of them still diving into a pool of apple sauce, however. Without fish, though, the pool was quiet, slices of apples floating about the surface like soggy leaves.

My "comments" had been "noted," and, the manager wrote, "will be shared with our Marketing Staff." Piñatas did not intrigue folks on the Marketing Staff, and the correspondence ended. I was disappointed. I expected the Mott's people to be livelier. "Bottlers of apple cider would have risen to the occasion," Vicki said. "Ideas ferment in cider. Apple sauce jars are sterilized, and the contents pureed. The people at Cadbury thought you a crank. No one dared approach closer than a rubber handshake."

Being foisted off with a paragraph of pasteurized words did not bother me, for I had just received a letter from one of my crank friends. Instead of being confined by a single identity, cranks revel in personalities. For the purposes of this particular letter my friend assumed the identity of Mrs. Neeoscaleeta Pemberton. A decade ago Mrs. Pemberton founded the Carts for Weenie Dogs Foundation, dedicated to "Defending the

Rights of Weenie Dogs on Carts Everywhere," in other words aiding crippled dachshunds. In the letter Mrs. Pemberton noted that recently she had become more than simply the founder of the CFWDF, as she put it. She was now Grand Worthy Advisor and Fundraising Secretary for Weenie Dogs on Carts Subcommittee (GWAAFSFWDOCS)." According to Mrs. Pemberton, Rush Limbaugh, the political commentator, had mounted an attack against the rights of weenie dogs. "We must be ever vigilant in our campaign to assure that every weenie dog that needs one is provided a cart," Mrs. Pemberton wrote, adding, "*But that's not enough. We must assure that every weenie dog is guaranteed basic rights to protection from the elements while riding their carts.* That's where you come in, Mr. Pickelring. We're asking that you join in our fundraising efforts to provide each cart-bound weenie dog a sweatshirt (see enclosure)."

Stapled to the letter was a page from a mail-order catalogue. Prancing across the lower right-hand corner of the page was a beagle wearing a four-legged sweatshirt complete with hood. The sweatshirt came in three leg sizes, twelve, sixteen, and twenty inches long. "Your pet will be the talk of the block in this authentic hooded sweatshirt," the advertisement stated. Although mostly beagle, the dog was a pizza of ingredients. A touch of pointer coursed under the sweatshirt, and the animal's nose pointed at an advertisement on the lower left-hand side of the page. The advertisement consisted of two pictures, both of a blond woman wearing a blue sweater. In the left-hand picture the woman stood demurely, lips pressed together. In the picture on the right side of the advertisement, the side nearest the hound, she leaned backwards smiling, her chest lumpier than a bushel of honeydew melons. "INFLATABLE BOOBS," the advertisement stated, "grow before your very eyes! Squeezing concealed air bulb transforms anyone, male or female, into a voluptuous Triple E! Wear it like a bra under sweater or blouse. No one will notice until you hil-AIR-iously start to develop. Use as a 'booby' trap on dates, for Halloween, or at parties."

For a crank, dignity is a suit of clothes, a costume worn to fit mood, something easily shed or put on. Cranks resist platitude and glib consistencies buttressed by appeals to custom. Perusing the coatrack of identity, cranks are playful, nosing out the bogus and the moth-eaten lurking under the twill of high seriousness. Mrs. Pemberton was born in the South. More cranks seem to come from the South than any other part of the nation. Southerners rarely see life as a progress. For Southerners of my generation, education did not so much shape the future adult's success, social or financial, as tidy appearance and spread plaster thinly over the wallboard of character. What lay behind the plaster eventually seeped into daylight, not so much shaming the individual as binding him to family, giving delight to friends who traced anecdotal similarities to kin-folk three and four generations removed. Since people rarely escaped family to become their achievements, achievement lost stature. Instead of providing the exoskeleton of identity, achievement was the flabby, insub-stantial stuff of a moment. As a result Southerners were not so ambitious as other people. Instead of striving to reach goals, people meandered through hours, appearing to outsiders as triflers or eccentrics.

Whether this interpretation of Southern character is correct is a matter of little importance, at least to a crank. On the Saturday after Ground-hog Day, the telephone by my bed rang at 11:30 at night. On the line were a group of women with whom I had grown up in Nashville. They and their husbands were at Bill Weaver's house celebrating Groundhog Day. For the occasion the men had special ties woven. Across the front of the ties scampered dens of groundhogs resembling the ordinary weave of animals trapped on club ties except that the rodents had massive tes-ticles, "bigger and hairier than Georgia peaches," said a woman over whose feet I stumbled during the waltz contest at Fortnightly Dancing School in the seventh grade. "Only in the South," Vicki said later when I de-scribed the telephone conversation, adding "I bet you would like one of the ties." "Damn straight," I answered. "If you wore it up here," Vicki said, "people would not understand. They would think that you had finally gone round the bend."

Despite Vicki's view, some folks in Connecticut are playful. Certainly Eliza is, and she has spent little time in the South. Last week she wrote a story entitled "Zany Xen," an account of a nun who forsook the church and joined roller derby. Xenalla was an unconventional nun. Because she suffered from corns on her feet, she rode a unicycle around the abbey. "Under her habit," Eliza wrote, was "a great mass of frizzy pink hair." Every night Xenalla combed "the mop" with an electric hair brush and styled "it with Crisco." Xenalla's transformation into Zany Xen, "Queen of the Roller Derby," probably did not surprise other nuns at the abbey. Once when the Mother Superior sent Xenalla to town to buy candles,

Xenalla spent the money for "a ten-foot-long tapeworm for sale at the local pet store, the Pigsty." Of course Eliza's story, literary merit aside, may result more from family than from place. "Nuns on unicycles and tapeworms resembling clothes lines are," Vicki said, "the sorts of things I would expect to tumble out of a piñata stuffed with apple sauce."

Outside of story Xenalla would not have become Zany Xen. Fiction, however, works miracles. Writers are cranks who know some things that happen and a lot that don't happen. Truth is often small. In my essays I embellish days. I stretch truth to make life colorful. Away from my books, Carthage is a small town in Smith County, Tennessee, a slow, country place I have not visited in a decade. On the page Carthage is lively with story, and no matter the expense of flying from Connecticut to Tennessee, I travel to Carthage once or twice each month. There I meet all sorts of people. In fact I would not be surprised if Zany Xen wandered through town someday. Corns will force her to retire from roller derby. Not only did she learn to play the organ at the abbey, but she memorized a sacristy of prayers. With her knowledge of music and penchant for the frizzy, she could buy an accordion and after changing her name to Sister Grace or Full Redeemer could lead Fire Baptized Holiness Rallies or Body of Christ Foot-Washings and Blood-Drinking Communions. Even Latin prayers could be transformed into the seed of honest American money by helping her speak in tongues. A *venite* planted in Red Boiling Springs and a *dominus* watered in New Middleton would grow greener than tobacco.

At this moment, though, Xen is still with the roller derby, her toes redder than hot dogs. My last visit to Carthage was lively nevertheless. After failing the eleventh grade at the Male and Female Select School, Odometer Hackett, or Odo, as his friends called him, left Carthage. For eleven years he wandered the South, collecting scrap iron in Alabama, cooking barbecue in Arkansas, and then finally his most successful venture, selling fertilizer in North Carolina, a home brew of phosphate, potash, and cottonseed meal. Odo did so well with fertilizer that he returned to Carthage and bought Bascomb's grist mill. Before settling down to the grinding routine of business, Odo renewed old acquaintances. One morning he realized that he had not seen H. B. Povey around town, and on meeting Loppie Groat outside Read's Drugstore, he said, "I have not run across H. B. How is he doing?" "H. B. is just fine," Loppie answered, "but his wife, Beevie, isn't doing so well." "I'm sorry to hear that," Odo replied, tilting his head and nodding sympathetically before asking, "what's wrong with her?" "Well," Loppie said, "she's having a hard time adjusting to being a widow."

On my pages funerals bloom in Carthage. Hink Ruunt's fourth wife, Zeura, died last week. At the funeral Hink threw himself on the coffin and moaned, "the light of my life has gone out." "Knowing Hink as well as I do," Turlow Gutheridge said the next day at Ankerrow's Café, "it won't be long before he strikes another match." Talk in Carthage is more enjoyable than at most universities. Sawyer Blodgett had long been a reprobate. Nevertheless after his daughter Bettie Claire took him to Nashville and bought him a set of false teeth, he behaved worse than ever, suddenly making malicious remarks about his neighbors. Although Judge Rutherford devoted years to bettering education in Smith County, Sawyer bitingly dismissed the Judge's concern for others, saying, "he's the kind of fellow what will piss in his trousers and not care which leg it runs down." At Ankerrow's the lunch crowd speculated about the cause of Sawyer's meanness. "Ever since Sawyer got false teeth," Googoo Hooberry said, "he lies something terrible."

Even casual talk in Carthage is spirited. After Albert Hennard renounced strong drink for the eighth time, his wife, Amanda Leigh, invited Carthage's first citizens to a celebratory dinner. Albert had a fine garden, and last year his beets won a blue ribbon at the Smith County Fair. Amanda was proud of Albert's vegetables, and before the party she visited Walduck's candle manufactory. To surprise Albert she ordered a giant wax beet as a centerpiece for the dining room table. As large as a gilt duroc, the beet was an impressive table decoration, especially after Amanda wrapped yards of blue ribbon through the greens. Judge Rutherford and Turlow Gutheridge arrived at the party early and, wandering into the dining room, saw the beet. "Gosh, I have never seen anything like that," the judge said, then asked, "what do you suppose Amanda will serve for dinner?" "Damn," Turlow exclaimed, his attention so drawn to the table decoration that he did not hear the judge's question, "that beat's all."

Cranks forever pump truth up so that it reaches a fetching "triple E." Recently my friend George wrote an essay for the student newspaper. In the essay he urged the university to shed the Reserve Officers Training Corps, or ROTC, as Mrs. Neeoscaleeta Pemberton calls it, because the Corps refuses to enroll students who admit being homosexual. The article was lively, and George hoped to provoke reaction. Rarely do words stir readers to write. Three days passed, and when George did not receive a letter, he looked despondent. Not even talk about piñatas could bring a smile to his face. "What's the use of words?" George said in response to my wondering whether I should write the chairman of Cadbury Schweppes. "Nobody pays attention to words." That afternoon I sent George a crank letter. First I cut a picture of Fidel Castro out of *Time* magazine. Next I pasted the face on a sheet of white paper. In the middle of Castro's forehead I stuck three small American flags, these sliced from address labels sent to Vicki by the Veterans of Foreign Wars. Actually I stuck little flags randomly over the page, more flags than the number of stars visible in Dessert Pizza, thirty-nine flags in fact. With a red marking pen I drew an arrow pointing to Castro. Under the arrow I wrote, "Is This Your Heroe Pinkoe?" I wrote on both sides of the paper, using Eliza's marking pens. I pasted pictures over the paper, including the masthead from the *Daily Worker* sliced from an article in the *Manchester Guardian*, and several pictures of babies, all decapitated. Beside the pictures I scrawled in big yellow letters, "I bet you don't like babies either." Next I took a pair of Vicki's underpants, never worn I must add for the sake of propriety. On the rear of the pants I wrote in blue, "boys who don't fancy ROTC should wear these." Lastly I stuffed the pants and letter into a book bag. Around the edge of the bag I pasted a border of American flags. Then after misspelling George's name on the address, I mailed the bag. Two mornings later when George walked into the Cup of Sun, he seemed a new man. His step was brisk, and his eyes sparkled. "You won't believe what I received in the mail," he said, spring racketing in his voice as he pulled the book bag from his satchel.

Cranks envision different worlds. Willow trees were once human. At the crucifixion they were fishermen. Not imaginative enough to see beyond themselves either to believe in a savior or sympathize with a man wrongly executed, they refused to stop fishing to mourn. As a result they were changed into trees, doomed to spend eternity leaning over creeks, fishing through rain and snow, heat and drought, never landing a fish, their twigs always without hooks. Because cranks are imaginative they can pour new wine into old bottles, transforming ordinary plonk into the richly intoxicating. Examinations bore me. While students hunch over desks, I pace the room, silent except when I imitate a clock and scratch the time on the blackboard. This semester 256 students took my course on the short story. During the mid-term examination the room was so crowded that walking was difficult. For a while I collapsed behind my desk.

The baseball cap, however, has replaced the tee-shirt as the most popular item in the undergraduate wardrobe. Students wear caps in classes, something I have railed against, labeling the wearers sartorial Goths and Visigoths, Huns, Aztecs, Methodists, and Texans. As I sat behind my desk, the examination stretched wintry before me, at least until I noticed caps blooming in clusters. Instead of resembling the pupae of blow flies fattening on the corpse of manners, the caps suddenly resembled flowers, the blossoms composed of a big disk and a single petal, the bill. In some blossoms the petal jutted forward; in others it stuck out the rear, hanging down the stem or the neck of the wearer. During the test flowers bobbed, and colors winked. Some cultivars were local. I counted fourteen Huskies, including three of UCONN Lacrosse. Among other local varieties were Hooligan's, the name referring to a bar in South Eagleville; Watch Hill, Rhode Island, the location of a beach near the university; and several cultivars, their taxonomy in Greek letters, Sigma Chi and Kappa Kappa Gamma among others.

Most caps were imported, however, cultivars fragrant with the names and nicknames of distant schools: Ohio State, University of Oklahoma, Notre Dame, Virginia Tech, Washington State University, Ithaca College, Georgetown, and University of Colorado. Frolicking among the nicknames were Tarheels, Wildcats, Gamecocks, Beavers, Gators, and Jayhawks. Several standard professional varieties also grew atop heads, including, Boston Red Sox, Pittsburgh Steelers, San Francisco Forty-Niners, and Chicago Blackhawks. Although most caps came from commercial haberdasheries, amateurs created hybrids. One girl stitched Jennifer across the disk of her hat in calico letters. A boy sewed a turtle on the petal of his cap; on the disk he wrote Goofy. Although most caps only bloomed for a season or two before they vanished into the mulch of the misplaced, a few caps were perennials. At the end of the third furrow blossomed an ancient cultivar. The flower had once been blue and red, or perhaps orange. Years drained vitality out of the colors, and, resembling blight or the scorch, dots speckled the cap in swatches of yellow and white. Printed on the front of the cap were the words *Fighting Illini.*

Reading the words was difficult. A piece of green tape obscured the final three letters of *Illini.* "How long have you owned the cap?" I said to the student as I leaned over him, trying to read the words on the disk. "I have worn this cap," the student said, "since seventh grade. I wouldn't sell it for anything." "Oh," I said, "you have answered my next question."

For the crank days are infinitely various. Amid the small lurk interest and pleasure. Last week I received a letter from Wellington, New Zealand. Enclosed in the envelope with the letter was a photograph of five puppies, all Jack Russell terriers. On the right side of the picture stood a sturdy puppy named Pickering. Pickering had a brown head; a white body with a puddle of brown on his right hip; then a brown tail, the tip of which appeared to have been dipped in white paint. "I don't know whether you'll accept this as an honor or an insult," my friend Tony wrote. "An honor," I said, practically barking with pleasure. "Crowds have children named after them," I said to Vicki that night at dinner, "but how many people have dogs for namesakes?" Later that night Edward handed me a story he wrote. Entitled "A Day to Remember," the story described a baseball pitcher's first appearance in the Major Leagues. "Spike stood on the dirt mound, warming up in the waning midday sun, his shadow stretching before him. He loved the clap-clap sound of the ball hitting the mitt as it was thrown back and forth. As Spike waited on the mound, he remembered years in the minor leagues: the sweltering heat, swarming flies, the long rides in the musty old buses and the roadside meals." Edward's story did not startle; Spike won the game. For me, though, dog and story made the day one "to Remember." Just as memorable was next morning in my office. At eleven o'clock Ben brought me his latest essay. He handed the essay to me in a blue folder in which he kept notes from the class. Across the front of the folder he wrote in big, black letters, "Nature Writing, English 268W. Mr. Pickmenose."

Not all matters warm the hearts of cranks. Some make them hot under the collar. According to legend the gall bladder in a drowned body bursts after nine days, causing the corpse to rise to the surface of the water. In the bodies of some live cranks gall always bubbles like champagne. "Look at this," Josh said, slapping an article from the *Advance,* the university newsletter, onto my desk. The article described a meeting held at the university and sponsored by the Institute of Violence Reduction. Three hundred people attended the meeting, including police, social workers, and representatives from three Hispanic gangs in Hartford. The article implied that "dialogue and compassion," as Josh put it, would help solve the problem of gang violence. "Kindness to the wolf is cruelty to the lamb," Josh said. "Still," he continued, "the grammarians who organized this meeting are on to something. Rich with high-cholesterol words, English lends itself more readily to subtlety and discussion than to deed. Compassion won't stop violence, but English will. Teach the rabble proper English, and debate will clog their days. After only three grammar lessons gang members will become as muddle-headed as sociologists and forget why they were angry at each other."

Josh occasionally sips the milk of the wild ass. Consequently he brays. Although I often find his criticism of what he dubs "lambent dullness" in poor taste, he is a stimulating crank. Yesterday he returned to my office. He heard that the Alumni Association commissioned a statue of the school mascot, the husky dog. On completion the statue was going to be placed outside the basketball coliseum. "But only one canine," Josh exclaimed. "Do the alumni inhabit an Age of Lead? Have they not heard of the Lady Huskies?" Two statues of equal size, Josh said, had to be forged, one of a dog, the other of a bitch. "For the sake of conventional propriety," he said, "the creatures should stand side by side, or, better, sniff one another's noses. Under no circumstances should they greet one another as common canines greet each other at the pound." If forging a male husky was sexist, gelding the statue was worse. An hermaphrodite would, Josh said, expose participants in athletics to wounding ribaldry. "Adolescent sports persons will suffer permanent psychological damage, leading," Josh assured me, "to a pack of lawsuits and ultimately the bankruptcy of the university." To muzzle the howl of protests, Josh suggested that the husky wear boxer shorts. The pair, he suggested, could be stylish, "the fabric hanging over the dog's backside adorned with the mascots of Connecticut's rivals in the Big East athletic conference: along the right buttock, the eagle of Boston College; over the left haunch, Villanova's wildcat; in between a friar representing Providence College."

Cranks don't discover truths. Because cranks spend hours observing the world, life always seems in motion. Instead of becoming possessed by dogma, cranks collect clutter. Days are various, and when a crank holds a mirror up, say, to Nature, he does not see truth reflected. Consequently insight does not blind him. Change flows across the mirror like mood through an impressionistic painting. Instead of being confined within a frame, vision sweeps outward drawing miscellaneous details into attention, much as a tide strands matter high on a beach.

In March I spent three days in Cedar City, Utah. I made a speech and taught classes at Southern Utah University. I flew from Hartford and left home before Vicki and the children got out of bed. "Vicki," I said as I dressed in the dark, "there is a monstrous snake loose in this room." "Don't take it with you to Utah," Vicki said, flicking open her left eye, "Delta will charge you a fortune for excess baggage." Solomon got things wrong. Not the way of a man with a maid but the talk of a wife to a husband is wonderful. No eagle hung under the clouds above Bradley Airport, and Solomon would have been disappointed. Still, birds bustled about, if not wondrously, at least in ways I noticed. Pigeons blew up from the asphalt then fell dusty onto the roof of the terminal. Starlings sputtered like grit around trucks and baggage carts. A crow flew through the horizon. The bird resembled a zipper, its wings the zipper's teeth, its body the tab, and the flight itself first dividing then sealing the sky into a metallic whole.

The dishes ladled out by daily life are thick with roughage, not entrées that appeal to culinary and intellectual exquisites. Cranks are hardy tren-chermen. Amid the low gastronomic fare of airline meals I always dis-cover crumbs which appeal to my literary taste. On the flight from Hart-ford to Cincinnati Delta served a "Snack," a Biscoff "original speculoos biscuit." Although distributed by The Gourmet Center in San Francisco, the biscuit was a "Lotus product of Belgium." The biscuit was nibble-sized, weighing 6.25 grams, or 3/16 of an ounce. In contrast writing on the wrapper surrounding the biscuit was a mouthful. "All Natural" and containing no tropical oils and no cholesterol, the biscuit was cobbled together, the label informed flying gourmands, from "wheat flour, sugar, partially hydrogenated vegetable oil (contains one or more of soy bean oil, sunflower oil, peanut oil), soy flour, brown sugar, leavening (sodium bicarbonate), salt, spice (cinnamon)." I washed the biscuit down with Minute Maid Orange Juice. Minute Maid, the can informed me, was a division of Coca-Cola Foods, its main office located in Houston, Texas. Printed on the can was a request, followed by a command: "Please Re-cycle" then "Deposit Me."

The snack whetted my appetite for lunchtime reading. Shortly after the plane left Cincinnati, a stewardess handed me a Blimpie sandwich to peruse. Consisting of a roll stuffed with turkey, lettuce, and tomato, the sandwich had been manufactured by Blimpie Subs and Salads in New York City. To season the sandwich, I received a packet of "Blimpie Special Sub Dressing," a blend of distilled vinegar, soybean oil, water, guar gum, xanthan gum, "Calcium Disodium EDTA to protect flavor," and "certified color," red numbers three and forty and blue number one. A side dish of Rocheleau Potato Salad accompanied the Blimpie wrappers.

With its head office in Chicago, Rocheleau was a division of Blue Ridge Farms of Brooklyn, New York. The salad weighed four ounces. Stamped on the label of the plastic pot containing the salad were eight lines of ingredients, the print too small for me to read. I did notice, however, that the salad contained two dollops of artificial color, yellow numbers five and six. Dessert was not a slice of Mott's pizza but a Dutch Treat Brownie. The bar weighed 1.2 ounces. Fantasia Multifoods in Sedalia, Missouri, baked the brownie with, the label assured me, "Hershey's." Topping off the meal was a can of La Croix Pure Sparkling Water, La Croix itself being a division of the Winterbrook Beverage Group in Bellevue, Washington. Seeing me writing through the meal, the man sitting next to me asked what I was doing. On my explaining that at lunch on planes I often used a pencil more than a knife and fork so that I could bake pages for books with, as the Consumer Services Manager from Mott's put it, "kid appeal," my companion gave me his address in Garden City, New York, and asked me to send him a copy of the finished menu. Later when I handed my tray to the stewardess, she said, "you must not have been hungry." "On the contrary," I said, "I found the meal wondrously filling."

Stuffing notebook rather than stomach served me well on the flight from Salt Lake to Cedar City. The plane was small, a Fairchild Metro III, the sort of aircraft in which one bends over like a staple in order to reach one's seat. For an hour the plane yawled through dark clouds above the Wasatch Mountains, the whirling propeller outside my window a gray blur. No snack was served on the flight, and I studied E. A. R. Classic "Plugs," as the wrapper put it, "for Hearing Protection," manufactured by the Cabot Safety Corporation in Indianapolis, Indiana. A half inch in diameter and three-quarters of an inch tall, each plug was yellow and resembled a hunk of bubble gum. "Keep away from infants," the wrapper warned. "These earplugs are non-toxic, but they may interfere with breathing if caught in windpipe." When the aircraft dropped out of the clouds onto the runway at Cedar City, I thought the way of a pilot with a plane wonderful. At Cedar City Solomon would have found marvelous feathered matter. As the plane taxied toward the terminal, a golden eagle pulled himself off the ground and bumped upward into flight.

If a person sucks the "tit" of a sow with piglets, Loppie Groat told me, he will see the wind. When I am on the ground, I watch the wind rush through trees, twirling and cascading, sweeping branches into currents, tossing them aloft, bouncing them in great sprays off boulders of air. Flying, in contrast, gets the wind up in me. In planes I create still pools in which letters function like heavy leaves, blanketing turbulence and keeping fear from slapping me about. I concentrate on reading and rarely talk to people sitting near me. Once on the ground, however, I pitch myself into streams of conversation.

Because a storm delayed planes throughout the West, I did not fly directly back to Hartford. Instead I flew to Boston, waited two and a half hours, then took Business Express to Hartford. The flight from Boston left from gate eleven in Terminal E. People waiting outside gate eleven appeared dull, and I joined a crowd at fifteen. "So you missed me," a large woman said, after her husband smacked her bottom as she walked out of the gangway into the terminal. Another woman sat down across the waiting area from me. In her right hand she carried a pet carrier. "What are you going to put in the carrier?" I asked. The woman was traveling from Louisville to Albany. Her sister-in-law bought a Maine coon cat from a dealer in Albany. "I am picking up the kitten for her," the woman explained. "She paid my expenses." "And how much would that be?" I asked. The flight cost $230, and a motel room in Albany, $53. The woman did not know the price of the cat, but, she said, she thought it "cost a bundle."

"The next time you run an errand for a relative," I advised as the flight to Albany was announced, "find out the cost of the pet and don't let her book you into a cheap motel. Insist on staying in a room that costs at least one hundred and fifty dollars. And," I concluded, as the woman stood and picked up the carrier, "eat extravagantly this evening. Go to a place in which the food is served on silver platters by gigantic Egyptians wearing white robes decorated with golden birds. Treat your palate to peacocks' tongues floating in Blimpié sauce, black caviar La Croix, and truffles à la Rocheleau." "Is there such a place in Albany?" the woman asked. "Absolutely," I answered. "In New England exotic restaurants are as common as barbecue pits in Kentucky."

"Ski Utah," urged license plates in Cedar City, "the Greatest Snow on Earth." "Advertising gruel," Josh said when I mentioned the slogan, "but not so bad as the moronic pap expressed by most states." Josh particularly dislikes the phrase "Virginia is for lovers." "I have motored through every county in Virginia," he told me, "and never have I seen an amorous pair coupling on the right of way, much less disporting themselves against a bridge abutment. Yokels in the northern and western deserts of the state are not known for gallantry. But in the tidewater where the tribes pride themselves on ancestry and aristocratic abandon, I expected to see clots of blue bloods writhing amid asphalt and gravel." Both days and shoulders of roads in Cedar City were cool. Above Main Street mountains rose in red heaps, a lace of sagebrush, juniper, and pinion pine skirting the lower slopes. From peaks snow splattered down, slipping into high canyons like feathers. Behind a rumple of cloud and drizzle, tops of the mountains were often only shadows. I dreaded the return flight to Salt Lake, and I spent much time searching the horizon for creases of light.

The morning after I arrived in Cedar City, I spoke to eight hundred people. Although many were students, a large number were adults living in and around the town. As I arrive at airports well before my flights are scheduled to depart, so I arrive at speeches early. I wander audiences and visit, particularly with older people who also get to engagements early, though I should say that in Cedar City when I appeared at 9:14 for a speech scheduled for eleven o'clock, I was the only person in the auditorium. Later an older woman for whom I found a seat near the front said to me, "there are a lot of Mormons in this room." "Ma'am," I answered, "I don't mean to contradict you, but there is not a single Mormon in the auditorium." "What do you mean?" she answered. "I'm a Mormon, and I know most of these people. They are my neighbors, and all of them are Mormon." "Ma'am," I said, "I know Mormons, too. They come to my house in Connecticut every month. Mormons wear black suits, and there is not one black suit in the room."

During the trip I talked to many students who had been on missions. Most had gone to Central America or New England. "Connecticut isn't God's restored Israel," Josh said when I mentioned my findings about missions. "A person would have more success winding a sundial than he would in saving sinners in Fairfield County. Old Coaly has those folks by the bank accounts." After my talk the audience asked questions. Several people commented on the speech. "If a scientist put your brain into a woodpecker's head," a woman said, "the bird would fly backwards." Not all statements are mysterious. "There ought to be a law against a person outliving his children," my friend David Lee said that evening. "Yes," I answered, and for a minute both of us sat silent, our thoughts on family, our books meaningless scribbles.

In Cedar City I stayed at the El Rey Best Western Motel. At six o'clock each morning I ate breakfast next door at Sullivan's Café. Afterward I walked Main Street. Not many people were about, and most of the words that flowed through the walk came from signs. Still, outside the State Bank of Southern Utah, a man greeted me. "Good morning, Sam," he said. "I forgot your last name, but I heard your talk, and I enjoyed it." Beside us on the sidewalk stood blue plastic barrels, pansies blooming from the tops. Above our heads flashed an illuminated sign. Along with advertising IRA's, the bank wished the boys' and girls' basketball teams from Cedar High "GOOD LUCK AT STATE B-BALL." Just down the street at Holmes Barber Shop two men got haircuts, the clock on the wall reading 8:13. Next door the Chinese Garden served "Chinese and American Food." Atop the sign over the door of the restaurant stood a metal Chinese girl, a red hibiscus in her hair and a dress clinging to her like the skin of a mermaid. While the special at Pizza Factory was key lime pie, the "Big Catch Platter" at J. B.'s Restaurant cost $4.99 and consisted of shrimp, fish, and scallops. Walking through downtown was not easy. Streets were broad, and for old people crossing was difficult. Four lanes ran down Main Street, and on both sides of the street cars angled into curbs to park, making the street six lanes wide.

The problems old people faced were on my mind. A week after returning home from Utah, I flew to Texas. My father's only brother, Coleman, lived in Houston. Coleman and Amanda, his wife, did not have children. Four years ago Amanda died, making me Coleman's last relative.

Coleman was a stranger. I met him a handful of times when I was a child. But I had not seen him for twenty-nine years, and on that last occasion I visited with him for only ten minutes. He and Amanda stopped by Montgomery Bell Academy where I was teaching and talked to me in the school parking lot.

Because Coleman was Father's brother, I tried to keep up with him during the past few years, telephoning him every fortnight when I was in Connecticut, writing him occasionally, mailing him copies of my books, and then on Christmas, sending presents, usually food ordered from catalogues. Although Coleman chatted genially on the telephone, he never wrote me or returned a call. For years Father complained that Coleman neglected their mother. To get Coleman to write Grandma Pickering often took Father several telephone calls and letters. Why Coleman was a loner, I do not know, genes, I suspect, for at times I, too, imagine escaping into silence, not from family, however, but from words, essays that importune and demand to be written, the very writing of which not only makes me seem petty, but also immerses me in a clamorous, often vulgar, world.

This past Christmas Coleman sounded weak, and when he asked me to visit him, I said I would. "We are on this earth to help others," Quintus Tyler told his class in the Male and Female Select School in Carthage. For a moment the class was silent. Then Billie Dinwidder spoke. "That's all well and good, Mr. Tyler," he said, "but what are the others here for?" Quintus could not answer Billie's question. For half a minute he stumbled through the Sermon on the Mount, bruising his shins against alms and good works, trying to describe those treasures which neither moth nor rust can corrupt, things that middle-aged people understand better than twelve-year-olds. Only the bell for the next class saved Quintus from rolling all the way down the Mount and collapsing in an incoherent moral heap. "I'm not going to Texas because Coleman is Daddy's brother," I explained to the children. "He is an old man, and he needs someone. When people need help, other people have to act. After all," I concluded weakly, echoing Quintus, "if we are not here to help others, why are we here?"

I landed in Houston late one Saturday afternoon. At Hobby airport I rented a car. I knew Coleman lived on Terrace Drive, and I telephoned him from the airport and asked directions to his house. "I don't know where I live," he said. "I am too old to know." Houston is huge. I was tired, and finding Coleman's house seemed impossible. Still, I asked if he lived near a park or a lake. He said, "I think Memorial Park is nearby." Dollar Rent-A-Car did not have maps of Houston. A clerk gave me directions to the highway, saying I could purchase a map at a filling station. Reaching the highway took a long time. Shortly after leaving the airport, I noticed the windshield of my car was badly cracked, and so I returned to Dollar. After another clerk recorded the crack on an invoice so that I would not be responsible for replacing the windshield, I started into Houston again. I found a service station and bought a map, not without difficulty because the manager of the station only spoke Spanish. Print on the map was too small for my eyes to decipher, and I could not read the names of streets. Nevertheless I found Memorial Park, a green circuit-breaker hammered into a grid of highways and streets, traffic rushing through them in great electric bursts.

Reaching the park took an hour. Headlights of other cars flickered in the dusk, and I drove slowly in right-hand lanes. Near the park I stopped at a convenience store. The manager was Chinese. She lived an hour from the store and had not heard of Terrace Drive. In the store I tried to read the map again. I failed. On the map streets hung around Memorial Park like bundles of loose wires. I considered checking into a motel and searching for Coleman's house the next morning. Cranks, though, are persistent. Instead, I stood at the door of the store. I asked each customer who entered if he knew the location of Terrace Drive. The fourteenth person not only knew the street, but she found it on the map. The street was only one turn and a quarter of a mile away.

Coleman's house was a ranch shaped like an *L*. At the end of the foot was a two-car garage. Outside the garage sat a 1971 Plymouth. Once yellow, the car resembled a tired custard, dumped from a mold and sagging out of shape and color. Catkins basted the car and, washing into seams, clotted and turned sour. Coleman had not driven the car in three years, and wasps' nests hung from the ceiling in patties. "When the bees leave," Coleman said, "I will drive." The last time he drove he parked in the driveway of a house four lots down the street. The next day George, a man who mowed Coleman's yard and brought him groceries, removed the starter motor.

I stayed six days in Houston. Several times a day I walked around the house. Across the front of the house a hedge of azaleas bloomed pink and purple. In damp along the foundation behind the house grew fans of Venus maidenhair fern. A gray squirrel ran up an oak tree, and a fat rabbit nibbled grass beside a broken bird bath. By a wooden fence lilies peeled into white trumpets. Chameleons hunted about the house, gleaming in the sunlight like veins of emeralds. A green ravine marked the back boundary of the lot. Years ago George's uncle trapped raccoons in the ravine. Properties on Terrace were small, most ranging from a quarter to a half an acre in size. Close to the park, the neighborhood was fashionable. Joggers coursed down Terrace like white corpuscles through veins, and sprawling ranches were being ripped out and replaced by compact townhouses. In 1965 Coleman paid $22,400 for his house, signing a twenty-year mortgage and paying six percent interest. In a shoe box I found a schedule of payments, the last having been made on 18 August, 1985. "I can probably sell this house for twenty-five thousand, so I won't have to worry about money," Coleman said, a statement that made me worry about him.

Inside, the house was tired, a candidate for the bulldozer, not renovation. Next to the garage along the foot of the L was the kitchen. China turned greasy on shelves; doors slipped off cabinets, and roaches bigger than my thumb scurried across the floor. When I stepped on a roach, it snapped like a kernel exploding in a popcorn popper. Boxes of books soiled a breakfast nook. Sides of the boxes bulged and broke, and the books spilled across the floor in dry puddles. Every room in the house contained books, most selections from the Book-of-the-Month-Club. Coleman did not throw books away, and in two rooms I counted twenty-nine telephone directories. From the kitchen a hall led along the base of the L to a dining room, then a living room, and finally a sunken study. Along the hall beyond the kitchen and opposite the dining room was a small addition consisting of a bathroom and bedroom. After the first night I slept in the room, turning a desk and a coffee table at the foot of the bed into work areas as I tried to make sense out of Coleman's finances. Down the leg of the L beyond the study were two bedrooms and a bathroom. Coleman slept in the second bedroom at the end of the house.

The back door was open, and when I walked into the house, I did not know what to expect. Coleman was in bed. "Is that you, buddy?" he said when I called his name. "I had given you up for lost." During my visit he always called me buddy. Never did he address me by my name, simply, I think, because he forgot it. After I had been in Houston for four days, I asked him if any other Pickerings remained on our branch of the family tree. "I've got," he said slowly, "a cousin or a nephew or something. He lives in Connecticut and teaches school, I think." "He teaches," I said. Lights in Coleman's room were off, but the television stayed on night and day, the sound noisy but providing company. Although the picture tube was broken and no image appeared on the television, the machine exuded a silver light that turned objects in the room ghostly. I spent the first night in the room next to that of Coleman. The television was so loud that I slept little. No matter the number of pillows I piled over my head, I heard the soundtracks of movies, most westerns, all featuring gunfights near corrals. Unable to sleep I dressed at four-thirty and explored the house.

When I saw Coleman in bed, I knew he was a Pickering. He lay in the same position as that in which Father slept and as Francis and I now sleep, on his left side, head resting on the upper part of his left arm, the rest of the arm crooked upwards like a post blown askew; right arm pulled into the chest, left leg straight, the right bent across it at a right angle. Coleman slept in his clothes, even wearing a sport coat. He wore slippers with rubber soles. Occasionally he kicked them off, but usually he kept them on in bed. On a bedside table were a broken radio, false teeth in an ashtray, and an empty bag of cookies. Every evening I bought him a bag of Chips Ahoy and a quarter-pound bar of Hershey's dark chocolate. He kept the cookies and candy bar by his bed and nibbled on them throughout the day. George told me not to let him eat chocolate, explaining that chocolate made Coleman's hands shake. Pickerings love chocolate. Every Easter I sent Father seven pounds of chocolates from Munson's, a candy company located in Bolton, Connecticut. At eighty-four Coleman could eat, I decided, as much chocolate as he could wedge into his mouth. At dinner and breakfast his hands shook like branches in a storm, and coffee sloshed out of his cup like rain pouring off magnolia leaves.

Coleman's hair was soft and white. He had not had a haircut in years, and hair hung over his shoulders, making him resemble a celluloid colonel in the Confederate army. Before I left Houston, I took him to a barber shop. Once his hair was cut, he resembled his father. At night I rubbed his back until he dozed. As my hand moved, my thoughts traveled through generations, from Grandfather's strawberry patch in Carthage to my daffodils in the dell in Storrs. "Oh, God," I thought, "don't let me grow old alone. Kill me before I totter into the arms of a stranger." Coleman slept days and nights, getting out of bed only to go to the lavatory or to the kitchen where he snacked on cereal. I asked him many questions, but only rarely did he answer. At Vanderbilt Coleman majored in French, and during the Second World War, Father told me, Coleman managed a bread factory in France. When I asked him what he did during the war, however, Coleman said he could not remember.

He did say that William B. Pickering, my great-grandfather, once ran for the House of Representatives. He ran against Cordell Hull, a next-door neighbor and later Secretary of State. "Grandpa," Coleman said, "was one of the most popular men in Smith County, but Cordell Hull had a rich wife." He also told me that Father had been sent to Kentucky Military Institute, not because the schooling was superior to that in Carthage but "to straighten him up. Samuel read so much he stooped," Coleman said, adding that KMI not only straightened him but also "taught him to cuss." Several times Coleman said that Uncle Nelson Fisher used to pick him up and swing him when he was a boy, always saying, "Coleman Enoch Pickering Brown. His feet fly up and his head hangs down."

Amanda and Coleman ate their meals, breakfasts included, at restaurants. They often ate in One's A Meal, half a mile away on Memorial Drive. Both owned cars, and, neighbors told me, they drove separately to the restaurant "in convoy, Coleman behind Amanda." At the restaurant they parked side by side, ate together, then drove directly home, Coleman again following Amanda. Although Coleman had not been out of the house in months and complained that he wanted to stay in bed, he walked easily, and I rousted him out of the bedroom mornings and evenings and took him to One's A Meal. Because Coleman rarely talked I kept track of what we ate. Every morning he ate pancakes, and I had two eggs sunny side up, patty sausage, toast, grits, and coffee.

At dinner both of us ate hamburgers. I tried to vary the mix, one night having a cheeseburger, another night adding bacon to the cheese, still another night eating the hamburger on toasted pumpernickel. In the evening Houston policemen stopped for coffee and pie. One evening six policemen sat at a table next to us. Occasionally I chatted with them.

"Today," one policeman told me, "people need safety tools. Once a man had to work hard to get possessions. Now he has to fight to keep them." Because people in the country generally kept safety tools handy, burglars, the policeman said, avoided farm houses.

Coleman was blind in one eye, and dark confused him. When I parked in his driveway after dinner, he said, "Whose house is this?" Once out of the car, he felt his way forward toward the house, moving past my car. As soon as he touched his Plymouth, he said, "What is this?" Inside the house, he knew where he was. But until I helped him through the back door, he was lost. Besides jaunts for meals I took Coleman on two trips: to get his hair cut and then before I left Houston to obtain Power of Attorney for myself.

I did not know what I would find in Texas. Moreover my responsibility for Coleman was not clear, at least not to me. After two days in Texas, however, I realized matters could not continue as they had done. I learned that before George began bringing him meals Coleman almost starved. I spent part of a morning walking the neighborhood looking at signs put out by real estate agents. One man handled most of the houses in the area. A neighbor said the man was honest. Moreover he lived nearby and for twenty-five years had sold most of the houses in the area. Before leaving Houston, I put Coleman's house up for sale, not for twenty-five thousand dollars but for considerably more, enough to take care of Coleman for several years. I investigated nursing homes, asking them to mail brochures to Connecticut. I paid bills and rummaged through papers, trying to discover things such as Coleman's Social Security number and the state of his accounts in two banks and the Postal Credit Union. Strangers were helpful. Rules at the Credit Union prohibited giving information even to relatives. After I explained that I lived in Connecticut and described Coleman's situation, a kind woman said she could not release information about accounts, adding, however, that the amount in Coleman's account was between two figures, the numbers she cited being only two hundred dollars apart.

Coleman had less than two thousand dollars in his accounts. For twenty years he worked for the Post Office. Still, the income from his retirement and Social Security was only twelve thousand dollars a year, not enough to maintain him in the house. Delving into Coleman's financial life made me uncomfortable. Because I was executor of and heir to half his property, I felt guilty. Against my will I found myself dreaming of discovering stocks which would pay for the children's years in college. Integrity matters to me. Last Christmas I refused a book from a student. The book cost $9.95. The student left the book on my desk along with a card. Because I did not want to bruise the girl's feelings, I wrote her, explaining why I could not accept the gift. "Your smiling presence in the class," I wrote, "was the best present you could have given me."

Discovering Coleman had little means relieved me. Instead of coveting, I could serve, my actions not soiled by self. Responsibility burdens, and once or twice at night while I searched for information I became melancholy. "Is a person's life paper," I thought, "scraps to be thrown away when a house was sold, erasing existence in an afternoon?" When I felt despondent, I telephoned Vicki and the children. To intrude my mood into their days would have been selfish, so I forced myself to be cheery, in the process brightening the time in Houston. To manage the sale of the house for Coleman, I needed Power of Attorney. I hesitated to obtain it, in part because I did not know how to proceed and in part because I did not want Coleman to think I was manipulating him.

I had not planned the trip to Houston. Before leaving Connecticut I should have gotten the name of a good lawyer from friends in Nashville. I took a copy of Coleman's will with me to Houston, however. Stamped on the will was the name of the lawyer who drew it up. On the fourth day in Texas I telephoned him and asked him to draw up the Power of Attorney. I explained that I needed it the next day. The lawyer did not remember Coleman, but he said he would do it and told me that Coleman and I should be at his office at two o'clock the next afternoon. The cost was $75. During the trip to Houston I paid for groceries and the meals that Coleman and I ate. Not once did Coleman thank me. When I left town, though, he wept. Although I have traveled the world, I don't know my way around financial institutions. Not until I telephoned a bank and learned that I could receive an advance on my charge card was I certain that I would have enough money to pay the lawyer. Seventy-five dollars is a small amount, but small matters nagged me throughout the trip. Before the real estate agent hammered his "For Sale" sign in the front yard, I went to the houses of neighbors and as a courtesy told them what I was doing. I visited one house four times before I found anyone at home.

The lawyers whom I know in Nashville have offices in tall glass and steel buildings, the sides of which flow into corners glittering like silver dollars. The lawyer who arranged Coleman's will was country, not corporate. His office was in a small brick house in an industrial zone. Railway tracks sliced through the area. Modest frame houses leaned together in clumps, almost as if they were defending themselves against the heavy warehouses that pressed upon them, besieging the remnants of neighborhood. The lawyer shared the building with "Live-In Senior Care," run, the man said, by a reputable and dependable woman.

To reach the office, I drove along Washington, the map of Houston in the middle of the steering wheel. Coleman sat in the back. Usually when I drove, he muttered, his comments below hearing, *shit* the only word I could distinguish, breaking from his lips with more vehemence than anything else. Perhaps because I drove in early afternoon, Coleman said more on the trip to the lawyer's office. "You don't know where you are going," he said, then added, "turn around and take me home." "Hell, no," I responded, "I've come fifteen hundred miles to take care of you, and I am damn well going to do it." "You're lost," Coleman said a minute later. "Of course I'm lost," I said. "I don't live in Houston. We will probably never get back to your house."

Forty-three years ago the lawyer had been a fine softball pitcher. In a frame on the wall was a newspaper article describing his pitching two no-hitters, followed by a one-hitter. Gentle and gracious, the man would have been a good partner for Turlow Gutheridge in Carthage. Coleman was too weak to write his name. At the office he placed his left hand on my right wrist, and I signed his name. "Just like I signed Daddy's name when he was sick," Coleman said.

When not driving around Houston, I roamed Coleman's house, not searching for information but pacing, following thoughts as I pondered how to act. Plastic flowers sprayed out of pitchers in every room: foxglove; daisies; philodendron, the leaves catching streams of dust; pink chrysanthemums; dogwood; and peonies sagging and cracking out of texture. Mounds of wax fruit moldered in bowls: grapes and apples, green and red varieties of each; oranges; bananas; pears; and strawberries big as fists. On a sideboard in the dining room a silver service was so tarnished it sank out of sight. Amid the pitchers hunkered a small cup, the size of a big daffodil blossom. Engraved on the side of the cup was "CEP 1912." A diminutive tiger stood on a shelf in a china press and blew a post horn. Beside the tiger sat a lustreware cream pitcher.

Five plates decorated with English country scenes leaned against wire stands. Four massive black horses pulled a coach across the center of one plate. In the background towered a yellowish inn, balconies hanging off it like chins. On another plate two fox hunters leaped a hedge then a ditch. Beside them ran four hounds, one clamoring out of the ditch and resembling a broken bundle, white tissue breaking through brown wrapping paper. Throughout the house blue and white country china stood on stands. Pink roses wound around borders, and in the center of a bowl a cavalier knelt on one knee beside a lady. Once the plates and saucers of Sunday meals, the china was now the stuff of lost family memory. I ran the index finger of my right hand over a small bouquet of yellow flowers on a cream pitcher, in the vain hope that touch could make recollection vital.

A cut-glass chandelier hung over the dining room table, hunks of glass resembling tears. Legs of chairs and tables bowed out then turned down to ball and claw feet. Above a cherry chest hung an octagonal mirror, on either side lithographs of green parrots. Over the mantle in the study was a thin watercolor. A shallow blue stream oozed through a country flatter than a sheet. From the water humidity rose in a silver haze. On a table sat an ashtray made from the bottom of a shell casing. Engraved on the side was "France 1945" and "To Daddy From Coleman," palm trees on each side of the ashtray pushing the words together like bookends. Above the ashtray stood an imitation Tiffany lamp, the body of the lamp as exotic as the palms, three struts bowing inward and up into a triangle joined at the top. At the bottom of each strut was a hoof, fur just above the nail flaring out like leaves. Staring from the top of each strut was a ram's head, the horns twisting like snail shells. Behind the lamp sat a black telephone, the first two digits in the center letters, *u* and *n,* rather than numbers.

In the living room a picture window faced the street. To prevent the window from shattering during a storm, someone had stuck plastic tape over the glass. The tape formed a checkerboard, making the window resemble faded oilcloth. In front of the window sat a mahogany love seat and two mahogany chairs, their backs cut into the shape of urns and the wood so dark they resembled shadows. The love seat and chairs came from Carthage, as did much furniture in the house. In a chest I found a letter written to Coleman by Father on 12 December, 1963, shortly after Grandma Pickering's death. Father and Mother spent a weekend cleaning Grandma's apartment, taking a few items for themselves but leaving most of the furnishings behind for Amanda.

"We probably threw out some stuff which was questionable," Father wrote. "However we spent two days working, and it was quite a job. Couldn't feel that mother's clothes should be sold. I sold the car," Father continued, "to the Dudney's next door for $125. They had been mighty good to mother, as had their dog, Sugar. They wanted it for their boy, Larry. Mother was fond of them and the boys, so I asked what they could pay and just sold it. Could have gotten more, but not much and felt mother would have wanted it that way." The apartment in which Grandma Pickering lived after selling her house in Carthage was small. Coleman's house was much larger. During the summer Vicki and I would drive to Houston, and, I planned, would sell the furniture, even pieces which had been in my family for 150 years. Already my house in Storrs resembled a warehouse, the furnishings of generations piled high in attic and basement.

Coleman's house was a gallery of pictures. In a small plastic frame by Coleman's bed Francis, Edward, and Eliza stood smiling. "He loves your children," a neighbor told me, "and he is so proud of you." The statement made me uneasy, for I knew that in summer I would toss the pictures into the garbage. Throwing away many pictures would be easy, for they were of strangers. From a frame measuring three by four inches, a farm boy stared out of the past into Amanda's bedroom. Gold hung in a scalloped curtain around the boy. The color did not lessen the young man's unease, and he sat stiff and uncomfortable in his best clothes, bunting glued to the edges of his coat, his hands nailed immobile to his knees. In an oval frame a young woman sat before a writing desk, a bowl of roses atop the desk and a quill pen in her right hand. The picture was romantic. The girl herself was a rose, gold encircling her like a wedding band, her head tilted to the left, a loose braid of hair flowing down over her shoulder, her eyes gazing dreamily into the distance.

On the mantelpiece in the living room were family pictures. My grandmother stood beside her two sisters, all three girls dressed in lace, brown hair heaped high upon their heads. While Grandma stared at the camera, her sisters looked to the sides, making them appear weak. "Mother was very bright," Coleman said. In front of Grandmother sat a fourth girl, her face scratched out. What, I wondered, angered Grandmother so much that she defaced the picture? Across the bottom of the photograph curved a banner with the name of the photographer and his place of business stamped upon it, "F. M. Irwin, Lewisburg, Tenn."

In another photograph Father and Coleman sat on a white pony, Father appearing five years old and Coleman three. The picture was taken outside the home of Grandma's sister, Aunt Lula, in South Nashville. In front of the pony stood a boy, six or seven years old. Coleman wore a dark sweater, white leggings, and a stocking cap. Father wore a short coat and a sailor cap with the brim turned down. Stitched to the sleeve of the coat was a patch decorated with the wheel of a boat and three stripes shaped like V's. The other boy, Cousin Jerdan, was dressed in a double-breasted jacket with a velvet collar, on his head a pie-shaped hat, a ribbon encircling it then tied in a bow. Jerdan, Coleman said, "was the smartest boy in Hume-Fogg." At Vanderbilt Jerdan suffered a breakdown and spent much of the rest of his life in mental institutions. One December he disappeared on a farm in Williamson County. Search parties could not find him. A heavy snow fell, and his body was not discovered until one day in early spring when the wind was right.

In a chest I found a battered nine-by-twelve-inch picture that had been colored and varnished. The man in the photograph had red hair. Glued to the back of the picture was a scrap of paper, identifying the man. The paper was torn. All that remained of the writing were the last four letters of Tennessee, the *e* I assume of Carthage followed by a comma, and then the name Pickering. Francis has red hair. Vicki and I have brown hair, and we have often wondered what ancestor bequeathed red hair to Francis. Unfortunately, the picture will not solve the mystery. Old photographs humble, however, showing viewers that they are not free agents but products of heredity, ruddy imprints of dusty ancestors. In another picture taken shortly after Grandma Pickering's marriage, long before Father was born, I saw Father. Grandmother's eyes resembled Father's, and the left side of her mouth turned up in bemusement, an expression that crossed Father's face every day of his life, an expression I now see on Edward's face.

In another picture two teachers and forty-two students stood on brick steps in front of the elementary school in Carthage. The children were young, most appearing under ten. The girls had bangs and wore sack-like dresses made from checkered cloth. Father stood on the third step. He was the best-dressed boy in the photograph. He wore knickers and a coat that looked as if it were made from velvet. Over the shoulder of the coat a white collar spilled out like a ruff. Coleman was not in the photograph. Pictures of Coleman sat on tables throughout the house. I wondered how many to keep. For my children Coleman won't even be a stranger. He will be a shade from the past, a mysterious image fading on a photograph.

On a chest stood two pictures of Coleman, the first taken in 1931 when he was twenty-one, the second in 1943 when he was a captain in the army. In a drawer I found pictures taken when he was a member of the Vanderbilt track team. His legs were slender and bowed, muscle wrapping his calves in sinewy bundles. He looked as if he could run forever. In a box on top of the pictures were medals he won running: three for winning the "Intramural Cross Country" at Vanderbilt, two dated, 1929 and 1930; another for being part of the championship mile relay team at the "Southern Conference Meet"; and the last for being a member of the winning four-mile relay team at the Southern Relays, held at Georgia Tech in 1930. On the front of this last medal a runner handed a baton to a teammate, their arms a diameter stretching across the medal.

In several places in the house were pictures of Amanda and Coleman's wedding, taken in 1939 at West End Methodist Church in Nashville. Coleman wore a double-breasted dark suit, a white carnation in the lapel. In her left hand Amanda carried a bouquet of white clematis, pale orchids hanging down in thin tresses. Because I knew Amanda even less well than Coleman, I won't keep pictures of her. Amanda's students were her family, and from the time she moved into the house on Terrace Drive until her retirement, she kept every note students sent her. Bundles of letters and cards tied together by ribbons filled a score of drawers. The letters were ordinary, the sort of correspondence all teachers receive. Yet they made me sad. Before Coleman's house is sold, I will send the letters, and in a sense Amanda's teaching life, to the dump.

Amanda taught third and fourth grade. Many letters were thank-you notes written in May at the end of the school year. "Dear Mrs. Pickering," Kathy wrote in 1969, "You are the sweetest teacher in the whole school. You have done so many things for us, and you do everything right. I love you more than any teacher in the whole wide world." "I wish you were my teacher all through school," Claire wrote, adding, "P.S. I mean everything I've said." Tina did not want summer vacation to begin, writing, "I wish we had three more months left." "I loved being in your room," Julie wrote. "In third grade I wanted to be in it so much. You have made me feel so good with all the things you taught me in fourth grade." Amanda was popular with children. "You are the nicest teacher I ever had and I don't blame you for getting mad at me," said Roger. I remember little about Amanda except that she was talkative, something to which Alice alluded, writing, "I want to thank you for the wonderful year I've had even though your favorite subject is talking." "People told me when I was in third grade that you were very hard. They said to hope that I don't get you," Debby reported. "Now I'm glad that I got you. You have taught me more than what I'm supposed to know in fourth grade." Vyvianne thanked Amanda for helping her enroll in "Academically Able."

In 1966 Bill's success did not match that of Vyvianne. Nevertheless he was fond of Amanda, and although his family was moving to Australia, he wanted her "awdress." "I will miss you very much and I will still write to you," he declared. "You have teach me very much about oldthing long ago people and some other things. Could you come onday to see me in Australia. I will miss you if you don't." Laura drew a border of pink tulips and blue and orange daisies around her note. "You have been so nice to me," she wrote. "I love you. I have tried to be a good student this year. I hope you appreciate me." As I looked at the flowers blooming around the page, I imagined Laura. She, herself, was a bud, kind words falling over her like spring rain. Although the notes were formulaic, behind them I glimpsed children and then Amanda herself. "To a GREAT teacher," Chris wrote on the envelope containing his note, adding, "From the Smartest kid in class (dumest)." "Thank you for the frog," Scot wrote at the conclusion of his letter, "and please come over and swim sometime and visit him." "Dear Mrs. Pickering," Grace wrote, "I have enjoyed being one of your daughters, and I tried to please you. But the future years have yet to come when I will be a teacher too." Cheryl made a card from a piece of waxed cardboard, nine inches long and six and a half inches wide, removed from the bottom of a flat box of cookies. On the card gold and silver sprinkles swirled through blue paint. Inside Cheryl pasted cardboard letters spelling "I Love You," the first letter of each word green, the other letters yellow.

I have taught for twenty-five years, so long that I don't know the effects of education. Yet as I read the letters, I wanted to believe that Amanda had daughters. I wanted to believe that somewhere in Texas a forty-year-old woman remembered her. Amanda received many letters during summers. After moving to Pennsylvania, Jenni wrote a three-page letter. While the state bird of Pennsylvania was the ruffled grouse, she wrote, the state tree was the hemlock and the state animal the white-tailed deer. At the end of the letter she drew three lines of O's and X's, five O's and five X's on each line. In July, 1971, Rachel sent a card from California. She and her family were "having alot of fun." They had visited Palm Springs and were "getting reddy to go to Sanna Barbara." "I'm sending you a free ticket," Jimmy wrote in July, 1966. "I hope you enjoy it." In the envelope was a green rectangle, three and a half by two inches. Printed on it was "This is a FREE TICKET. It's not good for anything. It's just free." When Amanda's mother died in 1970, students wrote her. "I'm very sorry for your mother's death!" Erin said. "But you've got somebody right here who loves you! You were my favorite teacher and I learned a lot! At least you didn't load us up with homework! Mr. Brown, my teacher, really scares the wits out of you when he bangs the ruler on his desk! You were a really interesting, fun, nice and a loving teacher!"

Scattered through the letters were notes from parents. Kelly missed school on Tuesday, his mother explained, because "he had bands put on his teeth Monday and his mouth was *very* sore." John was late because his sister Missy was sick, and his mother "had to wait for the maid to come." "Preston," his mother wrote, "has a cold and feels bad, so I let him stay at home yesterday. If you think he is too droopy to be at school today, just send him home. I think he probably spread all the germs Monday and might as well attend today, in case of learning something!" "Would you please see if you can help Roger to find his text books. They are not at home," a mother requested. "Does Pamela concentrate in class when you are explaining how to do math?" another parent asked. "Apparently she's not or something. If she's not listening maybe a firmer hand would help from you as from me. Her grades are terrible."

Amanda liked mathematics. "I did the arithmetic teaser to Daddy and he got the trick the first time," Julia reported. "I told him Mrs. Pickering wants to know this! But he replied, 'but Julia I know Math'. I wasn't surprised a bit." "We were all so pleased and excited over Kathy's 'E' in conduct," another parent wrote. "I congratulate you because I know it was your insight and ability that helped made the 'E' possible. If Kathy had learned nothing else in school work this year, the time would have been well-spent." In a drawer was a stack of report cards for the Houston Public Schools, "Kindergarten through Grade Six, 196_–196_." On the card Conduct was divided into six categories: "Disciplines Himself," "Reports Promptly And Willingly," "Is Courteous," "Works And Plays Well With Others," "Respects Property Rights," and "Is Attentive."

Amanda also kept school correspondence. In 1968 she taught at Edgar Allan Poe Elementary School. "Will you please be in charge," the principal asked her on October 15, "while I am at a 3rd grade reading demo. at Montgomery School 8:30–11:30." "This introduces," another note from the principal stated, "Mrs. Cardwell. She is a parent at another school and she will be a teacher next year. She is also a very active member at Bering Memorial Methodist. I have given her permission to visit your class for an hour, 9:00 to 10:00. Thank you." In 1968 seven children in Amanda's class sent a package to South Vietnam, the contents of which were given to a child of a soldier in the South Vietnamese Army. "Your fine friendship packet arrived today," Major Jambeck wrote, "and without being here to see the children, you can't begin to know how happy they are. Your box was given to a child whose father is a private in the 3rd Ranger Group. Every thing in the box brought joy to their faces and their parents were so glad to get the soap and toothbrush, so they can take better care of their children. I am a father of 3 small children who are blessed to live in America and I am very grateful to you. Your kind act makes our job of helping the Vietnamese people to a better life and a life of freedom much easier."

After death only bits of a life remain, flecks of paint peeled from a portrait, never the portrait itself. Splotches cluttered Amanda's chests. A Victorian hairbrush with a purple and yellow iris painted on the back lay at the bottom of a drawer. Folded under the brush was a "Notice of Appointment" for the school year 1965–66. The Houston Independent School District paid Amanda $7,750 for teaching third grade. Amanda chose to receive her salary in twenty-four payments rather than eighteen. Beside the brush lay an emery board four and a half inches long. Printed on the back was "SMOOTH OUT THE ROUGH SPOTS WITH LIFE INSURANCE. National Life and Accident Insurance Co., Nashville, Tenn." In another drawer was a small booklet, *49 Delightful Ways to Enjoy Karo,* "America's Favorite Table Syrup." On the back of the booklet Dr. Allan Roy Dafoe stated, "Karo is the only syrup served to the Dionne Quintuplets. Its dextrose and maltose are ideal carbohydrates for growing children." "KARO," the booklet explained, "gives you smooth, fine-grained and full-flavored desserts." The syrup made "frequent stirring unnecessary" and was "a boon to busy women." The booklet cloyed with desserts, among others, maple custard, greengage cream sherbet, caramel tapioca, grape snow pudding, oatmeal hermits, and chocolate rice parfait. The booklet would have disappointed the marketing staff at Mott's, for not a single recipe used apple sauce.

Amid bundles of letters lay an old postcard, the back crazed and mottled by time. Printed by the Auburn Post Card Company in Auburn, Indiana, the card depicted the Jackson County Courthouse in Gainesboro, Tennessee. The courthouse was a square brick building three stories high, fourteen windows and one door on each side, the door and four windows on the first story, and five windows on both the second and third stories. Above the third story was a pediment decorated with pendants. From the center of the roof rose a clock tower, the time on the clock 10:45. Also in the drawer lay a "Postal Card." Printed on the front were two ovals, the one on the left depicting a bald eagle, wings outspread and a banner curving beneath his beak and reading "E PLURIBUS UNUM." In the oval on the right was a bust of President William McKinley, the dates of his birth and death, 1843 and 1901, printed below. On the card J. T. Anderson, Assistant Cashier at the Bank of Gainesboro, acknowledged receiving two hundred dollars from C. S. Brown of Granville, Tennessee. The card left Gainesboro on February 26, 1903, and arrived in Granville the next day.

In Houston I noticed small things. In a Bible belonging to Miss Lillie Vantrease was a lock of golden brown hair. Fifteen and a half inches long, the lock was woven into a tight braid and had been used as a bookmark. Attempts to separate the spiritual from the commercial never succeed. Also in the Bible were an order form for and envelope addressed to the

Mail Order Department of J. Bacon and Sons, on Market Street in Louisville, Kentucky. According to the form Bacon and Sons had offices in London, Paris, Berlin, and New York, in addition to Louisville. Printed in heavy black type on the bottom of the form was "AGENT FOR DEMOREST SEWING MACHINES, $16.89 FOR MACHINES WORTH $55." Bacon instructed customers who wanted to see samples of cloth, rather than machines, to enclose a two-cent stamp with their request. When writing "it is best," the company suggested, "for a married lady to give her husband's initials."

Money changers feed on old people. George told me that unscrupulous individuals had bilked Coleman out of thousands of dollars. Amid a stack of bank statements was a letter addressed to Coleman from a lottery in Germany. "Dear Mr. Pickering," the letter began, "Surely you have just forgotten to send me your payment for classes 1 & 2 of the running 94 Lottery. Keep in mind, 663,100 prizes of more than 719 Million Deutsch Marks are still to be won." "For the time," the lottery agent concluded, "I have advanced the money for you and your ticket is definitely in the game and plays for your account if I receive the Balance due of DM 328.96 or of US $199.37 not later than Jan. 10, 1994." The letter angered me, and I imagined ordeals to which I would subject the agent, all of which would slowly turn him into a castrato soprano.

I did not create many ordeals. As I sharpened my imagination, the telephone rang. Forest Park Funeral Home buried Amanda. For his part Coleman prepaid his funeral, starting payments on the 24-B Barrington Service in 1981. On the telephone was a woman from Forest Park. "Could I speak to Mr. or Mrs. Pickering?" she said. "Forest Park has counselors in the area who would like to talk to them." Counselor was a euphemism for salesman. "Talking to Mrs. Pickering will be difficult because you buried her four years ago. Still, if you must talk to her," I said, "she is in your graveyard. Dig her up. As for Mr. Pickering, he has already paid you for his funeral, and I doubt that your counselors will be able to convince him to be buried twice."

On top of one of Amanda's chests lay *A Child's Garden of Verses*. Above a skyline of towers decorating the cover of the book floated an inscription written by a child in pencil: "This Belongs to Mrs. Amanda Pickering, Given By: Kathy Haden." On a shelf in Storrs was another edition of Stevenson's poetry, this one published by Charles Scribner's Sons, a present given to me by my parents in 1945 and costing $1.75. I can still recite many of Stevenson's poems. "I should like to rise and go / Where the golden apples grow," I said, as I held Amanda's book. "Where below another sky / Parrot islands anchored lie." Books broke out of boxes and slipped from cases throughout Coleman's house. In the entrance hall books eddied across the floor then gathered against walls forming slippery hurdles. Books jammed the garage, crates piled atop each other sagging in dusty heaps, spider webs drooping between them. Coleman's affairs worried me, and I didn't sleep well, so I read at night. Sleeping was also difficult because the hot water tank beyond the wall to my bedroom was defective. Although large, the tank held little water. Moreover what water it contained cooled rapidly, and the gas heater burst into flame six or seven times an hour. The flame was so powerful that it caused the tank to buckle and thump. The night before I returned to Connecticut I tried to adjust the thermostat. I succeeded only in frightening myself. I worried that I extinguished the pilot light. After I left, gas, I imagined, would blow the house and Coleman to heaven. Then police would accuse me of murdering my uncle in order to sell his property.

During nights I read a shelf of books: an omnibus volume containing three mysteries by Josephine Tey, all of which I read before but which were hazy in memory early in the morning; Christopher Morely's *Parnassus on Wheels,* a comic novel describing the life of a bookseller who traveled in a horse-drawn wagon; Eric Ambler's thriller *The Light of Day;* and *A Moveable Feast,* Ernest Hemingway's memoir of the rich literary time he spent in Paris in the 1920s. Never have I spent time around writers, and in the quiet dark, my life seemed sterile, as musty as Coleman's house. People who read, however, are not slaves of mood. Changing books changes attitudes. Almost as soon as I put *A Moveable Feast* back on a shelf, I began *We Die Alone,* a Book-of-the-Month-Club selection in 1955. The book described the fate of "Norwegian saboteurs" who sailed from Britain to Norway during the Second World War in order to destroy a German airfield. Betrayed by a countryman, eleven men died. Two months later, the single survivor reached Sweden, carried across the border by Lapps, having endured being buried for a week under four feet of snow and amputating nine of his toes, among other trials.

In the living room I found several books from Carthage. My great-grandfather William B. Pickering owned *Guide to the Royal Arch Chap-*

ter: A Complete Monitor for Royal Arch Masonry. He marked several passages in the book, all the selections prayers. "Make us to be as living stones," one prayer implored, "tried and accepted of thee, to be built up in that spiritual building, that house not made with hands, eternal in the heavens." On the title page of *The Last of the Mohicans* published by Macmillan in 1919, Father wrote "*S. F. P.* 1st Year High School. November 7, 1921." Father gave the book to Coleman who started reading it, Coleman wrote, on January 16, 1924. In margins throughout the book Coleman wrote his nicknames in red ink: Colie, Little Pick, and Kildee, Jr. On page 381 he wrote "Little Kildee an' everything!"

After the death of his first wife, my great-grandfather married Etta Haynie, or Cousin Etta as she was known. In the living room was a book she owned before she married, *Father Ryan's Poems.* Inside the front cover she wrote "Miss Etta Haynie," the tops of the letters swirling up and turning over like small waves along a placid seashore. Opposite the title page was a print of Abram J. Ryan. He was short and stocky and wore a dark ecclesiastical robe. His right hand rested on the back of a chair while his left pressed into his haunch, elbow akimbo and a white handkerchief hanging down from his sleeve like the corner of a sheet. His face resembled a muffin, and shreds of hair hung doughy to his shoulders. Published in Baltimore in 1880, the collection of Ryan's verse was 348 pages long. I read the poems. "Yes, give me the land where the ruins are spread, / And the living tread light on the hearts of the dead," Ryan wrote in "A Land Without Ruins," explaining in a head note that "a land without ruins" was "a land without memories."

Ryan was once famous, the poet of the Confederacy, "whose spirit," it was said, "shall keep watch over the Stars and Bars until the morning of the Resurrection." A Vincentian Father who taught at Niagara University in Niagara Falls, New York, then later at the diocesan seminary at Cape Girardeau, Missouri, Ryan joined the "Confederate service as a freelance chaplain" in 1862. "Until the Conquered Banner was furled at Gettysburg," Ryan "shrived the dying on the battlefield and carried wounded to safety." His contemporaries said that "of himself he had no thought and of death he had no fear." After the war he served as a priest throughout the South, in Biloxi, Nashville, Knoxville, Clarksville, Macon, and Mobile. He made frequent lecture tours, donating fees to "victims of recurrent plagues" and to the widows and orphans of Confederate soldiers. When smallpox erupted in Gratiot Prison in New Orleans and the chaplain decamped, Ryan was the only divine who ministered to the sick.

In contrast to a life quick with incident, Ryan's poetry was slow and melancholy. Suns set in the west. Vesper bells rang. Nights were starless, and valleys, shadowed. Shrouds of grass covered graves, and icicles of woe hung in sorrow's vale. Despite the clouds that lowered over Ryan's lines, the verse was popular, and "The Conquered Banner" and "The Sword of Robert E. Lee," Richard Purcell declared, "were long sung in households and schools of the Southland." For my children born in Connecticut the Civil War has vanished from history. In contrast the Civil War was the central historical event of my childhood. I had not thought about the war in years, however, and as I looked at pictures of Coleman to make a stranger vital so I read Ryan's *Poems* in hopes of awakening memory. I did not succeed. Family and time have changed me, and the war poetry had little appeal. Instead I enjoyed Ryan's lyricism. "Song of the River" began gently. "A River went singing, adown to the sea, / A-singing-low-singing-/ And the dim rippling river said softly to me, / 'I'm bringing, a-bringing-/ While floating along-/ A beautiful song'." In "Life" a mother died when her son was young, and Ryan wrote: "Her humble grave was gently made / Where roses bloomed in Summer's glow; / The wild birds sang where her heart was laid, / And her boy laughed sweet and low."

In the drawers lurked the stuff of my identity. In a chest I found two weekly newspapers, the first the *Williamson County News* published in Franklin, Tennessee, on Thursday, February 11, 1915, the second the *Carthage Courier* published in Carthage on Friday, but also dated February 11, 1915. In the papers were obituaries for Grandma Pickering's sister, Mary Innis Griffin, who died in Cape Girardeau, Missouri. "NOBLE WOMAN CALLED HOME," declared the headline in the Williamson County paper. The obituary described family, in the process mentioning the members for whom Coleman was named. Born in 1876, Mary Innis was a daughter of the "late Daniel and Nancy Brown Griffin." Daniel Griffin was a rounder and was stabbed to death. "When a child she went with her widowed mother," the article stated, "to live with her uncle Coley Brown, in the Sixth district of this county, where she grew to young womanhood, later going to Nashville to reside." In 1901 she married a doctor and later moved to Missouri. Among the relatives surviving her were two uncles, Coley Brown of Belleview and Enoch Brown of Franklin. "She was an exceptionally bright and attractive young woman," the article stated, "and her early death is greatly deplored. Truly it could be well said of her, 'She looketh well to the ways of her household, and eateth not the bread of idleness. Her children arise up and call her blessed; her husband also and he praiseth her'. For it was in the home she shone the brightest and will be missed the most."

I read the papers closely. The *News* was eight pages long, four columns to a page, each page measuring eleven by sixteen inches. A year's subscription cost a dollar. Headlines on the front page described sensational happenings: BIG FIRE FOR SPRING HILL, FATALLY KICKED BY A MULE, ACCIDENTALLY SHOOTS LITTLE BROTHER, and TEN YOUNG LADIES PEPPERED WITH SHOT. "In the Cow Creek locality, near Beattyville, Ky," the article referring to this last headline recounted, "ten young ladies were peppered with shot Saturday night. The daughter of a man named Macintosh had been married and the young ladies had arrived to shower congratulations and bestow presents. Hearing animated conversation near the house, supposed to be a charivari party, the old man emptied both barrels of a shotgun in the direction of the voices, and screams followed. Macintosh was jailed."

The *News* printed little national or international news. "The sailing of the Cunard line steamer Lusitania under the American flag for the purpose of avoiding being torpedoed by German submarines is the occasion of a great deal of talk here," began a report from Washington. "The captain of the Lusitania did only what any other commander would have done if he had reason to fear a hostile warship, particularly a submarine," the report declared, "though his choice of the American flag was not regarded as particularly clever, as the whole shipping world knows there are no such giant vessels as the Lusitania running under the American flag." In May the Germans sank the *Lusitania* as she approached the Irish coast after sailing from New York. Twelve hundred people died. From the eastern front the Russians reported that the Germans were withdrawing to a position west of Lodz. The retirement, Petrograd claimed, was "the first stage of a general retreat from Poland." The report was optimistic. By November 1915, the Germans had taken all of Poland and had captured Pinsk in the Ukraine and were threatening Minsk in White Russia. In December 1917, Russia retired from the war.

The paper printed some national news under the heading "Brief Dispatches." Lester H. Kennedy, president of the Mound City Butterine Company in St. Louis, a dispatch noted, had been "indicted for coloring oleomargarine." "Members of the Christian Endeavor Society of the Viroqua (Wis.) Congregational Church will install bowling alleys and shuffle boards in the basement of the church in hopes of increasing the attendance," another dispatch recounted. From South Bend, Indiana, came the announcement that preparations for the "entertainment of the annual convention of the Indiana Laundry Owners' association" were well "under way."

I like towns more than cities, and local doings interest me more than national. From Beachville came the report that "Little Miss Sarah Spencer has been suffering with tonsillitis." In Franklin "the Embroidery Club met Tuesday with Mrs. Daniels, who has rooms with Miss Florence Napier on Third Avenue." From Antioch came news of the death of Uncle Ben Collins. "The old stoop-shouldered man who has for the past thirty years met every passenger train" passing through Antioch was dead, the article stated, "and one of the unique landmarks that greeted the eye of the southern traveler has been removed." Uncle Ben, who was sixty-four years old, the article declared, "never tired of waiting for the train that was to bring his mother back to him." He "passed quietly away" at the home of his sister Mrs. Annie Smith. "He had been sick but one day with pneumonia."

"The majority of travelers and trainmen, to whom Uncle Ben waved his cheery greeting as the fast express train sped by," the article explained, "believed his whim for watching every train due to a promise his mother made to him when he was a child. She went away on a journey, tradition has it, and promised her son to return the next day. The next day came, but no mother, and the day after that. His mother, according to the story, was killed in a wreck. Time went on and the months stretched into years and the years into decades. Uncle Ben never missed being at the side of the railroad tracks when the trains came, unless he was unavoidably detained. Daily disappointments did not discourage him, however, and he held firm to the belief that his mother was coming back—because she told him she would." Fiction expanded Uncle Ben's life. Truth shrank it. Relatives explained his watching trains mundanely. Ben, they said, never recovered from a brain fever that struck him down in childhood. As a result, his actions resembled "those of a 5 year-old child." Ben, the article concluded, was "not only known to the regular transients who pass Antioch frequently but his face was familiar to those who passed that way once in five years. There was something about his expression not easily forgotten."

The *Courier* was only four pages, but each page measured sixteen by twenty-two and a half inches. Since my grandmother lived in Carthage, Mary Griffin's obituary appeared on the front page. The paper reported several other deaths. "POPULAR YOUNG LADY HAS PASSED TO HER REWARD," stated one headline. Carthage, the article related, "was shadowed with a cloud of sadness last Sunday afternoon about 1 o'clock when it was announced that Miss Bessie Day, one of the town's most popular young ladies, had succumbed to her lingering illness of tuberculosis. Miss Day was only twenty-three." "For a long time," the paper declared, "she was a very efficient operator in the Cumberland Telephone office and through her kindness and gentle disposition in this position she won a host of friends not only in Carthage but throughout the county."

In Nashville Mrs. Bettie Allgier Fitzpatrick died in a sanitarium, where, the *Courier* recounted, "she had been carried hoping against hope that she might be benefited, but her frail body was too weak to withstand the storm." "A pure, unassuming gentlewoman," she "died as she had lived, a quiet, peaceful death and her going," the obituary said, was "only the ending of one more pure Christian life." Several people died in communities around Carthage. "The grim reaper of death," reported a correspondent, has visited Brush Creek, "taking for its victim Mrs. Crook, the devoted wife of Tillman Crook." "We are very sorry to report that the death angel has again visited our community," the correspondent from Horseshoe Bend began her column.

The death angel blazed the way for commerce. On the second page of the *Courier* was an advertisement for J. P. Carter, a funeral director in Rome, Tennessee. Carter's advertisement measured three and a half by four and a half inches. Across the top of the advertisement rolled a horse-drawn hearse. "No trips too long, too cold or too hot," Carter declared. "Coffins, Caskets, Robes, Burial Suits from the cheapest to the best. Quar-

ter-sawed Oak Caskets, Metallic Caskets, burglar-proof steel vaults, Cabi-
net-finished outside boxes carried in stock for ready use." "In fact everything to care for the dead," Carter assured readers, adding, "I have a branch
house at R. A. Waggoner's in South Carthage and can have my new funeral car there within 2 hours. I have uptodate funeral cars, one for white
and one for colored, both rubber-tired."

All the people who died during the previous week in Smith County
seemed to have been women. For those women who hoped to delay traveling in Mr. Carter's new car, Cardui advertised its "WOMAN'S TONIC."
"Before I began to use Cardui," Mrs. Sylvania Woods of Clifton Mills,
Kentucky, testified, "my back and head would hurt so bad, I thought the
pain would kill me. I was hardly able to do any of my housework. After
taking three bottles of Cardui, I began to feel like a new woman. I soon
gained 35 pounds, and now, I do all my own housework, as well as run a
big water mill." In contrast to advertisements directed toward people nervous about the agricultural doings of the grim reaper, W. H. Davis, a
nurseryman in Smithville, said he wanted "live wire fruit agents" to "sell
our 'Model Home Orchards,' and all other kinds of fruits, vines, shrub-
beries, ornamentals, trees, etc." In Brush Creek the reaper ignored commerce. "Thos. Ferrell, traveling salesman," the correspondent for the community reported, "was here last week shaking hands with our merchants
and taking orders for a nice bill of groceries." My grandfather was also
shaking hands in Brush Creek. "Sam Pickering of Carthage," the correspondent also reported, "agent for the Home Insurance Co., was here
last week writing insurance."

Houston was so big and the traffic so heavy that I did not like leaving
Coleman's house. Accounts of matters in and around Carthage appealed
to me, smacking of slower, less-crowded times. The correspondent from
Sullivan's Bend wrote only a paragraph, but the paragraph was rich with
life. "We are having a few days of sunshine and the farmers are making
good use of them," the correspondent wrote. "Mrs. Arthur Rogers is quite
sick at this writing. Henry Grisham sold a nice buggie horse to Andrew
Ford for $125. R. D. Overstreet was here Saturday buying corn. Rev. L.
B. Dickens of Maggart who has been confined to his room for some
time on account of serious illness is not expected to recover. J. B.
Overstreet of Macon county is visiting his daughter, Mrs. Frank Henry.
Mrs. John Russell is confined to her room this week with lagrippe. L. R.

Boulton purchased a colt from Roosevelt Overstreet, paying $75. S. N. Thackston was in Nashville the past week."

The first item on the editorial page was a maxim, "it's a long way from the flour barrel to the biscuit pan." Next came a complaint that the clock atop the courthouse in Gainesboro did not strike "with due regularity." In Smith County tobacco was a big crop, and a discussion of tobacco prices followed next. Unlike breadstuffs tobacco was a luxury, and the war in Europe hurt exports. Those "in charge of the Upper Cumberland Loose Leaf Warehouse Company," the editorial assured readers, "are men of good judgment and experience and are doing everything in their power to establish for Carthage and themselves a reputation for honest and fair dealings."

The last editorial praised the energy of the new county school superintendent, Professor F. E. Huffines. Professor Huffines had just returned to Carthage from a tour of schools, and the *Courier* published his report on the front page. The school at Elmwood, he noted, had an enrollment of 137 students. At his visit a goodly number were present "notwithstanding high water and deep mud." The principal, Professor Neal, was a graduate of Lincoln Memorial College and was "full of enthusiasm." Elmwood was a fine community, the superintendent stated, and every man was "proud of the school." Every seat in Professor D. M. Johnson's class in Monoville was occupied while Johnson's assistant "Prof. Sam Key had the primary students 'sardined' in his room." Huffines's next stop was the Central Point School, "a one-room building in charge of Prof. W. W. Taylor." "Prof. Taylor," Huffines wrote, "is a promising young teacher and great things are expected of him. He has quite a number of wide-awake young men in school." Many students attended Piper's School who had not attended class for a long time. Because the teacher, Professor Calvin Gregory, was also a preacher, Huffines said, "I naturally expected to find a well-ordered school, and I was not disappointed." At Pleasant Shade every student knew his place, and all had "certainly learned to work." With fifty pupils Mace's Hill was the largest one-teacher school. Professor G. W. Goad, Huffines wrote, "is my oldest teacher, having been in harness for 31 years. All these years have been spent within a few miles of where he now is, which speaks volumes for a teacher. I found that these 31 years have not been wasted for he knows exactly how to drive a fact home, even to an unwilling student."

All was not work in Smith County, however. At Gordonsville, the Junior and Senior basketball teams played games against visitors from Elmwood. While Elmwood won the Junior game 9 to 7, Gordonsville won the Senior game 7 to 4. Outlined with black on the front page was an account of the meeting of the Get Together Club. Seventeen members spent "a very pleasant hour in the dining room of the Chapman Hotel." At six o'clock Mrs. Chapman served "a most excellent" dinner. Over dinner the members decided to invite ladies to the next gathering. "Those in charge of the function at once began arranging and executing plans of a very interesting nature. There are to be many unusual details and the occasion promises to be the greatest social event of the year." The article mentioned "charming features" of the program. W. E. Myer was slated to discuss "object of the meetings." L. B. Flippen was in charge of "Ladies and Flowers." Miss Ethel Fisher was going to read, and Mrs. J. M. Gardenhire was asked to sing. At the end of the meeting J. M. Cox would open the "Chestnut Burr" after which "The Crowd" would sing the Doxology. Like the burr some items on the program were mysterious, being listed under topics such as Law, Love, and Luck. Grandfather Pickering was scheduled to present "His Western Experience," probably an account of time spent in Cape Girardeau.

My flight left Hobby Airport for Dallas at seven-thirty in the morning. Coleman did not own a clock with a working alarm. Nervous that I would sleep late and miss the flight, I stayed awake all night. Because traffic was bad in Houston and I worried about getting lost while driving to the airport, I decided to leave early. As a result I left Coleman's house at three o'clock in the morning. I arrived at the airport at 3:25. I regretted leaving Coleman. He was no longer a stranger. Several times I walked along the corridor to his room and, standing in the glow of the television, looked at him curled in the bed. Before telling him good-bye, I rubbed his back. "You take care, Uncle Coleman," I said, a catch in my voice. "Vicki and I will come back this summer." "All right, old buddy," he said. "I will miss you. Come back soon."

I was the first passenger to arrive at the airport. When I walked through the door, a cleaning man stared at me, wondering, I guess, why a sane person would arrive so early. Later, I was the first person at the counter of American Airlines. The clerk said I could take an earlier flight to Dallas, one leaving at 6:22. Hobby was small, and so I took the flight in hopes of buying a croissant and a good cup of coffee in Dallas. Almost as soon as I changed flights, I began worrying. Was I tempting fate? I wondered. Suppose the new flight crashed? On the other hand, I thought, suppose my original flight was doomed, and changing planes saved my life? Once my plane landed in Dallas, I imagined the story I would tell if the later plane crashed. Such thoughts made me feel guilty, and I pushed the subject out of mind and searched for coffee and a croissant.

As soon as I reached my seat on the flight from Dallas to Hartford, I smelled insecticide. A friend told me the climate in Houston resembled that of Calcutta, and for a moment I imagined that the airline had sprayed the plane to eradicate insects, probably fire ants. Then I looked at the woman sitting next to me. She wore a denim jacket. Sewed on it were patches celebrating bass fishing tournaments. The woman spent the morning fishing. To keep mosquitoes away, she bathed in bug spray. The aroma was so strong that I turned my head toward the aisle, at the same time elevating my nostrils in hopes that air streaming down from the nozzle in the ceiling would be fresh. "You flew to Hartford with that big nose hovering over the aisle?" Vicki said. "It didn't take you long to return to form. Here is a welcome home present." She handed me a piece of waxed cardboard, a sleeve which contained six 3.9-ounce tubs of Mott's Apple Sauce. Printed on the cardboard was a recipe for and a picture of Mott's Snake Pit. "Mix Mott's apple sauce with finely crushed graham crackers," the recipe instructed. Next "mix in gummy worms to form a snake pit." Atop a small tub curled six worms. Half of each worm's body was red. The other halves varied in color, three orange, one green, and two translucent, all the worms, however, resembling leeches who had just washed apple sauce down their gullets with a belt of blood. "You're sure to get giggly," the recipe stated, "when you try this wiggly treat." "Look," I said, "*gummy* is spelled with a *y*. On the recipe for Dessert Pizza *gummie* was spelled with an *ie*. Such inconsistency demands a letter."

there have
been changes

In March, Helen, a friend from childhood, wrote from Nashville. In her letter she described the fortunes of mutual acquaintances. "Matt," she wrote, "is hanging in there, but there have been changes." Once time seemed a still pool, years sifting through it without a ripple. Now time resembles a hard wind winnowing days, not only separating the vital from the infirm, but bending the hardy, exposing roots, drying and pulling people from the earth. In April two members of the English Department retired, and I attended a party in their honor at a friend's house. Midway through the evening the department gathered in the living room, and one of the men read a passage from Henry James's novel *The Spoils of Poynton.* Immediately afterward the second man read the concluding section of "Little Gidding" from T. S. Eliot's poem *Four Quartets.* "We shall not cease from exploration," the man read, "And the end of all our exploring / Will be to arrive where we started / And know the place for the first time." "Wrong," I thought. Many of my friends no longer had energy enough for future exploration. Just clinging to the present sapped their strength. "And all shall be well," Eliot declared, envisioning a golden eternity, ignoring people curled in their beds like nuts, not hearing the mewing of the aged but imagining the trumpets of the heavenly host, the voices of seraphim and cherubim rising like roses. "Good Lord, deliver us," I muttered, quoting the Litany.

I heard only snatches of "Little Gidding." Instead of standing in the living room, I sat on steps in the hall. In my hand I held a brandy snifter. In the bottom was a puddle of flat soda water. I held the glass in my right hand. My left arm lay crooked in my lap. Three weeks earlier I gave blood. The man who drew the blood was inexperienced. Instead of jamming the needle cleanly into my arm, he delicately embroidered my vein, causing the needle to stitch in and out. After I gave blood, the head nurse slapped an ice pack on my arm. Nevertheless blood seeped under the skin down to my wrist, drying brown and caked like a mud flat. Every time I straightened my arm, the mud peeled and cracked then shred into tingling, burning flakes.

Over my left knee my trousers bulged. In January I had a bicycle wreck. At six-thirty one morning as I rode to the gymnasium, a delivery truck pulled out of a dormitory driveway in front of me. The morning was rainy, and I held an umbrella above my head in my left hand. With my right hand I steered the bicycle and grasped the lever for the front brakes. Because the umbrella occupied my left hand, I could not apply the rear brakes. When the truck suddenly blocked the road, I slammed on the front brakes. The back wheel of the bicycle pitched upward, and I flew over the handlebars, landing on the road in the middle of the umbrella with a heavy clattering. Embarrassed by the fall, I ignored a wracking pain in my knee and, after extracting myself from the umbrella, hurried on to the gymnasium. Six months have passed since the accident, and, filled with water, my knee resembles an over-ripe cantaloupe. I tell people that my hormones have gone haywire and I am growing a bosom on my knee, a statement that embarrasses the children. In contrast some of the older faculty at the university find the knee fetching. When I walk about in shorts, the dollop of flesh is perky and jiggles invitingly. Twice I have noticed emeritus professors gazing at my knee, embers of affection glowing behind their eyes. The swelling has not hampered me. Indeed I recommend early morning bicycle crashes to all Christians. Because I have a built-in cushion, I am able to kneel in comfort whenever the Spirit moves me.

Last week my friend Richard wrote from Florida. Richard's father is ninety-two and has begun to slip out of lucidity. Still, Richard noted,

"Father has clairvoyant moments. At a family lunch he said the blessing. 'Give us the information we need,' he prayed, 'and the courage we want to face what we have to face'." After swimming each morning I ride to the Cup of Sun and visit with friends. Three mornings a week an older woman drives over from Tolland. She eats a muffin, drinks one cup of coffee, and then walks around the campus because, as she says, "the flowers are pretty, and I don't know how many more springs I have left to look at them." Last fall the woman had both knees replaced. Occasionally I walk with her. We talk about family. Her only child, a boy, died many years ago of leukemia. "My husband and I tried for nine years to have a baby," she said, "and when he died, it hurt so much." The woman is more lucid than Richard's father, but occasionally she, too, dozes. The day before Easter she said to me, "have a nice Thanksgiving, and don't eat too much pizza."

Actually I am a bit dozy myself. In May I fell asleep during the university commencement, awakening near the end when the chairman of the board of trustees spoke. The man asked members of the audience who had supported the graduates to stand, "parents," he said, "grandparents, husbands, wives, and significant others." "Significant others, surely not!" exclaimed Nina, a lively member of the history department sitting in the row behind me. "Half the bearded boys on this faculty will have to stand." "Alas," I said, turning around to face Nina, "twenty years ago the faculty would have risen stout-hearted like Lazarus. But there have been changes. If an ear of sweet corn fell onto their plates, not one of the toothless caterpillars in this nest could manage a nibble."

"White bucks with pink rubber soles," John said to me in the English Department last week. "They were shoes." John wore white bucks to the homecoming football game when he was in high school. His date was the homecoming queen. During half-time he drove her around the field in a new red Oldsmobile convertible. "Life doesn't get any better than that," he said. "No, it certainly does not," I answered, wondering what T. S. Eliot would say, doubting that he ever drove a convertible, much less one with a beauty queen perched atop the back seat shining like an ice cream cone.

Domestic change is cyclical, and wifely. Four years ago over my protest, Vicki bought a dachshund from a pet store. House-breaking "Henry" was difficult, and nine months later Vicki gave him to the mailman. One afternoon late in February just as green seeped into days, Vicki said she "wouldn't mind owning a Jack Russell terrier." Dark mood suddenly blew over Horsebarn Hill. "Jack Russells are the most difficult dogs in the world to housebreak," I said. "Don't think about getting a puppy before talking to me. Remember Henry." "Of course," Vicki said. "Henry was a disaster, and I will never buy a dog without discussing things with you first." Three weeks later I flew to Houston to visit an aged uncle. Before my plane was on the ground in Texas, Vicki had bought a Jack Russell. My uncle's affairs were confused, and the trip exhausted me. Six nights later, the evening before I returned to Connecticut, I telephoned Vicki. "Eliza has something to tell you," Vicki said. "Daddy," Eliza gushed, "we have a surprise here that will cheer you up." "Oh, shit," I said as I put the telephone down.

Penny weighed two and a half pounds. Except for a black spot the size of a nickel on her right ear, she was white. Her eyes resembled two shiny black marbles and her tail, a stubby paddle, always rowing the air. When I walked into the kitchen, I stumbled over a blue bucket. In it sat a roll of absorbent paper towels and a plastic bottle containing a quart of Nature's Miracle "Stain & Odor Remover." A piece of cardboard sealed the kitchen off from the dining room. Spread on the floor by the back door was the financial section of the *Hartford Courant*. Silently I slipped into the familiar role of dog-poop man. At three o'clock at night while Penny bounced about trying to lick my face, I sloshed Nature's Miracle across the linoleum. The comfortable lemon fragrance awakened dormant associations. Almost without thought I found myself outdoors at dawn. While Vicki and the children slept, I followed Penny as she pranced across the damp lawn. "Do your business," I implored repeatedly. Although not responses to prayers but to a puppy's sniffing blades of grass, my words were as fervent as the supplications in the Litany. When Penny obeyed my exhortations, "good dog" rose from my lips in thanks.

This spring domestic changes stemmed as much from the feminine as from the wifely. At the beginning of April Eliza started catching red-backed salamanders. She converted a plastic tub that once held two pounds of Stop & Shop Plain Nonfat Yogurt into a nest, lining the bottom with moss, oak leaves, and a layered gabbro rock, this last removed from the beach below our farm in Beaver River, Nova Scotia, and brought home by Francis six years ago. Cleaning up after Penny was tiring, and I did not want to forage for salamander food. Consequently I encouraged Eliza to keep salamanders for only a night. Each morning before boarding the school bus, Eliza freed her salamander in the woods. After returning from school in the afternoon, she caught another salamander. Eliza named all the salamanders Lady Macbeth, differentiating between them by adding Roman numerals after the name. Lady Macbeth XIV was Eliza's last salamander. One morning after heeding my pleas and attending to business, Penny wandered into the study and crawled under the sofa. She reappeared with what seemed a length of dark twine in her mouth. When the twine wiggled, I realized Lady Macbeth had escaped the nest, or throne, as Eliza called it. I rescued Lady Macbeth. She was in good shape, having lost only a sliver of tail, and when I put her under a mound of leaves in the backyard, she twisted away swiftly.

Much as the failure to train Henry did not deter Vicki from buying Penny, so Lady Macbeth's near-death experience did not stop Eliza from catching animals. After I turned Lady Macbeth loose, Eliza tossed the throne under the forsythia in the side yard. For a week the tub remained empty. Then one afternoon Eliza said, "Daddy, I want a tadpole." Shortly afterward Eliza caught King Tut in the creek behind the high school baseball field. The King has thrived, his tail becoming legs, not a snack for Penny. Soon Eliza must free him. She won't miss him, however, for she is now trying to convert Dusty, the hamster she received for Christmas, from a nocturnal to a daytime creature. To this end she wakes him throughout the day. Whenever one of her friends visits, Eliza takes Dusty outside and lets him poke about in the grass. In comparison to Penny, Dusty is a slow learner and has not formed acceptable lavatory habits. Four days ago after Sarah put him down her shirt, Dusty scampered about, causing giggles until he descended into Sarah's trousers and urinated. "I can hear the urologist," Vicki said after outfitting Sarah in a pair of Eliza's shorts. "'What an unusual case! The ailment is quite common in rodents, but this is the first time I've seen it in the urinary tract of a human'."

Some people attach English names to houses: Rokeby, Abbottsford, or Northumberland. After Penny took up residence, I called our house The Kennel. In April I changed the name to The Shelter. No longer do I think the addition of animals to the household solely the result of wifely or feminine inclination. Spring is the season of the animal. One Saturday morning in April I went to the compost pile in the woods. In my left hand I carried a sack of rinds, in my right a shovel. Penny and George accompanied me. As soon as George rounded the lilacs beside the garage, he bolted across the backyard. At the foot of a big oak he tumbled, flinging something hairy into the air. I hurried over. A young squirrel lay on the ground, its eyes glazed and half its tail bitten off. Gingerly I scooped the squirrel up with the shovel. I lined a cardboard box with newspaper, and after dipping the bloody tip of the animal's tail into Mercurochrome, I wrapped him in two towels and laid him in the box. The animal was in shock and did not stir for ninety minutes. When he moved, he dragged his left hind leg, and I named him Tiny Tim after the crippled boy in Charles Dickens's "A Christmas Carol."

Vicki's interest in animals did not extend to rodents. She and the children spent the morning shopping for raincoats. When I showed Tiny Tim to her, rain had started falling. "You should treat the squirrel the way the ancient Greeks treated lame offspring," she said. "Call him Oedipus and expose him. Stick him into a puddle in the woods. He will disappear and won't bother us." "That it may please thee to defend, and provide for, fatherless children, and widows, and all who are desolate and oppressed, even down to the scampering creations," I said, emending the Litany to include Tiny Tim.

That afternoon I drove to East Brook Mall. At Puppy Love I bought two containers, or sixteen fluid ounces, of Just Born, "Milk Replacer for Kittens, Ready-To-Use Liquid." I could not find an eyedropper in the store. Another customer heard me ask the clerk where I could purchase a dropper. "Take one of these," the customer said, handing me a plastic eye-dropper. "I am raising two rabbits, and the vet gave me a handful." "Don't you love spring?" she continued. "I am selfish in winter. But in spring with all the little animals around I'm a changed person." Instead of changing my character, Tiny Tim made me more mobile. Before dinner I made a second trip to Puppy Love. This time I bought a plastic container of FleaTrol, "Zodiac Flea Spray for Kittens & Cats." Tiny Tim was infested with fleas. "Charity begins with dead parasites," Vicki said, forbidding me to bring Tim into the house until I defleaed him. Because the weather had turned cold, I wanted to keep Tim in the basement. I bought Step 4, the weakest insecticide sold in the store. I sprayed FleaTrol on a damp paper towel. Then I rubbed the towel over Tim, brushing against the nap of his fur. Next I removed the towels from the box and sprayed them. Afterward I stuffed them into a blue "Pet Taxi" Vicki purchased the day she bought Penny. Lastly, I set the taxi at the foot of the basement steps.

I fed Tim six times a day, the first feeding at 5:45 in the morning, the last at midnight. I poured boiling water into a coffee mug. After filling the eyedropper with Just Born, I stuck it into the water to heat the formula. I cradled Tim in my left hand. Although he never bit me, I held him in a washrag. I tilted him backwards, his belly up, my palm supporting his spine, and inserted the eyedropper into the corner of his mouth. I squeezed the dropper slowly, and Tim sucked down the liquid. I sat on the fourth stair from the bottom of the basement steps. Edward and Eliza often watched Tim eat, and occasionally they also fed him. I supplemented the formula with solid foods, filling tops removed from Hellmann's mayonnaise with peanut butter and mushes, Tim's favorite mush being a blend of aged banana, corn flakes, and formula. I fed him both natural and packaged peanut butter. Tim preferred the latter. When I mentioned Tim in my class on Nature Writing, Alecia said, "Everybody's daddy raises a baby squirrel." Tim's tail healed quickly, and after a week his leg knit. I enjoyed feeding him. Afterward I rubbed the white fur behind his ears, and he shut his eyes. The basement was quiet, and as I sat on the steps, the yapping hurly-burly of life seemed far away. At the end of a week I took the taxi outdoors and set it under a beech. Twice a day I let Tim out for exercise, and he scurried through grass before I picked him up and put him back in the taxi. By the eleventh day Tim had recovered. When I placed him on the ground, he dashed to a white oak. Before I could grab him, he climbed seventy feet. "He's just going to be a squirrel," Vicki said, looking upward. "Now you can't ask him to be something else. He and you will have to get on with your separate lives."

Although Tiny Tim abandoned his crutch, animal season had not ended. Two years ago the university commissioned a bronze statue of a husky dog, the mascot of the school's athletic teams. In May workmen created a garden near the entrance to the basketball arena. In the center they raised the statue, all the while keeping it wrapped in a brown tarpaulin. Shortly before graduation, the statue was unveiled. Vicki and I took George and Penny to the ceremony. I expected pounds of dogs to be in attendance. I was disappointed. Packs of trustees and administrative officers of the university milled about, but Penny and George were the only canines at the ceremony. When the president of the university pulled the tarpaulin from the statue, Vicki and I held Penny and George above our heads so they would not miss anything. The husky posed nobly, his muzzle thrust upward, his nostrils elevated. Sniffing the chicken fat and beet pulp of spiritual Eukanuba, he was, I told pet lovers, "a role model for all the dogs in eastern Connecticut, those with four legs and those with two."

As spring unraveled, changes occurred in the Mansfield Library, not in the books but in the patrons. One Thursday night I overheard a woman ask the librarian to find every novel written by D. H. Lawrence, explaining that she wanted to read the books on vacation. The woman was forty-five. Her hair was gray, and her skin had begun to thin and turn silver. The landscape of Lawrence's novels is the melodramatic stuff of adolescent fantasy. While women bathe in pollen, red stallions thunder across lush fields. What had happened, I wondered, to transform a middle-aged woman into a reader of Lawrence? Where was she going on her vacation and with whom? I studied the woman as she stood in front of the librarian's desk. Except for a glint in her eye, she showed no signs of an elevated temperature. She seemed the sort of person who would take Barbara Pym's novels or, at her most daring, P. D. James's mysteries on vacation.

I did not analyze long. Another patron of the library, also a woman and a stranger, interrupted my study. "Read this," she said, handing me a small volume. "This book will make a difference." The book contained short stories written by Banana Yoshimoto. I had not heard of the author, and her first name did not appeal to me. I don't find edible Christian names palatable. Still, if I were compelled to select names for offspring at the grocery store, I would choose a blend of fruits and vegetables, the traditional and the homegrown, choosing, for example, Peaches and Poke Sallet. In the first story in the book a man rode a train. When an alcoholic sat beside him, the man looked away for a moment. When the man turned back, the alcoholic had become a sultry woman. "Good Lord, deliver me from such stuff," I muttered.

The hounds of spring had treed winter, not simply in the woods and at the edges of fields but in colonials and raised ranches. The first woman, I decided, was taking Lawrence's novels to a sunny tryst. In mornings she would stride barefoot across sand dunes, white grains sticking between her toes. In afternoons she would read, a tall palm waving over her like a fan. "And at night, the silly thing," I mumbled, shutting Yoshimoto's book, "will misbehave." I removed *Antiques* from the periodical shelf and, walking to the rear of the library, sat at a cubby-hole desk in the children's reading area. Although I studied highboys and china presses, I pretended to read the short stories until the person who thrust the book at me left the library.

Despite my misgivings season influenced life. Francis bought a new pair of basketball shoes. "Size 13," Vicki said. "He is growing like a weed." "I hope not," I said. "If you must compare our son to a plant, I prefer that he be compared to a cultivated, preferably hothouse, variety." For her part Eliza began a story describing the effects of spring upon an invalid's personality. "The sun shone brightly that morning," Eliza wrote. "Its rays were like birds swooping through Mabel's open window. All the flowers on the mountainside seemed to bloom for her, and her alone."

Scattered amid change was enough continuance to be reassuring. Last spring when I donned short pants for the first time, Vicki dubbed me "Cellulite." This May she said I resembled Wilbur Gufgarten. Two years ago Edward played on a baseball team coached by Paul Ridzon. This spring he played for Paul again. One night Edward's team played on a field below Hampton town hall. David, Joe, Bill, Thor, and I, or the Fathers' Club, as we dubbed ourselves, sat on a high bank beyond center field. Grass slipped from the slope down to the field like water trickling into a green lake. Yellow with new, translucent leaves, trees ruffled in a border behind the field. Beyond a forest the distance stretched blue and misty. Edward hit a triple in the first inning. Later he pitched and played shortstop and first base. Still, the game occurred in a haze. Joe treated the club to beer and pizza. We leaned on our elbows and talked about our baseball careers, the strikeouts and dropped balls of the past becoming the sustaining mulch of the present.

Amid continuance one change rippled tradition. Since the Civil War, Pickerings have been Republicans. Although I usually voted for Democrats, I remained a Republican until April. "In this country one hundred and thirty years is considerably more than a century," I explained whenever Vicki wondered why someone who advocated gun confiscation, free access to abortion, and stringent environmental regulations stayed a Republican. "You could not stand on a splinter of that party's platform,"

Vicki said, "you just enjoy being contrary." "Finally you have come out of the voting booth," a friend said after I switched parties, adding, "what's next?" What came next was Eliza's birthday party at Ron-A-Roll Skating Rink in Vernon. Eight ten-year-old girls, Francis, Edward, Vicki, and I attended the party. I had not skated in forty years. At first I crept about the rink. Worried about my arthritic back, I pulled myself around the floor using the railing. But then on the third lap years rolled away, and I skated like a ten-year-old, actually better than a ten-year-old. Neither the boys nor Eliza's friends could keep up with me. "Nothing has changed," I said to Vicki as I clattered into the wall at the end of the rink, adding, "they up and call me Speedo, but my real name is Sam Pickering." "You mean Wilbur Gufgarten," Vicki said. "Now get off the floor before you have a heart attack."

Spring is the season of noticeable change. So many changes occurred in wood and field that transformations seemed continuance, a covenant between earth and plant promising eternal renewal. Bloodroot bloomed white in the dell then melted overnight. Male flowers on willows flickered like short circuits. On alder, buds resembled candles, new leaves peeling back in small green flames. On ash, leaves untwisted like strips of soldered metal rusting apart. Barberry leaves resembled small spoons, so many spoons bushes seemed gluttonous with green. On sugar maples, leaves opened like pie crust, damply sweet and rolled airy thin. Before I fell asleep at graduation, I heard a speaker urge students to give "total commitment" to each task they undertook. "Will you be able to look back and say," he declared, "'I gave it one hundred percent'." The world is too various for a person to devote much energy to a single activity. Only zealots are capable of narrow concentration, and even then their commitment is rarely deeper than platitude.

This spring, as all springs, my vision wandered truant. Sometimes I paused beside fields resembling green streams, dandelions shining like nuggets of mica, tree swallows diving over them, glistening in the air. Like my meanderings colors were watery. Winter cress turned the Ogushwitz meadow into a yellow bayou. From patches of Quaker ladies blue drained out into violets. Robin's plantain flowed weakly purple and alcoholic down hillsides. Swallowtails puddled on a dirt road. Hayscented ferns bubbled in green rivulets through woods while sensitive ferns leaned backwards and unfurled, the leaflets resembling delicate, tapering fingers.

In the marsh behind the beaver dam crinkleroot sprayed white through heavy spatulas of skunk cabbage. Above the marsh the trills of gray tree frogs fell down the ridge like streams pinched between sharp rocks. An oriole flew into a small white oak. From an alder a kingbird threw himself into the air after insects, his white breast resembling a kite, suddenly tumbling loosely then just as suddenly planing upward. On the ground lay a limb broken from a yellow birch, the bark a shiny sleeve, the wood underneath shredded and rusty.

Calls of wood thrushes cracked out of shadows like light refracted by crystal. Under plywood at the edge of a field black racers wove themselves into loops. Red-winged blackbirds swayed atop high grass in Valentine Meadow. Morgan horses grazed on the side of Horsebarn Hill, brown and gleaming, the light sticking to their muscles like oil. In the backyard birds blossomed in an umbel of reds. Two cardinals clung to bittersweet. A red-bellied woodpecker bustled up the trunk of a black birch, and a rose-breasted grosbeak foraged under the forsythia, pink falling down its chest in a triangular bib. Four flickers gamboled through the woods. Later a male hollowed out a nesting cavity in an oak outside the study window. He worked all Mother's Day, drilling then stopping to toss wood chips to the ground. He filled his bill with chips then flicked them to the side, sometimes spraying them ten feet away from the tree. I wondered whether he preferred to toss the chips left or right, and so one morning I studied him for an hour. I am not much naturalist. I concluded that sometimes he threw the chips to the left, other times to the right.

Unlike my observations of the natural world, my friend Josh's remarks about human nature bite. Josh usually damns the fashionable. In May he brought a broadsheet to my office. Printed on pale yellow paper eight and a half by eleven inches, the sheet announced a "Free Public Talk," given by a "visiting English Buddhist monk." The man wore glasses, had a ruddy face lumpy as a potato, and was, Josh said, the real Wilbur Gufgarten. "Successful Living," "Satisfying and meaningful success," the sheet proclaimed, "Practical techniques which help to eradicate stress and anxiety." "The way to cope with the ills of personality is to work, not to sit flop-doddled and cross-legged on your behind," Josh said. If the whole of "pale-skinned Christendom," to use Josh's phrase, turned Buddhist, however, I wouldn't notice. What irks me are changes in language. Few people make the distinction between *farther* and *further,* the latter having, as one linguist puts it, overwhelmed the former. Still, when an editor recently changed all the *farthers* in a manuscript of mine to *furthers,* I was miffed. In polishing my prose the editor also changed *shined* to *shone,* and *verandah* to *veranda.* On a verandah one relaxes in a soft chair, a tall minty drink standing atop a coaster on a nearby table, beads of moisture big as pearls on the lip of the glass, in the background quiet servants in white coats. On a veranda one hunkers on splintery steps, scratching oneself or a hound, ticks as big as pumpkin seeds dangling from the dog's ears in swollen clutches.

Recently I attended a christening in an Episcopal church. Some members of the congregation wore blue jeans, their dress appropriate both to Wal-Mart and the New Revised Standard Version of the Bible used in the service. That morning the congregation read a selection from Psalm 104. "O Lord," the King James version reads, "how manifold are thy works! in wisdom thou has made them all: the earth is full of thy riches. So is this great and wide sea, wherein are things creeping innumerable, both small and great beasts." "Yonder is the great and wide sea," the second half of the excerpt declares in the New Revised Standard Version, "with its living things too many to number, creatures both great and small." People who sit barefoot on verandas point to small, wooden buildings and say, "yonder is the outhouse. It's a four-holer, and folks both great and small can squat at the same time."

I don't oppose all linguistic change. Would that I could say there have been changes in my personality, changes which elevated language and thought. In May I gave the Phi Beta Kappa address at the university. In past years speakers discussed, among other topics, "Global Aspects of the Human Environment," "Liberal Education and the Technocratic Society," and "Higher Education and the Social Contract in a Democracy." I entitled my speech "On Being a Crank."

Crankishness twists through my DNA. My character has hardened. If a surgeon tried to splice my genes, his scalpel would shatter. Still, sometimes I wish I were more solemn. This spring Edward played on the town twelve-and-under soccer team. On Memorial Day the team participated in a tournament near Danbury. The referee of the first game was poor. Rarely did he shift his position from mid-field, and only occasionally did he look at the line judges. Near the end of the second half the father of one of Edward's teammates stepped on the field and called the referee a turkey. Immediately the referee forfeited the game to the other side. An artist, the father is a mild man, and the referee's action provoked laughter more than exasperation. Three nights later I sent a letter to the father of Edward's teammate.

Francis created a letterhead for me on the computer: a black and white soccer ball three and a half inches in diameter. Circling the ball in bold black letters were the words "Connecticut Soccer Association." Supposedly the writer of the letter was Annette D. Barcombaker, Worthy Grand Matron of the "CSAss." and a resident of 476 Post Hole Road in Darien. "Dear Mr. Zinsser," the letter began. "This morning I received a letter from Mr. R. F. (Fred) Jaggerson, director of the Newtown Kick-Off Tournament. Fred informs me that during this past weekend you used fowl language on the athletic field, calling one of the referees a turkey. Actually I understand that the phrase used was more personal and that you said, 'you turkey' to Mr. Igot Highballs, one of our most respected officials. The use of such language is reprehensible. If you had called Mr. Highballs a coxcomb, we at the association would be more understanding. But to give a man of his distinguished appearance the bird is shocking. By the way did you hear about the sick man whose doctor advised him to eat a piece of pullet? The man refused, saying it might lay on his stomach. Ha, ha! We at the Association are a lively flock. There are no flies on our giblets."

"I can only assume," the letter continued, "that hormones triggered your behavior. Are you middle-aged, Mr. Zinsser? Many soccer fathers your age experience problems with testosterone. I recall that on one occasion a former all-American football player and father of a lovely blood child aged twelve started growing breasts after he passed thirty-eight. From this distance I do not presume to analyze the effects of hormones upon you, but I do advise you to seek professional help. Fred tells me that not only did you call the official a turkey but that you stepped upon the field to do so. Only once before has one of our fathers violated a field to address an official. That happened, as I recollect, in 1986 during the first half of a game between the Greenwich Bandits and Milford Darlings. Like you the man was an artist. He encroached upon the field not to criticize but because he was overcome with passion. The official that day was Mr. Billy Capon, a man with the most divine buns and who played the organ at St. George's Episcopal Church in Woodbridge."

"The father couldn't control his lust, and he embraced Mr. Billy near the thirty-yard marker, disrupting a breakaway. All ended happily, however. He and Mr. Billy eloped the next day. They now own an antique shop in Westport. As I recall the man behaved a great deal like you, calling Mr. Billy 'my itsy-bitsy turkey gobbler'. Mr. Zinsser, examine your motives for stepping on to the field. Did desire master reason? I leave the probing of your parts to you alone. I must now stop to prepare Cornish hen for my beloved spouse. But I want to stress that all of us in the Connecticut Soccer Ass. are praying for you. We think of you as a member of our extended family."

Instead of change variety filled days this spring. One morning hemlocks were tipped with green, and sunshine bounced off the surface of the Fenton River and shimmered along banks like thin cirrus clouds. In the afternoon Ms. Barcombaker telephoned to inquire if the healing had begun. Last Sunday she asked Father Fox to cook up a special prayer for Mr. Zinsser. A week ago a slick magazine reviewed my last collection of essays. The review began, "Sam Pickering is the most publicized unknown writer in America." Yesterday a friend wrote from Nashville. Her first cousin, she informed me, read my books to his "Sunday School classes." On the radio an hour ago I played a tape entitled *Bushland Dreaming*. Vicki bought the tape in Sydney the day before we left Australia. In the middle of a tune called "Summer Wind" Vicki blew into the study. Her arms twisted over her head like braids of hair. In her right hand she held chimes, notes tinkling like bird song. "Here I am," she said, "your Kakadu wood nymph."

junebug

Twenty feet away from me near the road a robin hunted worms. Two catbirds flew into the side yard, one stopping and perching for a moment on the silverbell, the other disappearing into the forsythia. From the far side of Mrs. Carter's yard a kousa dogwood shined. The white blossoms hung over the lawn in shelves. Lightning bugs fell through the shadows behind the blossoms in a yellow patter, ticking like rain against the dark. "What are you doing on the stoop?" Vicki shouted from the kitchen. "I'm having deep thoughts about lightning bugs," I said. "I hope they are illuminating," Vicki answered. "They are," I said, turning to look at the mock orange I pruned last fall. Instead of bushy the mock orange had grown leggy. In the dark it resembled a cross jabbed into dirt atop a grave. Rather than tumbling out loosely in pale fans, flowers clung tightly to switches, looking as if a florist had wired their stems to twigs.

School shapes my life. Despite what I said, I don't have illuminating thoughts in June. The academic year ends in May, and I amble through June. Instead of mining significance out of observation to impress a class or a colleague, I gaze about me. I read books for story, not meaning, and I wander Storrs just to see what I can see. Eliza's hamster Dusty lives in a ten-gallon aquarium. Although Dusty gets bushels of fruit and vegetables to eat, he has a drab life. Because Dusty is nocturnal and stirs only after the children go to bed, Eliza rarely plays with him. In June I had the leisure to feel guilty about Dusty's stark existence. Early in the month I set a folding chair in the dell, and many afternoons at four o'clock I carried Dusty outside in hopes that he would find excitement amid the remnants of my daffodils. Once a nocturnal animal, always a nocturnal animal. Instead of scampering about twitching his nose at bud and beetle, Dusty rolled into a fist and fell asleep, his favorite bed being next to a stump where he fashioned a bower out of tall grass. I let Dusty sleep undisturbed, reckoning that dozing outside was better for him than sleeping inside amid a pile of wood shavings. Some afternoons I also slept. I always awoke with a start, at first fearful that Dusty had escaped, then disappointed that he was still in the bower.

Other afternoons I sat immobile. Voles bustled along trails near my feet. Above my head a flicker fed ants to young in an oak. A leathery grape fern grew beside a boulder. The fern's leaflets fanned out coarsely, resembling rivulets of water that drained into puddles, coloring the dirt green before sinking and leaving their outlines behind. Because I sat still, I saw things I had not noticed before. A wood tick crawled atop my knee, using minute yellow hooks at the ends of his legs to hoist himself up. This summer ticks were plentiful. During June I removed eighty-nine deer and wood ticks from myself and the dogs.

Insects interest me, and while sitting in the yard, I watched small brown mosquitoes feed on my forearm. The mosquitoes' wings resembled slivers of stained glass, blue and gold in the sunlight. A gypsy moth caterpillar clung to a Norway maple. The caterpillar was as beautiful as a cathedral. Its skin was mottled white and black, resembling kettlehole bogs seen from a height. Rising along the caterpillar's back behind the head were four pairs of velvety blue nodules then six pairs of scarlet nodules, hairs growing out of them in sheaves. Other hairs bristled over the insect's body, black and blue, then down the caterpillar's sides, blond, silver, and red.

Sitting in the folding chair, I imagined myself an explorer. For a moment patches of moss on the maple became tropical forests. Lichens spilled down bark like glaciers off ridges. Instead of an everyday insect the caterpillar became treasure, sapphires and rubies glittering in seams along its back. When I was young, I dreamed of wandering exotic lands. Years ago

I said good-bye to faraway places and countries I will not visit. Time has transformed lesser things into greater. My heart leaped when I saw a minute club fungus growing on an oak log. The mushroom was a quarter of an inch high. Small red clubs grew atop thread-like black stalks. When I flicked the clubs with my index finger, spores flew out in smoky wisps. I had not seen the fungus before, and for a moment I imagined a mushroom named for me, *geoglossum pickeringia,* one of the earth tongues. "A mushroom with my name, now that," I thought, "would be a real achievement."

Imaginary achievements last no longer in the mind than actual achievements do in daily life. Most afternoons the dogs ended my explorations. George chased Penny through the yard. Low and with a heavy, shovel chest, George bowled Penny over. For her part Penny was faster than George. When he charged, she jumped aside, spun around, and leaped on his back, throwing herself high on his neck, much as a cowboy bulldogging a steer. The dogs were noisy. To frighten Penny, George barked, and as the dogs bounded through the grass, the tags around their necks rang. The play made me smile, and I liked watching the dogs. In June, though, my attention drifted like a bank of heat, and eventually something distracted me from the dogs: the white plastic urns beside the garage, pansies blinking from one, from the other, geraniums flowing like gouts of red water, or the hollyhocks beside the front door, blossoms larger than teacups, twisting around stalks in sugary pink braids.

In mornings I often took the dogs for walks. Curled under plywood was the skin of a black racer, five feet nine inches long. Beside a hedge of multiflora rose lay a dead star-nosed mole. When I picked up the mole, a small praying mantis the color of sand scurried away from my fingers. Green aphids with spidery black legs lurked beneath flats of yarrow. On walks Penny chased chipmunks, their cries ringing. Eye gnats swarmed about my face. Oddly they lit only at the corners of my left eye. Near Schoolhouse Brook a great horned owl blew silently through the woods, resembling a brown curtain shaking in a breeze. Near the top of Bean Hill velvet grass bloomed in a red haze. Often I stopped and examined plants: staghorn sumac, yellow and green above Unnamed Pond; pink corn cockles on Horsebarn Hill; and below the sheep barns, bristly St.-John's-wort, the yellow so warm that black specks on the petals danced like motes.

During walks I often drifted, pondering things I read, wondering why, for example, medieval Britons labeled the starling Satan's dove, or speculating about the breed of dog that nipped Christ's ankles while He carried the cross. According to French tale, the dog was changed into the bulldog after the crucifixion. The animal's nose was crushed so that it could not smell myrrh, saffron, and cinnamon and follow their scents to Paradise and the well of living water. A Welsh version of the same story said the dog became the greyhound, so ashamed of its behavior that it carried its tail between its legs and ran, not because it enjoyed the chase, but in the fruitless attempt to escape guilt. I like stories that explain the habits of animals. According to a folktale popular among Magyars, the woodpecker was once the greatest sculptor in the animal world, famous for carving flowers delicate as clouds. Because his fellow creatures praised him highly, the woodpecker became proud. One day he bragged that he created not only man and woman and all the generations of the earth but that he had carved heaven itself out of a juniper bush. The Lord overheard the woodpecker's boast, and the next morning when the bird tried to carve a piece of olive into a scarab, all he could do was drill a hole.

While walking I carved old chestnuts into new tales. Onnie Feathers owned the finest Poland China hogs in Smith County. Four years in a row he won blue ribbons at the State Fair in Nashville, this past year for a giant boar named Hallelujah. Like his pigs Onnie was fond of swilling. One night early in June, he bolted a trough of strong drink at Enos Mayfield's Inn in South Carthage. At the end of the evening Onnie insisted upon walking home, so, as he put it, he would not founder. Beagon Hackett had been out late attending an experience meeting in Buffalo Valley, and he met Onnie on the bluff above the Cordell Hull bridge. "Drunk again?" Reverend Hackett said. "Don't you worry none about it," Onnie answered, fixing the reverend with an eye as bright as a window in a liquor store, "I'm going along pretty well myself." Beagon was the last person to talk to Onnie in this world. The night was stormy, and before Onnie stepped onto the bridge, he picked up a rock and threw it into the air to see which way the wind was blowing. Unfortunately the rock was large, and instead of being blown east or west, it fell south and hit Onnie on the head, causing him to stumble and fall off the bluff.

Onnie bounced two or three times before he catapulted into the river. "Onnie was stone dead before he hit the water," Loppie Groat said later. Onnie's reliability was suspect, and aside from his wife, Juno, few people in Carthage mourned his loss. Hoben Donkin summed up feelings in Ankerrow's Café when he said, "There's no telling what a man who kills himself when he is drunk will do when he is sober."

Although Sheriff Baugham organized a search party the morning after Onnie's fall, the body was not found for four days. Clay in the river stained Onnie's skin. "What with the bloating that will naturally occur in hot weather," Loppie said, "Onnie looked like a ham, all of him smoked except his face." Catfish grazed over Onnie's jowls and forehead, and his skull, Loppie said, "resembled a good head cheese, chuck full of onions, celery, carrots, parsley, even a few peppercorns."

Hogs were Onnie's great love, and in his will he asked to be buried on the rise behind his pig yard. Although Onnie was a Baptist, Beagon Hackett refused to bury him. "God didn't make Baptists," Beagon said, "to be brothers to hogs or companions to chickens." After Beagon refused to officiate at the funeral, Juno asked Slubey Garts to trim and salt Onnie for eternity. Slubey accepted. "Baptists might look down their noses now," Slubey said, "but things change. In the morning Mr. Turkey Buzzard is so high in the sky that he is just a speck. By afternoon he is squatting by the side of the road eating polecat." In part Slubey buried Onnie because Carthaginians had enjoyed a remarkably healthy spring. "Aside from a mite of a child," Isom Legg, the gravedigger, said before the funeral, "I haven't buried a living soul for six weeks." For the funeral Juno tied black ribbons around the necks of Hallelujah and Hallelujee, Hallelujah's favorite sow. The day was sunny, and Slubey preached a sermon rich with the hocks and knuckles of sugar-cured country religion. When the wind whistled through knotholes in Onnie's chicken house, Slubey called the sound "the music of God's own organ."

Inside the house in June I behaved much as I did in the yard. The end of the school year erased deadlines, so I observed the doings of family. Before turning out the light in her bedroom at night, Eliza performed a ritualistic "door tattoo." Starting in the upper left corner of her bedroom door and moving to the right then down and finally back to the left, she quartered the door, lightly hitting each section of the wood twice with her right hand, after which she smacked the center of the door three times with her left hand. "How long have you been doing that?" I asked. "Since last August when we returned from Australia," Eliza said.

In June I read the newspaper carefully, something I rarely do during the rest of the year. One morning in the *Hartford Courant,* I found a provocative article. A batch of conservative churches in Branford, Connecticut, refused to admit a Congregational church to a softball league, claiming that the Congregational flock was too soft on sin. Besides lowering rails to the fold so that homosexuals could bound in, the Congregational church did not have a "Virgins' Club." Most habitués of the club, I gathered from the article, were teenagers who pledged to remain celibate until marriage. I read the article to friends at the Cup of Sun. Old-fashioned Episcopalians and hard-ball players, none of us qualified for membership in the club. Still, we wondered whether Congregationalists might be able to attend meetings as virgins emeritus, thereby becoming eligible for the softball league. In June I also had the leisure to listen to conversations. A friend failed most students who took his classes. "Don't give them F's," a dean told him, "they will just take the course from someone else and fail again. Give them D's. I consider the D an F *cum laude.*"

The more observant a person is, the odder life appears. One afternoon as I sat outside in the folding chair, Dusty asleep in a wad of grass next to the house, and George and Penny dozing in the driveway, I noticed a red Plymouth Reliant station wagon coming slowly down the wrong side of Hillside Circle. When the driver saw me, he jerked the car to the right side of the pavement. Then he accelerated and sped past the house, turning around in a driveway three houses down the street. As he drove back past the yard, this time on the near and correct side of the road, his companion leaned out the window, holding a camera in his hands. The companion took two or three pictures of the house. Once the car was past the yard, the driver again sped up and, running the stop sign at the end of Hillside Circle, disappeared onto the university campus. That night at dinner the family speculated about the photographer's intentions. "You are famous, Daddy," Eliza said, "and the man wanted a picture of you." "Maybe we have won the Publishers Clearing House drawing, and the man was taking pictures in order to plan the award ceremony," Vicki said.

The man who cleans the gutters on my house has long hair. Four days earlier I left a message on his answering machine. "This is Sam Pickering," I said, giving him my address, then adding, "could you clean the gutters soon?" Perhaps the man had gotten into trouble with the police. "People with flowing locks often run afoul of the constabulary," I said. Maybe the sheriff had tapped the man's telephone, and the phrase "clean my gutters" meant "deliver a bale of marijuana." If that is so, I told Vicki, then the men in the Plymouth worked for the DEA. "Some night," I said, "they will batter down the front door. They will smash every antique in the house looking for dope, and we will be lucky if they don't shoot us."

I caught up with my reading in June. In March after buying a collection of my essays, a man in Kentucky sent me a book: Samuel Stearns' *The American Oracle. Comprehending an Account of Recent Discoveries in the Arts and Sciences, with A Variety of Religious, Political, Physical, and Philosophical Subjects, Necessary to be known in all Families, for the Promotion of their present Felicity and future Happiness.* Published in New York in 1791 and costing two dollars "in boards," the *Oracle* was 645 pages long. "The book resembles your essays," my correspondent wrote, "and is literary Brunswick stew. Everything is in it, not just okra and corn, but possum, squirrel, and coon, the tail of a red fox, probably even a good shaking of big green junebugs."

A miscellany, the *Oracle* began with a chronology, the first date being the creation of the world in the year 0, followed by pages of happenings, including Noah's flood in 1656 B.C., the "Invention" of purgatory in 250 A.D., and in 1624 A.D., the "First neat cattle imported to America." Stearns included a volume of his own verse in the book. The first poem printed was "A Description of the Author's Philosophical Contemplations, Astronomical, and other Labours." "In profound studies," he wrote, "I take much delight, / At high noon day, and in the silent night, / Of wond'rous things I aim to find the cause, / By diving into Nature's secret laws. / Sometimes I sit, and with myself converse, / And contemplate upon the universe; / Sometimes, when on my downy bed I lie, / My wand'ring thoughts to distant objects fly." Stearns was a doctor, and medicinal duties often brought his high-flying thoughts back to earth. "Whilst at my studies," he explained, "I am sitting still, / I'm often call'd to visit persons ill: / Then I haste where malignant ills do rage, / And against them with all my skill engage. / Sometimes I bleed, sometimes I puke and purge: / I use such things as Nature seems to urge."

No regimen of physic could purge study from Stearns' system. Included in the *Oracle* were lengthy discussions of geography, electricity, climate, money, astronomy, the slave trade, and drunkenness. Stearns wrote histories of several religious sects, the Moravians and Shakers, among others. He advised readers "how to chuse a good Wife, and a good Husband." He prescribed remedies for a pest house of maladies and suggested a medicine cabinet of nostrums for baldness. Stearns lived in Pennsylvania, and several of his "Epistles of Philadelphus" appeared in the book, the first entitled "Admonitions against the Usage of bad language." A list of the "gods of Heathenish Nations" was five pages long, the strangest deity, to me, being Anatis, "goddess of prostitution among Armenians." In his advice Stearns was delphic. In a discussion of funeral customs, he wrote, "when people die of putrid disorders, their bodies ought to be buried soon, to prevent the spreading of infectious distempers. But if they die in a fit of apoplexy, or very suddenly some other way, it may be proper to keep them a few days, because some have come to life, that have appeared dead."

Stearns also described American wildlife, devoting several pages to my favorites, reptiles, advising readers that the thorn-tail snake had a stinger at the end of its spine and was "very venomous." Although poisonous, rattlesnakes were a boon to man. Oil of rattlesnake, he declared, was the "most penetrating and relaxing of all animal oils, and is esteemed excellent for quinseys, stiff joints, and corns." Because they were constrictors, black snakes should be avoided. "When a black snake gets round a person, 'tis best to cut it in two," he wrote, "hence the necessity of travelling with a pen-knife; for whether they are round a person's neck or waist, they draw themselves tighter and tighter as he fetches his breath, and at last put an end to his life."

Everything was matter for Stearns' coiling intellect. In a poem about heat and electricity he described a moment that sparked inspiration. "In seventeen hundred eighty-eight, I sat / In a large room, with a good natur'd *Cat:* / She soon jump'd up, and stood upon my knees; / I strok'd her back, which did not her displease. / As she purr'd round, and grew exceeding bold, / I found her hairs were stiff'ned with the cold: / When I strok'd them—behold, the sparks did fly! / Like flaming lightning through the azure sky."

Much of the *Oracle* resembled sections taken from an almanac. June, "the Farmer and Gardener's Calendar" advised, was the time to "hoe Indian corn, weed your garden, and kill black flies, worms, and spiders, which devour your plants, by the fumes of tobacco, conducted to those vegetables, through some proper pipe, or tube." If the month was dry, plants should be watered early in the morning, Stearns suggested, adding that in hot weather, people should watch their bees "lest they swarm, and fly away." "Begin to mow grass, as soon as it is ripe, or in the bloom," he urged readers. "Rake and cock your hay every evening before the dew falls, spread it out the next morning, and cart it into your barn as soon as it is fit; but let it not be dried too much. Keep your barn-doors shut tight, to prevent the ingress of the air, for a free admission of that element will cause the hay to generate heat by fermentation, and will make it musty, and sometimes cause it to take fire; but if it is kept from the air, it will look green, and have an agreeable flavour the next year."

The activities Stearns thought appropriate to June did not appear on my calendar. Twice during June I mowed grass, but instead of raking it into hay I mulched it and left the cuttings on the yard. In Pennsylvania June was berry-picking month, and Stearns urged readers to gather cherries, currants, gooseberries, and strawberries. On afternoon walks I often ate wild strawberries. Still, berry season did not begin in Mansfield until July. Early in July raspberries ripened, while at the end of the month blackberries began to come into season. Even worse, the Calendar did not mention the hamster whose habits determined the course of much of my June. Moreover instead of devouring plants, the insect creation, particularly mosquitoes, feasted on Vicki. Vicki does not smoke, and rather than using tobacco fumes to drive them away, I lit citronella candles.

My June rituals were familial not agricultural. Late in the month Vicki and I drove the children to camp in Maine. We spent a night in Portsmouth at the Sheraton in a room facing the Piscataqua River. During the afternoon we wandered the town, rummaging through shops and eating sweets, much as we do every June. This year we ate ice cream in Harbor Treats Chocolates on Congress Street opposite the North Church. Edward had vanilla; Eliza, chocolate chip cookie dough; Francis, orange sherbet; and Vicki, a scoop of chocolate walnut fudge, topped off with Mississippi mud.

For my part I ate German chocolate cake ice cream, "a good choice," the girl behind the counter said. Nothing exciting happens on our trips, but I always notice small things. A girl with green hair came into the shop. She ordered strawberry ice cream, "to match her hair," Edward said. We sat at a round table. Three colors ran across the tablecloth in bands: purple, red, and blue. Ox-eyed daisies bloomed down the center of each color, turning the bands into flower beds. The tablecloth was thirty-six beds wide. At each side of the cloth, however, were portions of a row, one-half a row on the left, and two-thirds on the right. "Nobody but you would count the rows," Vicki said later. "I don't know about that," I said, turning to Edward and asking, "how many rows of color were there on that tablecloth?" "Thirty-six," he said, "with bits of cloth at each side." That night in the hotel room we watched television. The Three Stooges threw pies at people. "So far," Eliza said in the middle of the program, "they have thrown eighteen pies."

Vicki and I did not stay long at the boys' camp. When we left, Edward was playing basketball, and Francis was walking through the woods with his friend Alan. We stayed longer at Eliza's camp. Although Eliza was an experienced camper, having first gone to camp when she was eight years old, she did not want us to leave. When she started to cry, I walked into the woods. Yellow pollen sifted down from pines and dusted the leaves of moosewood. Midges swarmed through a shaft of sunlight, the insects spiraling around each other in strands. On the way home from Maine Vicki and I stopped for dinner at the Publick House in Sturbridge. We had never been there. "I bet," I said as I turned off the interstate, "that the Publick House will be an open-faced turkey sandwich sort of place." Sure enough, the sandwich was the sixth item on the menu, and so instead of eating in the restaurant, we bought sweet rolls and ate outside under a white trellis, feeding not only ourselves but a chipmunk that perched on a stone wall and begged. "This is living," Vicki said, as she tossed crumbs to the chipmunk.

July Fourth ends June. This year Vicki and I went to the Boombox Parade in Willimantic, "the event of the summer," my friend Rachel said. Participants carried radios tuned to WILI, the local station. The station played band and patriotic music, Sousa marches and "Yankee Doodle," for example. I took folding chairs, and Vicki and I sat on the curb of Main Street and watched the parade. Anyone can march. A radio announcer wore the uniform of the University of Connecticut's basketball team, adding a top hat to raise himself to playing height. Strapped to his feet were radios shaped like yellow shoe boxes. Uncle Sam tossed candy to children. A school of green fish swam past followed by a vegetable garden carrying a banner reading "Let There Be Peas on Earth." Flamingoes fluttered around an ambulance. A young man carried a wooden cross, and a family sat on the flatbed of a farm truck, American flags planted about them like corn. A butterfly winked by on roller blades. The butterfly's forewings rose high over her thorax. Along the costal margin of each forewing six white stars floated in a blue sea, glittering like sharp icebergs. From the sea red and white bars radiated out to the inner margins of the wings.

A man imitating Elvis Presley sat atop the back seat of a white convertible. A banner pasted to the side of the car read, "Elvis Lives in Willimantic." A recess of children rode past on bicycles. Many of the children rode bicycles equipped with training wheels. Beside the bicycles trotted a parents' association of fathers, ready to grab their offspring if the training wheels tilted. A little girl pulled a Radio Flyer decorated with flags and carrying a kennel of stuffed dogs. The Windham Whirlers, a square dance group, do-si-doed past. The Whirlers were middle-aged. The men wore red vests, white shirts, and blue trousers while the women wore red skirts and white blouses. A tractor pulled a hay wagon. A barnyard of children sat on the wagon, all of them wearing rubber noses, resembling the snouts of pigs. "Jesus Loves You," proclaimed a banner while another banner assured spectators that "This Land Is Your Land."

Many churches marched in the parade: the Open Bible Baptist, the Abundant Life Community Church, and the Light on the Hill Christian Fellowship, among others. A woman stepped out of the parade and handed me three religious tracts, each measuring two by two and a half inches and containing thirty-two pages. Entitled *Personal Bible,* the first tract contained "Verses of Comfort, Assurance, Salvation." The verses were familiar. An excerpt from Isaiah was typical: "Come now, and let us reason together, saith the Lord: though your sins be as scarlet, they shall be white as snow; though they be red like crimson, they shall be as wool." The second tract was *Happy is the Man,* the title taken from Proverbs,

"Happy is the man that findeth wisdom, and the man that getteth understanding." Questions and answers filled the last tract. "If your best friend knocked at the door of your house, what would you say to him?" a question asked. "You would say 'come in,' wouldn't you?" stated the answer. "Friend," the tract then declared, "the Lord Jesus is knocking at your heart's door right now. Will you receive him? Will you invite him into your heart and life?" For "extra copies," the final page of each tract instructed, write "Sowers of Seed," listing a post office box in Fort Worth, Texas, then adding, "Brethren, pray for us." "Thank you," I said to the woman who handed me the tracts, "there ain't a tree big enough to block out the blazing sun of God's truth." "Amen," she said. "What did you say?" Vicki asked after the woman rejoined the parade. "Just something Slubey Garts might have said in a sermon," I answered. "The language seemed appropriate."

That night Vicki and I celebrated the Fourth in high domestic style. I put the card table up at the end of the driveway. On opposite sides of the table I placed folding chairs with blue-and-white vinyl bottoms. Vicki found a bottle of 1991 Beaujolais that she stored in the basement before we went to Australia. She cooked corn and hamburgers in the kitchen and made a salad from peas we picked at Pleasant Valley Farm. For dessert we had homemade fudge cake and strawberries and cream, the berries also picked at Pleasant Valley. For our candelabra I set a yellow citronella candle in the middle of the table. We ate at the end of the drive and looked at passersby, occasionally waving at acquaintances. After dinner we walked Penny and George on the campus. It was dark when we returned home. A crocus geometer moth clung to the screen above the kitchen sink. The moth's wings were yellow and speckled with red. "Our fireworks," Vicki said.

We enjoyed the July Fourth celebration so much that we repeated it the next night. That morning Vicki bought a Hibachi grill on sale at Stop and Shop for $5.99. Putting it together took us two hours. On a shelf in the basement Vicki found a can of coconut milk. She poured me a sample and asked if I thought the milk musty. Although the milk clung to my teeth like dried moss, I said no, and Vicki made piña coladas. At Caldor's she bought two plastic schooners. The schooners were six and a half inches tall. Above a yellow base rose a green saguaro cactus with two arms. Perched atop the cactus like the nest of a buzzard atop a bluff was the bowl of the schooner. I cooked skewers of chicken on the grill. Once again we had a pea salad, this time, though, with potato chips swirled around it like scallop shells. For dessert we again had fudge cake and strawberries and cream.

The mail arrived late that day, and we read it at dinner, sitting at the end of the drive. Edward sent a card. "Camp has been okay so far," he wrote. "Most of the guys in my cabin are OK, but I haven't found any real friends. I'm not good at riflery and am *horrible* at archery. Shop is too hard, so I won't make anything there. I read most all of my free time, and I probably won't win one award. I can't say I've been enjoying camp so far. P.S. They changed the swimming system to levels 1–7. I'm in 4, and I hate it." "Well," I said, refilling the nest above my cactus, "that's quite a card. The five apostles could not have done better." "Four apostles," Vicki said; "there were only four apostles." "Five," I said, "Matthew, Mark, Luke, Anne, John." Eliza wrote a letter, and I opened it. Recently she had eaten breakfast in the woods. "Breakfast was delicious," she recounted, "chocolate chip pancakes and mugs of hot chocolate with red, white and blue marshmallows in the shape of stars floating on top." "A chocolate heaven shining with stars," I said, topping up my nest, "now that's the way to end June."